"Grant's ability to quickly convey complicated backstory makes this jam-packed love story accessible even to new or periodic readers."
–Publishers' Weekly

"Donna Grant has given the paranormal genre a burst of fresh air…"
–San Francisco Book Review

"The premise is dramatic and heartbreaking; the characters are colorful and engaging; the romance is spirited and seductive."
–The Reading Cafe

"The central romance, fueled by a hostage drama, plays out in glorious detail against a backdrop of multiple ongoing issues in the "Dark Kings" books. This seemingly penultimate installment creates a nice segue to a climactic end."
–Library Journal

"…intense romance amid the growing war between the Dragons and the Dark Fae is scorching hot."
–Booklist

SKYE DRUIDS SERIES

Iron Ember ~ Shoulder the Skye ~ Heart of Glass
Endless Skye ~ Still of the Night ~ Blood Skye ~ After Midnight

DARK KINGS SERIES

Dark Heat ~ Darkest Flame ~ Fire Rising
Burning Desire ~ Hot Blooded ~ Night's Blaze
Soul Scorched ~ Dragon King ~ Passion Ignites
Smoldering Hunger ~ Smoke and Fire
Dragon Fever ~ Firestorm ~ Blaze ~ Dragon Burn
Constantine: A History, Parts 1-3 ~ Heat ~ Torched
Dragon Night ~ Dragonfire ~ Dragon Claimed
Ignite ~ Fever ~ Dragon Lost ~ Flame ~ Inferno
A Dragon's Tale (Whisky and Wishes: *A Holiday Novella*,
Heart of Gold: *A Valentine's Novella*, & Of Fire and Flame)
My Fiery Valentine ~ The Dragon King Coloring Book
Dragon King Special Edition Character Coloring Book: Rhi

DARK WARRIORS SERIES

Midnight's Master ~ Midnight's Lover
Midnight's Seduction ~ Midnight's Warrior
Midnight's Kiss ~ Midnight's Captive
Midnight's Temptation ~ Midnight's Promise
Midnight's Surrender ~ A Warrior for Christmas

CHIASSON SERIES

Wild Fever ~ Wild Dream ~ Wild Need
Wild Flame ~ Wild Rapture

LARUE SERIES

Moon Kissed ~ Moon Thrall

Moon Struck ~ Moon Bound

WICKED TREASURES

Seized by Passion ~ Enticed by Ecstasy

Captured by Desire

Books 1-3: Wicked Treasures Box Set

✦ . ✢ . ✦ . ✢ . ✦

✦ HISTORICAL PARANORMAL ✦

THE KINDRED SERIES

Everkin ~ Eversong ~ Everwylde

Everbound ~ Evernight ~ Everspell

KINDRED: THE FATED SERIES

Rage ~ Ruin ~ Reign

DARK SWORD SERIES

Dangerous Highlander ~ Forbidden Highlander

Wicked Highlander ~ Untamed Highlander

Shadow Highlander ~ Darkest Highlander

ROGUES OF SCOTLAND SERIES

The Craving ~ The Hunger

The Tempted ~ The Seduced

Books 1-4: Rogues of Scotland Box Set

THE SHIELDS SERIES
A Dark Guardian ~ A Kind of Magic
A Dark Seduction ~ A Forbidden Temptation
A Warrior's Heart
Mystic Trinity (a series connecting novel)

DRUIDS GLEN SERIES
Highland Mist ~ Highland Nights ~ Highland Dawn
Highland Fires ~ Highland Magic
Mystic Trinity (a series connecting novel)

SISTERS OF MAGIC TRILOGY
Shadow Magic ~ Echoes of Magic ~ Dangerous Magic
Books 1-3: Sisters of Magic Box Set

THE ROYAL CHRONICLES NOVELLA SERIES
Prince of Desire ~ Prince of Seduction
Prince of Love ~ Prince of Passion
Books 1-4: The Royal Chronicles Box Set
Mystic Trinity (a series connecting novel)

DARK BEGINNINGS: A FIRST IN SERIES BOXSET
Chiasson Series, Book 1: Wild Fever
LaRue Series, Book 1: Moon Kissed
The Royal Chronicles Series, Book 1: Prince of Desire

DRAGON MARKED

Cover Design © 2025 by Hang Le
ISBN 13: 978-1-958353-47-9
Available in ebook, print, and audio.

Peek at DRAGON FORGED

Glimpse at STORM WOOD

www.DonnaGrant.com
www.MotherofDragonsBooks.com

DRAGON MARKED

A DRAGON KINGS® NOVEL

NEW YORK TIMES & USA TODAY BESTSELLING AUTHOR

DONNA GRANT

Shecrish
Orgate
Belanore
Stonemore
Human Land
Flamefall
Dragon Land
Iron Hall
Cairnkeep
Rannora
Zora

DRAGON KINGS INDEX

Alasdair (AEL-aeS-Deh-R) – King of Amethyst
- Dragon tattoo on his chest
- Power is energy absorption
- Story in DRAGON ARISEN & DRAGON KISS
- Mated to Lotti
  - Youngest Star Person

Anson (AN – sən) – King of Browns
- Ying yang dragon tattoo on back
- Power to take possession of someone's mind for a short period
- Story in BLAZE
- Mated to Devon
  - Descended from Druids
  - Gift from Con is a smoky quartz bracelet, both round and princess cut stones

Arian (AR-ee-ən) – King of Turquoises
- Dragon tattoo on his left leg
- Power to control the weather
- Story in DRAGON KING
- Mated to Grace
  - Gift from Con is a rose gold link ankle bracelet with a turquoise heart pendant

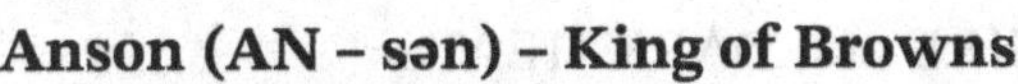

Asher (ASH-er) – King of Hunter Greens

- Tattoo on his left arm from wrist to shoulder
- Power to heal burns caused by dragon fire
- Story in DRAGON FEVER
- Mated to Rachel
  - Journalist
  - Gift from Con 4-strands of faceted chrome diopside necklace

Banan (BAN-yen) – King of Blues

- Tattoo of two intertwined dragons upon his chest
- Ability to make someone hallucinate
- Story in DAWN'S DESIRE and DARK HEAT
- Mated to Jane
  - Gift from Con is a silver cuff bracelet with a dragon, wings spread, covered in sapphires

Brandr (BRAND-er) – Dragon King

- Son of Con and Rhi
- Gold and beige dragon
- Ability to dispel magic

Cain (KAYN) – King of Navy

- Tattoo on chest
- Ability to use a cone of hot sand
- Story in FLAME
- Mated to Noreen
  - Dark Fae
  - Gift from Con was platinum wire wrapped lapis earrings

Cináed (KIN-ay) – King of Moonstone
- Tattoo on left leg from his knee up to hip
- Power that he can learn and master anything
- Story in DRAGON CLAIMED
- Mated to Gemma
  - Gift from Con silver Celtic cuff bracelet with moonstones at the ends
  - Druid who can sense another Druid's magic

Constantine aka Con (KAHN-stən-teen) – King of Golds, King of Dragon Kings
- Tattoo on his back
- Power to heal anything except death
- Best friends with Ulrik
- One of two Kings who never slept away centuries
- Puts the Dragon Kings and their future above his own happiness
- Story in INFERNO, HEART OF GOLD, OF FIRE AND FLAME, and DRAGON FROST
- Mated to Rhi
  - Gift from the Dragon Kings: a crown with a jewel for every color Dragon King
  - Royal Light Fae

Cullen (KUL-ən) – King of Garnets
- Tattoo on left arm
- Power to breath fog
- Story in DRAGON UNBOUND
- Mate to Tamlyn (no ceremony yet)
  - Banshee from Zora

Darius (də-RIE-əs) – King of Dark Purple

- Tattoo on his back looking over his shoulder
- No discernable special ability
- Story in SMOLDERING HUNGER
- Mated to Sophie
  - Doctor
  - Gift from Con are cushion cut dark Siberian amethyst dangle earrings over 5 carets each

Dmitri (DMEE-tree) – King of Whites

- Tattoo draped along the back of his shoulders
- Has the ability to cancel someone's thoughts
- Story in FIRESTORM
- Mated to Faith
  - Archeologist with ties to Skye Druids
  - Gift from Con is a narrow bracelet made of gold interlocked with a single pearl

Dorian (DAWR-ee-ən) – King of Corals

- Tattoo down his left side from his chest to his leg
- Has the ability to turn invisible
- Story in DRAGON NIGHT
- Mated to Alexandra
  - Gift from Con is a large, round sunstone gem set in a narrow rose gold beveled band

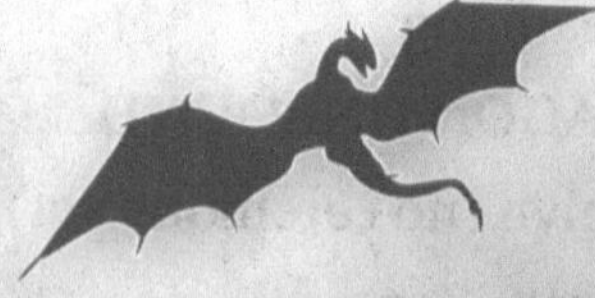

Eurwen (AYR-wen) – Dragon Queen

- Daughter of Con and Rhi
- Peach dragon with gold wings
- Tattoo along her spine
- Has the ability to shield herself
- Story in DRAGON MINE
- Mated to Vaughn
  - Gift from Con Montana sapphire

Guy (gai) – King of Reds

- Tattoo on back
- Power to erase memories
- Story in NIGHT'S AWAKENING and DARK HEAT
- Mated to Elena
  - Gift from Con is a teardrop ruby nestled in a platinum band

Haldor aka Hal (HAL-door) – King of Greens

- Tattoo on front and wrapping
- Ability to breath sleeping gas
- Story in DARK CRAVING and DARK HEAT
- Mated to Cassie
  - Gift from Con is a large emerald pendant necklace

Kellan (KEHL-ən) – King of Bronzes

- Tattoo on chest and extending to his left arm
- Power to pull wounds into himself
- Story in DARKEST FLAME
- Mated to Denae
  - MI5 agent
  - Gift from Con are smoky quartz earrings

Keltan (KEHL-tən) – King of Citrines

- Tattoo on right ribcage
- Ability to cook anything
- Story in FEVER
- Mated to Bernadette
  - Cryptozoologist
  - Gift from Con large oval citrine pendent on gold chain necklace

Kendrick (KEHN-drik) – King of Siennas

- Dragon Tattoo on back
- Power to camouflage
- Story in DRAGON LOVER
- Mated to Esha
  - Sun Elf
  - Asavori Ranger

Kiril (kih-RIHL) – King of Burnt Oranges

- Tattoo on his chest
- Breath of ice
- Best friends with Rhys
- Story in BURNING DESIRE
- Mated to Shara
  - Gift from Con is a Padparadscha (one of the rarest gems in the world) emerald bracelet.
  - Dark Fae who turned Light Fae

Laith (LAY-th) – King of Blacks

- Tattoo on his back
- Ability to breath paralyzing gas
- Runs The Fox and The Hound pub
- Story in HOT BLOODED
- Mated to Iona
  - Ancestor to Warrior, Hayden Campbell (Dark Sword series)
  - Gift from Con is a large black peal and diamond pendant necklace

Melisse (MEH-LihS) – Queen of Violets
- The very first Dragon King and Dark Fae offspring
- Tattoo winding up her left leg
- Ability to breath a cone of burning venom
- Was kept prisoner by the Dragon Kings for eons
- Store in DRAGON BORN
- Mated to Henry
  - JusticeBringer with his sister; part of an ancient line of Druid enforcers
  - Brother to Esther (Truthseeker)

Merrill (MEHR-əl) – King of Oranges
- Power of breath a beam of searing light
- Loves to give pep talks
- Best friends with Varek
- Tattoo on back mid-flight
- Story in DRAGON MARKED
- Mated to Katla
  - Gift from Con is a pear shaped Spessartite garnet pendant

Nikolai (nyi-ku-LIE) – King of Ivories
- Tattoo on right arm and right side of his body
- Ability of projected thermography (once he sees something, he can paint or draw it)
- Story in HEAT
- Mated to Esther
  - Gift from Con of mother of pearl earrings
  - Sister to Henry (JusticeBringer)
  - TruthSeeker with her brother; part of an ancient line of Druid enforcers

Rhys (REES) – King of Yellows
- Tattoo on his chest and shoulder
- Ability to call the night and shadows
- Constantly pushes Con, testing boundaries
- Best friends with Kiril
- Story in NIGHT'S BLAZE
- Mated to Liliana aka Lily
  - Daughter of nobility
  - Helicopter pilot
  - Gift from Con is a 5-carat cushion cut yellow sapphire ring set in a thin band of platinum

Roman (RO-mən) – King of Pale Blues
- Tattoo on his chest
- Ability to control metals
- Story in DRAGONFIRE
- Mated to Sabina
  - Gypsy
  - Gift from Con are teardrop aquamarine dangle earrings

Royden (ROI-dən) – King of Beiges
- Tattoo on his back
- Power of blinding light
- Story in DRAGON LOST
  - Mated to Annita
  - Gift from Con raw druzy cluster ring

Ryder (RIE-dər) – King of Grays
- Tattoo wraps his entire torso
- Ability to project weakness into someone
- Has an affinity for jelly donuts
- Designs, creates, and implements all electronics
- Story in SMOKE AND FIRE
- Mated to Kinsey
  - Talented hacker
  - Gift from Con is a gray star sapphire ring, large oval set in a thick platinum filigree band

Shaw (SHAW) – King of Sapphires
- Tattoo on right hip, waist, and thigh
- Ability to create illusions
- Story in DRAGON ETERNAL
- Mated to Nia

Sebastian (sə-BAS-chən) – King of Steels
- Tattoo on his right leg winding upward to his abdomen
- Can breathe lightning bolts
- Story in DRAGON BURN
- Mated to Gianna
  - Gift from Con large octagonal gunmetal blue stone pendant necklace

Thorn (THAWRN) – King of Clarets
- Tattoo on his chest
- Power of sound manipulation
- Story in PASSION IGNITES
- Mated to Lexi
  - Gift from Con are curving French wire 5-caret multifaceted rectangular garnet earrings

Tristan (TRIS-tən) – King of Ambers
- Tattoo on his chest
- Power to get into someone's mind
- Reincarnated Warrior, Duncan Kerr
- First new Dragon King in eons
- Story in FIRE RISING
- Mated to Samantha aka Sammi
  - Half-sister to Jane

Ulrik (OOL-rik) – King of Silvers
- Tattoo on his chest and neck
- Power to bring people back to life
- Best friends with Con
- One of only two Kings who never slept centuries away
- Banished from Dreagan for the war with humans
- Story in TORCHED
- Mated to Eilish
  - Gift from Con are platinum teardrop earrings
  - Powerful Druid
  - Wears silver Celtic finger rings that allows her to teleport

Varek (VAHR-ihk) – King of Lichen

- Tattoo on his left arm
- Power is energy draining shadows
- Best friends with Merrill
- Kidnapped from Earth and brought to Zora
- Story in DRAGON REVEALED
- Mated to Jeyra
  - Warrior
  - Gift from Con are green amethyst stone armbands

Vaughn (VAWN) – King of Teals

- Tattoo on chest
- Ability of dream manipulation
- Attorney for all things Dreagan
- Story in DRAGON MINE
- Mated to Eurwen
  - Gift from Con full finger ring with teal stones wound in a delicate, beautiful pattern from the base of her finger to her nail

Vlad aka V (vuh-lad) – King of Coppers

- Tattoo on his back with wings on the back of each arm
- Ability to mask himself while in dragon form
- Story in IGNITE
- Mated to Claire
  - Gift from Con is a 5-caret copper zircon set in rose gold
  - First mate to become pregnant

Warrick aka War (WAWR-ik) – King of Jades
- Tattoo on the right side of his body from shoulder to hip
- Power of protection
- Story in SOUL SCORCHED
- Mated to Darcy
    - Was the Druid who unbound Ulrik's magic
    - Gift from Con is a gold bracelet with five jade beads

DRAGON MARKED

A DRAGON KINGS® NOVEL

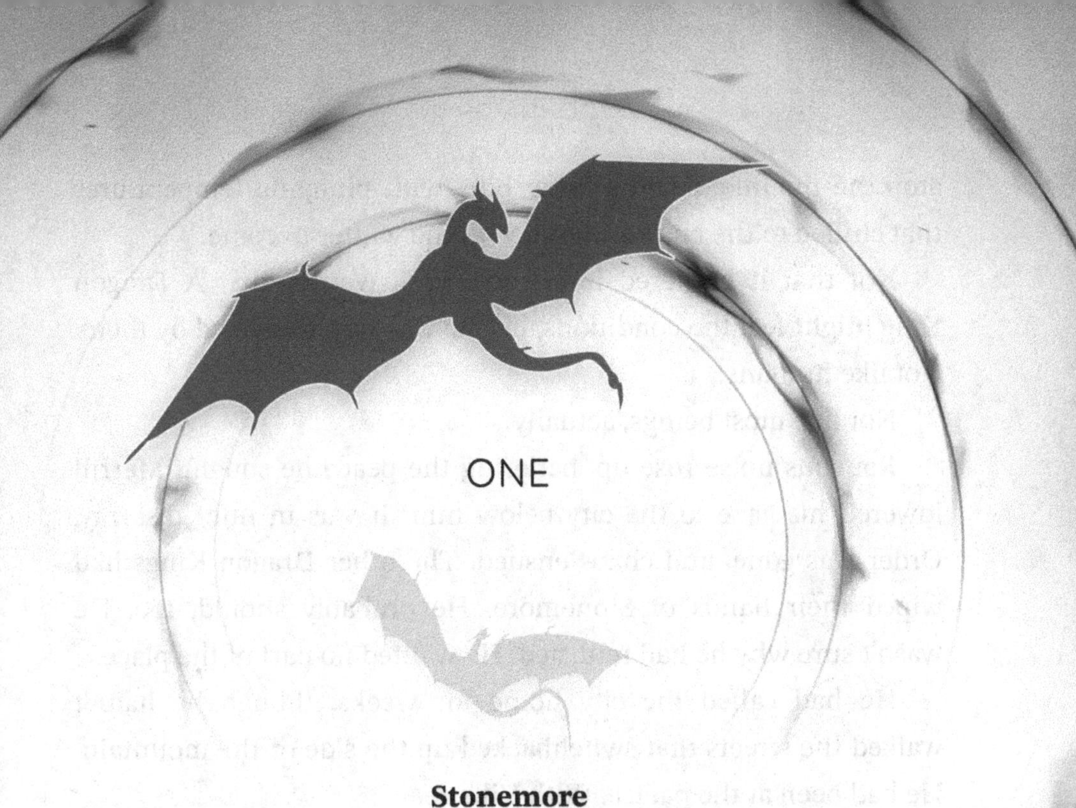

ONE

Stonemore

An invigorating wind swept through the city streets, scraping crisp leaves to rustle against stone. The air whistled past Merrill to rasp against his face and ruffle his hair that brushed his shoulders. Most considered the fall season as one of death, with winter darkness to follow. But he always thought of autumn as a period of renewal. Something about the scent of fallen leaves, damp earth, and pine, with the vibrant carpet of gold, orange, and red beneath his feet was energizing.

At least he had felt that way on Earth. He was still struggling to find his way on Zora.

The palace balcony offered a scenic view of the Ferdon Woods before him. Rising on either side of him were the majestic Tunris Mountains, silent guardians watching all with disdain, their jagged peaks not yet dusted with snow. All around him, the land was draped in autumn's warm, comforting hues. But the weather atop the mountain had a bitter bite, with plunging temperatures that chilled to the bone and hinted at the winter to come.

Not that it bothered him—hot, cold, wet, or dry. A Dragon King might feel the conditions, but he was never affected by them. Not like humans.

Not like most beings, actually.

Raucous noise rose up, battering the peace he sought. Merrill lowered his gaze to the city below him. It was in utter disarray. Order was gone, and chaos ensued. The other Dragon Kings had wiped their hands of Stonemore. He probably should, too. He wasn't sure why he had returned. He wanted no part of the place.

He had called the city home for weeks, though he hadn't walked the streets that switchbacked up the side of the mountain. He had been at the palace. With Villette.

Even now, thinking about her made him cringe.

The first time he had entered Stonemore was with Shaw. They had been sent to figure out who ruled the city in hopes of preventing more children with magic from being killed. Shaw had completed the mission. He, on the other hand, had been ripped apart.

He had been unprepared and completely caught off guard by the change that overcame him. All the anger, despair, and resentment he had carefully—and purposefully—locked away had found its way out, and he hadn't been able to stop the emotions from flooding him.

And, once released, he hadn't wanted to.

He had *wanted* to hurt others. Those who looked at him. People who crossed his path. Anyone.

Everyone.

The uncontrollable need to lash out and inflict as much misery as he had experienced seized him. And there was no turning back. Eons and eons worth of wrath had been unleashed. In the blink of an eye, he'd become someone else. Someone who didn't care about others. Someone without restraint.

Merrill couldn't return to the other Kings like that. They had dealt with their pain. He had helped them through those times. But they would see his. There was no way he could hide such rage, even if he wanted to. He wasn't sure what he was capable of. Or what he might do to them.

So, Merrill had made a decision that day. He'd watched Shaw shift into his true form and fly away with Nia, and then Villette had found him. At first, he hadn't known who she was, but he discerned that she was much more than she claimed. Her offer to remain at the palace had allowed him to put off deciding his next steps. Villette had been a distraction that'd lasted weeks.

All while his brethren fought against her and searched for him.

He had been unaware of it all. Villette's power had prevented any dragon from reaching out to him telepathically, and he hadn't sought out his kind, which allowed her deception to last even longer.

When he learned that Villette ruled Stonemore as The Divine, he didn't leave. He remained when he discovered that she possessed magic that allowed her to roam galaxies at will with the power of gods. He didn't fight her. He didn't try to return to the dragons. Even when he realized other Star People were on the realm, he did nothing.

But he wasn't exactly hers, either.

Merrill's internal wrath prevented her from controlling him. It was a small saving grace. Because if Villette had been able to manipulate him as she wanted, he never would've met Derek.

Discovering a Dragon King Merrill didn't know changed everything.

Derek's lack of knowledge about his heritage had spurred Merrill into action. Battle lines were drawn, sides chosen, and he once more joined his brethren. The Dragon Kings and their allies emerged victorious, but it came at a price. Villette was still out there somewhere. And Stonemore…

He studied the people below him. Someone needed to take charge of the city. There had already been a wealth gap, with the rich forcing the poor to live on the four lower levels while the affluent took the other three. The palace sat at the summit of the mountain. The divide had been easy to see and maintain.

The recent battle had forced guards stationed at each level from their posts, and the underprivileged now mingled with the prosperous. Most of the wealthy had barricaded themselves in their homes. It wasn't just the lack of food and the disappearance of the guards that began the riots, though. It was the sight of Merrill and his kin in the skies.

For centuries, Villette had spewed propaganda about the dragons and magic, making everyone fear those with special abilities. Yet none of the residents of Stonemore had known they had a powerful being governing them.

Villette's hatred for the dragons and her campaign to wipe them out had started long, long ago when the Star People enslaved the dragons. Her brother had set Merrill's ancestors free, creating Earth as their home, and that's where the dragons lived for millennia—free and prosperous. Until Villette found Earth.

Everything that had happened to Merrill and his clan, family, and friends was because of her. And he had chosen her over his own. He hadn't known about Villette's involvement then, but that didn't make his actions any less atrocious or shocking.

None of his brethren had said anything about it. But he knew the facts. He had lived them. Chosen them.

And those actions spoke loudly.

The problem was what to do now. Did he attempt to forget and go on as if he hadn't let the demons of the past loose? It seemed the best option. It was certainly what his friends wished for him. But he couldn't. Mainly because he hadn't faced those demons as all the other Kings had, and he couldn't rejoin everyone until he did. He was a powder keg waiting to detonate, and that was the last thing anyone needed.

Merrill clenched his hands, then spread his fingers. He'd always had his mountain in the Highlands of Scotland to escape to on Earth. Dreagan was where the Kings had hidden after the war with the humans. It was their home, their oasis. Their paradise.

They'd stayed hidden from mortals for thousands of years until dragons turned to myth and legend. Only then did the Kings emerge from their isolation and venture into the world. They took their skill of distilling to create Dreagan whiskey and become a multi-billion-dollar corporation. They lived in wealth right under humanity's noses.

But they were caged. Waiting for storms to return to their true form and take to the skies. At least on Zora, within the borders of the land the dragons had claimed, he could shift at will. He could fly as far and as high as he wanted.

It had been glorious.

Yet it caused him to think of when he had roamed Earth. Free and powerful. Before the humans arrived. Before the war. He had shoved all those difficult emotions away, locking them down deep so they would never see the light of day.

He could never have known that coming to Zora and finding the dragons would cause the crack that broke the barrier in his mind where he had shut away all things he didn't want to face. But it had. And there was no rewinding the clock, no ignoring things. The unruly demons had been sprung from their prison, and they were intent on destroying him.

Merrill turned and retraced his steps back inside the palace. It was all but abandoned now. Only a few servants remained. That wouldn't last long. Someone, somewhere, would realize the opportunity and seize it. Maybe Constantine should. He was the King of Dragon Kings. Con had kept everyone in line during those first few centuries after the war on Earth. He would be an excellent ruler for Stonemore. But he wouldn't take the job. The humans wouldn't allow it.

Merrill's heels thumped on the red sandstone floors as he strode to the stairs. The palace was vast and sprawling, but people had always moved about its many halls and stairways. Now, there was only the rare sighting of a servant going about their duties because they didn't have anywhere else to go.

He made his way out of the palace, only to pause atop the steps to look out over the exquisite garden across the road. It had once been a place where the affluent would come and stroll, enjoying the beauty of the flowers while hoping to enter the palace. How long until the garden was filled with people forced to live in squalor for years? How long would it take those who had slept on the street to run the wealthy out of their homes?

He figured it would be a matter of hours, not days. The sound of the mob making their way up the mountain was growing louder. Merrill walked down the steps and out into the unusually empty street. A few guards remained at the gate leading into and out of the eighth level, but there weren't nearly enough to keep out the coming crowd.

As Merrill approached the gate, he spotted the red-robed Priests of Innus who had joined the handful of Stonemore soldiers. Three of them wore armor. Merrill had a particular hatred for the religious sect established by Villette, mainly because the priests selected those who had magic—and carried out their death sentences.

On children.

Anger coiled within Merrill. Magic surged through him, waiting to be released—along with his wrath—upon the priests. They deserved it. They had taken countless innocents' lives. All because Villette had deemed it so. And they wouldn't stop. They would continue even now with the city in disarray.

He could stop them. Easily. No one would miss the murdering priests. But if he started, he wouldn't be able to stop with the three currently here. He would have to wipe them all out.

One of the armored priests noticed Merrill. He whispered something to the others, and they all turned toward him. He hadn't been looking for a fight, and as tempting as it would be to give in to the mounting rage, it would lead him down a road he wasn't sure he could come back from.

Tension was high as he neared the group. He took in the measure of each, noting who he'd need to strike first. Merrill wouldn't have to shift into his dragon form to take out the group of ten staring at him. But as he reached them, the soldiers merely opened the gate and let him through.

Disappointment rubbed Merrill as he walked past. Maybe he

did want a fight. Not that a human stood a chance against a dragon—especially not a Dragon King. Long-ago memories of the battle with the humans on Earth surfaced. It took everything he had to walk away and not rid this world of mortals.

A Dragon King didn't murder. If he were still on Earth and had his clan, the magic would have replaced him as King of Oranges for even contemplating such an action.

The humans began the war. They killed and forced the Kings to send the dragons away. The mortals took everything.

Bloody hell. It would be so easy for him to give in. He hadn't given in on Earth. But this wasn't Earth. Merrill shook his head to clear it of those thoughts as he fought to temper his ire.

"Hold up!"

The voice cut through the noise rising from the lower levels. Merrill halted and inwardly smiled. Then, he slowly turned to face the group. A fight it was, then.

One of the soldiers asked, "When is The Divine going to put the city in order?"

Merrill almost laughed out loud. Through the battle that'd featured dragons and Star People, as well as Druids and a hellhound, none of the residents understood that Villette was The Divine. And he wasn't going to tell them. They wouldn't believe him anyway.

"I wouldna wait around for order if I were you," Merrill replied.

His gaze lingered on the blond-haired, armored priest glaring at him. That one would be an issue that needed to be dealt with. That was if Merrill planned to remain in the city. This time, when he walked away, no one stopped him.

The streets on the seventh level were virtually deserted. It was the same on level six—no guards at the gates. When he reached the access to level five, he encountered a swarm of people. They didn't pay him any heed as they ransacked businesses for food. Merrill almost felt sorry for those whose homes were being destroyed by the crowd. Almost. All of it could have been prevented. The residents now paid for the decisions they made—and the edicts they had followed.

As he approached the gate to level four, he looked toward the temple used by the priests. The top portion had been blown away, and not by any of his friends. No one seemed to know what'd happened. He wished he did so he could commend whoever had managed to desecrate the building.

Merrill didn't hide his grin as he passed the temple and saw the priests murmuring in agitation as they shot worried glances at the ruins of their holy sanctuary. They were more concerned about the temple than the state of the city or its people. He wondered what they would do if he razed what was left of the temple to the ground. It wouldn't stop them from killing innocents in the name of some made-up god.

Indignation gripped him, its fingers digging into his chest. The dragon within fought to get free, to show the priests just why they should fear those like him. Fire burned in his lungs, begging to be released. He could cleanse the city and remove any trace of the humans. And Villette.

The temptation was great. Merrill came to a halt and faced the priests. He wanted to see the looks on their faces. Just before he shifted, he sensed Druid magic. Its touch was supple and heady, yet also powerful and compelling. He had felt that particular magic before. Merrill quickly scanned the faces of those rushing about.

Then he saw her.

It wasn't the first time he had laid eyes on the stunning Druid. And just like before, he was unable to look away from her incredible beauty. Unable and unwilling.

She leisurely walked up the incline of the street toward him while taking in everything going on around her. Hair as black as a raven's wing hung down her back in soft, luxurious waves. The length was parted down the middle with the sides clasped loosely behind her head, a strand or two falling free to brush her cheeks.

Her elegant, heart-shaped face was mesmerizing. She had a sultry mouth with wide, full lips meant to be kissed—and often. High cheekbones and a delicate nose added to her appeal. Gently arching brows sat over large, stormy gray eyes.

A thin, gray blouse skimmed over the swell of her breasts and tucked into a black, wide-legged split skirt that hung to her calves. A simple black belt wrapped around her waist, showing off her mouthwatering curves. Her feet were encased in black boots.

The Druid's name was Katla. She had recently fought against Villette, though not in the same battle as Merrill. She was the same Druid who had been taken to the top of the tower. The one who might very well be responsible for demolishing the temple. For that alone, Merrill wanted to thank her.

Unable to look away, he followed her with his gaze. And he wasn't the only one staring. A growl escaped when he noticed a priest watching her. They had hauled her to the tower to begin with. They'd had their chance with her.

He would make sure they didn't get another.

Merrill stepped in front of the priest who'd started after Katla and met the man's startled gaze. Villette was directly responsible for the deaths in Stonemore, but the priests were more than ready to kill for their false god. Outrage filled him. The fury from before returned with a vengeance. Everyone would be better off if no more of the red-robed men were walking around.

Is this who you've become?

Merrill didn't like the question. And he didn't like that he couldn't come up with an answer even more. He didn't know *who* he was anymore. He barely remembered who he had been. It was his dragon power, the same potency the magic on Earth had seen and used to appoint him King of the Oranges. That dragon wouldn't take a life without cause. *That* dragon would never have considered killing so freely.

Merrill managed to gain control of his bloodthirsty ire. He stepped closer to the priest and dipped his voice low, making it menacing. "Don't even look at her."

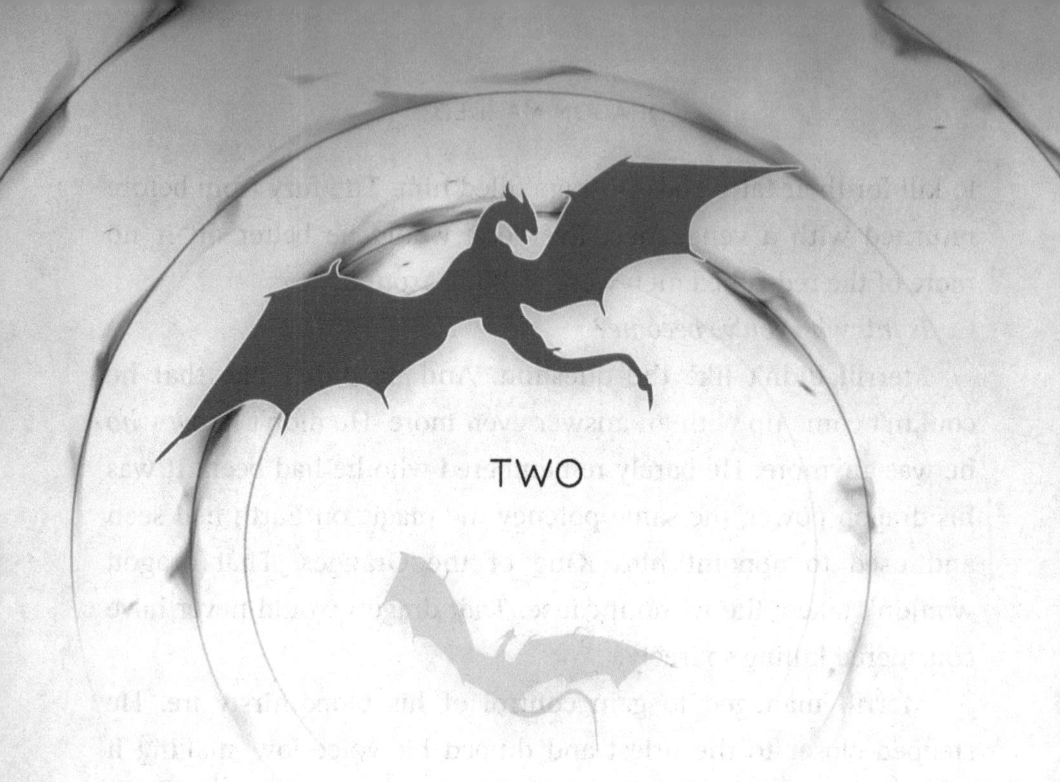

TWO

Returning to Stonemore had been a mistake. It was worse than Katla had imagined. Fear and hostility ran rampant through the streets. It contorted the faces of those plundering homes and shops in search of food. It creased the visages of the owners endeavoring to protect what was theirs.

Katla refused to look at the temple, but the scene from days before still played out in her head. The city held nothing but death and destruction. She turned to leave. She had been gone too long already. But she hadn't gotten two steps before she spotted the gathered priests.

She had no wish to hurt anyone, but she wouldn't allow them to take her again. If any soldiers or the red-robed clerics came for her, she would unleash the full extent of her powers. She wasn't sure what they were yet, but she was ready to find out. She faced the group, only to see she hadn't caught their attention. A tall, imposing, formidable man had.

The stranger stood nose to nose with one of the priests. The man was severely outnumbered, but he didn't back down. Not even when they surrounded him. The priests wearing armor moved closer as they pulled their swords from scabbards. The man lifted his head, his scowl directed at each one. Then, he looked at her.

The glare vanished. Even from a distance, his gaze grabbed her, held her. There was an intensity about him, a potent power that swirled around him as purposefully as the wind. He was hard and unyielding, fierce and arresting. Something about his barely leashed violence drew her, beckoned as if her very essence recognized him. She studied his ruggedly handsome visage, taking in his prominent cheekbones and brows to the hard line of his jaw and wide lips, the bottom fuller than the top. She couldn't see the color of his eyes, but she wanted to. She wished to be close enough to pick out all the colors of his irises.

His hair brushed his shoulders. She wouldn't call it blond, nor would she claim it was light brown. It was an interesting mix of both. Her eyes lingered on his wide shoulders. His shirt was a blue so deep it was nearly black, and he had the sleeves pushed up to show off his corded forearms, hinting at what lay beneath. Black trousers molded to trim hips and muscular thighs. His black boots had a different look to what others wore, setting him apart. Just as his bearing did.

Her gaze ran back up his body to meet his eyes once more. The wind swirled, grabbed the hem of her split skirt, and whipped the material against her legs. It whistled past as it caught her hair, lifting the ends momentarily before whooshing toward the priests and the man. The strong gust caused some to lose their balance, but the stranger with the penetrating gaze didn't seem fazed.

One of the soldier priests waved a sword before the man's face, severing their connection. The man cut his gaze to the cleric as more priests circled him. She peered through the bodies to watch the stranger. Magic skated just beneath her skin. She knew exactly what the priests were capable of. She had been in their custody only a short time ago.

Katla thought about helping the stranger, though he looked capable. He might even get out of it himself without her interference. She gripped the legs of her skirt with both hands, her mind drifting back to the valley and the hatred that had ruled her every decision. It would be easy to turn that animosity on the priests. So very easy. But it would bring attention to her. And others were waiting for her, counting on her. She couldn't let them down.

Her thoughts halted when the stranger moved with lightning speed, knocking away the sword and taking it for himself. There were shouts of dismay. More swords were drawn as the priests moved in. The stranger turned and pivoted, fighting off attack after attack as if he were swatting away pesky bugs.

Then, an unmistakable boom of magic laid out the priests, leaving the stranger the only one standing. He threw down the sword with contempt, his lip curled in disgust.

That's when she realized who he was. Or rather *what* he was: a dragon able to change forms. Only recently had she learned that some had that ability. Stonemore was close to the border of the dragons' land. She had even been warned they were fighting Villette at Stonemore. She should've expected to encounter one.

Nothing, however, could have prepared her for her reaction to this particular dragon.

That didn't stop the apprehension from settling uncomfortably in her belly. His gaze slid back to her. Was he here for her? Had the dragons decided to seek justice for what she had done to them?

The dragon stepped over a fallen priest and moved toward her. The day would come when she had to pay for her crimes, but it wasn't now. It couldn't be. Katla didn't try to talk to him. She ran. And didn't stop. She barreled through people until she reached the first level and darted to the open gate. She didn't slow, even when she was out of the city.

She ran headlong into the Ferdon Woods, weaving between the giant trees. She pushed herself, pumping her arms and legs to put as much distance as possible between her and the dragon. The earthy smell of the forest surrounded her, and colorful leaves danced upon the air as they tumbled to the ground. She knew her destination and traveled the straightest line to it, no matter how harsh the terrain.

Katla's lungs were on fire and sweat trickled down her face. She slid down a steep embankment and then scrambled up the other side. Birds scattered as she raced past. When she saw the twisted tree, she finally slowed to a walk. Her breathing was loud as she scanned the area for danger. As she drew closer to the tree, she checked the ground for signs that man or beast had come snooping. A relieved sigh escaped when she found the area undisturbed.

She pressed her thumbs together and lifted her hands before her, then moved them as if separating curtains. Her magic revealed the three sleeping children lying side by side within. Katla briefly closed her eyes, silently giving thanks that the kids were still there and unharmed. She knelt and touched the blond locks of the eldest of the three—just seven years old. The girl's brown eyes fluttered open and focused on her.

"Shh," Katla murmured. "It's just me, Aven."

"Did you find food?"

Katla forced a smile she didn't feel. "Not yet. But I will."

"Don't leave us again," Aven said, gripping Katla's hand tightly.

"I have to, but I won't go far."

Maely rolled onto her back and rubbed her eyes. Her straight black hair was cut at her shoulders. She sat up and stared at Katla with dark eyes that had seen too much in the five years she had been alive. "We'll go with you."

"Yes," Aven said loudly as she also sat up.

The commotion woke four-year-old Perick, the youngest of the trio, who was cocooned between the girls. He had a wild mop of dark curls and green eyes. "Katla?"

When he reached for her, she pulled him into her arms. He wrapped his arms and legs around her and rested his head on her shoulder. It made her think of her daughter and how she had loved to be held in such a way.

From the moment the priests had thrown her into the tower with the children, Katla had known she would do anything to keep them alive. And that was before she gained their trust. Now, she would tear down the world for them. Would protect them as she hadn't been able to with her daughter or nieces.

They'd eaten the last of their food that morning and could only survive on berries for so long. She had hoped to find something at Stonemore, but if she had known the state of the city, she never would've gone. Never mind encountering the dragon. Their only choice now was to keep going until she found another village. She hated moving the children, but the farther away from Stonemore they got, the better it would be for all of them.

Katla smiled at the girls, then kissed Perick's cheek, holding him close. She got to her feet and walked into the sunshine, Maely and Aven following. "It's time to feel the sun on your faces. We'll also fill the waterskins."

"There's that berry bush I found yesterday," Aven said.

Maely groaned as she twisted her lips in distaste. "More berries?"

"I don't mind them," Perick said, lifting his head from Katla's shoulder. "They're sweet."

He wiggled to get down. Once Katla had set him on the ground, he danced around with the energy of a child. It amazed her that the three could smile and play despite what they had been through. It proved how resilient children were. When did that leave a person? Why was it so difficult for adults to face hardships in the same manner?

"Berries. I want berries," Perick said happily.

Maely wrinkled her nose and released a long sigh. "I'll take him."

"Stay within sight," Katla warned.

Aven tucked a strand of blond hair behind her ear. "I can try to hunt. There are plenty of animals in the woods."

It was a job Katla should be doing, but she couldn't quite manage it. However, she had run out of ideas and had no choice but to hunt now. She would have to put her aversions aside for the children. "We'll do it together. Help me keep an eye on the other two."

An hour and a half later, Katla was plucking feathers from a bird. Each time she looked at the wings, she thought about the dragons and lifted her gaze to the sky, peering through the canopy of trees. There hadn't been any large shadows overhead that heralded their arrival. Would she have enough time to beg them to spare the children if they came?

She had ignored the scared, mournful calls of the dragons she'd captured. What made her believe they would treat her any better? Or that she deserved more? But the dragons weren't searching for the children. She held on to that hope.

The sun was sinking as Katla watched Perick and Maely gather rocks to form a circle around sticks of wood while Aven ignited the fire with her magic—the reason the priests had targeted the children. They possessed magic, and to the residents of Stonemore, that was enough reason to kill them. Katla encouraged all three to use their abilities but had also cautioned them on when and how. Everyone was a potential enemy.

With the porunea roasting over the fire, Katla had more time to think. Instead, she watched the children. She hadn't allowed herself to dwell on her daughter after the loss, but being around kids again made her heart ache for the family she'd once had. Katla grinned when Perick found a bug and brought it to Maely, who shrieked and ran away. A laugh bubbled up when Aven joined in the fun of chasing Maely.

Soon, their interest turned to the colorful, falling leaves as the girls made a bouquet of them. Perick dug in the dirt for more bugs. Katla would never get tired of watching them or hearing their laughter.

For these few moments, she could almost forget who she was and what she'd done. She immersed herself in the present. Even contemplated being a mother again. But those flashes never lasted long. The past was too fresh, the truths she had learned too raw. And her complicity in everything too great.

As much as she wished she could move forward, free from it all, the reality was that she couldn't. Then there was the constant, gnawing fear in the back of her mind that she would revert to who she had been. She had hurt so many. The last thing she wanted to do was harm the children.

Katla shivered and held her hands to the fire to warm them. It would take her a while to get used to the fluctuations in temperature again. She had spent too long in the valley without sun, rain, heat, or cold. Her stomach growled at the smell of the cooking bird, but the thought of taking a bite made her queasy.

The moment she called to the children that the porunea was ready, they rushed over and devoured their meal. It was just enough for them. She boiled some villeali leaves for herself as the kids licked their fingers clean. It was a recipe she'd used while still with her village. The drink would help sustain her until she could have a proper meal.

Aven rubbed her hands over the thin sleeves of her tunic and huddled next to Perick. The weather was getting colder every day. In addition to food, the kids needed clothes and shelter. Katla had to figure out something for them, and soon. They couldn't remain in the forest. It was no life for children.

"Katla," Maely called softly.

She looked across the fire to the girl, but Maely was staring over her shoulder. Katla turned and found the man from Stonemore standing behind her. He leaned a shoulder against the trunk of an oak and nodded to the kids, his lips softening.

"I mean no harm," he told Katla.

THREE

The Druid quickly jumped to her feet, moving to stand between him and the bairns. As if he would harm the children. Merrill had spent the day tracking her. She hadn't made it easy, but he had been determined to locate her. Though he wasn't entirely sure why.

"What do you want?" Katla asked.

Merrill lifted his hands, palms out. He used to be good at finding the right words. At one time, his brethren had come to him for advice and guidance. Now, words deserted him. He glanced at the bairns once more and remembered how they had gobbled the bird as if starving. That was something he could rectify.

"I'm hunting. I saw the bairns and thought I could help," he offered.

The eldest girl perked up as she cut her brown eyes to Katla. The wee lad licked his lips in anticipation. Only the middle child, with her dark eyes, kept her features even. Reserved, just like Katla.

"Why?" the Druid demanded.

Merrill never liked lying. It took too much effort to remember each falsehood and keep up. Because once one lie was spoken, more always followed. "I saw you in the city."

"I know," she replied.

He shook his head. "Before today. It was in a pub."

Her brow furrowed slightly, but she didn't reply.

"I heard the priests took you." Merrill tipped his head to the younglings. "I assume they were taken, as well?"

The lad nodded and scooted closer to the eldest girl. All three children's faces tightened in remembrance of their time in the tower.

"No one will harm them again," Katla declared in a voice laced with warning.

Merrill met her stormy gaze and shook his head. "Nay, they willna."

The Druid's eyes narrowed, but she didn't relax. She had no reason to trust him. And he hadn't given her one yet. His enhanced senses locked on her, his dragon eyes piercing the growing shadows to see that her gaze remained tempered like steel.

She was strong and resilient, just like the metal.

"I know what you are," she said.

"And I know what you are."

Her throat bobbed as she swallowed. She said nothing, only stared, no doubt calculating her odds if she ran.

Merrill once more searched for words, something that might convince her to let him help. Then he remembered a connection he could use. "Kora is well. As is Derek."

"Were you part of the battle we heard?" the lad asked.

Merrill briefly met the boy's green eyes. "I was."

"Which side?" the younger girl asked.

Merrill dipped his chin. "Against Stonemore, of course."

The lass tipped her head slightly in acknowledgment.

Katla asked, "Is Villette dead?"

"Nay. But her sister Miena is."

"The brunette with the bright green eyes?"

Merrill straightened from the tree. "That's her."

"That's who came to the tower," the eldest girl murmured.

The lad beamed as he looked at the Druid. "The one Katla saved us from."

Merrill met Katla's gaze once more. "I can help with food. Allow me to do that for the bairns."

"What's a bairn?" the lad asked.

Merrill grinned. "It means children where I'm from."

"And where's that?" This from the eldest.

Merrill thought about his beloved Scotland. The Highlands, the moors, the lochs. The land was as much a part of him as he was of it. He ached to walk the glens once more as heather blossomed. "Somewhere far, far away."

"Can we go there?" the boy asked hopefully.

Before Merrill could answer, Katla asked, "Did they send you for me?"

Merrill tilted his head to the side as he regarded her. "No one sent me."

"Then why did you follow me?"

"You were out of place in the city today."

"So were you."

"I'm out of place wherever I go." He blew out a breath. "You can ask all the questions you want after I return with food."

The Druid hesitated and looked back at the kids. Reluctantly, she nodded. Merrill waved at the children and turned on his heel to stride away. He could've used magic to create whatever he wanted, but he opted to give Katla some time alone. Besides, it had been a while since he'd hunted.

Merrill crafted a bow and a quiver of arrows and set out. The Ferdon Woods wasn't as magnificent as the Caledonian Forest in Scotland, but he had to admit it was still beautiful. The realm quieted as night descended. Stars twinkled in the navy sky as the last rays of sunlight faded.

He drew in a deep breath as he wove through the trees. With each step, his tense muscles eased. He paused and opened his hearing to pick up the sounds of animals. After a moment, he turned slightly to the right and began moving slowly.

As a dragon, he had spent all his time in nature, soaring high into the clouds and diving deep into the oceans. Even after becoming a Dragon King, he'd spent most of his time with his clan. It wasn't until the Kings sent the dragons away that things had changed. They each spent more time in human form than they did in their true ones.

They had lost their connection to the Earth. Or maybe he was the only one who felt that disconnect. So many of his brethren had not only found a way forward but had also found mates. Merrill couldn't rewind time. He couldn't change the decisions he'd made. At one time, he had been sure of so many things. He feared he might never find the dragon he'd once been.

He stopped when he saw the deer-like creature. It was smaller than a red deer, its coat tan, and its chest solid white. Merrill nocked an arrow and took aim. The deer's head jerked up, her big ears twitching. Just before he released the arrow, a fawn stood.

Merrill lowered the bow as the two wandered off. About thirty minutes later, he came upon a buck. He took the deer down with a clean shot.

Merrill walked to the slain animal and knelt beside him, placing his hand on the animal's neck. "Thank you for giving your life so others may live."

He removed the arrow and slung the deer over his shoulders as he started back. The children were on the lookout for him. The moment they spotted him, they rushed to Katla, who rose to her feet. She remained by the fire as she watched him enter the camp. Their eyes met before he lowered the buck to the ground.

"What do we do with it?" the lad asked.

The eldest stepped forward. "We skin it."

"First," Merrill said, straightening and looking around for a tree, "we hang the deer to drain the blood. Who wants to help?"

The boy jumped up and raced toward him. "Me."

Merrill held out his hand. "I'm Merrill. And you are?"

"Perick," the lad answered with a bright smile.

Merrill noticed Katla clutching her hands as if she wanted to grab Perick and pull him against her. He shook the lad's hand. "Nice to meet you."

"I'm Aven," the eldest girl said as she stepped forward.

Merrill nodded at her. He slid his gaze to the remaining child.

She wrinkled her nose. "I'm not getting anywhere near blood."

"I wouldna dare ask it," he replied with a grin.

The girl stood beside Katla. "My name is Maely."

"I'm pleased to meet all of you," Merrill replied.

Perick jumped around. "Can we hurry? I'm hungry."

"Ugh. You're always hungry," Maely muttered.

Merrill reached behind his back and called some rope to his palm. He then handed it to Perick. "Can you hold that for me?"

The lad eagerly took it. Aven grabbed one of the deer's legs and dragged it after Merrill as he searched for a tree. He found a good location and held out his hand for the rope. Perick handed it to him. The boy attempted to reach for the end after Merrill tossed it over a limb, but Aven beat him to it.

In no time, Merrill had the deer hoisted off the ground. Blood was already draining from the wound. Aven moved to stand beside him, her gaze expectant. He used magic again to create a dagger and sliced the deer open. Aven didn't hesitate to reach in and gut the animal.

"I used to help my dad," Aven said. "Before we were forced to relocate to Stonemore."

Anger twisted Merrill's gut. He fought against it, refusing to let it take him. Not when the bairns were nearby. He concentrated on skinning the deer. Aven helped, but she didn't speak any more about her family. It took far longer than Merrill liked to get his ire under control. Each time he thought he had, he saw Aven and thought about how Villette had conquered villages, burning them to the ground and forcing the people to an already overcrowded city.

By the time he'd situated the deer to cook over the fire, he had finally gotten control of his emotions. For now. But it became harder and harder each time. He looked up to find all three bairns sitting around the fire, licking their lips in anticipation.

Merrill, however, found his gaze returning to Katla as he buried what remained of the deer. She was the only one who seemed uninterested in the meat. She barely even looked at it. Merrill straightened and turned toward the sound of burbling water. He didn't have far to go until he reached a stream. It flowed slowly, the shore dotted with rocks worn smooth.

He stopped at the edge and watched the flowing current for a moment. Then he knelt and plunged his hands into the cold water to scrub away the blood and dirt. Soft, unhurried footsteps approached. He splashed his face before sitting back on his haunches and looking over his shoulder at Katla. She stared at him, wariness in her gaze.

Merrill swung his head back around to look across the stream to more trees. He hadn't been sure what to do or where to go for weeks. His time in the forest had given him some clarity.

"Why are you here?"

The Druid's voice was rich and warm as it washed over him. He liked the sound of it. Even if he didn't like that she didn't believe him. "I've already told you."

"The children are innocent."

"I know." He wiped his hands on his pants and got to his feet to face her.

A small frown puckered her brow. "Let me get them somewhere safe before you take me."

"Take you?" he asked in confusion. "Take you where?"

"To the Kings."

He studied her, his bewilderment growing. "Why would I do that?"

"To punish me."

Now, he understood. He should have realized that she would construe his arrival. "No one sent me. And there has been no talk of punishment."

Gray eyes raked over him slowly, much as she had done at Stonemore. "Do you know who I am?"

"Aye. Kora has been searching for you."

"Then you don't know who I am. If you did, you wouldn't be so willing to help me."

Merrill ran a hand through his hair to shove it out of his face. "You're a Druid who no' only got the bairns out of the city but also destroyed the temple in the process. And you've taken on the duty of looking after the children. That's enough for me."

"I'll go peacefully if you only allow me to take the children somewhere safe. That's my only stipulation."

He studied her for a long moment, noting her unease and the tension radiating from her. Nothing he said or did eased her, and he was beginning to believe that nothing would. "If I had come for you, I would've taken you at Stonemore. I'm no' here to mete out whatever justice you think the Kings demand."

Irritation flashed across her face. "You expect me to believe that you came to bring food?"

"I honestly doona know why I came. I offered my assistance when I saw the bairns. You have magic. Why no' use it to get food?"

Katla wound her arms around her middle as she turned her head away. "The children can't return to Stonemore."

Merrill shifted his weight to his other leg. "I agree."

"They need somewhere safe."

He thought about Iron Hall. The underground city in Raynia Canyon was where his brethren looked after other bairns saved from Stonemore. Merrill almost mentioned it to Katla, but she hadn't believed anything he'd said up to this point. And he doubted that would change anytime soon.

"Thank you for the food. The children were sick of berries."

"What about you?"

She frowned as she looked at him. "What about me?"

"Are you sick of berries?"

Her face shuttered. "I like them fine."

"But no' the meat." The smell of it hung in the air, and his mouth watered for a taste.

"Merrill!" Perick shouted as he came running toward him. "I'm starving. Is it ready?"

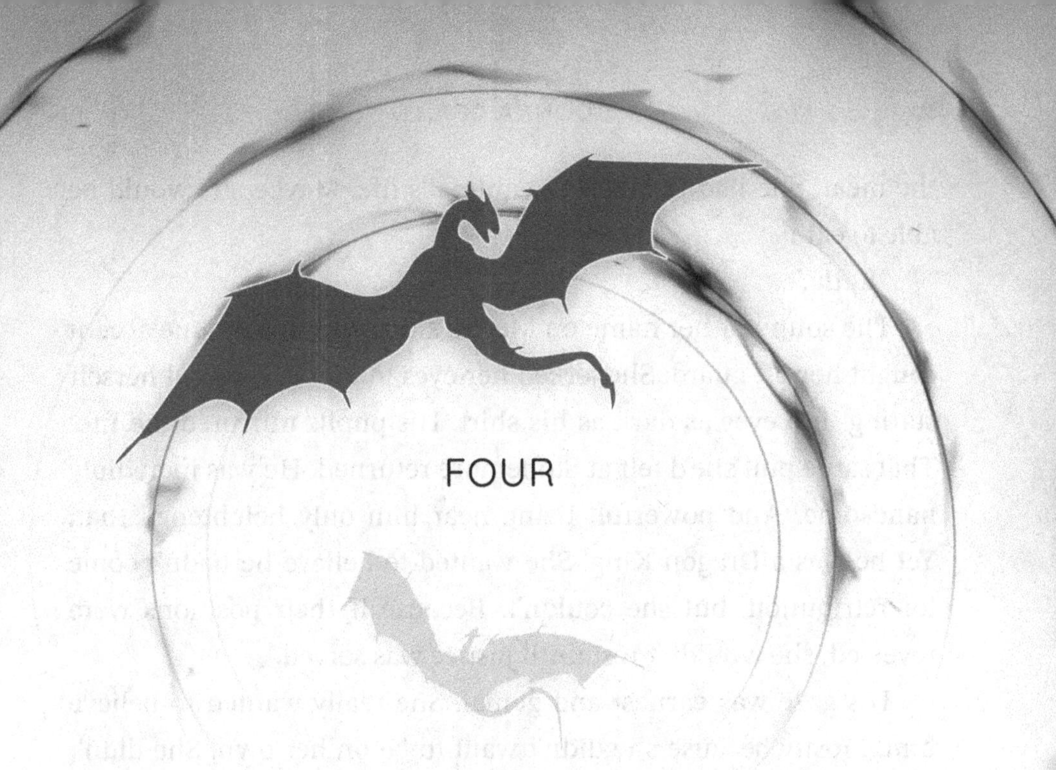

FOUR

Katla's stomach growled with hunger as she returned to the fire, Merrill two steps behind her with Perick in tow. She took her place and inhaled the delicious smell. Even her mouth watered as Merrill passed the meat around.

"There's plenty," he said, offering her a large slice.

She looked away and shook her head. "I'm not hungry."

"I can hear your stomach from here," Maely said around a mouthful of food.

Merrill rose and walked around to squat beside Katla, the slice of meat still hanging from the end of his dagger. "Is it that you doona like the taste of this animal?"

"That isn't it."

"Then what is it?" he asked softly. "There is enough to fill everyone's belly several times over."

She was hungry. Starving, actually. The villeali leaves hadn't done much, and she couldn't stomach another berry. Katla eyed the meat. She hadn't taken the animal's life. Maybe she would be able to eat it.

"Katla."

The sound of her name on Merrill's lips with his unique accent caught her off guard. She jerked her eyes to him and found herself staring into eyes as dark as his shirt. His pupils mirrored the fire. That same pull she'd felt at Stonemore returned. He was incredibly handsome. And powerful. Being near him only heightened that. Yet he was a Dragon King. She wanted to believe he hadn't come for retribution, but she couldn't. Because if their positions were reversed, she wouldn't rest until justice was served.

His gaze was earnest and genial. She really wanted to believe him. Mostly because she didn't want to be on her own. She didn't know anything about this world or who to trust. She was tired of being alone. And she didn't want to shoulder everything herself. But this was about more than her. It was about Aven, Maely, and Perick.

"Eat," Merrill urged softly.

She needed her strength. It was the only reason she pulled the meat from the blade and bit into it. She waited for her stomach to rebel, but nothing happened. The taste was pleasant. Katla devoured the piece within moments. Merrill had another waiting for her. She didn't know how much she ate before finally waving him off. Katla looked at the children to find them on their backs, pointing at the stars. She watched them, smiling when they laughed and genuinely enjoying their presence. They were the only ones she didn't doubt. They were innocent and pure of heart.

"I can attempt to locate their families in the city if you'd like."

Merrill's offer jerked her out of her musings. Katla had forgotten that he was there. She glanced over to see him sitting beside her. Had he been there all along? "That would be the right thing to do."

"No' if the parents decide to remain in Stonemore."

"It isn't as if I can force them to leave."

He reclined on his hands. "I can. And I will. There isna anything in the city anymore. You saw that yourself."

"What happened with the priests?"

"We had a disagreement."

She quirked a brow as she looked at him. "I see."

"I didna kill them. That isna to say I didna want to. I did. Which is why I didna."

She wondered if she would've had the same control. "You're a better person than I."

"You didna go after them. And you had the chance."

"Maybe I should." Her gaze swung to the children. Perick had his head in Aven's lap, his eyes barely able to stay open while the girls talked. "Then no one else would get hurt."

"The religion is too ingrained. You remove those priests, and more will take their place. Likely even more fanatical ones than are there now."

She looked at him. "Is that why you didn't kill them?"

"That's one of the reasons."

"Villette could stop it. She's the cause of all of this."

Merrill grunted. "She's part of the catalyst, aye. But she didna do it alone. Miena began it. Villette turned on her sister and locked Miena away."

That's why Katla hadn't heard Miena's name before. "How did Villette get away?"

"As difficult as it is to understand, she joined us to battle Miena."

Katla shook her head in disbelief. "You mean you had a chance to take her out and didn't?"

"Sometimes, you have to set aside one villain to go after another who's more dangerous."

"I don't believe that."

"How much do you know about the Star People? They're extremely powerful."

"I know," she stated icily.

He shook his head and sat up. "I'm no' sure you do. Villette is strong, but Miena was stronger. Star People doona die easily. They can take each other's lives, but the only other being that can kill them is a hellhound."

"Kora," she replied, thinking about their brief meeting.

"Aye. It took several Kings, three other Star People, a Fae, *and* Kora to bring Miena down."

Which meant Katla wouldn't be able to rid the realm of Villette on her own.

Merrill took a deep breath. "None of us wanted Villette's help, but we needed it. And Miena was going after her, so Villette needed us. The enemy of my enemy is my friend."

"You said three other Star People. Who are the other two?"

"Eurielle. Another sister of Villette and Miena, though she keeps to herself. I doona know much about her, but she has aided us in the past. There is also Lotti, who is mated to a King."

Katla glanced at the kids to see Perick asleep. "How many Star People are there?"

"I doona know an exact count. My guess is many, many more."

That's what she was afraid of. "Where is Villette now?"

Merrill shrugged. "Your guess is as good as mine. As soon as Miena breathed her last, Villette vanished. Our agreement was only until Miena's death. If she's smart, she'll go to another realm. But she has a deep-rooted hatred for my kind. She's worked hard to create an atmosphere of hate here. I doona believe she'll leave."

"Because the Star People enslaved the dragons," Katla said, remembering what she had learned from Henry in the bramble forest.

A muscle clenched in Merrill's jaw. "You know the story?"

"I know Villette's brother freed the dragons and created the world you come from."

"Earth," Merrill offered.

She nodded. "And Villette brought humans to your realm, as well as here on Zora."

"Her goal is to wipe out every dragon and then create her own to enslave."

"But...why? If the Star People are as powerful as you say, why do they even need slaves?"

Merrill shook his head. "Power. Miena and Villette found our dragons here after we sent them away. Those two destroyed our homes, families, and lives. They nearly destroyed us."

"But you're still around."

"To what end? We've endured many wars. We doona want another."

Katla stirred the fire with a long stick. "There is much hatred and fear for dragons."

"There is much hatred and fear for magic," he said, looking pointedly at her and then the kids.

"I feared and hated."

He looked up at the sky through the branches. "Most do in some form or another."

"Even you?"

"Even me."

Katla moved some hair from her face. "Until quite recently, I didn't know dragons could shift forms."

"Henry shared a lot about us."

"He wanted to save Melisse."

Merrill scratched an eyebrow. "They're mates."

"Henry isn't a dragon."

"That doesna matter. He's a Druid," Merrill replied and looked at her.

She propped the end of the burning stick on a limb. "That's something else I hadn't heard until Henry."

"There are many Druids on Earth. It was Druids Villette brought to our planet."

"But what *are* they?"

He grinned. "You mean, what are *you*?"

"Fine. What are *we*?"

"Druids are as vast and differing as trees. Some can manipulate water or fire, others can communicate with the wind or trees. Even animals. Many more doona have special abilities but can still create magic with spells."

Katla leaned on one hand, angling toward him and lowering her voice so she didn't wake the now-sleeping kids. "Spells?"

"That is how Druids use their magic. They also have a special connection to nature."

"I've never known anyone who had magic or used spells."

His dark blue eyes were steady as he watched her. "No one?"

"No one. Our village was isolated and relatively small. Everyone knew everyone. If someone had such abilities, it wouldn't have remained hidden for long."

"You had to get yours from somewhere."

Katla glanced at the ground. "Villette."

"She may have ignited things, but she couldna *give* you Druid magic as she isna one."

"Meaning?" Katla asked, her brain trying to sort the new information.

Merrill propped a foot on the ground and rested his arm on his knee. "Meaning, if she gave you anything, she gave you part of her magic."

Did she really have a Star Person's magic in her? Could that be what tainted her? What made her do the things she had done? Nay. She was the only one to blame. She'd had a choice, and she let grief and rage rule.

"I don't know any spells. That isn't how my magic happens."

"But you are no' like the Druids on Earth, so that makes sense."

She wasn't so sure about that. "Do you sense Star Person magic?"

"Your Druid magic overwhelms any other. It's verra strong. So strong that it drew Henry across realms. That's why I have a diffi-cult time believing you didna have magic before. I doona sense any other magic, but that's no' to say it isna there."

Katla drew her knees to her chest and wound her arms around her legs. Merrill knew Henry, which meant he must know who she was—and what she had done. He hadn't said anything about those horrible acts. Hadn't even hinted at them. She didn't know what to make of that. Was it because he didn't care? Or was he trying to get close so he could turn on her?

She hadn't meant to have such an open conversation with him. It had just happened. She was also lonely, and it was nice to converse with an adult—especially about things she was trying to sort out. Did she dare believe him? That was the real question.

"You still doona trust me," Merrill stated.

It wasn't a question, and she didn't treat it like one. "I've made poor choices in the past."

"Everything I've told you is the truth."

She turned her head to him. "Why would you help me?"

"Should I no'?"

"Don't do that. You know of what I speak."

He sighed, his lips flattening briefly. "You believe I should be angry with you."

"I do."

"Why?"

She closed her eyes for a heartbeat, attempting to retain patience. "You know why."

"Say it."

Katla glared at him, but he held her gaze. She was tired of skirting around the issue, and apparently, so was he. When the words came, her voice wobbled. "I killed dragons. I lured them into the vine forest and held them for Villette."

"Did you personally take their lives?"

"I trapped them."

"Did you take their lives?" he repeated, his voice firm. Unyielding. Just like his stare.

She swallowed. "I might as well have. I could have released them." If she hadn't held such hatred, she never would have done the things she had.

"Why did you trap them?"

That wasn't part of the story she wanted to think about. She had already revisited those memories when Henry confronted her. She couldn't do it again.

"Why?" Merrill pressed, his voice softer.

Katla shook her head. "Stop." She didn't want to hear the screams reverberating in her head again. Didn't want to feel the heat of the fire, smell the burning flesh, or experience the pain.

"Who hurt you?" he coaxed gently.

The backs of her eyes burned with unshed tears. The memory formed of its own volition, wrapping her in urgency and terror. And death. "The first dusting of snow coated the valley overnight. The sun was bright as the children played. We were simple people, living simple lives surrounded by a stunning landscape. The village sat at the base of a mountain at the start of the valley, where it was the narrowest. No matter the season, it was exquisite."

One side of Merrill's lips curved slightly. "What was your favorite season?"

"Winter. It could get frigid, but there was something captivating about that first snowfall. The way the snow dusted the evergreens and the water froze. I loved how everything was blanketed in white."

"Aye, lass. I know exactly what you mean."

She found herself smiling as she thought about the winters in the valley. But that picture shattered when she grasped that she hadn't seen snow in a very long time. Following on the heels of that thought were the events of the past that had upended her life. "Our tranquil existence was extinguished when the raiders came. They arrived from the road and down the mountain. There were so many. Our small village couldn't fend them off. A few attempted to take a stand but were ruthlessly cut down."

Katla clenched her hands as she remembered the fear that had choked her. "We were outside washing as my daughter played with my two nieces. I heard the invaders' war cries. I saw people being killed. My husband turned to get his sword, and I knew if he faced the enemy, he would be struck down, as well. I shoved our daughter into his arms and took hold of my nieces. I tried to find my brother and his wife, but everyone was scrambling by that point."

The memories were so clear. It was like she was back there, surrounded by chaos and death. She lowered her legs to sit cross-legged. This was why she didn't want to talk about the past. It was still too raw and painful. Too gut-wrenching.

Merrill's hand covered one of hers that rested on her knee. The touch was light. His gaze held sympathy and support, both of which gave her the courage to continue. Unfortunately, when he dropped his hand, he took his warmth with it, leaving her skin chilled.

"We couldn't fight them, so we tried to run, but the attackers blocked our escape. Then, they began surrounding us. Some pleaded for mercy while others screamed and cried. I couldn't wrap my head around the fact that such violence had come to our peaceful home. I can still hear the sound of their blades swinging and the splatter of blood as it landed on the ground. I couldn't find my husband or my brother and was panicking. Then, I heard someone shout my name. I looked over and saw my husband as he shoved his way out of the crowd. I didn't know where he was going or why, but I trusted him. I picked up my youngest niece and put her on my hip, dragging the other after me. That's when I spotted what my husband and a few others had. The invaders hadn't surrounded us completely. There was an opening to get free. We believed it was their mistake."

"They left the space on purpose," Merrill said.

Katla nodded before taking a long drink from the waterskin. "Once others saw what we were doing, they began to follow. We ran in the only direction we could—straight toward the dragons' border. The valley was long. We heard the dragons, of course, and I caught a glimpse of one once, but no one dared to venture too near the border. But that day, it was the only way for us to escape. We ran to the only place we could."

Merrill briefly lowered his gaze to the ground. A muscle in his jaw jumped, but he said nothing.

There was nothing to say. She drew in a ragged breath, remembering the uneven ground and how many times she'd tripped. "I couldn't carry my niece. I set her down and hauled both her and her sister with me. My husband was ahead of me, clutching our toddler to his chest. She lifted her head and looked at me. I saw her tears and how she dug her little fingers into her father's neck. I ran faster, all the while thinking the invaders would stop when we reached the boundary. They gained on us quickly, cutting my friends and family down."

Perick murmured as he turned over. Katla watched him for a moment. Then she licked her lips and continued. "The others ahead of me saw what was happening and crossed the border. It went against the very law of the land, but we were fighting for our lives. I heard the attackers coming up behind me and knew the girls and I were next. I watched my husband and daughter rush onto the dragons' land. Certain death was behind us, and a promise of death before us. Yet we crossed without hesitation. I was certain the invaders would halt their pursuit. We all believed it. There was no celebrating, though. We knew what dangers awaited in traversing onto sacred land. We searched the skies for dragons, but it appeared clear. Just when I thought we had escaped all of it, someone was cut off mid-scream. The raiders followed us across the border, chasing us deeper into dragon territory."

Merrill's jaw muscle jumped again as he closed his eyes for a heartbeat.

"A dragon's roar deafened the screams and the sounds of slaughter. The sight of the enormous beast caused pandemonium. I lost hold of my nieces somehow. One moment, I had them. The next, they were gone. There wasn't time to look because the dragon swooped toward us. It flew so close, the wind from one beat of its wings knocked me down. The villagers spun and ran straight to the waiting invaders. We were trapped between them and the dragon."

Katla swung her gaze to the fire. Wind whipped through the flames, making the blaze dance and pop. "That's when I saw my husband. He fought one of the raiders while our daughter hid behind him. She was screaming for me, her arms out. I knew the moment I called out to her that I had made a mistake. She jumped up to come to me, just as the dragon flew over and breathed fire. My husband turned and covered our daughter with his body as the blaze cut a path before me."

Her eyes closed as she recalled the size and scope of that one breath of fire. "The heat was so severe it blistered my skin. I watched the invader flail around, screaming as he burned. The flames were too high to get through, but I couldn't stop searching for my family. Even though I knew nothing could survive that inferno."

She forced her eyes open. She could still smell the burnt bodies and scorched earth. "Smoke billowed in the air. The screams of the dying were fading, and raiders and villagers alike lay dead all around me, some bodies burned so badly I couldn't distinguish who they were. I found one niece dead, a spear in her back. I never found my youngest niece or the rest of my family. I wanted to stay and search, but the dragon swung back to make another pass. I ran back over the border, and that's when I discovered I was the sole survivor. I swore retribution for my family and village that day. I was so overcome with grief and hate that nothing mattered. I don't know how long it was before Villette found me. She offered me a way to get revenge, and I took it without a second's thought."

Katla spread her hands on her thighs. "I never should have blamed only the dragons. The raiders held more responsibility. Everyone knew crossing onto dragon land meant death. Grief clouded my judgment." She swallowed and glanced at him. "Henry told me the dragon in question, Eurwen, was trying to help us. She saved my husband, daughter, and a few others and took them to a safe place. Maybe if I had remained, she would've taken me with them. Instead, I spent the next fifteen hundred years taking my vengeance out on your kind."

FIVE

Merrill had heard Katla's tale from Henry, but it had only been the basics. Listening to her speak of that dreadful day had put him into the memory with her. He understood her hatred, animosity, and bitterness. Every Dragon King did. Because they had lost everything, too. While Katla had focused on the dragons for revenge, the Kings had fixated on the humans.

Yet neither the dragons nor the humans were to blame. The fault lay squarely with the one who had instigated both. Villette.

Merrill inwardly winced when Katla dashed away a tear so he wouldn't see. The old Merrill would know what to say to alleviate her sorrow and self-loathing. Instead, they sat together, listening to the fire pop.

"I know that was hard. Thank you, lass," he murmured.

She sniffed and nodded but kept her gaze on the fire. He recognized that she needed to be alone with her thoughts. He had pushed her to dredge up those memories and regretted it. For just a moment, he had been the old him. Then, when she needed comforting words, he was left wanting.

Merrill noticed the bairns huddled together for warmth. He rose, magically materializing blankets in his hands. After he'd tucked the blankets around them, he glanced at Katla. She had a faraway look in her eyes. He wondered if he should leave, or at least watch over them from a distance. Katla didn't trust him, and she had every right. No amount of denial and assurance could make her believe that he hadn't come to exact justice for the dragons.

His gaze slid to the bairns. They were only some of those who'd borne the brunt of Villette's endeavor to wipe out those with magic. Merrill had seen enough wars to last an eternity. And there were never really any victors. There was just death, destruction, and loss. But there was no getting out of what was coming.

Villette might have joined with the Kings to put an end to Miena, but that in no way meant she'd had a change of heart. Villette's loathing ran too deep. And she had stirred up too much discontent across Zora, not just with dragons but also against anyone with magic. Generations had been educated to hate and fear. And that wouldn't stop with Villette's death. The seed hadn't just been planted, it had sprouted and spread like a contagion. And, like any disease, it had to be eradicated.

Which meant war.

Merrill wanted to remain, but he needed a good excuse to convince Katla. And he had it—Villette. Their common enemy deserved to face those she had wronged to be punished. It undoubtedly meant that he would have to open himself to Katla and share things he didn't want others to know, but it was worth it if he could stay near her.

He studied the bairns. She was right that the woods were no place for them. He might be able to persuade her to bring the children to Iron Hall. The bairns were the reason she remained in the area, after all. Once they were seen to, Katla could set out to find Villette.

Merrill felt a push against his mind. He opened the mental link at the sound of Varek's voice. *"Aye? Is everything all right at Iron Hall?"*

"Everything is fine," Varek said. *"I'm checking on you. You didna return."*

Merrill rubbed the back of his neck and turned away from the fire. Varek was his best friend, the one dragon who knew him better than anyone. And yet, he couldn't tell Varek how he really felt. His friend would want to help, but no one could help him. This was something he had to do alone. *"Stonemore is as bad as we feared. You should also be aware that I had an altercation with some priests."*

"I'm no' surprised. They're looking to show their might."

"It didna go as planned."

Varek chuckled. *"I bet it didna. I wish I could have been there. Their hold on the city shouldna last long."*

"I wouldna wager on that. I'll be surprised if they doona retain control."

Varek grunted. *"You may have a point. So, want to tell me what's really going on?"*

"Leave it, brother."

"I can no'. You have been there for all of us when we needed it. Let me be here for you."

Merrill ran a hand down his face and sighed. *"I appreciate the offer."*

"But?"

"I'm no' the dragon I was. I can no' find the words to offer comfort or wisdom. I can no' even find it in me to smile. I'm broken."

"You're no' broken, brother. You're suffering. It's finally coming to the surface. You know how low I sank, and you refused to let me go through it alone. I willna allow you to deal with this on your own."

"But I need to."

Varek was silent for a moment before he exhaled. "Merrill—"

"I know what you want to say, and I'm telling you no' to. There is nothing left of the dragon I once was. You have no idea how hard I fight against ire at every moment. It nearly took me at Stonemore with the priests."

"But it didna."

Merrill looked at Katla. It hadn't because he had seen her. It hit him then that the entire time he'd been with her and the bairns, the anger hadn't reared its head. "It could have. Had it, there wouldna have been anything left of the city. You and the others would've had to hunt me down."

"It willna come to that."

"You doona know that. Neither of us does."

"I know you. You're a good man!"

This was why Merrill hadn't wanted to tell Varek anything. He put his back to the fire. "Maybe it was always meant to happen. Maybe coming to Zora instigated the release of all I had locked away. The why doesna matter. It happened. And I have to sort through it."

"If this is about you and Villette, no one is upset."

Merrill felt a familiar anger begin to bubble within him. "You should be."

"Come back to friends. Perhaps you need to return to Earth and Dreagan."

"It willna matter what realm I'm on. Let me do this the way I need to. Please, brother."

Varek released a long sigh. *"All right. If you need me, I'm here."*

The tension melted out of Merrill. *"You'll be the first I reach out to."*

"I'll hold you to that. Stay in touch."

"You have my word."

Merrill severed the link. He probably should've spoken to Varek before leaving Iron Hall. After what he'd put his brethren through, Merrill at least owed them an explanation. But he had left without a word. Again. What did that say about the person he had become? More than he wanted to delve into, probably.

He looked over his shoulder toward Katla. She hadn't moved from her spot. He wanted to go to her. Instead, he walked to the stream and stood at the water's edge. Zora's double moons were a sight to behold. They were near enough that you could stare at both together. One was closer to the planet than the other—much closer than Earth's moon was to it. He studied each before taking in the vast sky of stars and contemplating the enormity of space.

At one time, his ancestors had flown through the universe with the Star People. What they might have seen and experienced was overshadowed by the fact that the dragons had been slaves, bowing to the whims of a more powerful race. If it hadn't been for Redis, who'd freed his ancestors, the dragons would likely still be in the service of the Star People.

Merrill closed his eyes and tuned out the sound of the water as his hearing expanded, moving through the woods and over the border to his kin. He listened to the dragons call to one another for several minutes, imagining that he was with them. It took him back to the time when his clan was still on Earth.

It didn't take anything for him to delve into the past and think about flying with other Oranges around him. Of how he used to sit atop the highest region and stare out across the land the magic had deemed him worthy enough to rule. Of what a sight it was to behold when a large grouping of Oranges flew together. Oh, how he missed his clan and family.

Merrill felt Katla before he heard her. He waited for her to speak, but when she began to turn to leave, he bade, "Stay."

"I don't wish to disturb you."

"You are no'."

"What are you doing?" she asked.

Merrill grinned. "Listening to the dragons."

"You can hear them?"

The surprise in her voice pleased him. "I can hear their wings flap as they fly, and their roars as they call out to others."

"What are they saying?"

"Dragons doona speak as humans do." He opened his eyes and turned to her. "We speak through our minds."

Her head tilted to the side. "You read minds?"

"That would be an invasion of privacy. We have the option of ignoring someone. If a dragon wishes to speak with me, they say my name. I hear it in my head. Then, I can open the link to allow communication or keep it closed."

"That's incredible," she murmured.

"The link stretches over vast distances, as well."

She glanced at the water, her lips twisting. "I had no idea. I always assumed the roars were words."

"There are many reasons for a dragon to roar. Sometimes, it's for intimidation. Or perhaps to get another's attention. There are nuances in each, but not for conversing as we are now."

"The roars all sound the same to me."

He jerked his chin to her. "I think it's how a human's ears are constructed that prevents hearing such depths."

"But you can."

"I may have your form, but I retain my dragon senses."

She raised a brow. "Which are?"

"Highly enhanced. I can hear things miles away. We're able to see as clearly in the dark as we can during the day, but we can also see far into the distance. We discern smells that humans and even some animals wouldna be able to pick up."

Katla held his gaze for a heartbeat. "What do you look like? In your true form, that is."

"Are you asking me to show you?"

"Nay," she said hurriedly. "I'm wondering what color you are."

There was still a great deal of fear within her about dragons. He wouldn't have shifted anyway. This wasn't the place. "Orange."

"And you choose this form?" she asked, motioning to his body.

"I didna choose it. It was bestowed upon me. On all the Kings."

Her brows snapped together in puzzlement. "By the Star People?"

"Nay. The magic of Earth. However, it could conceivably be Redis's magic. He's the Star Person who created our world and set my ancestors free. In his last act to keep the realm hidden, he gave up his life to do so. It worked for a long time, but Villette eventually found us. And when she put the Druids on Earth, things changed. Con called the Kings together after their arrival. We had no way of communicating with the mortals. They were terrified at having dragons around them."

"I can imagine," Katla said.

"We were trying to figure out how to speak to them when we suddenly shifted forms. This was the body the magic gave me."

She walked a step closer to the shore. "You never wanted to change it?"

"I can no'. Just as I can no' change what I look like as a dragon."

"Then you were able to talk to the humans?"

Merrill turned his head away as he let his mind drift back through the memories. "Our magic allows us to learn languages quickly. Once we could understand and speak their language, we learned that they had no memory of how they had gotten to Earth or where they had come from. They knew nothing of our world or its dangers. Had we let them go about things on their own, they would've died within hours. We made a vow to protect the humans. And that promise led to our ruination."

"I don't understand."

Merrill had known he would have to share about his past, but that didn't make the truth easier to impart. He had never told anyone about this. It didn't matter that it had occurred millions of years ago. To him, it was still fresh, still painful.

"You don't have to tell me."

"I want to. Because I want you to understand."

She nodded once and waited for him to continue.

"We carved out land for the mortals. We showed them how to hunt and fashion weapons. We aided them in every way. When their numbers grew, we gave them more land. The Kings split our time between our clans and the mortals who had settled in our territories. We explored life in these bodies, and even took mortal lovers." Merrill inhaled deeply before releasing it. "It was as close to harmony as our two cultures ever got. Yet it wasn't enough for the humans. They wanted more. Then they demanded more. Most respected the boundaries we set, but others pushed and pushed and pushed. Smaller dragons were hunted. In retaliation, some dragons hunted the humans."

Merrill knew how it sounded, but he couldn't care. Talking about the past had opened old wounds. And with them, the fury he fought to keep from exploding. "The lines blurred between who was right and who was wrong. Perhaps we should've seen how things would eventually turn out. Or maybe we believed that, as Kings, we could control everything. And that might have been the case with a dozen or so humans. We lost that ability when their numbers swelled to the tens of thousands. Things came to a head when Ulrik, the King of Silvers, fell in love with a human."

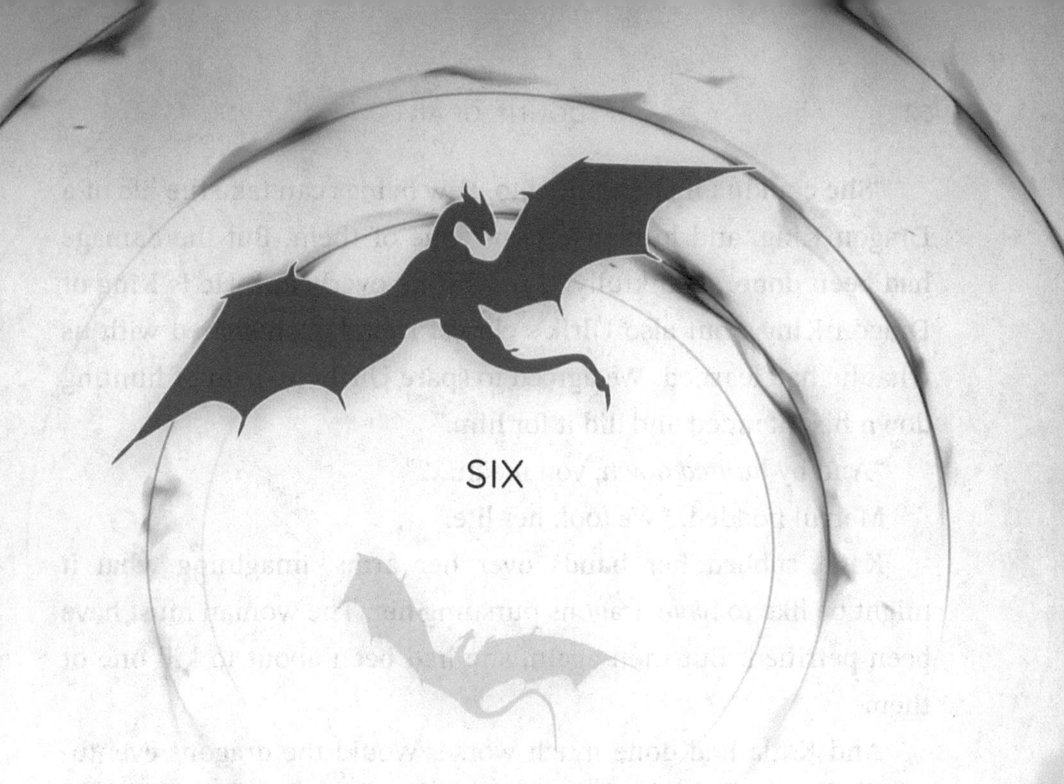

SIX

"That should've brought everyone together." Katla watched the play of emotions on Merrill's face. The revulsion, the disgust. The anger.

He grunted softly. "We had learned by then that mortals couldna carry a bairn to full term. Many miscarried immediately. The few who managed it bore stillborn babes. It meant any King who took a human as a mate would never have children. Ulrik made his choice, and we respected it. Everything might have gone fine, but Ulrik's uncle believed *he* should've been chosen as King."

"Chosen?"

"The magic of Earth picks each King," Merrill explained as he turned to her. "It sees who we are. A King must be physically strong but also have mental strength. And his heart must be pure. Mikkel's wasna. He turned Ulrik's lover against his nephew, convincing her that she must kill Ulrik."

Katla raised her brows as the story took a turn she hadn't expected. "Tell me she didn't."

"She couldna if she wanted to. Few beings can take the life of a Dragon King, and humans are no' one of them. But the damage had been done. Thankfully, Constantine overheard. He is King of Dragon Kings, but also Ulrik's closest friend. Con shared with us what he had learned. We agreed to spare Ulrik the pain of hunting down his intended and did it for him."

"And by *hunted down*, you mean…?"

Merrill nodded. "We took her life."

Katla rubbed her hands over her arms, imagining what it might be like to have dragons pursuing her. The woman must have been petrified. But then again, she had been about to kill one of them.

And Katla had done much worse. Would the dragons eventually come after her like that?

"We only told Ulrik after," Merrill continued. "His fury was immense. It was unlike anything I've seen. Yet he didna take it out on us as we anticipated. He directed it at the humans he had sheltered and protected. In that instant, the war began. The mortals were all too ready to stand against us. And we were all too ready to be rid of them. All of us except Con. Like many of the Kings, I had dealt with countless affronts. Decades of outrage and insult boiled over that day. We joined Ulrik in the effort to rid Earth of humans."

"You wiped them out?"

Merrill slowly ran a hand around the back of his neck and rubbed before letting his arm drop to his side. "There's a reason the magic chose Con as the King of Kings. He reminded each of us of our promise, slowly bringing us back to his side, one by one. Ulrik wouldna listen, though. Con demanded that he stand down and call off the Silvers, but Ulrik was too lost in his grief."

"I know something about that." Their gazes met. She watched the moonlight shine upon his dirty blond locks, making them appear as if they were glowing.

"You can no' imagine how bad it was. For every King, there was at least one human settlement. Everyone rose up against the other. Nowhere on Earth wasn't embroiled in conflict. Con didna allow his Golds to harm any mortals, but that didna stop the humans in his territory from attempting to hurt the Golds. By then, only Ulrik and the Silvers were fighting the humans, but they didna care. They wanted to be rid of us as much as we wanted them gone."

Katla couldn't look away from Merrill. His gaze stayed directed at the water as he spoke.

"Some Kings ordered their dragons to protect the human settlements from the Silvers, but things had already progressed too far by then. I watched too many dragons slaughtered by mortals who had given into fear, and those dragons not defending themselves because they were ordered to guard the very ones taking their lives."

Katla grimaced at the horror his words created. "By the stars," she whispered.

"That's when I knew we had lost the war. How do you come back from something like that? We had opened our lands to the humans. We could show our power and control them, but it would happen again. The mortals would never trust us, and we could never trust them again. But nothing could be decided until Ulrik and the Silvers were dealt with. Con took control of all but four of the largest Silvers who wouldna leave Ulrik's side. It took all our combined magic to force those Silvers into a dragon sleep and cage them. Then, we had a decision to make."

"You mean what to do with the humans."

Merrill blew out a long breath. "We were divided. Half wanted to rid the realm of mortals and return our world to what it had been. The other half stood with Con after he reminded us that we had vowed to protect the very beings we were at war with."

"But it was your world first."

Dark blue eyes met hers. "That may be, but if we'd killed to end the war, none of us would be Kings any longer. We would be murderers. Not the pure of heart the magic demanded."

She swallowed as she leaned closer, needing to hear the rest. "What did you do?"

"We stood by our promise, but even as we did, we recognized that the war would continue. Neither dragons nor humans could live together any longer. Since we couldna send the humans to a new world, we created a bridge with our magic and sent our clans to find a new home."

Katla had more questions but she didn't ask. She couldn't, not with the anguish cutting across Merrill's face. His voice had dropped to barely a whisper, as if speaking the words had cost him everything he had.

At that moment, she understood that if anyone could appreciate how she felt about losing everything, it was him.

The silence stretched out for so long she thought he'd finished the story. She was about to leave when he sucked in a breath.

"We had no idea where the dragons would go," Merrill continued. "We could only hope they found a home. They didna want to leave. Some balked. *We* didna want them to leave, but someone had to. Otherwise, the war would have continued indefinitely. Our beautiful world was gone. The stench of blood and death hung in the air. The wails of both dragons and humans were unimaginable. We promised to protect the innocent, and we stood by that. I hated the mortals for putting us in that position. I hated myself for making the oath. I still hate myself for it," he said, his lip curled in disgust. "It was our world. We should've protected the dragons, no' the mortals. I would've gladly given my life to ensure my clan had a home. I should have. We all should have. Even though we had convinced ourselves that we could bring the dragons back, we all knew it would never happen."

His torment was so powerful that it swarmed her, forcing her to take a step back. He looked away, putting his face in profile. His hands were clenched at his sides, showing white knuckles, and his body was rigid. Katla thought about reaching out to offer him comfort, but it had been so long since she had done such a thing. She wasn't sure she remembered how.

"That was the beginning of the end," Merrill told her. "The Kings, as a collective, bound Ulrik's magic so he was forced to remain in human form and banished him from Dreagan." Merrill looked at her and grunted. "It sounds harsh—and it was—but he wouldna stop attacking the humans. He left us no choice."

She refrained from giving her opinion. It was easy to look back at someone's decisions and judge. She didn't want hers weighed, so she wisely kept silent.

He shoved his hair from his face with both hands before dropping his arms to his sides. "We left Ulrik to his fate and hid away on Dreagan. Each King went into their mountain and remained, sleeping through time until the day humans forgot dragons were real. Only two Kings remained awake during that time—Con and Ulrik. Con visited each of us every ten years and updated us on what was happening in the world. Eventually, we began to wake and live among the mortals. But the Kings had a difficult time controlling their loathing."

"You didn't?" she asked.

He shrugged one shoulder. "My brethren needed me. It started with Varek. I saw that he couldna manage his wrath. If he saw a mortal, he would've killed them immediately. So, I helped him through it. Then I helped others."

"What about you?"

His lips twisted. "I shoved my feelings down. Ignored them. I always intended to deal with my resentment eventually, but it was easier to keep bottling it up. And I locked it away in the deepest, darkest part of my mind, then forgot about it. Millennia passed as we tried to locate the dragons, hoping against hope that they'd survived. It turned out a verra powerful friend of ours had seen everything unfolding on Earth. Erith created Zora in Earth's image and directed the dragons here. She kept the information from us. She claims to have had her reasons, but I still have issues with it. Eventually, she told us everything. Without her, I'm not sure what would've happened."

"Villette would've found the dragons."

He nodded irritably and looked away. "Most likely.

"You were reunited with your clans. That should be cause for celebration."

"It was. Definitely. But things have changed. The dragons are no longer in clans. Nor are they ruled by Dragon Kings. They're governed by Con and Rhi's twins, Eurwen and Brandr. In fact, the dragons despise the Kings. The story of how we sent their ancestors away has traveled through generations. Am I glad the dragons survived? Aye. Am I happy I saw them? I think it would've been better had I stayed on Earth."

Katla nibbled on the side of her lip. "If you hadn't come, Villette might have succeeded in annihilating the dragons. I would still be helping her. Your reunion might not have been what you imagined, but it has changed a great many things."

"If I had remained on Earth, I would still be the man I used to be." He paused. "Instead, I'm filled with rage."

"Against the humans?"

Merrill swung his head to her. "Against myself for not making another choice. Against Villette for everything. Against every Star Person who knew what she did and didn't stop her. The Druids she brought to Earth were puppets. What happened on our realm might have been avoided. When her plan didna work out there, she focused it here. Once again, she brought in humans to mix with dragons. And this time, she made sure the mortals feared and hated the dragons right from the beginning."

"She's trying to get things to play out just as they did on Earth."

"I think so."

Katla shivered in the night air. "Then don't let her."

"Killing her willna stop what she began."

"Maybe not, but if she isn't around to stir things up, there's a chance people can change."

Merrill ran a hand over his face. "You have more faith than I do."

"Hope. Not faith. I was a good person before. I have much to make up for."

"You already began that journey," he said, motioning toward the sleeping children.

She looked at them. It warmed her heart to have children with her once more. She'd had an ache in her heart the whole time she believed her daughter had died, only made worse by the knowledge that she had lived a long, full life. Katla could've been a part of that, but she had chosen vengeance instead.

"Other bairns have been saved from the priests," Merrill said, breaking into her thoughts.

Her gaze slid back to him. "How do you know that?"

"A friend of mine named Tamlyn. She is a Banshee and knows when a child with magic is about to die near her. She and her friends were drawn to this area because of what was happening at Stonemore. She has saved many from the priests."

Katla was surprised and pleased to learn that. "Really?"

"She has taken in several bairns. They are safe and loved. She would be delighted to have three more."

There was a catch. There had to be. "And what would she want in exchange?"

"Nothing," Merrill replied. "However, you should know she's mated to a Dragon King."

Katla probably should've seen that coming, especially when Merrill said she was a friend. She looked at the children once more. It would be better if they had a stable, protected home. What could be safer than having a Dragon King as a protector? It was the right thing to do. Yet Katla didn't want the children to leave. She knew it was selfish, but she wanted to keep them with her. Their presence made her remember the mother she had once been.

"Iron Hall isna far," Merrill added.

Under her care, the children had gone hungry. All because she had feared using her magic to kill an animal. She might not have killed the dragons, but they died because she'd trapped them. It was close enough.

Merrill moved a step closer. "You can visit them anytime you wish."

And it would be harder to leave each time. She couldn't do that. But she had wished for a safe place for the children. And Merrill offered one. She should be excited to know they had a place to go. And she would be. One day. Just as soon as her heart stopped aching.

"They'll be treated well?" Katla asked.

"They'll be loved and cherished beyond measure. The Kings and their mates live there, and, as I said, there are other bairns."

Could she trust a dragon? Did she dare? She had made so many wrong decisions. This had to be the right one.

"I'll take you to Iron Hall. You can see for yourself."

Katla jerked her head to him. Was this the trap, then? Would he use the children to get her to the Kings instead of chasing her? "So I can be locked away?"

He sighed, his lips flattening. "If we wanted to punish you, we would have already."

She couldn't argue that point. Merrill had found her. If he wanted, he could bring down all the Kings upon her. He hadn't. As much as she wanted to make a home with the kids, she couldn't. She wanted redemption, and the only way to get that was to hunt down Villette. She couldn't do that with the children in tow.

If this was a trick, and the Kings locked her away, then so be it. At least the children would never have to worry about the priests again. "All right."

SEVEN

Katla's words had barely registered with Merrill before she made her way back to the children. He watched as she carefully lifted the blanket over Aven and curled beside the lass. Merrill stared for a moment longer, but he had to look away from the cozy scene as it brought back memories of his older sister and her family.

Delving into the past stirred up his already agitated emotions. Merrill couldn't remember the last time he had thought about any member of his family. He had pushed away any notion of them to survive the devastating pain of their departure. In the process, he had barred the pieces of him that he needed, glossing over the yawning voids with smiles. When it became too much, and he ended up drowning in misery, Varek had been fighting the same torment.

Merrill had helped his friend and, in the process, found momentary relief for his sorrow. From then on, he'd made the conscious decision to plod onward without confronting his grief. It was easier to elbow it away than give in to the driving need to eviscerate every last mortal. Wiping them from existence and returning his clan and family were the only ways he could heal. He had comprehended the gravity of his hostility.

Choices had been made. There was no going back. Merrill had felt—and seen—how banishing Ulrik had affected the Kings—especially Con. He refused to follow that path and force his brethren to banish him. So, that left him with one option. And he gladly took it, grasping it tightly with both hands. Otherwise, he would have gone to a place he would never have returned from.

Yet here he was. Facing those same arduous emotions all over again millions of years later. And they still terrified him. Mostly because he knew there was still a chance they could swallow him whole.

He listened to the dragons in the distance. Many were settling in for the night, but some preferred the moon to the sun. The dragon within urged him to shift and soar toward the stars. He closed his eyes and imagined the wind in his face, brushing against his scales and wings as he spread them and glided upon the night air.

Merrill opened his eyes, cutting off the image. He wanted nothing more than to return to the dragons and stand among the Kings as he once had. But to go now would be a disservice to all of them. He had wounded his brethren enough. They deserved better. It was time he confronted the past and whatever it held.

First things first, though. Merrill reached out with his mind. *"Cullen?"*

"Aye, brother," Cullen answered immediately.

"Do you have room for three additional bairns?"

"Of course. There's plenty of room. I take that to mean you returned to Stonemore."

Merrill grunted. *"It's worse than we feared."*

"Wonderful," Cullen muttered. *"Are you bringing the children tonight?"*

"Tomorrow."

Cullen was silent for a beat. *"Is anything amiss?"*

Merrill should've known Cullen would pick up on the fact that something wasn't right. He looked toward the fire where Katla slept with the kids. *"The bairns were in the tower with Katla."*

"The Druid saved them, then."

It wasn't a question. *"She did. She also knows who I am and where the bairns will be going."*

"Does she intend to remain with them?"

"She only wants them somewhere the priests will never harm them again."

Cullen made an indiscernible sound. *"They'll have that at Iron Hall. Are the bairns or Katla injured?"*

"If the kids were, she took care of it. I'm no' sure about Katla. She's hesitant to trust."

"No' surprising. I didna think we'd ever see her again."

"I think she'd prefer it that way. She's sure I've been sent to mete out justice."

Cullen exhaled loudly. *"Villette manipulated Katla. It also helps that she fought alongside us. She isna without blame, though. She had a choice."*

"So did I. And I made the wrong one."

"You didna kill dragons."

Merrill briefly squeezed his eyes closed and turned away from the comforting sight of the bairns. *"I did something worse. I turned my back on all of you."*

"That isna your fault."

"If Katla is to blame for what she did, then so am I," Merrill insisted. *"We've all been manipulated by Villette."*

"Aye, we have. No one intends Katla any harm. Let her know she'll be welcome if she wishes to visit the bairns."

The muscles in Merrill's shoulders relaxed. *"Thanks, brother."*

"See you soon."

Merrill hadn't realized how much he needed to hear that the Kings wouldn't harm Katla until Cullen said the words. Merrill would wait until morning to tell her the news. There would be no sleep for him, however. Dragons didn't need to sleep like humans. Instead, he patrolled the forest. Katla stirred only once, rising to look around groggily. He wondered when she'd last allowed herself to rest. She set up a barrier around her and the children before lying down again.

Her magic rolled across the ground. He stilled and waited for it to sweep past him. The moment it made contact, it paused and wrapped around him. Then, it moved on. Maybe it was because he had been waiting for it, but Merrill felt something unusual. It was subtle, faint, just a whisper of a deviation from the Druid magic he was familiar with.

Then he reminded himself that they were on another planet. Zora was similar to Earth in many ways, but there were also differences. It stood to reason that a Druid's magic on Zora would feel different than it did on Earth.

The sensation of Katla's magic stayed with him as the hours passed and dawn approached. He had encountered many animals on his patrol, each more unique than the last. He could compare most to creatures on Earth. Though some weren't recognizable. The more time he spent on Zora, the more apparent it became how distinctive the realm and its inhabitants were.

When the first rays of sun broke the horizon, Merrill returned to the fire. He studied the sky as it steadily lightened, and one of the moons sank below the skyline, leaving only one visible in the heavens.

Perick was the first to wake. The lad sat up and shoved away the blanket, pulling it away from the girls on either side of him. Maely grunted and turned over before yanking the covers to her shoulder. Perick rubbed his eyes sleepily. It took a full minute before he noticed Merrill. He climbed over Maely and walked around to drop down next to Merrill, leaning his head against Merrill's arm as he yawned.

Merrill gazed down at Perick's head of dark curls. After a moment, the curls faded, replaced by orange scales as a memory surfaced of how his nephew used to lean against him just like Perick. He had lost that recollection until now. Part of Merrill wanted to stay with it, open to more memories. The other part resisted because of the pain it would dredge up.

His thoughts halted when Aven stirred and rolled onto her back. She stretched her arms over her head and yawned. A moment later, she sat up and looked for Maely and Perick before searching for Katla. Aven seemed pleased to find the Druid sleeping beside her. She carefully extracted herself from the covers and got to her feet. To Merrill's surprise, she came to sit on his other side.

"I've not seen her sleep," Aven whispered as she looked at Katla.

Merrill's gaze was drawn to the Druid. He kept his voice low as he said, "Then we shall let her rest."

"I'm hungry," Perick declared loudly.

Katla startled and sat up.

"Well, there goes that," Aven muttered angrily.

Merrill fought a grin as he handed the lad some leftover meat. Perick ate it with his eyes closed. Katla rose and folded the blankets, gently rousing Maely. Soon, everyone was breaking their fast.

When their bellies were full, Katla took them to the river to wash up. Merrill used that time to wrap up the last of the deer. His magic created a bag he used for the blankets and the meat. The bairns giggled and splashed handfuls of water at each other. He leaned a shoulder against a tree and watched them.

The kids had been taken from their families and hauled into the tower to be executed. Yet there was no anger within them. They adjusted to each day and whatever Fate threw at them. If only it were that easy for him. Merrill knew exactly what they had lost: family, shelter, love, security.

Katla's approach pulled his attention from the bairns. She combed her fingers through her long length of hair as their eyes met, then quickly turned her gaze to the children.

"Do you still wish for the bairns to go to Iron Hall?" he asked.

She nodded.

"I spoke with Cullen last night. They're making room for all three now. It is farther than I originally thought, however. It will take us days if we walk."

"Are you suggesting you'll fly us there?"

He shrugged. "It's an option."

"Not a good one. It wouldn't be good to show yourself on this side of the border, and I'm certain the dragons wouldn't care to have humans on their land."

"I had another idea."

Her head swung to him as her stormy gray eyes met his. "Oh?"

"I have a friend who can teleport us."

Katla hesitated, her gaze returning to the bairns. "You trust them?"

"With my life."

"And they wouldn't harm the children?"

"Never," he replied. "

Her shoulders lifted as she inhaled. "The kids have endured enough. They haven't complained despite being out in the elements with little to eat and nowhere to go. The three of them are innocent. They didn't ask to be born with magic or to live at Stonemore. I want the fear they try so hard to hide to vanish. Forever."

"It will at Iron Hall."

"Then take them."

Merrill frowned as he stared at her. "You're no' coming?"

"I know what I've done and what the dragons think of me. I don't want that to taint the children."

"It willna. Cullen has said you're welcome to come anytime."

Her smile was fleeting as she glanced at him. "I appreciate that, but my presence is a reminder of what was done to your kind. I don't want that for the children."

"I willna let it."

Gray eyes slid to him. "I'm trusting you to bring them to safety. Please don't make me regret that."

"I've spent centuries defending my world and the mortals living there from threats. I protected the descendants of the ones I went to war with. I give you my word that nothing will ever harm those bairns."

"I believe you."

Merrill didn't want her to leave. There was still much about Katla he wanted to know. More than that, he liked being around her, which wasn't something he said about many people at present. She cared deeply for the bairns. The only reason she would leave was to protect them. "Bloody hell. You're going after Villette."

"Someone needs to, and I have much to make up for."

"Villette manipulated you. Why can you no' accept that?"

Katla grinned and waved when the bairns showed her something. "I accept it. But that doesn't erase what I did." She turned to face him. "Last night, you said something I've not been able to stop thinking about. You said the women you took as lovers on Earth weren't able to carry a baby to term."

Merrill grimaced at his carelessness. The humans on Zora were unable to procreate. Yet, somehow, infants appeared all over the realm. "I shouldna have spoken about that."

"I'm delighted to learn there are worlds where women can become pregnant. But I began wondering if dragons were affected like us or if they are like the other animals and can reproduce."

He knew where Katla was going with this. He wished there was a way to lessen the blow, but nothing he could say would change the facts. It was better to state the truth as simply as possible. "Aye, dragons can produce offspring."

Tears quickly welled in her eyes. She blinked hastily as she fought to keep them from falling. "It's as I thought, then. I took children from their parents. From families."

"Doona go down that road."

"Too late," she whispered.

He took a step toward her. "Katla," he began.

"I need to tell the children what's going to happen."

Merrill clenched his hand to keep from reaching out to her. Instead, he watched the soft sway of her hips as she walked away.

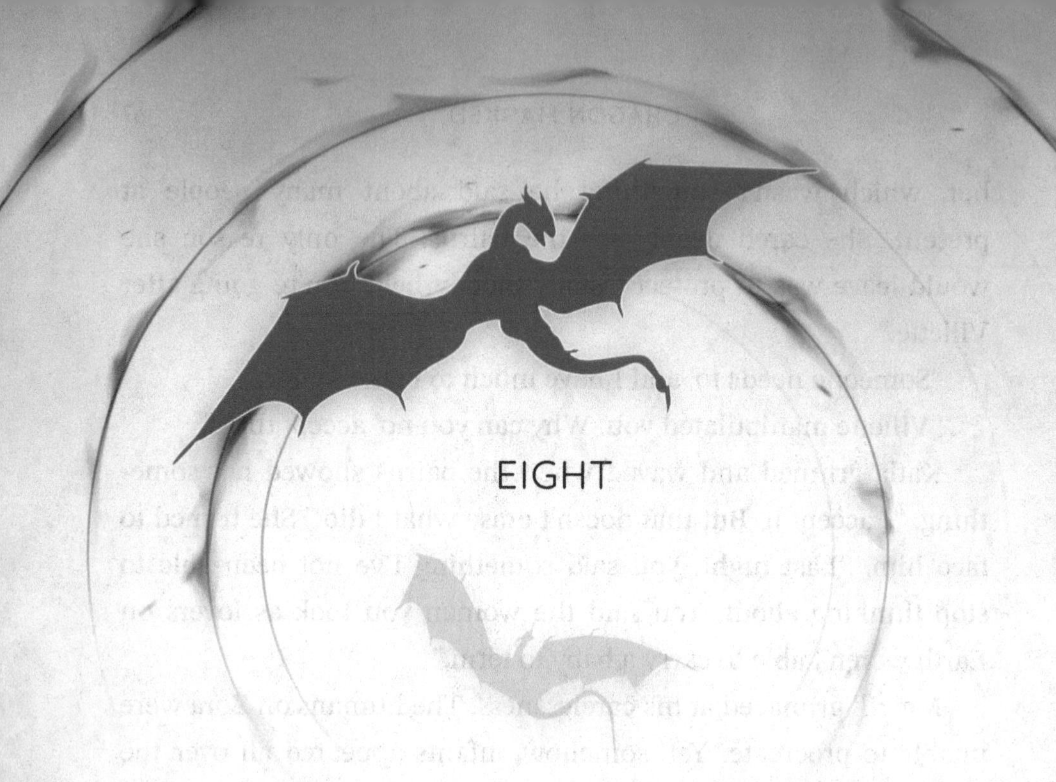

EIGHT

It was the right decision. Why, then, did Katla's heart feel like it was being ripped out of her chest? Her feet felt heavy, and each step was excruciating. Maely, Aven, and Perick played at the water's edge, unaware of her struggle.

She'd had only a handful of days with them, but they were as much her children as her daughter had been. She had fought for them, protected them, cared for them. Loved them. In the darkest hours of the night when she despaired about how to keep the three of them safe, she had wondered if she was the right one to watch over them. After all, she hadn't been able to keep her nieces alive.

When morning came, the children opened their eyes and looked at her with smiles full of trust and devotion. That had been it for Katla. She had let her daughter and nieces down. She wouldn't let these three beautiful, innocent children down, too. So, she had plodded on, facing each day with new resolve.

Now, there was Merrill, who seemed to be the answer to all her worries. She was leery of dragons. Especially the Kings. After all, she had trapped countless dragons in the vine forest to give to Villette, who then tortured and killed them. But she didn't want the children to be afraid. Not if they would be living with the Kings and their mates.

At Iron Hall. She knew nothing about the place, but she had been ignorant of so very much for so very long. Villette had made her believe she was the sole remaining human on Zora. Which further inflamed Katla's hatred for dragons. And it kept her in the valley, surrounded by the vines, waiting for the next dragon she could lure into a trap.

She would still be there if Melisse—who appeared human but had been trapped like the dragons—hadn't entered the brambles. Henry had come after her. Through Henry, Katla learned that some dragons could shift their forms. He told her about the many villages and cities on Zora where humans lived and thrived. It was Henry who'd unraveled her world one piece at a time, showing her just how foolish and naïve she had been.

Katla had a second chance now. Few were offered such opportunities, and with the children taken care of, there was nothing stopping her from making Villette answer for her many crimes.

Saying goodbye to the children would take more fortitude than she had, but she would do it. For them. It didn't redeem her for her past actions, but it was a start. And, perhaps, the kids would think back fondly on her when they got older. It was all she could ask for, really.

She swiped at a tear that fell. Another quickly followed. She looked away and fought against the sorrow that swelled in her chest, making it feel as if it might burst open from the pain. Katla couldn't let them see her like this. She had to put a smile on her face.

For them.

She felt Merrill's gaze on her. Katla glanced over her shoulder and looked into his eyes. There was pain there. He didn't hide it. He probably wasn't even aware of it. But beyond that, she saw a good man. It was there in how he spoke to the kids, how he treated them. Even in how he dealt with her. That was why she trusted him with Aven, Perick, and Maely.

Merrill shook his head and mouthed *doona*.

She would miss his accent and how he said words such as *doona*. Oh, how she would've liked to see his world. She had no right to wish for anything, but she hoped Merrill and the dragons stopped the war from happening on Zora. The dragons deserved peace—everyone did.

Katla turned back to the children and called to them. When they looked up, she waved them over. Her throat tightened with emotion, and she blinked back another rush of tears as they ran up. She squatted before them, looking at Aven, then Maely, and finally Perick. She took Aven's and Perick's hands.

"Are you ready for an adventure?" Katla asked.

Perick immediately nodded his head. "Aye!"

"What kind of adventure?" Maely asked skeptically.

Aven said nothing as she stared at Katla.

She gently placed her hand on Aven's cheek before answering Maely. "A grand one."

"When?" Perick asked, jumping up and down.

Maely put her hand on his shoulder to keep him still. She looked at Aven before sliding her dark gaze to Katla.

They might be children, but they had experienced more than

most adults. They knew that something was going on. Katla wasn't fooling them. So, she stopped trying. "There is a place where other children who were saved from the priests have been taken. It isn't just safe. It's somewhere the priests will never find you."

"Can such a place exist?" Aven asked.

Katla nodded. "Merrill knows about it."

"He could be lying," Maely said.

Perick yanked his hand from hers and glared. "He wouldn't."

"I wouldna," Merrill said, his voice rising to reach them.

Katla pressed her lips together. "I don't know the area. What I do know is that the three of you deserve a real home, with people who will look out for you. And other children to play with." She hesitated. Did she tell them now? It was better they knew who they would be living with beforehand. "And powerful protectors."

"How powerful?" Aven's voice was a whisper as she looked past Katla.

She knew the child was staring at Merrill. He looked like a man, but there was something different about him that set him apart from others. Maybe the children had noticed that, too.

"Very," Katla answered. "There will be dragons there."

Perick's eyes widened in excitement. "Can I ride one?"

"How many?" Maely asked.

Aven continued staring at Merrill.

Katla squeezed Aven's and Perick's hands. "The dragons are friends. Never forget that. Some will look like dragons, and others will look like—"

"Merrill," Aven replied.

Katla's heart skipped a beat. She glanced behind her, but Merrill hadn't shifted forms. Katla looked at Aven. "That's right. How did you know?"

"He's different." Aven dropped her gaze to Katla. "If they wanted to hurt us, the dragons would've crossed the border long ago."

Katla grinned and nodded. "That's right. There are many lies told about the dragons. Just as there are lies about those of us with magic."

"Why?" Perick asked. "We've not hurt anyone."

Maely's lips flattened. "There are those who have."

"The point," Katla said, getting their attention, "is that each of you has the power to decide to use your abilities for good or evil. People will always lie. Usually, out of fear of what they don't understand. And there have been too many lies about magic. Regular people can't see the truth because it's been too clouded by falsehoods. It's important to remember that."

"Do I get to ride a dragon?" Perick asked again.

Before she could answer, the child raced toward Merrill. Katla stood, turning to watch as Merrill caught Perick as the child threw himself at the Dragon King. Merrill held Perick against him as the child rattled off question after question.

"Are you sure about this?"

Katla looked over at Maely, who had asked the question. She looked between the two girls. She hadn't delved much into their magic. There hadn't been time, and it'd been the last thing on her mind. Now, she wished she had spent more time talking to them about it. "Merrill and his friends have actively fought against Stonemore and the priests. I think it's the best place for you."

"You mean it's the best place for all of us," Aven corrected.

This was the part Katla wished she could skip, but there was no getting around it. She had to go through it. "Do you remember the woman who came up to the tower?"

The girls nodded.

"That was Miena, Villette's sister," Katla explained. "Both are from a powerful race of beings known as the Star People. Not all of them are bad, but Miena and Villette are."

Maely's brow furrowed. "Miena wanted to hurt us."

"She intended to steal the bairns' magic," Merrill said as he walked up. "It's how she became stronger than the others."

Katla was shocked by the news. "I didn't know what she'd planned. I just knew it wasn't good."

"You made the bright light," Perick said with a smile.

Katla tried to smile but wasn't sure she succeeded. "Miena is dead, but Villette is still out there. I'm going after her."

"It doesn't have to be you," Aven argued.

Katla smoothed a lock of blond hair from the girl's face. "It does, actually."

"What about us?" Maely asked, anger and panic sparking in her dark eyes.

Katla cupped the girl's cheek in her hand. "I'll return for a visit as soon as Villette is dispatched."

The misery on the children's faces was wearing her down. Katla struggled against another wave of tears. The longer they stared at her, the harder it was to remain stoic. A sound behind her drew their attention. She used that moment to brace herself for the final farewells. All she had to do was get through them. After the children were gone, she would cry. But not before.

Katla turned and saw someone speaking in low tones to Merrill. The woman was stunning with her silver eyes and thick, black hair that fell down her back. She was dressed in an all-black, form-fitting ensemble, but it was the boots with their incredibly high heels that caught her attention.

"Katla, this is Rhi," Merrill said.

For a moment, Katla thought she recognized the woman.

Rhi inclined her head. "We didn't get to meet, but I was at the battle with Villette."

That's where Katla recognized her from. There had been a number of people, as well as dragons, in the valley that day. But she had been focused on ending Villette.

"I'm going to take all of you to a very special place," Rhi said to the children as she leaned forward, bracing her hands on her thighs.

Perick cocked his head to the side. "You talk funny."

"It's an accent," Rhi told him. "Those on my world call it Irish, but it's really a Fae accent."

Maely asked in a curious voice, "What's a Fae?"

"A race of beings with magic," Rhi replied with a smile, looking at each child.

Aye, Katla had made the right choice in sending the children to Iron Hall. She would miss them, but they would be alive and free. And well cared for.

Aven eyed Rhi. "What kind of magic can you do?"

"Well, for one, I can teleport," Rhi said.

Perick's face scrunched up. "What's tele...tele...?"

"It's like jumping from one place to another in the blink of an eye," Merrill explained.

Rhi straightened, her smile growing. "It won't hurt. Though it might tickle your tummy."

Aven, however, wasn't finished with her question. "You're friends with the dragons?"

Rhi's silver eyes turned to the girl. "Actually, I'm mated to one."

"And no' just any dragon," Merrill said. "Con is the King of Dragon Kings."

Perick's eyes widened at that. "Really? Can I meet him?"

"Of course," Rhi said. "Everyone is waiting for your arrival. Shall we go?"

All three kids turned to her. Katla smiled and nodded. "It's a good place."

Aven made a choked sound and threw herself at Katla. She wound her arms around the girl before pulling Maely against her. Katla could no longer stem the flow of tears. Through them, she saw Perick squirm out of Merrill's hold and run to them. Katla closed her eyes and hugged all three against her as tightly as she could.

Then, she forced her eyes open and leaned back to look at them. She softly wiped the tears from their faces. "This isn't good-bye. It's only farewell for now."

"Come with us," Aven begged.

Katla cupped her face and kissed her forehead. "I'll be there soon." She repeated the kiss on Maely's and then Perick's foreheads.

All three were crying softly as they reluctantly walked to Rhi. Katla smiled at them one last time before she looked at the Fae. Rhi dipped her chin in silent acknowledgment.

Then, they were gone.

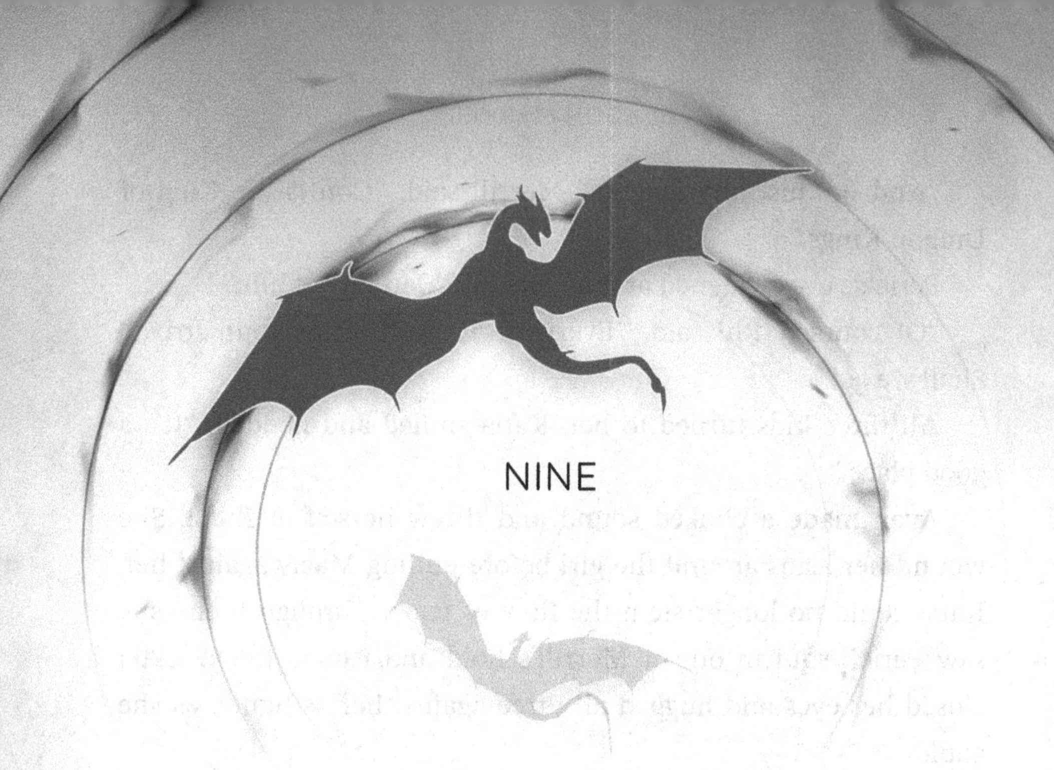

NINE

Merrill didn't move as Katla buried her face in her hands and sobbed. He had never been good at watching women cry. Usually, he tried to offer comfort, but he wasn't sure she would want it from him. He debated whether to walk away when she finally lifted her head.

Her dark lashes were spiked from the tears that had left trails down her face. She jerked at the sight of him. "Why are you still here?"

"You are no' the only one who wants to see Villette punished."

Katla shook her head and wiped her cheeks. "I don't need anyone's help."

"I didna say you did, lass."

Instead of arguing, she walked to the stream and knelt along the shore. There, she splashed water onto her face a couple of times, then flicked her hands and wiped them on her clothes as she stared across the stream at the trees beyond. Merrill ran a hand down his face, wondering if he had made the right decision. He'd made so many wrong ones of late that it was hard to know.

If he had been able to convince Katla to go to Iron Hall, he would have. But he recognized her stubbornness. Mainly because he had the same obstinate streak. Her first goal had been the children and their well-being. Merrill knew she had assumed he would accompany the bairns to Iron Hall. He hadn't dissuaded her of that notion because there would have been a clash. By remaining quiet, she had been able to focus solely on the children.

Katla got to her feet and spun. She strode past him to the fire without even looking in his direction. Merrill turned with her. The misery that had been etched into her face was gone, carefully disguised behind a mask of aloofness. She believed hiding her pain would protect her. But nothing could shield someone from such misery.

"You will see them again," he told her.

She waved her hand over the flames, dousing them instantly. "I doubt that."

"We would never keep the bairns from you. Or you from them."

"You should return to your people."

He didn't like that she refused to look at him. "I can no'."

"I'm not someone in need of saving," she snapped.

"I never thought you were."

Her stormy eyes lifted and flashed dangerously. "Then why have you remained?"

"You say you want redemption. Well, so do I. I willingly remained at Stonemore with Villette. I didna know what she was, nor did I know her machinations. All I knew was that I couldna return to my brethren. I didna reach out to them, and I didna even care that none of them tried to contact me. I wanted to be on my own. Away from them."

She stayed silent, waiting for him to continue.

"I became suspicious of Villette verra soon, yet still did nothing. I contemplated leaving, but I didna. Varek, my closest friend, said I wouldna have been able to, even if I had tried. He may be right, or he may have said that to make me feel better. But that isna the point. The point is I didna gather information. I didna follow her. I did nothing for weeks. No' until Alasdair and Lotti came to Stonemore to find me. They interrupted Villette's magic enough that Alasdair got through and told me who Villette was. But I didna leave with him. I said I would remain and learn what I could." Merrill twisted his lips. "It wasn't an outright lie. I stayed because I wanted to. Even after I knew who Villette was."

Katla shoved her hair over her shoulder. "You're angry."

"You're bloody right, I am."

"If that's the worst you've done, then you have nothing to worry about."

He snorted and looked away. "We'll have to disagree on that."

"You didn't lure dragons into a trap. You stayed at Stonemore and didn't reach out to the dragons. That's nothing."

"I was her lover."

Katla stilled, the action showing her surprise. "If she hates dragons as much as you say, why did she take you to her bed? Why not kill you?"

"She planned to use me against my kin."

"Villette is good at that. It's why she needs to pay for her crimes."

Merrill nodded. "Aye, she does. We have a better chance of success if we work together."

"You don't want to be around me. Everything I touch ends up destroyed."

"No' those bairns. You saved them."

She huffed and shook her head. "They were practically starving. I might have gotten them away from Miena, but I didn't improve their situation."

"They would disagree. So would I," he replied.

"I plan to spend what time I have left making amends for the lives I've taken. I won't stop looking for Villette. No matter how long it takes."

He held her stony gaze. "I doona intend to stop looking either."

"You have people to go back to. Return to them. Find some peace while I handle Villette."

"I'm no' sure there will ever be peace for me. And you willna be able to fight her on your own."

Katla shrugged one shoulder. "So you've said. But I almost killed Villette. All I need to do is get close again."

"She willna let you," Merrill called when Katla turned and started walking away. He blew out a frustrated breath and followed.

The Ferdon Woods was heavily trafficked, but she kept off the main road. If Katla had a direction in mind, she kept it to herself. Merrill guessed that she was likely just walking to cover ground. Her footfalls were soft, her tread light. She stayed several paces ahead of him and didn't look back once.

She only veered from her path to avoid an animal or if she spotted some berries. She ate them by the handfuls, particularly the pale-yellow ones. To his surprise, she didn't stop for lunch.

Her strides didn't slow, even when the forest eventually gave way to miles of open grassland as far as the eye could see. A herd of some horned, hoofed animals spooked at the sight of them and bounded off. Merrill looked over his shoulder at the cover of the trees they'd left behind, then glanced at the clear sky and bright sun. It would help warm up the temperatures slightly. He eyed Katla's thin shirt. It would do nothing to protect her from the weather. But if she was cold, she gave no indication.

The afternoon crawled as they trekked through the boundless waist-high grass. It was a soft gold color, but he bet it was a vibrant green in the spring. It would likely be a sight to behold. Merrill studied the area, but other than the occasional bird, there wasn't another person or animal anywhere. The city of Orgate was some-where to the east, but after Varek's imprisonment there, it was better to avoid it. Thankfully, Katla kept to her northern direction.

The sun was near the horizon when her steps suddenly slowed. Merrill looked around her and spied the tops of some buildings ahead. She diverted slightly to the northwest and headed straight for them. He made out their dilapidated state before they reached the village. Even when she saw nothing but ruins remained, Katla continued into the town.

Merrill eyed what was left of a decent-sized community. It was close enough to Stonemore that it wasn't much of a stretch to believe the village had been attacked by Villette's army like so many others had. There was no one left inside the half-burned buildings. How many lives had been lost? How many more had been forced to relocate to Stonemore, only to starve on the streets? He feared what the answer might be.

Katla stopped next to a building with a door that stood ajar.

The structure was the least damaged of those still standing. She walked under the overhang and gently pushed the door open to peer inside. He made his way around the structure to get a better look at all the sides. There were scorch marks at the back that reached up to the roof, but other than that, the building looked surprisingly sturdy.

Katla was inside by the time he returned to the front. Merrill cautiously walked through the doorway and halted as he regarded the splintered pieces of wood on the floor and the thick dust covering everything. He followed her footprints into the first room on the left and paused when he found her standing in the middle of the room, holding something in her hands.

"This was someone's home," she said, turning as she held up a drawing of a man and woman with a baby.

Merrill took in the broken furniture that lay scattered across the floor. "I'm sure they willna mind if we use it for the night."

"What happened here? Where did they go?"

He began stacking remnants of wood to the side. "After Villette trapped Miena, she got complete power over Stonemore. She wanted more than that, however, and sent her army out. They attacked cities and killed those who stood against them. Whoever was left was ordered to Stonemore. Her army grew each time. But so did the number of those within the cities' walls."

"That explains the overcrowding I saw. But I don't understand sending everyone there. She had to know there wasn't enough food."

Merrill dusted his hands as he stacked the last of the wood and straightened. "She didna care about food or housing. She only cares about power. Those at Stonemore had to bow to her wishes."

Katla sighed. "I don't know how to find her."

"We didna know how to locate Miena either. She found us."

"I'd rather have the advantage."

"I'm no' sure that's possible."

Katla nodded absently, still holding on to the drawing. "She told me she's trimmed back the human population several times before. I couldn't bring myself to ask how."

"It's probably better if you doona know."

"She made me believe there were no more of my people anywhere, and I never ventured out to see if it was true."

Merrill walked over to her. "You saw everyone wiped out. Had you ever left your village before?"

She slowly shook her head. "I stayed right there for fifteen hundred years. I shouldn't have lived so long. I shouldn't be alive *now*."

"But you are. Wondering why willna change that fact."

"Villette told me to remain in the valley. I did everything she asked without question."

Merrill watched the play of emotions on her face. "You were vulnerable, and she took advantage of that."

"It was more than that." Katla looked down at the drawing again. "Hatred kept me going. Hate doesn't need to be fed. It thrives on its own, growing until it consumes everything."

"You are no' in the valley anymore. You got out."

"Have I? Sometimes, I'm not sure."

Merrill looked into her gray eyes. "You're free."

"How many others did she trap like me?"

"It willna do you any good to think like that."

She leaned back against the wall. "Why have none of her other siblings stopped her?"

"I've concluded that the majority of them doona care about anything but themselves."

"You're probably right."

Merrill spotted an unbroken chair across the hall. He brought it back to Katla and motioned for her to use it. "That means it's up to us to do something about her."

TEN

Katla lowered herself into the chair and barely held back a sigh of relief. It wasn't until that moment that she realized how badly her body ached. She had pushed herself hard. A sort of punishment, she supposed. And Merrill had remained with her. Always behind her, but still with her. No matter what direction she went.

She let her gaze slowly move over the Dragon King. She couldn't admit it to him, but she was glad she wasn't alone. He had reasons to want Villette dead as much as she did, but she couldn't help but wonder if he had an ulterior motive. Maybe he had been sent to watch her. The dragons might think she still worked for Villette. After all, she had deeply wronged them.

But she had hurt Villette at their last encounter. Maybe the Kings wished to use her for that. Which was fine with her. But if that were the case, she wished Merrill would admit it.

"I'm going to hunt," he told her.

Those deep blue eyes seemed to see past all her defenses into the darkest parts of her psyche, the bits she didn't want to acknowledge existed. She longed to ask what he saw there, but she wasn't brave enough to hear just how black her soul was. Redemption wouldn't save her from whatever fate awaited her, but it would help her face each day. Maybe even lighten the burden she carried a tad.

Merrill turned on his heel as he said, "You need more than berries."

Katla had to admit she was hungry. And definitely for something other than berries. She looked around the house before the chill in the air registered. There was a fireplace, but she needed wood. Merrill had stacked plenty against the wall, yet she couldn't bring herself to use it. It just felt wrong.

She stood and walked out of the building to the middle of what was left of the village. The sun cast an orange glow across the tall grass, the ruins, and the ground. She basked in the last rays of warmth as the horizon pulled the orb downward.

As much as she would like to stay and enjoy the sunset, Katla used what meager light was left to search the ruins for wood. It was everywhere, but much of it was either too burnt or too heavy. It was just a matter of searching through the skeletal remains of the buildings. A few looked ready to fall over at any moment. They most likely would during the next winter storm.

She could've started the fire with magic. In the valley, she had believed Villette had bestowed it upon her to carry out their plan. But Henry and Merrill kept telling her she had magic before Villette.

It was difficult to know what to do with that knowledge. Magic hadn't been a part of her life until she lost everything. She had thought it reasonable to use Villette's when she believed it was in the pursuit of justice for her family. Now, nothing about her magic felt right. Not the fact that she had it—and possibly some of Villette's mixed with hers—not anything. It made her hyperaware of every time she thought about using it.

Katla broke apart a half-burned piece of timber, holding it with one hand and stomping on it with her foot. She stacked what she could in her arms and carted it back to the shelter to pile next to the hearth. Then she returned for more. It gave her something to do and helped keep her thoughts from the children and her past, neither of which put her in a good headspace. Though she hadn't been in a good place in over fifteen hundred years.

She should have died long ago. Or found her husband and daughter and lived out her life with them as she had planned. Katla had had everything she could want: the love of a good man, a child to call her own, and a nice life. It had been enough.

An image of Merrill filled her mind. How long had he lived? Much longer than she. She complained about centuries, and he'd had untold millennia. Would she live that long? She wouldn't want so many years if she were alone. Merrill had the other Kings. She had no one.

Katla got another armload of wood and felt a flare of anger at what she had been denied. She squeezed her eyes shut. She had blamed the dragons for her grief, and she had been wrong. Her wrath should've gone to the invaders. It was easy to blame others, and while Villette did have a hand in things, the decision had ulti-mately been Katla's. She could've refused Villette. She could've walked away from the valley and her hate.

Instead, she had embraced it and worn it like a treasured garment.

She walked to the shelter as dusk gave way to night. She paused when she pushed the door open and saw Merrill stoking the fire. He turned his head, their eyes meeting briefly. His head dipped in greeting. She gave him a quick smile before stacking the wood with the rest. She stepped back and saw a large bird cooking over the flames.

Katla dusted off her hands, but her palms were blackened from the charred wood. She glanced down to see that her clothes were also soiled. Merrill held out a waterskin. She took it and walked outside to dribble the water over her hands to clean them. Unable to help herself, she also tried to remove the dirt from her top to no avail.

The smell of their dinner drifted outside, making her stomach growl. She returned inside to find Merrill sitting against a wall, his legs outstretched and crossed at the ankles. He turned his head to her, his eyes searching again. She had spent so much time alone that she no longer knew how to act in the company of others, much less recall how to carry on a conversation.

She sank onto the chair and stared at the flickering flames. It seemed the safest thing to do. Without the children, the silence stretched and became uncomfortable, making her more aware of it with every heartbeat. She should say something, but no words came to mind. But she didn't want to stay in her head either. The thoughts that kept running on repeat only made things worse.

Suddenly, Merrill rose and walked to the hearth. He turned the bird over before taking a small bag from his pocket. He dug his fingers inside and sprinkled something over the roasting fowl.

"Seasoning," Merrill told her when he caught her looking.

He cinched the bag closed and returned it to his pocket. Then he resumed his seat. Katla's skin warmed where his gaze touched her. She tucked her feet under the chair and focused intently on the dancing flames. Until she could stand it no more. She turned her head to him.

"Would you rather be alone?" he asked softly.

She had spent centuries on her own. Without the sound of birds, the warmth of the sun, or the feeling of rain against her skin. "Nay." She swallowed, hating that her voice broke on the reply. "It's just...I spent too much time alone. I don't know how to be in the company of others."

"You did fine with the bairns."

"They talked among themselves. I merely listened."

Merrill's fingers slid into his brownish-blond hair as he raked it away from his face. "You really had no one to speak with in all that time?"

"Just Villette. And she only came after I..." She trailed off when she realized what she had been about to say.

"Well, you have me now."

She shifted uncomfortably in the chair. "I...don't know what to talk about."

"Tell me about the valley."

"Why would you want to hear about that?"

Merrill shrugged. "I'm curious."

She waited for him to say more, but he merely looked at her, waiting expectantly. Katla licked her lips. "Winters were harsh but beautiful. Besides the snow, the trees would ice over and make stunning shapes. Then there was the rainy season. Summers could be blisteringly hot, and the spring when everything burst into color was lovely. Hunting was plentiful, and the soil was fertile for our crops."

"Sounds like an incredible place. And you never had worries about dragons?"

"As I mentioned before, we heard them. Often. It was a sound I got used to. They didn't come close, and we never ventured onto their land. We lived so near the border and tucked away in the valley that few risked coming our way. Once a year, we had traders come to us, but that was it. We were isolated. It made for a good life but also meant we didn't know how to defend ourselves."

"The raiders never came before?" Merrill asked.

Katla shook her head. "If they had, we would've been prepared."

"Villette orchestrated everything on this side of the border. The only thing she couldna control was what the dragons did, but she knew that if your people crossed that line, the dragons would retaliate."

She had to admit it made sense. "Possibly."

"Trust me. She had it all planned. It's what she does." He nodded to her. "Did Villette display power when you met her?"

"She didn't do any magic, if that's what you're asking. But I recognized that she was powerful."

He grunted and switched which ankle was on top. "That tells me she wanted you to know that. Did she promise to stop the dragon?"

"I wasn't chased over the border. Nay, Villette found me after I made my way back to the village. I hoped someone else had survived, but there was no one but me."

Merrill sighed softly. "You were hurting and vulnerable."

"I don't think there's a word that can accurately describe my emotional or mental state at that time." Katla slipped off the chair and sat on the floor near the fire, seeking its warmth. "I cried. I begged. I raged. I contemplated crossing the border again so the dragon would end my life. Anything to stop the pain. Just when I was thinking of giving in, Villette appeared."

"She had no doubt been watching you."

Katla brought her knees to her chest and wound her arms around her legs. She rested her chin on her knees and looked at Merrill. "She knew what to say. My grief was so raw that I wasn't in my right mind. I wanted someone to blame, and she pointed to the dragons. I latched on to that and never thought twice about it. Not until Henry asked why I hadn't blamed the invaders."

Merrill shook his head. "Doona blame yourself. Villette focused your attention where she wanted it. Had you attempted to switch your anger, she would've returned it to the dragons. She needed you to hate them for her plan to work."

"It worked, all right. I felt powerless before. After Villette's visit that first time, I believed I was in control. That, somehow, my rage would diminish with each dragon I lured into the valley. But it was all an illusion."

"No' everything, lass. You still have magic."

Katla turned a hand palm up and stared at it. "Because of Villette."

"Did she touch you?"

"I don't know. Maybe. The memories of that day aren't clear."

He scratched his cheek. "She may have made sure you couldna remember."

"I recall looking up and finding her there. I don't know how long I had been alone before that. The elation I felt at seeing another person was so great that my knees wouldn't hold me. She was kind and compassionate. I don't remember her words. I was in a daze." She shook her head. "She drew a bath or used her magic for one, I don't know which. It was just there, and she led me to it. I stripped out of my filthy clothes and soaked. She hummed the entire time."

"Hummed?" Merrill repeated with a confused frown.

Katla nodded. "I just remembered that. I was glad not to be on my own, but I also wasn't in the mood to talk. The humming soothed me. When I finally emerged from the bath, new clothes were laid out for me on the bed. She sat me by the fire and combed my wet hair. Then we ate. I had never seen so much food before."

"She was getting you to trust her."

"It worked."

Merrill cocked his head to the side. "She knew what to say and do to manipulate you. That isna your fault."

"She asked me what happened to my people. I told her all of it." Nausea twisted her stomach as she realized how devious Villette had been. "She comforted me. Told me that things happened sometimes but assured me I would get through it."

"Is that when she offered you a way to get revenge?"

"That didn't happen for a few days. I wanted to go back and look for my family members' bodies, but I couldn't because of the border."

Merrill's lips twisted. "Ah. That was the opening she was waiting for."

"It was. Villette started to say something but stopped. I urged her to tell me whatever it was. Still, she hesitated. I had to practically drag it out of her. That's when she declared her hatred for the dragons and told me how fortuitous it was that she'd found me."

"Because you could join forces."

Katla nodded. "I wanted retribution, and she gave me a way to get it. When I told her there wasn't much I could do, she took my hand and told me there was a way. She said she could help me. I told her I would do whatever was needed."

"Is that when she gave you some of her magic?"

"Maybe. I didn't feel any differently, but I could suddenly do things." Katla curled her fingers into a fist. "Villette warned me that I had to remain in the valley to get my vengeance."

Merrill uncrossed his ankles and bent one knee, propping one foot on the floor. "Did you create the vines?"

"I don't believe so. Though, maybe I did." She shook her head in frustration. "I can't remember."

"You've protected them."

Her gaze jerked to him. "They're alive. They proved that when they chose to help Melisse and Henry."

His gaze softened. "You felt betrayed by that action."

"I did," she admitted. "They were the closest things I had to friends, and they had always chosen me before."

"You still fought to keep the Kings from setting them on fire."

"The vines always did as I asked. Nothing is their fault. They shouldn't be blamed for my sins."

Merrill lifted his brows. "The same could be said about what Villette did to you."

"It's different," Katla argued.

"You just said the vines are alive. That means they can make their own decisions. If they should be forgiven, then so should you."

Katla parted her lips to argue when she realized that he was right. She drew in a deep breath and looked away.

"Do you still wish the dragons harm?" he asked.

"I do not."

"Exactly. You, like the vines, made a choice. If the vines shouldna be judged, neither should you. Now, I hope you're hungry. It's time to eat."

ELEVEN

Merrill ate while furtively watching Katla. Her stomach had rumbled when he sliced the bird, but she'd said nothing about being hungry before. She didn't devour the meat. She savored each bite like it was her first taste, then went back for seconds and even thirds.

"You nearly didna eat when I brought the deer back for you and the bairns," he said. "Was it the animal?"

Katla licked her lips and lifted her gray eyes to meet his. "It didn't have to do with the animal. It was more about me. Once Villette visited, I wasn't hungry or thirsty. It wasn't until after I left the valley that I experienced hunger. At first, I didn't realize what it was. I had forgotten that sensation—and many others. It wasn't until the children that I recognized my need for sustenance."

"With berries?" he asked, his brows raised.

She wrinkled her nose. "That was easy. It meant I didn't have to hunt."

Now, he understood. "Because it's a reminder of the past."

"My hunting of your kind." She turned pensive as her gaze slid to the fire. "It hit too close to home for me."

"You would've done what was needed for the bairns."

A small smile curved her lips at the mention of the children. She looked at him. "Aye, I would've. Thank you for both meals."

"You're welcome. What is the bird called?" he asked.

"I know it as a porunea."

"Porunea," he said, testing the word on his tongue. "Other than the color of its feathers, it looks similar to grouse on my realm."

That got her attention. "Are there many differences between our worlds?"

"As many as there are similarities."

"Tell me," she urged.

Her words were soft, curiosity winding through her voice. It glittered in her stormy eyes. She didn't look at him as if he were a wounded animal who needed to be handled with caution. She didn't treat him as if he were broken—when, in fact, he was.

Maybe beyond repair.

Each time she talked about the past, she retreated, her walls rising around her. She carried guilt and a wealth of blame that caused her to withdraw. But now, seeing her lit up from within took his breath away. He would talk for eternity, telling her anything she wanted to know, if only that look remained. He would break down every molecule between the worlds if it meant keeping her shining.

He had the chance to make her happy, and he would give it to her. "Where shall I begin?"

"Anywhere." Her brows drew together. "Though I don't know much about my own world."

That statement made her face darken as she traveled down the path to the past. She had spent enough time there, and he was partly to blame because he had asked her to return to those memories. But it was time she moved on. At least, for now.

"You know enough. How about I start with the Druids?" he offered.

The interest returned to her eyes as her entire body perked up. "I would like that."

"Henry can only sense other Druids, but dragons can recognize more than Druids."

"What does magic feel like?"

"No one has ever asked me to describe it before. Let me see if I can put it into words." Merrill searched for the right descriptive expression as he beckoned her magic close. "It weaves a silken, fluid thread that is both subtle and robust."

She was silent as her eyes lowered to the floor. "I wouldn't have used such words for my abilities."

"Call it what it is, lass. Magic. What would you have used?"

"Dangerous. Disturbing. Unstable."

He wondered if she was talking about herself and not her powers. "Do you fear your magic?"

She shrugged and looked at him. "I know what you said before, but I don't think it's mine. How can I trust it when it comes from Villette?"

"I'm no' sure Villette could give you something you didna already have. She might have woken your powers, however."

Katla's dark brows drew together. "Woken?"

"You could have been spelled for them to remain dormant forever or until the magic was needed. There are many scenarios. Many Druids on Earth are unaware of their abilities. Some bloodlines are diluted, so the magic doesna show up as it once did.

Unless they're around other Druids, a person wouldna know what to look for. Nor do we know where you came from."

She lowered her legs to sit cross-legged. "You mean not even the dragons know where the babies brought here hail from?"

"We doona even know who it is transporting the bairns to Zora."

"Which means I could've been taken from anywhere."

Merrill nodded. "Exactly."

"If the first mortals brought to your world were Druids, then every human is descended from them and, therefore, a Druid."

"But no' everyone has magic. Those first Druids on Earth didna have any. It's why they were chosen. However, as more humans were born on Earth, some had magic. They were drawn to each other, and a particular place called the Isle of Skye."

Her lips softened into a half-grin. "It sounds magical."

"It is. I'm partial to the place because it's part of Scotland."

"Your home. I remember," she said. "You say its name reverently. Same with Dreagan."

He put his elbow on his knee and flattened his hand against his head. "The magic of the realm is centered at Dreagan. It's why we chose the location as our central location. It might be what makes Scotland—and the Highlands in particular—so ruggedly beautiful. The gray rock peeking through the towering, green mountains and the rolling glens. Waterfalls at every turn. Some huge, some small, but all breathtaking. Forests that beg to be explored. And lochs deep and wide enough to hide even the largest of my kind."

"Lochs?" she asked.

"What you call lakes."

"I think I like loch."

She smiled, and he found his lips quirking at the corners. "And that's just the Highlands. Around the wild coastlines of my homeland are pristine beaches and water in colors you wouldna believe existed. The isles, like Skye, are a treasure trove even more picturesque. Then there are the people. We Scots stand apart from other cultures with our love of tartans, bagpipes, and whisky."

"Is a tartan a food?"

Merrill could have described it for her, but he decided to show her instead. He held out his palm and called his magic to create a ten-by-ten-inch plaid square. Her eyes widened as she crawled closer for a better look. She tentatively touched the red and yellow material accented with green.

"It's so colorful."

He handed her the fabric. "Each clan chooses a different tartan. That's how mortals recognize members of other clans. In the old days, there were even different patterns for hunting and special occasions."

"And bagpipes are?"

"An instrument."

She looked from the tartan in her hands to him. "Can you show me?"

"They're better heard than seen, but they're loud. You either love or hate the sound."

"You love it?"

He nodded as he thought back to walking through Edinburgh and hearing the pipes play. "Verra much so."

"What about whisky?" she asked eagerly.

"Now, *that* I can show you." He produced a bottle of Dreagan whisky and two glasses.

"A drink?" she asked, regarding the bottle. She ran her finger over the double-headed dragon logo and then lifted her gaze to him. "Dreagan. Does the word mean dragon?"

"It does, indeed. It's from the ancient language of the Celts. Whisky is favored among the mortals. We make this particular brand, but there are hundreds of different kinds."

Katla pointed at the label. "You call your whisky dragon and even put dragons on the bottle. Do humans still not know what you are?"

"They doona have a clue. And that's how we want it." He unscrewed the cap and poured a splash into a glass before handing it to her. He cautioned, "Sip it. It's strong."

She brought the tumbler to her mouth and inhaled. "It smells good."

"It tastes even better, though some claim it's an acquired taste." He raised his tumbler to her and then drank.

Katla watched him before she tipped the glass back and wet her lips.

"Let it sit in your mouth for a moment to feel the texture," he urged

The moment she swallowed, her face creased, and she gave a little cough. "It's strong, but I like it."

"It's perfect on a cold, wet night."

She studied the tartan in one hand and sipped the whisky with the other. "How else is our world different?"

"We only have one moon, while you have two. Also, while Zora is younger, I am surprised you're no' more technologically advanced."

Her head snapped up. "I don't understand that word."

"People on Zora move from place to place either on foot, by cart, boat, or horse."

"If you say so."

He took another drink. "On Earth, we have other options. Cars, trains, buses, and planes. Electricity runs everywhere, lighting people's homes as well as cooling and heating them. You can use computers to look up anything you want to know and find the answer. Devices we carry in our pockets can call anyone on Earth."

"I don't know what any of that means, but I want to know. It all sounds incredible. There are really things that cool and heat a home?"

"There are. Did I forget to mention plumbing that brings in fresh water to bathe and wash clothes?"

She gave a small shake of her head. "That's incredible. I wish we had some of that."

"You might have, but I think the culprit preventing that is Villette. She kept cities in conflict and displaced people to keep them focused on food and surviving each day rather than improving their lives."

"Another reason she needs to pay."

Merrill tossed back the rest of his whisky before pouring more. "It's just a guess."

"You're probably right. It goes with everything else she's done."

"That's why you and I will stop her."

Katla looked at him over the rim of her glass, then sipped. "We?"

"Who better? You no' only survived her, you fought against her."

Katla shrugged one shoulder. "I didn't win."

"You survived. That's more than most can say. You've stood against two Star People," he stated.

She lowered her gaze to the tumbler. "I didn't know that's what Miena was."

"How did you get away from her? More importantly, how did you destroy the tower?"

"Good question. I don't think I would've done anything had I been in there alone. I reacted to the threat to the children." She inhaled and lifted her head. "I felt their terror the moment I entered the tower. When I saw Miena, I knew she intended to do them harm. A wave of fury washed over me when she started toward us. I held up my hand to stop her, and everything happened all at once. A ripple of magic shot from my hand that swelled to surround us. I saw her fly backward right as a bright light flashed. There was a loud rumble, and then we were standing together just as we had been in the tower, except we were in the forest."

Merrill swirled the whisky, wishing he had witnessed the interaction. He suspected it was all Katla, but he had to ask. "Was it all your magic, or did the bairns help?"

"If any of the children did anything, they didn't realize it."

"That's why you were eyeing the tower. You wanted to see the damage."

She laid the tartan on her leg and smoothed her hand over it. "I was happy to see it damaged so thoroughly."

"I'd say it was more than damaged. The top is completely gone."

"Too bad the entire thing didn't come down." Her shoulders lifted in a half-hearted shrug. "We might have gotten away, but I didn't hurt Miena. I merely threw her back."

Merrill shrugged as he shifted to get more comfortable. "I

disagree. The fact that she wasna able to get to you says a lot. Besides, you hurt Villette."

"I can't take credit for that. It was a combined effort with your friends."

"I know you walked up to her and took her by the head. A bright light was described there, too. Which also took you to another place. Maybe you wanted to be away from the valley just as you wanted to get the bairns from the tower."

Katla sighed. "I was angry then, too. I turned that vengeance on Villette. I really thought I could kill her. It's why I went after her myself."

"What did Kora tell you about Derek?"

"That Villette was using him."

"Did she also tell you that Villette shared some of her magic with him?"

Katla stilled and stared at him for a long moment. "You know that for sure?"

"I do. I saw Derek go up against Miena. He was able to stand his ground with her because he had Star magic. You hurting Villette is proof that you have some, as well."

"Villette had to know I might turn against her. Why would she give me the power if it could harm her?"

"Control," Merrill said. "Villette never intended for you to discover the truth. Because for all her planning, she couldna have foreseen Melisse entering the vines or Henry going after her."

"I don't want her magic. How do I get rid of it?"

"You can no'. Think of it this way. It could be how we exact justice."

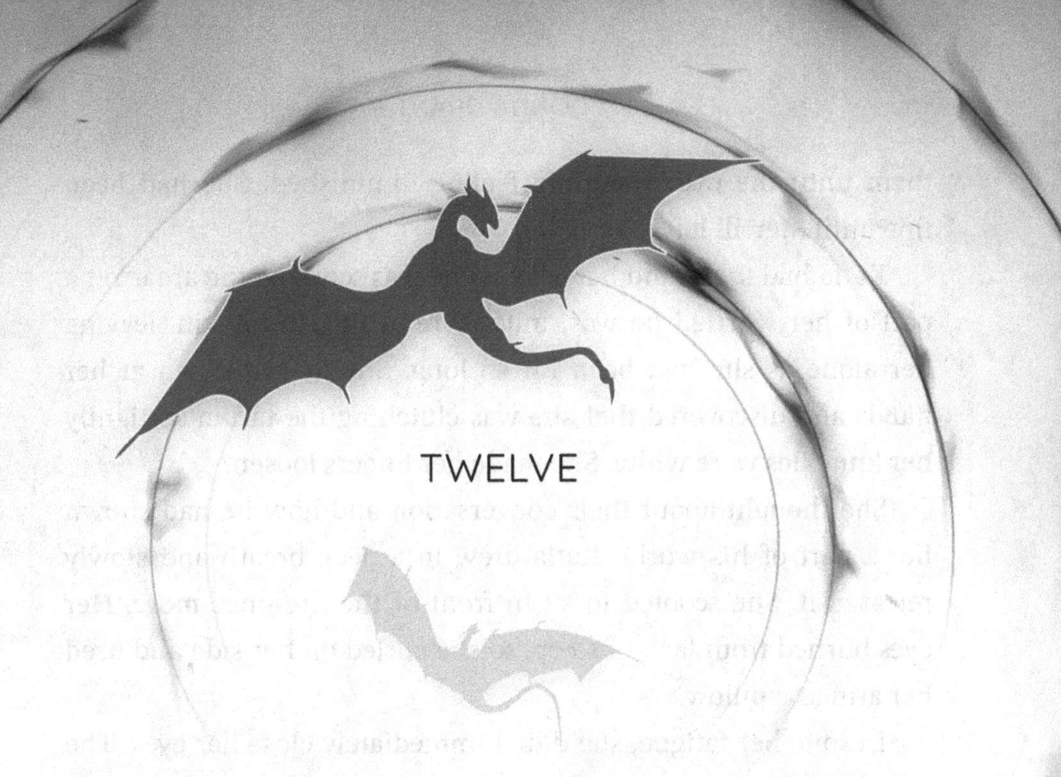

TWELVE

The idea of having anything to do with Villette made Katla ill. Still, if Merrill was correct—and the more she learned, the more she believed he was—she might be able to defeat her.

"Think about what I said," Merrill told her as he got to his feet. "I'm going to have a look around."

She followed him with her gaze, sliding down the back of his hard body and taking in his easy, long gait as he walked away. It was the gait of a commander, a leader. Someone used to being in charge. She watched him disappear into the darkness as the door closed behind him. She stared at the front of the house, longing to call him back. Or go with him. She'd had enough of being alone. But her lips wouldn't form the words.

The silence was heavy, oppressive. She had never noticed it before, but nothing was as it was. She was learning the world again. Her senses were overloaded at times. Whenever the sensation occurred when the children were with her, she'd fixate on them until the overwhelming feeling diminished. She had been fine until Merrill left.

Katla had to remind herself that he was scouting the area. Yet a part of her worried he was, indeed, returning to his kin, leaving her alone as she had been for so long. She looked down at her hands and discovered that she was clutching the tartan so tightly her knuckles were white. She made her fingers loosen.

She thought about their conversation and how he had shown her a part of his world. Katla drew in a deep breath and slowly released it. She scooted to sit in front of the fire once more. Her eyes burned from lack of sleep, so she curled on her side and used her arm as a pillow.

Despite her fatigue, she didn't immediately close her eyes. The flames were mesmerizing. She watched them dance until her eyes wouldn't focus any longer. As she lowered her lids, thoughts of Merrill filled her mind.

When she opened her eyes again, the fire still burned, but there was a stillness that only night brought. She rolled onto her back, only to realize a blanket covered her. She immediately looked for Merrill. He walked past the window outside. Knowing he was there was comforting. She turned onto her other side and immediately fell back to sleep.

The next time she woke, she lay unmoving, listening for the sound of Merrill's footsteps. Finally, she heard him. She released a breath she hadn't realized she was holding. Katla tried to return to sleep, but her eyes wouldn't stay closed. After several minutes, she sat up. She yawned and stretched before folding the blanket and rising. She went to the door and opened it to look around. Her gaze found Merrill as he rounded a building to her left and came toward her.

"It's a few hours yet before dawn," he said as he approached.

"I won't be able to sleep anymore. You can."

He stopped beside her. "I'm fine."

"Do you not need sleep?"

"No' like humans. We rest, and I can sleep, but it isna needed."

She folded her arms around her, missing the warmth of the fire and the blanket. "That must be nice."

"It comes in handy."

"See anything?"

Merrill shook his head. "Only a few animals. It's quiet out here."

"The vine forest was quiet. Here, there is an excess of sounds. The music of the night." She turned her head to him. "Do you hear it?"

"Aye," he answered softly as he met her eyes.

She looked up at the night sky littered with stars. "It's beautiful."

"One of my favorite times to fly is at night."

Her gaze slid back to him. "How high can you go?"

"Verra."

"That sounds amazing. You get to soar among the clouds, leaving the nonsense of the world behind."

Merrill gave her a half-hearted shrug. "It's a benefit, I'll admit." He lifted his gaze to the heavens. "Up there is…"

Katla watched him, waiting with bated breath for what he might say. She didn't look away. She didn't want to miss a single emotion that might cross his face.

Finally, he exhaled and lowered his gaze to her. "Solace. It's a place humans can no' reach. No' like we can. It's ours alone. There, we can be who we were meant to be."

"And what is that?"

"Fierce. Free. Commanding."

His words had a way of touching her that left her soothed and wanting more. "You are still those things."

"You see me as a human, no' a dragon."

"Are you not one and the same?"

His lips twisted. "I suppose."

"You don't sound sure."

"I'm no' who I once was."

Katla laughed dryly. "Who is? Change is inevitable. It's all around us. Look at the trees. The leaves are changing colors and getting ready to fall to the ground so the trees can pause for the winter. It sounds much like what you and the other Kings did after the war."

"Aye, we did. When we woke, it was with fury and bitterness. And a lot of rancor."

"Emotions have a way of clouding otherwise decent judgment. I should know. I'm far from the woman I once was. I'm walking in a world I don't recognize."

He nodded slowly. "It isna an easy thing to do."

"But you got through it."

"We supported each other."

She cocked her head to the side. "Is that why you're here? You don't think I can do this alone?"

"I think you can do anything you set your mind to. You have fortitude the likes of which I've rarely seen. You doona need anyone, lass. Certainly no' me."

That wasn't true. She needed someone for everything. She was tired of doing everything without help, weary of facing each day by herself. And worn out by carrying her numerous burdens alone.

She didn't have strength. It was just that no one could do it. She put one foot in front of the other because she had to.

"You're wrong about me," she said. "I didn't want to be the lone survivor. I prayed for death. I could've ended it just by crossing the border again, but I couldn't even manage that. Strength didn't guide me. It was spite. Determination doesn't keep me on my feet. I've just refocused my vengeance, moving it from your people to Villette. That isn't fortitude. It's fear and despair."

Merrill shifted to face her. "You could've taken your life. That would have put an end to your misery. Instead, you channeled your grief. I'm no' saying it was the right way, but you didna give up. You could've remained in the vine forest and continued your retribution against dragons. You saw the truth Henry revealed. You confronted Villette. You stood against her. You broke free of the prison she put you in. That isn't fear. Lass, that's perseverance and valor if I've ever seen it. And trust me, I've seen a lot. You may no' see yourself as courageous or resilient, but I do. I've seen many crumple under much less than what you've endured."

Katla was so unprepared for his words that she was still reeling from them when he walked away. She watched his retreating back until he was out of sight. Her eyes returned to the sky. There were streaks of pale pink and yellow mixed with the navy and gray now. Large, puffy clouds were a beautiful canvas to display the various colors.

She desperately wanted to be the woman Merrill spoke about, but she didn't feel it. All she saw were the wrongs she had committed, the violence and destruction she wrought. The wanton act of destroying a species that hadn't harmed her family. Dread had driven her for so long. She'd claimed other emotions. Rage. Bitterness. Revulsion. But every one of them was rooted in fear.

Emotion had dictated her decisions for as long as she could remember. It had even pointed her north. She didn't know why she had decided on that route. It wasn't as if she had knowledge of where Villette was. Instead, she had just taken off. Merrill had known and followed anyway. He hadn't asked her where she was going or why. He hadn't tried to make her deviate either. What he had done was remain with her so she wasn't alone. He had been a silent figure offering support when—and if—she asked for it. He remained, regardless of how many times she told him to leave. Steadfast and constant.

She wasn't sure what to do with someone like him. After so long on her own, she had forgotten how to ask for help. She had gotten used to depending on herself and conformed to that life. But she didn't want to stay like that. She yearned for change. And that transformation had to start somewhere.

Yet there was safety in remaining how she was. She knew what to expect and the ways to adjust. What if someone let her down? What if she depended on someone and they forgot about her? Someone could lie or deceive her.

That was the way of the world, wasn't it? It was always the chance you took. Fear didn't want her to change. It wished to keep her as a prisoner. She had been locked in that cycle for long enough. Change was terrifying. Anything could happen. Her life could turn out worse than it was, or it could be better. She wouldn't know unless she took a leap of faith. And she really wanted to be the person Merrill spoke about.

Katla entered the structure and walked to the fire. The warmth of it invited her closer. The flames reminded her of Merrill—strong and vibrant with the ability to offer comfort with its heat, cook meals, or light a dark room. But there was another side to the blaze. If she got too close, it would destroy her, devour her body and soul without hesitation.

Friend or foe.

Or something in between.

Merrill could be any of those things. The anxiety that usually reared up inside her remained silent now. Maybe it was because she was so desperate for company that she couldn't feel the warning. Or perhaps there wasn't one. Maybe there was nothing to fear with Merrill. The only thing she knew for sure was that she liked having him near.

She became aware of a presence in the room and turned her head to the door to find Merrill. His deep blue irises were trained on her, his expression unreadable. How she wished to know his thoughts. His eyes saw everything, filtering it into his mind to be stored with eons of images and conversations. What made her think she would stand out? Besides, someone as handsome as Merrill must have someone special.

"It's going to rain soon," he announced.

But her mind remained on her last thought. She wondered what he would be like as a lover. Would he be controlling or allow her to take the lead? Would he only see to his desires or pay attention to his partner's? Did he finish quickly or last all night? She eyed his muscular frame and imagined his endurance exceeding that of any human.

A lock of dirty-blond hair fell across his forehead. She wanted to smooth it back and let her fingers trail through the thick strands to see if they were as silky as they appeared. Her gaze fell to his lips, and her mouth went dry. Katla looked away, embarrassed about thinking of him in such a way.

More than hunger assailed her. She couldn't recall her husband's face or name—or the feel of his body against hers.

Her gaze returned to Merrill. She *ached* to have that kind of connection again.

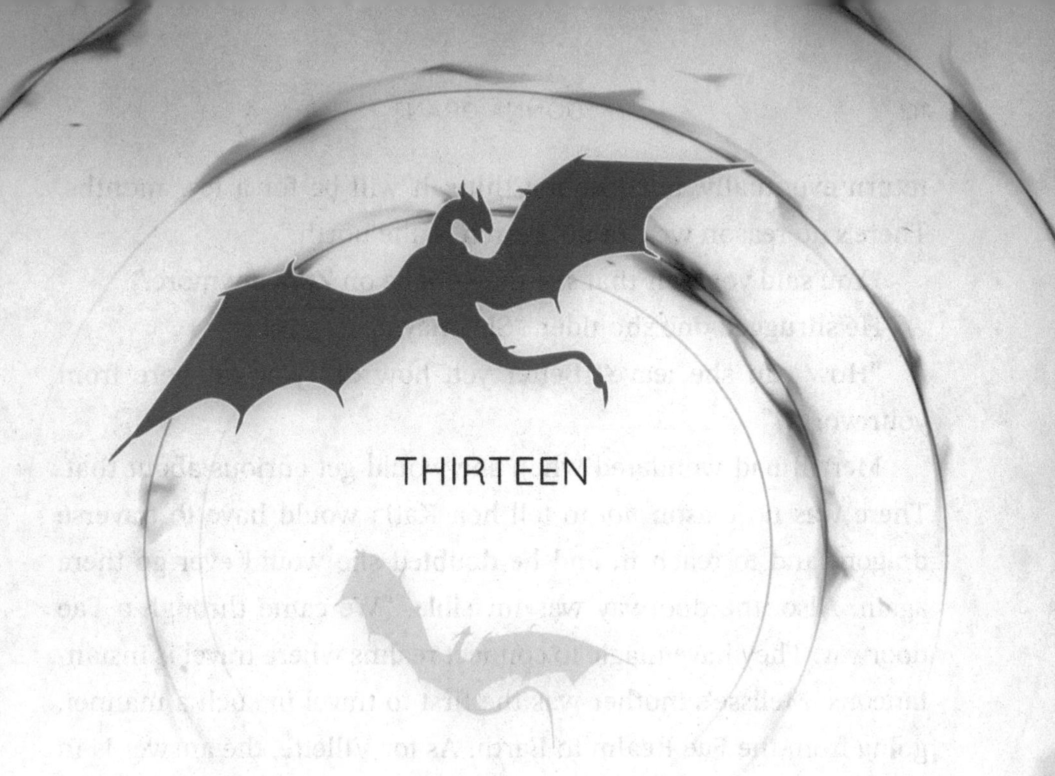

THIRTEEN

What drew his gaze to Katla again and again? She was stunningly beautiful, aye, but it was more than that. She had an aura about her that called to him on a primitive, primal level that made him want to throw back his head and roar. Push her against the wall and lay claim to her so everyone would know she was his.

Merrill noticed the flush to her cheeks. Desire coiled tightly, urgently, as it rushed through him. He burned for her with a need that could bring him to his knees. Yet he made no move to show his interest. His position was tenable at best. He was better off hiding his attraction lest she push him away again. *That* he wouldn't be able to stand.

"If you wish to continue north, I suggest we wait a few hours and let the storm pass," he told her once he knew he could say the words without the truth coming through his voice.

She absently picked at her shirt. "I have no destination in mind."

"Villette knows Stonemore will be watched closely. She may

return eventually, but I doona think it will be for a few months. There's no reason we can no' search in the north."

"You said yourself that she may not be on Zora anymore."

He shrugged one shoulder. "She may no'."

"How can she leave? Better yet, how did you get here from your world?"

Merrill had wondered when she would get curious about that. There was no reason *not* to tell her. Katla would have to traverse dragon land to reach it, and he doubted she would ever go there again. Also, the doorway was invisible. "We came through a Fae doorway. They have magic to connect realms where travel is instantaneous. Melisse's mother was the first to travel in such a manner, going from the Fae Realm to Earth. As for Villette, the answer is in the description of their kind. They move freely among the stars."

A cool breeze brushed past, sending Katla closer to the fire. "I still don't understand how."

"I've never seen it, so I can no' explain the how of it."

"Dragons used to be with them. Does that mean you can also move among the stars?"

The wind grew brisk, sending colder air into the building through the doorway and the windows without covering. He shut the door, fastening it so it stayed in place. "Maybe. We've never tried."

"In other words, I could be searching for Villette for the rest of my days."

"Possibly." He didn't add that they had no idea how long Katla might live.

She scratched her earlobe and pulled the chair to her as she sat. "I'm not good at this."

"At what?"

She clasped her hands and stared at the flames intently as if waiting for them to deliver a message. "I don't know how to ask for help."

Now, he understood her reluctance. Merrill was lowering himself to the floor when the first drops of rain began to fall. He leaned against the wall. "You just did. What would you like help with?"

"Finding Villette."

Her turbulent gray eyes cut to him, almost as if she were afraid to look at him head-on. They might have suffered similar losses, but she had been completely on her own, whereas he'd been surrounded by the other Kings. Ulrik had lost his mind when he was on his own, dying over and over, only to return and suffer through it all over again.

It was probably a blessing that Katla hadn't realized how much time had passed since her family's death—likely Villette's doing. And for once, Merrill agreed with her actions. Had Katla been aware of the passage of time, she wouldn't have continued trapping dragons. Villette's decision had served her needs, but it also aided Katla.

Merrill had difficulty asking his brethren for help, and they had been his constant companions. Which meant he understood exactly how hard this was for Katla. "I've already said I wanted to help."

"I tried to send you away."

"Notice how I ignored that." There was a soft curve of her lips when she looked at him. It wasn't quite a smile, but it was close. "Saying that, I would leave if you truly wished it."

Her brow furrowed as she shook her head. "I don't want you to go."

"Then we shall take this journey together."

"And if it takes months?"

He leaned back against the wall. "Then it does."

"What of your friends?"

"If they need me, they'll let me know."

Katla gathered her hair over one shoulder and ran her fingers through the long, inky length. He imagined grabbing a handful of the onyx strands and winding them around his hand as he held her head in place for a searing kiss. The vision was so clear and vivid that, for a heartbeat, he believed it was real. Blood rushed to his cock. When he blinked, he was still on the floor across the room from her. He swallowed a moan.

The rain began droning louder as the storm settled in. Droplets came through the windows. The instant he saw Katla shiver, Merrill rose and waved his hand over the windows. He could almost see Con shaking his head. The Kings' magic was powerful, but they used to be mindful of how often they used it and for what purposes. That directive was disregarded by all after coming to Zora—Con included. It was just another thing that was different on Zora.

"I'm beginning to think there isn't anything you can't do," Katla said.

He returned to his seat on the floor. "I was getting wet."

"I suspect you wouldn't have minded." She nodded at the fire. "None of the wood I brought in has been used. Is that your doing, as well?"

"It is. Druids on Earth can do such spells. I imagine you could, too."

At the mention of magic, her hands paused in her hair for a heartbeat.

"You shouldna be frightened of your abilities," he said after seeing her reaction.

"When I was in the vines, I knew my purpose and place. I knew where I fit in the order of things and why I was there. Some of the things I did with magic just happened. I didn't feel in control of it."

Merrill was fascinated by how her fingers nimbly moved as she plaited her hair. "Magic can feel like that. It can be instinctive at times, and then others, it won't come when we need it."

"Did that happen to you?"

He pulled his gaze away from her hair to look into her eyes. "No' in the way I know it has occurred with the Druids. Specifically, the ones who didna grow up with someone to teach them how to use their power." The disappointment that crossed her face was like a punch. "I can try to help. If you want, that is."

"I'd like that," she replied.

There was a vulnerability about Katla that hadn't been there before. She was opening up in small increments. It didn't diminish her. To him, it made her even stronger because it took a great deal of strength to take a hard look at yourself and want to change. It took even more to step toward that by asking for help. It was a different kind of strength. One inherently more potent.

"Would you like to begin now?" he offered.

She tied off the end of the braid before reaching for the waterskin. "Maybe not quite yet."

"There's no reason to be nervous." He watched her throat as she drank. He wanted to run his tongue along the vein before kissing down it and then behind her ear.

Katla lowered the waterskin and pressed her wrist to her mouth to dry it. "I don't trust myself. What if I hurt you?"

"We have to know the extent of your magic. How much of it is Druid, and how much from Villette. I'm also curious to discover if there are differences in your magic compared to the Druids from Earth."

She flipped the end of her braid over her shoulder to fall down her back. "Why help me?"

"I doona have an answer. I followed my intuition after I saw you at Stonemore. It wasna just because Kora and Derek wanted to know that you were all right. It was as if something told me we would be on this journey together."

"I'm not sure I deserve your help—*anyone's* help."

He held out his hand and waited for her to toss him the water-skin. He caught it easily and removed the lid to take a long drink. "I know that feeling well. I still think you're too hard on yourself."

"Then you are, too."

"We'll have to agree to disagree on that," he replied.

This time, he got an actual grin. It was fleeting, but it was there. She tore off pieces of meat from the porunea. Merrill produced rolls with his magic. She spotted the basket near her feet and grabbed one. The smell of warm, fresh bread permeated the dwelling, making even his mouth water.

"Delicious," she said after biting into the roll.

Her eyes closed in contentment as she chewed. He liked pleasing her. It made him want to do more. He was considering turning their space into an opulent chamber when he heard his name in his mind.

"Cullen wants to talk. Give me a moment," he told her.

She hurriedly asked, "Can you inquire about the children?"

He nodded and opened the mental link. *"I'm here, Cullen. How are the bairns?"*

"Settling in nicely. They're a wee bit overwhelmed, which is to be expected after what they went through. The other children are helping them more than we are. It tends to be how things are."

"That's good to hear. Any issues?"

Cullen chuckled. *"Only with keeping enough food for Perick. The lad is never full. It will take some time for them to fully settle in, but they're on their way. As you know, everyone is looking out for them. How are things with you?"*

"We're fine."

"No encounters with anyone?"

Merrill frowned at the question. *"Nay. Has something happened there?"*

"It's strangely quiet. It's put everyone on edge."

"We've spent so much time fighting that maybe everyone needs this."

Cullen sighed. *"That's what Tamlyn says, but we've no' seen the last of Villette."*

"I agree. I think she's forming another plan to hit back hard."

"If that's true, then you and Katla shouldna be out there alone searching for her."

The mention of her tugged Merrill's gaze to Katla. *"There is more to Katla than we think. I believe Villette gave her some Star magic."*

"I think you're right."

"Katla might be able to take down Villette."

"Merrill," Cullen said, worry lacing his words. *"You know how many it took to bring down Miena. If you locate Villette, contact us so we can get there to help."*

Merrill wanted to refuse, mainly because he wanted to end Villette on his own. But he knew that wasn't possible. Nor would he watch Villette harm Katla. *"Doona worry, brother. I plan on it."*

"You might want to reiterate that to Varek. He's concerned. We all are."

"Doona waste your thoughts on me. I'll figure things out."

"You can figure them out here."

Merrill remembered a time when he had said similar words to one of the Kings. He had always told them that family was there to lean on. It wasn't that he no longer believed that. Because he did. But this time was different. *"No' this time."*

"Varek said you'd say that." Cullen exhaled loudly. *"I doona like it, but I'll stand by your decision. Though, I will say I'm glad you're no' on your own."*

"Aye." Merrill was glad Katla was with him, too. Or was he with her?

"Where are you headed?"

"North at present."

There was a brief pause. *"No' to Orgate?"*

"We're steering clear of that city."

"Good to hear."

Merrill drained the last of the whisky from his glass. *"Tell the bairns Katla is thinking about them."*

"They'll be happy to know that. They miss her. Be safe, brother."

"You, as well."

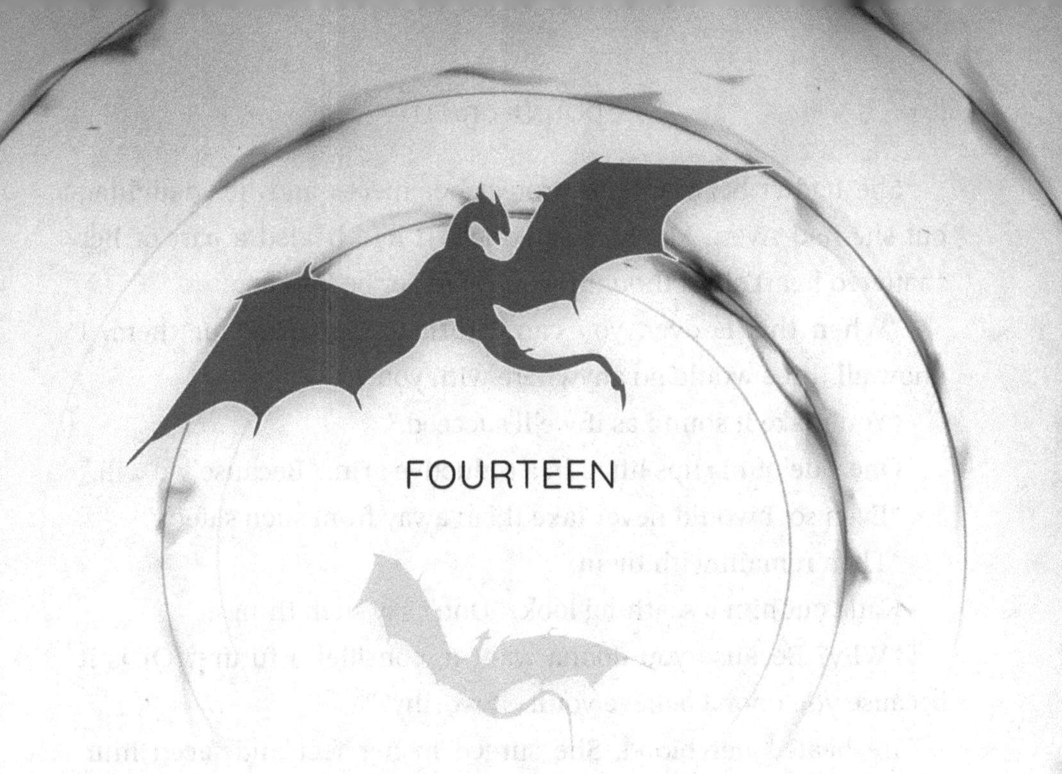

FOURTEEN

Katla tried not to stare at Merrill. It looked like he was just sitting there, but really, he was having a full-blown conversation in his head. She felt his eyes on her. She wanted to look at him but she kept her gaze on the fire. She had so many questions about the children. She wished she could talk to them herself, but she would have to be content with this—which was more than she had expected.

Merrill stretched out his legs and crossed his ankles. "The bairns are doing well. The other children have taken them under their wing."

"That's good," she said, looking down at her lap. With the other kids, they probably didn't even think about her. "I'm glad they're happy."

"They miss you."

Her eyes lifted to meet his. "Do you think so?"

"I know so. They wanted to make sure Cullen passed that on. They willna forget you, lass. You saved them."

She hadn't been able to protect her nieces and her daughter, but she had Aven, Maely, and Perick. It had healed a part of her shattered heart she'd thought would forever be broken.

"When this is over, you can return to Iron Hall for them. I know all three would go anywhere with you."

"You make it sound as if we'll succeed."

One side of his lips lifted in a seductive grin. "Because we will."

"Even so, I would never take them away from such safety."

"Then remain with them."

Katla cut him a scathing look. "Don't say such things."

"Why? Because you doona want to consider a future? Or is it because you doona believe yourself worthy?"

Ire heated her blood. She surged to her feet and faced him. "Both. Nor do I want to test how welcome I would be."

"No one would dare harm you."

He hadn't raised his voice, but there was steel in his statement. Enough for her to know he meant every word. Moreover, she believed him.

"Are you no' searching for redemption?" he asked.

"I am, but—"

"Ah. So, if you take out Villette, that willna be enough for you to forgive yourself and move on."

She didn't like that he knew exactly what to say to make her blood boil. "It will be a start."

"But no' enough. What would be enough? Or is there no such thing?"

"I don't know," she said, a hard edge to her words.

He quirked a brow. "You need some kind of bar to meet that will release you of sin."

"Nothing will wash away what I've done!"

She saw the sparks as her words echoed around the room. That's when Katla realized she had not only stood, but her fingers were also outstretched, her arms at her sides. Magic flowed through her so fast it was dizzying. She curled her fingers into fists to stop the sparks, but it was more difficult to turn the magic away.

"Doona fight it," Merrill cautioned as he got to his feet. "I saw the sparks and wanted to know how far I could push you. Forgive me. I shouldna have done that."

"I didn't even know it was happening." Katla turned away, flipping between humiliation and shock.

Her eyes slid closed as Merrill came up behind her. She felt his solid presence. It wasn't threatening or intimidating. He was like an immovable oak. Someone to lean on if she needed it. Or someone to shield her. Then again, perhaps she was imagining it because she yearned for just those things.

"Emotions rule you. Control is an illusion others convince themselves they have. Doona try to deceive yourself. It's about being aware of your feelings and your response, then adjusting to each circumstance."

His voice was smooth, husky. That unique lilt was like a seductive caress as it slid over her, around her. She could listen to him until the end of time. His nearness was too powerful to ignore. She opened her eyes and turned to face him. He was closer than she realized. She could have leaned back and rested against his chest. Her palms itched to smooth over his wide shoulders and down his chest. He was magnetic, drawing her in. And she had no desire to be anywhere else.

"You make it sound easy."

"Nothing meaningful ever is," he replied.

This close, she could see the thick eyelashes framing his captivating blue eyes. They ensnared, beguiled.

Tempted.

His very presence did. Was he aware of what he did to her? Was it on purpose, or just a byproduct of being a Dragon King?

"Call to your magic," Merrill urged hoarsely.

Her eyes lowered to his mouth. She pressed her lips together as she suddenly recalled how much she had enjoyed kissing. She remembered the motions, but she couldn't recall the feeling of her husband's lips on hers. Or his arms around her. Surely, he had held her in such a way. Why couldn't she remember? She hadn't made him up. She had once loved and been loved. But it was just an echo of memories she had once treasured.

"Lass?"

Merrill's voice pulled her from the darkness into the light. She focused on his mouth once more. Desire, seductive and ardent, heated her blood. She yearned to pull his head down for a kiss and hold him close. She craved the feeling of his weight lying atop her. Need throbbed at her center. She longed for things she couldn't have.

Katla lifted her right hand when she felt magic swirling in her palms. She looked down and saw teeny sparks coming from her fingertips. The magic within her was thick and clingy, but she still felt its vibrant potency. She focused on her power and could soon sense it throughout her body, flowing just beneath the skin, waiting for her command.

"Just like that." Merrill's words were as soft as a whisper.

She lifted her other hand and urged the magic to her fingertips. In the next instant, sparks shot from her fingers. Katla brought her hands side by side and watched the dazzling display for several minutes. Then Merrill's hand hovered over hers. She immediately yanked hers away.

"What are you doing?" she demanded.

"You willna hurt me."

"You can't know that."

He quirked a brow, refusing to move. "Return your hands," he bade.

Katla wanted to refuse. Merrill was the closest thing she had to a companion in centuries, and she didn't want to cause him harm. But at the same time, she needed to be able to direct her magic. He was teaching her.

"Trust me, lass," he pressed.

Those eyes. That voice. She was powerless to refuse him, especially when he called her *lass*. Katla slowly returned her hands to rest beneath his. He dipped his chin, telling her to proceed. She pushed her magic up through her fingers once more. The sparks moved around him, converging over his hand to shoot toward the ceiling. Wonder filled her as Merrill turned his palm up so she could see there were no burns.

"How?" she asked in astonishment.

His eyes softened as his arm lowered to his side. "The magic is a part of you. It feels what you feel, sees what you see."

"So, I'm controlling it." She stopped her magic and dropped her arms.

"Do you control your emotions?"

Katla started to say she did when she realized his ruse. "Sometimes."

"How?"

Despite how many years she had lived, it was easy to forget that Merrill had existed for eons longer. He had seen and experienced thousands of lifetimes more than she ever would. And he had come out the other side. Who was she to ignore whatever wisdom he wished to impart?

"Anger may come, but I can choose whether to retaliate," she replied.

"When ire comes, you'll be mixed in its storm before you know it. Your magic will respond and lash out simultaneously. What you speak of is irritation or frustration. You put it eloquently earlier when you said anger didn't need to be fed."

Katla blew out a breath. "I get your point."

Merrill gently wrapped his fingers around her wrist and lifted it. "Think of strong emotions. Abhorrence. Indignation. Terror." He paused, his gaze piercing. "There will be triggers that set you off. You'll react instinctively. We all do. But it's realizing what you're doing before the magic leaves you."

She had difficulty concentrating on his words with his fingers wrapped around her. His grip was firm but gentle, his touch warm. He hadn't done more than lift her arm, but her breath came in a rush as she silently begged him to pull her against him.

"You'll lift your hands without knowing it," he continued.

Lift. Yes, she could do that. Wait. What did he say? She blinked and tried to concentrate.

"The trick is to keep your arms at your sides. That way, if any magic escapes, it will shoot downward. Understand?"

She nodded since words no longer formed on her tongue. He lowered her arm and released her. One innocent touch and she could barely remain on her feet. She was desperate for human contact. She hungered for it as the ravenous did with food. Her need was so profound she was prepared to do anything for another whisper of a connection.

"It will take practice, but it's achievable." Merrill turned and walked away. "No' that I think either of us will be able to contain ourselves when we find Villette."

The mention of her nemesis yanked Katla out of her musings. She looked out the window, hoping the rain had stopped so she could get outside and walk off some of her restless energy before she did something embarrassing like throw herself at Merrill.

The storm was still going strong, however. It didn't look as if it would let up anytime soon. She smiled then because she hadn't felt rain in a long time. There were a few drops when she woke to find herself in the forest outside of Stonemore, but nothing like what was happening outside now. She might have lived for centuries, but she had been deprived of so many things that humans took for granted.

Katla strode to the door. She glanced at Merrill, their eyes meeting briefly before she walked outside and into the rain. It lashed at her body, soaking her instantly. The icy droplets pierced her like tiny daggers, but she didn't care. She spread her arms and threw back her head as she twirled in the storm.

Rain pelted her eyelids and ran down her face and through her hair. She shivered, but she remained. Katla hadn't truly comprehended how much she had missed rain until then. She had dashed out of a storm so many times, not wanting to get wet. Now, it was all she wanted.

Light flashed behind her eyelids and, a moment later, a thunderous boom brought her to a stop. It took her a moment to recall that it was thunder and lightning. She turned in a circle, looking for the direction the lightning had come from. She saw the zigzag of light just as it streaked across the sky in a dazzling display of raw power.

The autumn weather was putting on a stunning presentation, and she excitedly took in every moment. She didn't want to go inside, even when her teeth chattered from the cold. After being denied something as simple as rain, Katla knew she would never be able to see another storm and not rush into it.

She wrapped her arms around herself for warmth and reluctantly pivoted to return to the building. Merrill leaned a shoulder against the doorway, watching her. She couldn't see him clearly through the downpour, but she thought there might have been a smile on his lips.

Katla couldn't wait to get in front of the fire to begin warming up. Merrill moved out of the way as she hurried past him, but she came to a halt a few steps inside when her eyes landed on the oval tub sitting before the hearth.

"The water will stay warm for as long as you wish it," Merrill said.

She turned to look at him.

"Remain for as long as you want," he told her. "I'll be outside."

Then, he was gone. Katla turned back and saw the wisps of heat rising from the water. She hurriedly yanked off her clothes and sank into the tub.

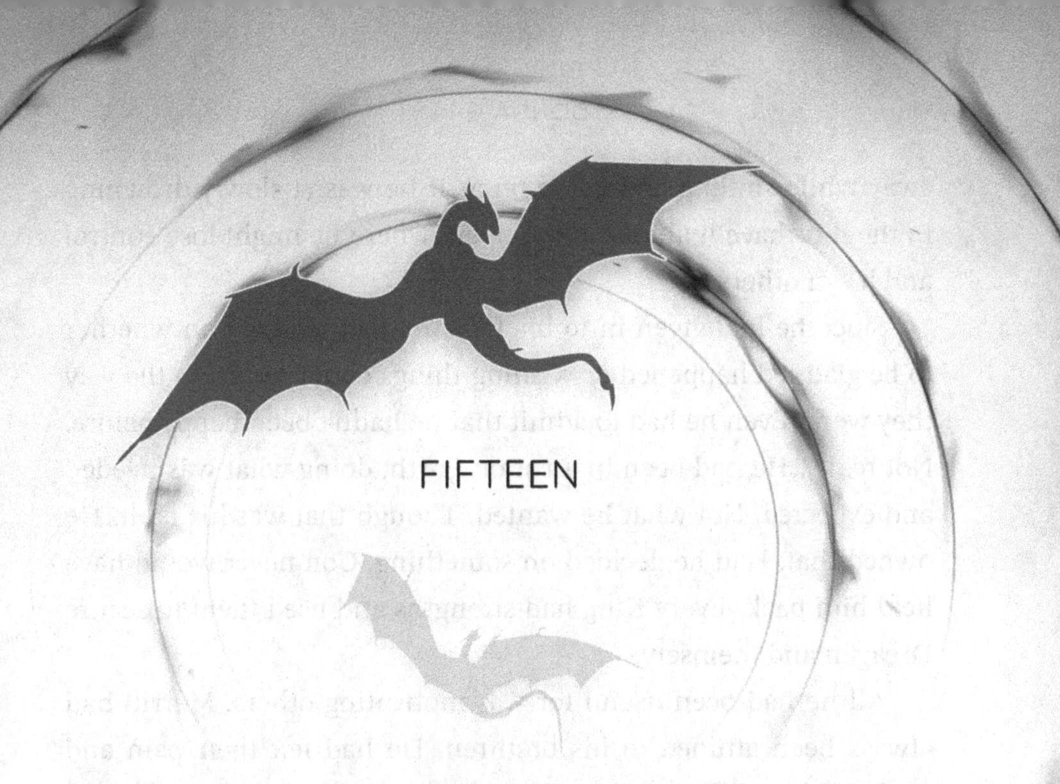

FIFTEEN

Merrill pressed his back against the building and stared at where Katla had danced in the rain. He couldn't get the sight of her jubilant expression out of his mind. The way she had spun with such abandon and joy had him transfixed. She had been a sight to behold: the rain upon her upturned face, her hair fanning out around her, and her saturated top molding to curves he couldn't look away from.

She had let go of everything for a fleeting instant and relished the moment. He thought about her description of the vine forest, where she had resided for the past millennium and a half. Somehow, she still found happiness.

It was something he hadn't been able to do in so very long—longer than he realized. He had put on a brave face for Varek and the others for a considerable length of time and was so good he had even fooled himself. Merrill would probably still be that person if he hadn't come to Zora.

He wasn't sure if it was better to have kept his emotions locked away while smiling and going on as if he wasn't slowly drowning in them or have it all out in the open, where he might lose control and harm others.

Since he had given in to his rage, he had teetered on whether to be glad it'd happened or wishing things could return to the way they were. Even he had to admit that he hadn't been happy before. Not really. He had been in a rut on Earth, doing what was needed and expected. Not what he wanted. Though that was his fault. He owned that. Had he decided on something, Con never would have held him back. Every King had strengths and used them to secure Dreagan and themselves.

All he had been useful for was motivating others. Merrill had always been attuned to his brethren. He had felt their pain and anger and could take it away. Just as they would have for him had he asked. Orange dragons were known empaths, but he had always believed his empathic abilities were stronger than others in his clan. How could he be upset about that when it had helped the Kings get to where they were today?

That wasn't what fueled his rage. *That* was reserved for the mortals. For the war. For the dragons being sent away. And for taking away his home and everything he loved. The humans weren't truly at fault. He knew that now. They were just doing what their species did. But that didn't diminish his suffering.

His wrath had intensified when the dragons on Zora rejected the Kings. He and his brethren had given up *everything* for their freedom, and the dragons despised the Kings. It was only now that he could admit that he was more hurt than angry by their response.

No, the true culprit was Villette. Merrill lay the blame for it all at her feet. Her actions and interference had destroyed countless lives, all in the pursuit of revenge. Her treachery stretched across multiple realms and was far-reaching. And he had bedded her. It sickened him to think that he had shared his body with her.

Granted, he hadn't known who she was. Nor had there been any romantic feelings. She had simply been someone to ease his needs. There came a time when he knew something wasn't quite right about her, but he had chosen not to look any deeper. Once he learned her identity, he refused her advances. But he should've recognized her duplicity sooner. He should have known. He was an empath, after all.

He never should've remained at Stonemore. That was where he had wronged not just the Kings but also every dragon throughout time. He had slept with the enemy, the mastermind of their ruination. Merrill would never be able to wash away that sin, not even if he assassinated Villette every day for a million years. It was a mark on his soul. And just one more thing he needed to atone for before he could return to the others.

Merrill became dark and broody whenever he thought about Villette and the part he'd unwillingly played, and he was never good company when he was like that. He had chosen to be Katla's companion. The least he could do was make sure he was somewhat agreeable. He closed his eyes and pushed Villette out of his mind, replacing her with thoughts of Katla. The tightness around his chest lessened, and his entire body released its tension as frustration and irritation melted away.

He focused his hearing to pick up sounds within the structure. The drone of the rain faded as he caught the pop of the fire. Water swished as Katla moved in the tub. He picked up the sound of a droplet as it cascaded down her arm before dropping back into the water.

But it was her sigh—a sound that was more a sensual moan than anything—that made his balls tighten with longing. He pictured her reclined in the tub, wet hair clinging to the side of her face while the rest hung over the back and dripped onto the floor. He imagined one knee bent and breaking the surface as her arms rested along the rim. The swells of her breasts would be visible, a hint of nipple showing.

He fought not to go inside and join her in the bath. The tub was big enough. He hadn't needed to make it that big, but he had. Because in the back of his mind, he pictured them there together, naked bodies slipping and sliding against each other as their limbs tangled. His cock grew so hard he had to palm it to adjust.

Katla had no idea of her beauty or allure. She could have him on his knees in a heartbeat if she wanted. He'd crawl through Hell just for a taste of her lips. He'd follow her to the ends of the universe for a smile. He would bestow untold pleasures upon her from now through eternity if given the chance.

But that wasn't what she needed from him—not that she required anything. He was here more for himself. Her nearness diminished his rage and soothed the violence. Though she had let it be known that she wished for his company. He imagined he'd feel the same if he had been alone for so long.

Water splashed within. He bit back a moan and adjusted himself again. He could ease his discomfort, but it would only give him a moment's relief. His craving for Katla ran deep—deeper than he had ever experienced before.

He opened his eyes and tried to drown out the sounds from inside, but it was too late. He was attuned to every noise that wrought carnal images, sending desire straight to his cock. He shoved away from the building with his teeth bared and stepped into the rain, hoping it would cool his body. It did nothing but make him think of Katla.

Something moved out of the corner of Merrill's eye. He spun around, staring through the sheet of rain, but saw nothing. He opened all his senses, reaching out to see what might be there. Could it be Villette? Merrill turned his head and looked through the window, seeing Katla in the tub. He pulled his gaze away and prowled the area. The rain washed away any tracks, but something had been there. He was sure of it.

Merrill supposed it could have been an animal, but without any tracks, he scratched that off the list. That left only two options. It was either a Star Person or the invisible entity. Their unseen foe targeted dragons. It'd killed fifty not long after the Kings arrived on Zora. It had nearly taken out Con and Rhi's twins, Brandr and Eurwen. Just a few days prior, it had attacked Derek and Hector. Had it come for him now?

If it was the entity, he would never be able to see it. There would only be a slight movement in his peripheral. And a smell. Alasdair had said there was a peculiar smell but couldn't name it. Merrill stalked around the ruins, searching every space for the enemy. The longer he remained in the storm, the more certain he was that something was out there. Why, then, didn't it attack?

He stood in the middle of the village street and waited for it. He had never been one to put things off. If something had come for him, then he wanted to face it now. But nothing happened. He blinked the rain from his lashes and turned in another slow circle. The entity always struck. There was no reason for it to wait. Unless it wasn't the invisible foe.

Merrill started back toward the structure but couldn't shake the feeling that something was out there. He stepped under the overhang just as Katla opened the door. Her hair was wet, her skin flushed from the bath. She took in his soaked clothes.

"Just patrolling," he explained.

Her gaze narrowed slightly. "Is something out there?"

"I thought there might be, but I didna find anything."

Her gaze moved past him to look outside. "No tracks?"

"No' a single one. Though the rain could be washing them away."

Gray eyes met his. "Star People don't have to leave tracks."

"I'm aware."

"You don't think it was them?"

Merrill hesitated. "It could be."

She motioned him inside. Then she faced him. "What do you think it was?"

"The dragons have an enemy we can no' see. It's concealed to us."

"Invisible?"

He sighed and nodded. "Aye."

"To just your kind? Or everyone?"

He raked a hand through his wet hair to get it out of his face. "Humans and elves can no' see it either. However, Star People can."

"Could it be something Villette created?"

"Doubtful since it went after her no' so long ago. Alasdair, Varek, and their mates, Lotti and Jeyra, tangled with Villette. While they were battling, the entity struck, attacking all of them. Lotti described it as a floating knot of angry, swirling, dark energy with wisps trailing behind it like arms waving. It moved swiftly and fluidly, making it challenging to track. There is no face or body, just a sense that it took pleasure in causing confusion and pain. It's gone after dragons, elves, and Star People."

Katla's brow furrowed as she listened. She absently finger-combed her damp hair. Merrill produced an actual comb, which he handed to her. She took it with a brief smile of thanks before sliding it through her hair. "This entity could be outside?"

"If it was, I think it would've attacked. It doesna like dragons."

"It doesn't seem to like anyone."

Merrill changed into dry clothes with merely a thought. "It isna an animal, or it would eat what it kills. The warrior dragons it initially took down were large, and it left them. As if it only wanted their deaths."

"Maybe it did. I didn't know dragons could shift as you can. I didn't know about Star People or Druids. I've recently learned about the Fae, and you speak of elves. Who knows what might be roaming the realm?"

"The elves live on the eastern side of the dragon border. They're fairly easy to identify by their pointed ears."

Surprise flickered on Katla's face. "I saw such a woman when I attacked Villette."

"That would be Esha. She and several other mates were there that day with the Kings." He sighed softly. "Maybe what I saw was a bird. I searched the ruins. There was nothing. If it was the entity, it would've come straight for me."

"To kill you."

Merrill nodded. "Aye."

"Surely, you can best it."

"If I could see it, maybe. But even Lotti and Villette's Star power didna stop it."

Katla's face creased as she winced. "That isn't good news."

"The Kings have no' been here long enough to explore this world. Brandr and Eurwen chose to stay within the dragon land borders instead of learning the rest of Zora. Which means we're heading into territory no one I know has traveled."

"In other words, we won't know what we might encounter."

"Precisely. I doona want to worry you, but you need to be informed. Just in case."

She finished combing her hair. "I'm glad you told me."

"And if the entity comes, you need to run."

"To do what? Leave you behind to possibly die?" she asked crossly.

He thought about her dancing in the rain. She should have many more years of that. "If it comes to it."

"But I might be able to see it. I could help."

The stubborn lift of her chin told him she wouldn't change her mind. Her words warmed his heart, but he had been in enough battles to know when they were unwinnable. Tangling with the entity was one of them.

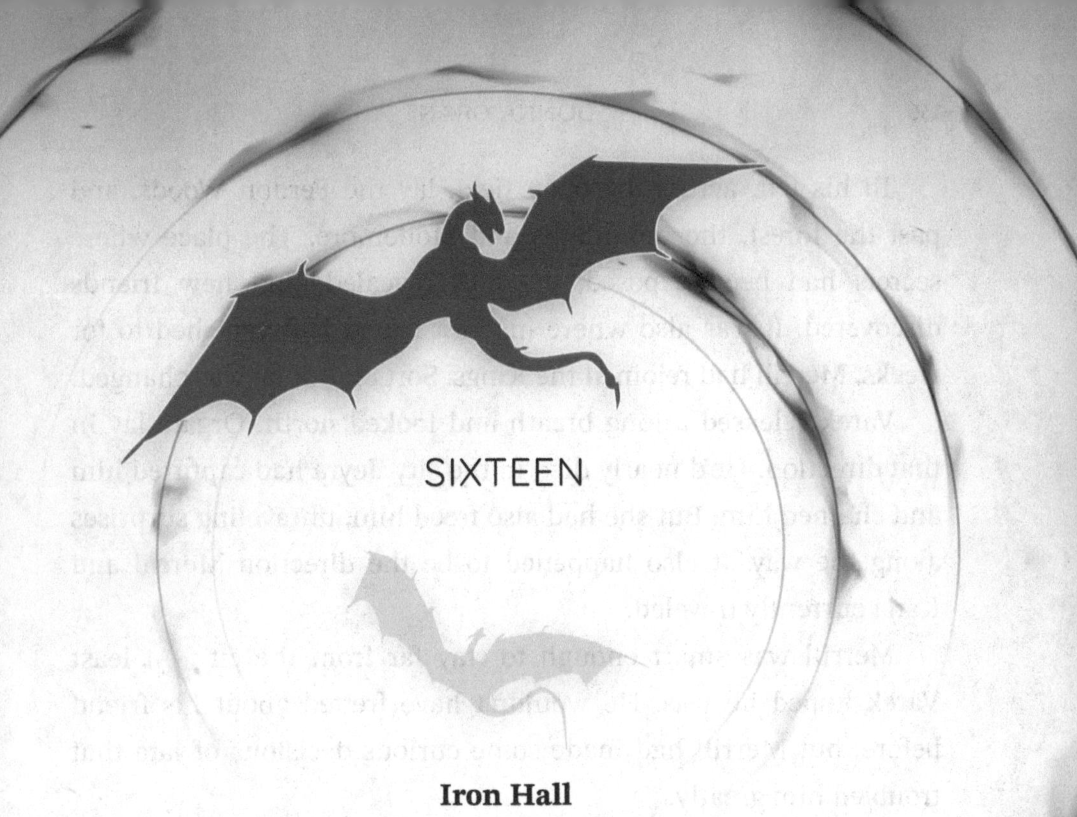

SIXTEEN

Iron Hall

Clouds blocked the sun, casting shadows on the ground. The air had a crispness to it that warned of winter's coming. Varek walked along the bottom of the canyon, his footsteps masked by its verdant plant life. Raynia Canyon was near the coast, which brought in the warm, wet weather, keeping the temperatures mild, especially deep within the canyon's crevices.

He looked up at the chasm's rim before jumping to the top in one leap. There wasn't another soul in sight. At least for the moment. If he looked east, he could gaze across the land belonging to the dragons. It was a large swath of terrain stretching far and wide. Despite its size, it was still a cage for his kind, limiting them while also keeping others out. The border was a field of magic imperceptible to all but dragons. They were alerted anytime someone crossed. This side of the border actually ran down the middle of the canyon.

To his left, across the open field, lay the Ferdon Woods, and past the forest, the mountains and Stonemore. The place where secrets had been exposed, enemies revealed, and new friends discovered. It was also where his best friend had vanished to for weeks. Merrill had rejoined the Kings. Sort of. But he was changed.

Varek released a long breath and looked north. Orgate lay in that direction. He'd nearly died in the city. Jeyra had captured him and chained him. But she had also freed him, unraveling surprises along the way. It also happened to be the direction Merrill and Katla currently traveled.

Merrill was smart enough to stay far from the city. At least Varek hoped he was. He wouldn't have fretted about his friend before, but Merrill had made some curious decisions of late that troubled him greatly.

The sound of footsteps behind him caught Varek's attention. He turned his head to the side and caught sight of Cullen approaching. The King of Garnets wasn't alone. Padding alongside him was Nari, the wildcat who had not only saved Cullen from the entity in the past but also befriended him.

Varek watched the large predator as she came to stand between them. She was as big as a lion with large, black spots amid her black fur. Nari lifted her head, and intelligent, green eyes met his before she looked away. Varek scratched her under the chin, but she leaned against Cullen, purring. They had an unshakable bond.

"I thought I might find you here," Cullen finally said as he gathered his long, dark blond hair at his neck and tied it off.

Varek sank his fingers into Nari's thick fur on the back of her neck. "I should be out there with Merrill."

"He can handle himself."

"It isna that I doona think he can." Varek flattened his lips as he shook his head and looked away. "I should've noticed something was wrong before he and Shaw went to Stonemore."

Cullen's pale brown eyes stared northward as a shadow of a cloud moved over them. "We all should have. We didna because he hid things well. Shaw never saw anything that would've caused him concern, and he was in Stonemore with Merrill."

All that was true, but it didn't ease the guilt Varek carried. "He pulled me out of the depths of despair so many times. And when he needed me, I was too wrapped up in other things."

"Other things being your mate." Cullen grunted. "You and Jeyra were sorting through your own things. No one blames you for that."

"I do." Varek pinched the bridge of his nose with his thumb and forefinger before letting his arm drop to his side. "We could've lost him."

"But we didna. Give Merrill some credit."

Varek cut his eyes to Cullen. "He was ensnared by Villette. For *weeks*."

"He was also one of the first to stand against her," Cullen pointed out with his own hard look. He tempered his expression and voice when he said, "I just spoke to him."

"And?" Varek asked impatiently.

"He sounds fine. No' the upbeat Merrill of before, though."

"He's still with Katla?"

Cullen nodded once. "He's protective of her."

Varek didn't know how to feel about the Druid. On one hand, she'd aided Villette in killing dragons. On the other, Villette had exploited Katla and coerced and manipulated her into doing her bidding. "He's a protector by nature. I think Merrill is drawn to her because of their comparable turmoil."

"Could be. I also think there might be some guilt on his part about Villette."

Varek wrinkled his nose. "He didna say it, but I suspect it, too. He doesna like to talk about his time at Stonemore."

"Would you?" Cullen asked, his brows rising when their eyes briefly met. "I wouldna wish to discuss taking our greatest enemy to bed."

"He didna know it was her."

Cullen lifted one shoulder in a shrug. "You and I both know that doesna change the fact that they were lovers. None of us hold that against him, but he has to get past it on his own."

"Even if he and Katla do find Villette, they can no' take her on themselves."

"I'm no' so sure their expedition is about Villette."

Varek jerked his head toward Cullen. "What do you mean? Do you think he lied about needing to be on his own?"

Cullen twisted his lips as he once more looked northward. "Merrill knows we're worried. Out of all the Kings, he'd tell you the truth. So, nay, I doona believe he lied. However, I do believe something might be tied to the Druid."

Varek thought about how the bairns brought to Iron Hall had talked excitedly about both Katla and Merrill. What if there was something between the pair? Varek wanted every King to find their mate. Especially Merrill. Jeyra's love had healed many aspects of Varek's past and put the future in a positive light. Something he hadn't believed was possible.

"Merrill is a fixer. If there's a problem, he's going to find a solution. If someone is in need, he's going to help them," Cullen said. "He did it for all of us. He's doing it for Katla."

To his own detriment, Varek realized. Because none of them had offered Merrill the same courtesy. Not even him. Varek could tell himself Merrill would've said something had he been in need, but he knew his friend better than anyone. Merrill put others before himself. It was the empath in him.

They had talked about how unbalanced orange dragons could become when they took too much of another's troubles and emotions onto themselves. Varek had failed Merrill over and over. But he wouldn't make that mistake again.

He ran a hand down his face. "Merrill lost the humor, but he gained a sense of self. It was there when we spoke before he left for Stonemore. I think you're right. He is helping the Druid, but I think he's helping himself, too."

"He might be stubborn, but if there's danger, he willna risk Katla's life. He'll reach out. I remember when you went missing. He went crazy trying to locate you."

Varek grunted as he recalled being pulled from Earth to Zora by the magic of a Star Person. "It's probably a good thing Jeyra and I got free of Orgate before all of you arrived."

"There would be nothing left of the city had Merrill gone in after you." Cullen looked at Varek. "None of us would've left it standing."

"Yet we didna go into Stonemore after him."

"If we had, the war Villette wanted would've begun."

Varek rolled his eyes. Everything always came back to that fucking woman. "She's going to get her war regardless."

"Maybe, but if it helps, think of it this way. Had Merrill not been at the palace, he never would've encountered Derek. We wouldna have a new Dragon King, and Miena would still be an issue."

"You're no' telling me anything I've no' already thought about. But it still feels like I let him down."

Cullen slapped him on the back. "You didna, and Merrill knows that."

Varek remained after Cullen and Nari walked away. His dragon eyes saw far into the distance, but no matter how far he looked, he didn't see his friend. Merrill was one of the strongest Kings. Not just physically but also mentally. But his empathy was his downfall. Merrill held himself to standards few could reach. He put family above all else.

And the Kings were his family. He would never purposefully hurt any of them. If Merrill thought he had let them down, he would want to rectify it before he moved forward. The only thing that gave Varek any peace was knowing Merrill wasn't alone. Katla was a wildcard in all of this, and while Merrill tried to find firm ground again, Varek trusted him to see into the heart of the Druid. Since Merrill remained with her, that told him a great deal.

About his friend.

And about Katla.

A distant dragon roar reached him. Varek closed his eyes and let the sound fill every cell of his body. Another answered. Then, a third replied. The roars were as different and unique as the dragons themselves. For a heartbeat, Varek could almost believe they were on Earth before the war. That if he opened his eyes, he would see the lichen-colored scales of his clan soaring above him.

But Zora wasn't Earth. It was, however, the dragons' new home. They had been driven out of one and refused to be driven out of a second.

He lifted his lids and looked across the barrier surrounding his kin's domain. Dragons dotted the skyline. He yearned to join them. Maybe one day they would forgive the Kings for the decision that had altered everyone's course. Maybe they would welcome the Kings to fly with them someday.

Until then, Varek and the others would continue fighting against Villette—and anyone else who tried to harm the dragons. The Kings had vowed to protect the mortals on Earth. They hadn't made that promise on Zora. Not that they wished to dole out death, but they couldn't allow Villette to win.

No one knew that better than Merrill. He would also be the first to sacrifice himself if it saved everyone else. That's what Varek refused to even consider. Merrill would survive.

Varek would make sure of it.

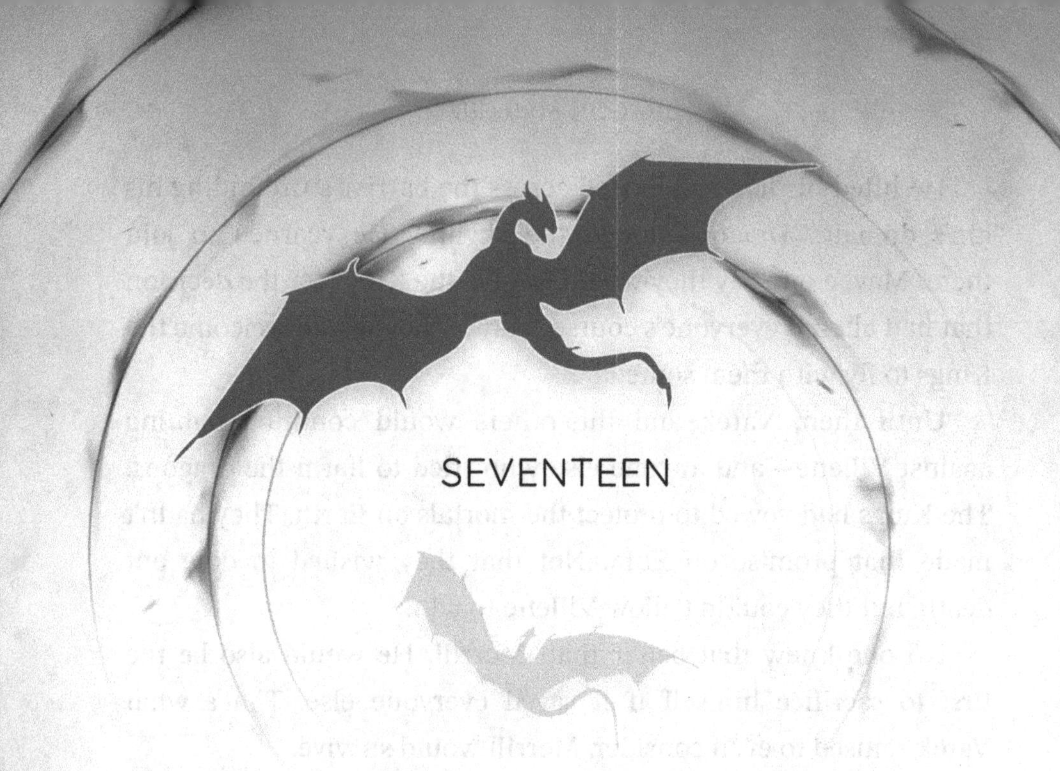

SEVENTEEN

There was something hypnotic and exhilarating about the storm. Katla stood at the window gazing out, watching the rain fall so hard and fast she couldn't see anything else. Only for the storm to taper off. It was a tease, though, because there was another dowsing a few minutes later.

Katla had never paid that much attention to rainfall in her previous life. That's what she called the time before the invaders came. And before she turned into a monster. This was the after.

Before, her life had been simple. Now, it was complicated and uncertain.

"What did you do in your village?" Merrill asked.

They had sat in silence for so long, and she had been so immersed in her thoughts that his voice startled her. She shifted to the side to look at him. He had returned to his position on the floor, leaning against the wall. He could create large tubs of steaming water and shields over the windows to block out the wind and rain, but he didn't use magic to fashion a chair for himself.

Katla wondered if he would've covered the windows had he been the only one here. She rather thought he wouldn't have. Everything he had done, had been to ease and comfort her. But not him. It said a lot about the man he was.

She raised her brows and asked, "What do you mean?"

"Did you have a skill?"

"I was sought out for medicinal remedies. Many knew what plants could be beneficial, as well as which ones were harmful, but few knew how to mix them properly."

Surprise flashed over his face. "Interesting."

"How so?"

"Tell me more about your village. What was your religion?"

Katla turned to put her back against the wall as she thought back to those days. "We prayed to many gods and goddesses, but the moon guided us. It was our focal point. Above all, nature was divine. We worked in harmony with it."

"And you considered all things interconnected. You also believed trees to be sacred."

She blinked in surprise. "We did, indeed. How did you know that?"

"Because Druids on Earth believe the same. Among other things."

"Like what?" she pressed, eager to learn more. It was shocking —and thrilling—to have that connection between their worlds, yet she had never heard the word *Druid* until recently.

Merrill thought for a moment before answering. "Ancestors are honored because it is believed they impart information from beyond the grave. Druids also believe that once someone dies, their souls are reincarnated to live again."

"Amazing," she murmured.

"There are eight main holy days. Imbolc, the spring equinox, Beltane, the summer solstice, Lughnasadh, the autumn equinox—"

"Samhain and Yule," Katla finished. "We had the same."

One side of his lips curved slightly. "You were a practicing Druid and didna know it."

"It seems impossible, but the more I learn, the more it seems it isn't." She looked to the side, recalling bits of memories from those holy days. "I wonder if those who survived the attack continued our faith."

"You could find out."

She immediately shook her head as she glanced at him. "I couldn't."

"Why no'? No one will know who you are."

"I shouldn't."

Merrill twisted his lips. "Think on it. You doona need to decide now."

"I'd rather consider what direction we head in next."

"Any way you want," he answered.

Katla blew out a breath and pushed away from the wall to walk to the fire. She wasn't chilled, but she still held her hands out to the flames to let the warmth touch her anyway. The tub was gone. Probably a good thing. She hadn't wanted to leave it. Had even fantasized about Merrill in the water with her.

"I have nothing guiding me. I never left the valley before now. I can't even fathom how big the realm might be, or how long it would take to traverse it."

"Well over a year," he replied.

She turned her head to him. "Where do you think we should go?"

"There's only one place I know that means anything to Villette."

"Stonemore."

He dipped his chin to his chest. "That doesna mean I recommend returning there."

"Then how else are we to find her? We could walk this realm many times over and never locate Villette."

"Verra true."

A bubble of irritation filled her as she faced Merrill. "I want to find her, not walk around searching for an enemy I probably won't find."

Merrill didn't react to her outburst. His deep blue eyes never looked away from her. "And after you've brought Villette to justice?"

"What?" she snapped, her voice raised louder than she intended.

"Have you thought about after?"

She dropped her arms and looked away. "I doubt I'll survive."

"Ah."

Her head swung back to him. "What about you? Have you thought about after?"

"I've faced many foes over many millennia. There were times when my brethren and I were nearly defeated, but we always managed to come out on top. I'd like to believe this will have the same outcome."

Which meant he expected a future. She wondered what that would look like for him. What if she survived? What then? It wasn't as if she had a home to go to. There was no one waiting for her out there.

Merrill climbed to his feet in one smooth movement. "I'll return to the other Kings. We might get a few weeks of peace, but Villette stirred hatred among others too deep for it to dissipate so easily. The priests at Stonemore will need to be addressed. And quickly. As will the religion as a whole. Above all, the innocents must be protected. That isna even considering all those with magic who remain in hiding. There is much to do. You would be an asset."

"Me?" she asked in astonishment.

"You're a survivor. Doona give up so easily when there is much more of life to be lived. There's a place for you."

She wanted to believe him. But she couldn't. "I'm not sure there should be."

His shoulders lifted as he drew in a breath. In a soft voice, he said, "I know well the need to thrash myself because of my actions and decisions. There is much shame for what I did, and I intend to make up for it somehow. I do it for myself because I doona wish to be the person who allows anger to consume me so that I turn my back on my family. It willna be easy to let go of all of that, but I want to. Perhaps you should consider doing the same."

Katla was never prepared when Merrill bared his soul. For such a strong man to reveal his innermost demons and conflicts was as astonishing as it was unexpected. Yet, by doing so, he compelled her to ponder alternatives.

As she considered things, he walked outside. It was only then that she noticed the rainstorm had passed. She followed him, her feet moving of their own volition. Cold air slammed into her. She wrapped her arms around herself since her thin shirt did little to help with warmth. Water dripped from the roof to splatter against the drenched ground. Soft sunlight spilled through the dense clouds, moving rapidly. She hadn't thought about the weather when she headed in this direction, but it would factor into where they went next.

Merrill stood a few feet away, scrutinizing the sky. She used the time to study him. He had a quiet, relaxed manner about him, but beneath it was inconceivable power. He reminded her of a mountain. Strong and imposing against any storms, but unmovable. Unyielding. Or perhaps a lake that might ripple against the elements but then steady, the depths as mysterious as they were dangerous.

"The storm has passed," he confirmed. He turned to face her. "Where shall we go?"

She licked her lips and considered her options. "If Stonemore is where she'll return to, then perhaps we should go back to that area."

"If we leave now, we could cover a considerable distance by nightfall."

"All right," she replied as she stepped toward him. Then she remembered the fire. "We need to douse the flames."

Merrill held out his hand. Hanging on his finger was a long, black coat. "Already done. You'll find this will help with the chill."

"Thank you." Katla slipped her arms into the white-fur-lined coat that fell to her shins. She buttoned it up and slipped her hands into the soft pockets.

Their gazes locked, held. Something in his eyes made her stomach flutter with excitement. But it vanished as quickly as it came. She was inexplicably drawn to him, even taking a step forward. Katla searched his gaze for another peek at what she had glimpsed, but it wasn't there. Or maybe she imagined it.

"Walk beside me this time," she said.

He inclined his head and swept his arm to the side, waiting for her to begin. She inhaled deeply, and as she released it, set out. He fell into step with her, their boots squishing in the saturated ground. The clouds were dissipating, allowing the sun to shine upon more areas.

They were halfway through the settlement when Merrill suddenly stopped. Katla paused to see what had caught his attention. His gaze was on the ground, and she soon realized why when she spotted the boot tracks. Alarm thundered through her. Merrill squatted beside a track and ran his finger along the indentation. Then he looked at her. Someone was near. She looked around as he straightened and slowly turned in a circle.

"Are they still here?" she whispered.

He said nothing as his eyes swept the area.

Katla swiveled her head to him. "Perhaps we should leave."

"Or we can follow the tracks and see where they lead."

Katla nodded when his gaze met hers. Merrill led, staying on one side of the tracks as he followed them across the road and around some ruins. A few tracks were easy to see, but she lost sight of most. Merrill, however, didn't have that issue. She followed behind him as the trail led them to the edge of the settlement and the shelter they had used.

"They stood here for some time," Merrill said. He crouched and pointed to the track midway in the road. "You can see that by how deep it is compared to when they walked."

"Man or woman?"

"By the size and depth of the track, I estimate it to be a male. Although…" he said, trailing off.

Katla waited for him to finish. Instead, Merrill lifted his head and peered into the distance. "Although what?" she finally asked.

"It could be an Amazon," he replied as he straightened.

"A what?" How many more varieties of beings were out there that she had never heard of?

"Amazons are fierce, female warriors known for their strength, agility, and art of combat." Merrill glanced at her as he paused. Then he said, "You can come out now."

Katla was surprised when a woman with a blond braid walked out from behind the ruins. She was nearly as tall as Merrill, and her brown eyes locked on him before sliding to Katla. The warrior wore a simple, short-sleeved, tan tunic with a metal breastplate over her torso. She didn't wear trousers but a leather skirt cut into strips that fell to just above her knees. Greaves covered her shins, and she held a sword in her right hand.

Merrill turned his head to look past Katla. She looked over her shoulder and saw another woman, her black hair in braids, dressed in similar attire. Katla's magic surged into her hands, and sparks began to shoot from her fingertips.

"Easy," Merrill murmured.

Katla looked between the two warriors. By Merrill's description, she assumed they were Amazons. Both women looked ready for battle.

Merrill focused on the blonde. "We were wondering what happened to you, Jenefer."

"How do you know my name?" she demanded as she took a step closer and raised her sword so the tip pointed at the sky.

Katla put up her hands on instinct. Merrill gently took her

hand in his and gave her a pointed look. Katla lowered her other arm to her side and curled her hand into a fist, remembering his advice about reacting.

"We met briefly," Merrill said as he returned his attention to the Amazon. "At Iron Hall. I'm one of Cullen's friends. My name is Merrill."

Jenefer stared at him with narrowed eyes before slowly lowering her sword. "I remember you. What are you doing up here?"

"It's a long story. One shared another time. Sian will be delighted by your return."

The tension left Jenefer's body as she sheathed her sword at her back, leaving the hilt to peek over her right shoulder. "It's been a difficult journey. Unfortunately, it didn't work out as I had hoped. I found Narin, but no others."

"I can get you back to Iron Hall immediately," Merrill offered as he shot a quick look at Narin.

Jenefer shook her head. "We can't go yet. We've been tracking a young girl. We believe she could be one of us."

"We need to find her," Narin said. "Most of our race has been annihilated."

Katla looked from one warrior to the other as they spoke.

Merrill's face was lined with concern. "We can help."

"Thank you, but it's better if we do it ourselves," Jenefer said. "If the young one is an Amazon, she won't trust anyone but us."

"*If* she trusts us," Narin murmured, her dark gaze looking east.

Katla's magic eased back. She should probably pull her hand out of Merrill's, but she enjoyed his touch too much to move.

Merrill dipped his head to Jenefer. "I understand. I'll pass on that I spoke to you."

"How is Sian?" Jenefer asked.

"She's good. Missing you."

Jenefer's lips softened into a smile. "I've missed her. As soon as we locate the young girl, we're heading to the canyon."

"Then we will leave you to it."

"There's something around here," Jenefer warned. "I don't know what it is. We've not been able to see it, but we've felt it."

Merrill's fingers tightened on Katla's hand. "Find the lass quick," he urged the Amazons. "Then get to Iron Hall."

"You know what it is," Jenefer said.

"It's invisible and began attacking us. But it's gone after others. Be grateful it left you alone," Merrill said.

Jenefer looked at Narin. The warrior nodded and slipped away. Jenefer's brown eyes slid to Merrill before she, too, turned and vanished into the grass.

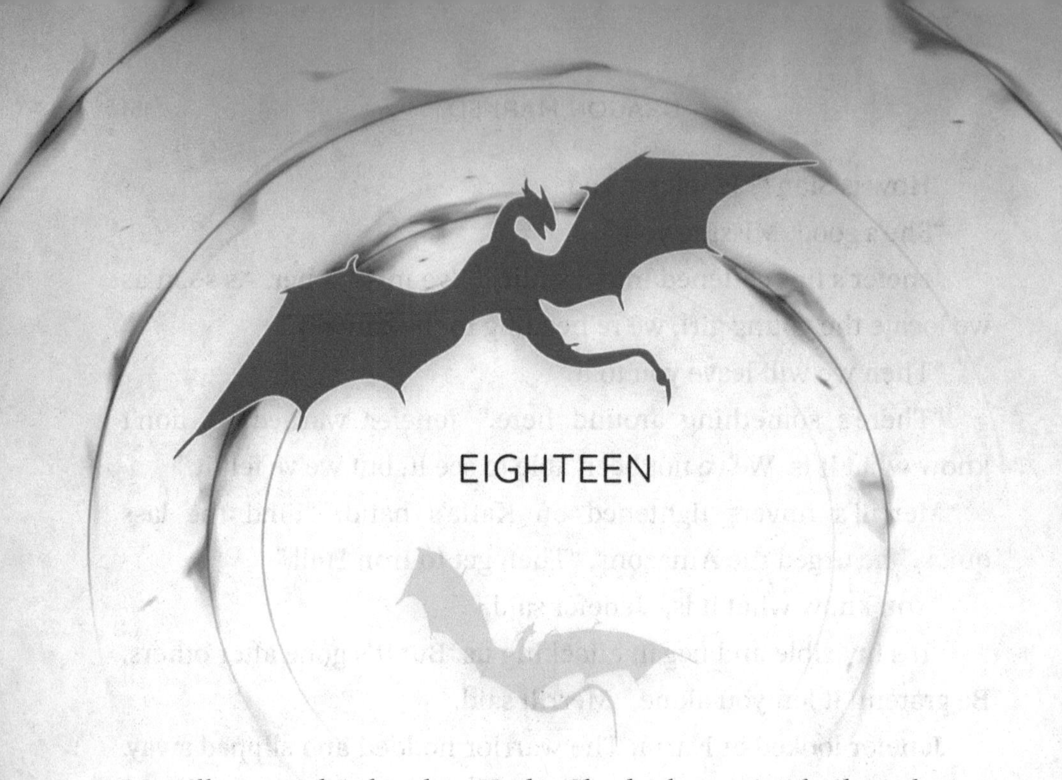

EIGHTEEN

Merrill swung his head to Katla. She had remained silent during the exchange with the Amazons. He glanced at their joined hands. He should release her, but his fingers refused to loosen. And she wasn't pulling away.

"What do you think?" Katla asked. "Should we remain here if something is out there? It would be better than it coming after us while we traveled."

He scanned the horizon. "Maybe. Though nothing here would be sufficient protection. A strong wind could knock over the buildings. There are no trees or mountains. Just openness."

"Then fly us."

Merrill hesitated before he met gray eyes that matched the tumultuous skies above him. Her words had been clear, but he still heard a slight wobble. She had spent decades hating dragons. Strong emotions like that didn't recede with the flip of a switch. Katla knew he was a Dragon King, but being with him as a man versus seeing his true form was altogether different.

The thing was, he wanted to take to the skies. It was instinct to prove his might and power. Nothing more. But it could get her killed. He wouldn't chance that.

"If it is the entity, and it strikes, it'll knock me unconscious. If we're in the air, we'll fall," he told her.

Katla's brow furrowed slightly. "If it strikes you, you'll be vulnerable. You shouldn't remain."

"*We* shouldn't," he corrected.

She kept speaking, ignoring him. "Call to Rhi. Get her to take you to Iron Hall."

"First, I'm no' leaving you behind. Second, I doona run from a fight."

"Maybe you should. Your friends need you."

He was acutely aware of the warmth of her hand in his. Her fingers were long and slim, her palm delicate. "Doona be so bold as to think you can face this enemy alone. It battered Villette easily."

"Justice finds everyone. Perhaps it's my turn. I always knew I would have to pay for what I've done. I had hoped to make some amends by executing Villette before then."

"Let me make this clear," Merrill stated frankly. "I'm no' leaving you."

She stared into his eyes for a long moment before sighing in resignation.

He nodded curtly. "Now that that's taken care of, I think we should continue on our journey."

"That has its own risks."

"There's a risk in every decision. I'd rather get us to a place where we have something to shield us if we are attacked. I might no' be able to see it, but it can no' go through walls. And I'm no' entirely convinced it is the entity. If it was, it would've already attacked me."

Katla stuck her free hand in her coat pocket. "All right, then. We'd better set out."

Merrill released her as they turned and began their trek. He curled his hand into a fist, missing the feel of her already. She hadn't indicated what she thought of his touch. Maybe she hadn't even noticed. But he had. He didn't think he would get the feeling of her hand in his out of his mind. Ever.

"For beings who recently came to my world, you've encountered several races I didn't know even existed," Katla said.

"I'm sure there are many, many more out there."

"What kind do you have on Earth?"

Merrill glanced over his shoulder as they reached the edge of the ruins. There was nothing there. He looked forward. If he stared hard enough, he could make out the forest's edge, but it was hours away. "There are only three. Mortals—including the Druids—Kings, and the Fae. Verra few humans know of our existence."

"Because you walk among them looking as they do?"

"Aye. The Fae are mistaken for humans all the time. There are ways to distinguish them that seem easy enough for me, but mortals doona always see it."

Curiosity colored Katla's words when she asked, "Like what? Please, I want to learn."

How could he deny her? "There are two kinds of Fae. Rhi is a Light Fae. A royal Light Fae, actually. The Light all have the same coloring: black hair and silver eyes."

"All?"

"All," he reiterated. "Every Fae is born a Light. They have to choose to become Dark."

Katla glanced at him. "I gather there are differences between the two?"

"Indeed. The first deed of evil will turn a Dark's eyes red. For each act after, silver streaks their black hair."

"Which means you can tell how amoral they are just by their hair."

Merrill glanced up when a bird squawked overhead as it soared past. "Exactly."

"If the mortals don't mind seeing the Fae, then they should be okay with dragons."

"That might be true if the humans knew *of* the Fae."

She made a sound in the back of her throat. "They keep themselves secret, too?"

"No' exactly. They look human, and it isna unusual for mortals on my world to color their hair different shades or wear contacts to change their eye color."

"That's incredible."

"The Fae can also use glamour to change their appearance. It allows the Dark to disguise their coloring and look like anyone else."

Katla wrinkled her nose. "Then how do you know if you're dealing with a Light or a Dark?"

"Humans can no' see through their glamour, but we can. The Fae are highly sexualized creatures. Mortals are inexplicably drawn to them. One bedding by a Fae will ruin a human forever. The Light are no' as bad as the Dark. The Dark feed off humans."

"Feed?" she repeated in shock. "How?"

"The mortals willingly have sex, and each time, the Dark drains their souls until there is nothing left but a husk of a body."

She gaped at him in shock. "And you allow them to walk your realm?"

He grunted. "There were the Fae Wars. You see, the Fae decimated their realm with a civil war and then brought it to ours. We sided with the Light, which brought an end to the fighting, but there was nowhere for them to go. A treaty was formed, and the Fae opted to settle in Ireland, an isle no' far from us. There have been issues throughout the years, but we've managed to contain them."

"How is it the humans remain unaware of you *and* the Fae?"

He shrugged as they walked. "Those who seek magic and magical things will find them. Those who close themselves off will never see them."

"Very similar to the humans on Zora, who are threatened by the rest of us."

"If you were no' a Druid, would you accept those with abilities?"

Katla nibbled on her lip. "That's difficult to answer. We respected the dragons. They never ventured across the border to harm us. But we also feared them."

"Because of their magic?"

"Because of their power and might." Gray eyes briefly met his. "Just as we feared and respected any flora or fauna with the ability to kill."

He tilted his head to the side. "I can understand that."

"I'd like to think my village would have welcomed anyone, regardless of whether they possessed magic or not. We were never tested, though. Saying that, I do understand those who are uneasy when someone with such power is near."

"Why?"

She turned her head to him, lines of bewilderment coloring her visage. "Those who have magic have the ability to kill."

"So do those without. And those mortals do it more ferociously and effortlessly than any others."

"That's troubling." Her eyes stayed trained forward, but her frown remained. "I never saw that in my kind. Nonetheless, I can believe it."

Merrill should've recognized that she would see herself in that light. "I wasna referring to you. You're nothing like that."

"You've not seen me when the rage takes over. Ask Henry and Melisse."

"I doona need to."

Katla swallowed as she huddled deeper in the coat. "I destroyed the tower."

"To protect the bairns and yourself."

"I wasn't honest before. I did want to protect the children, but I also wanted to hurt Miena." She shook her head slightly, her brow wrinkling. "That's not true. I wanted to kill her."

Merrill heard the quiver of apprehension in her confession. She feared herself, what she might be capable of. He knew a wee bit about that. "I saw you with the bairns. You would never have harmed them."

"I wish I was as sure."

"I know the rage you speak of. I fought my wrath while in Stonemore. I felt the residents' repugnance for me and my kind. Their hostility and disdain for beings they knew nothing about. I thought about the humans we allowed to live on Earth and what it had brought to my clan. To *all* the clans. And each King. I thought about the freedom we lost. And like so many other times before, I wondered if we had made the right decision."

Talking about it caused contempt to well within him. With that surge of emotion was violence that he seemed to constantly grapple with since coming to Zora. Merrill didn't push those feelings away. They would only return with a vengeance. Instead, he sat with them for a few breaths, letting them swell before they began to ebb.

"If the same decision came to us on Zora, I wouldna repeat our mistake," he told Katla. "Every day I was in Stonemore, I fought the need to scorch the city and everyone in it. I fight it still. It's why I can no' return to my brethren. No' until I have this resolved."

"And if you never get it resolved?" she asked.

Varek's face rose in Merrill's mind. His friend would only give him so long before searching him out. Merrill wanted to return to the Kings and take his place among them once more. He wanted to face the wrath within him and whatever else might arise. If he couldn't, then he had no business being a King. "That isna an option."

The conversation ended then. They walked in companionable silence for the next few hours. Merrill remained alert. They were out in the open, easily visible to all. Yet he neither saw or sensed anything. It set him on edge because he couldn't shake the knowledge that something was out there.

They paused briefly for lunch. Katla was deep in her thoughts, and he left her to them. She didn't pry into his. He wouldn't inquire about hers. Even though he was curious. They both carried a lot of guilt. It was a weight not easily set aside, especially when you held yourself responsible.

A frigid wind blew from the north as they set out again, causing Katla to nestle into the coat. Out of the corner of his eye, he saw her glance at him a few times. He said nothing, waiting to see if she would speak. The forest drew closer. He picked up their pace so they'd reach the woods sooner.

Katla cleared her throat. "Do you mind if I ask you a personal question?"

"Ask away. I can no' promise I'll answer."

"Fair enough," she murmured. Then, in a louder voice, said, "Did any Kings lose their mates when you sent the dragons away?"

Merrill's chest tightened. Of all the questions, this hadn't been what he'd thought she might ask. He didn't know how he continued walking. Somehow, he remained upright. Odd, since unimaginable sorrow cut through his entire body.

"I'm sorry. I shouldn't have asked," she hurried to say.

He tried to find his voice and ended up shaking his head. He cleared his throat, focusing on putting one foot in front of the other. She was waiting for him to say something. He had to form words. Finally, he got out, "It isna something we talk about."

"Ever?" she asked in a soft voice.

He shook his head again.

But maybe it was time.

NINETEEN

The haunted look on Merrill's face was one Katla would never forget, no matter how long she lived. She wished she could take back the question, but she had already given voice to the words.

"A dragon mating is never done lightly." Merrill's voice was soft, low with a thread of anguish. "Once a pair is mated, they are bound. Body and soul. Through life and death. When one dies, the other is taken."

When he said bound, he meant *bound*. Her thoughts immediately wondered if she had taken a dragon's mate from someone. And she knew what the answer was. It nearly ripped her in two. That meant she hadn't killed one dragon. She had killed two. The world tilted. Her knees wobbled, threatening to drop her to the ground.

As she was spiraling, Merrill's voice pulled her back to the present. "Finding a mate isna always easy. On Earth, our dragons remained in clans, based on color. We didna mix. No' like the dragons do here. It was always debated and considered, but there was so much pushback on it that it never happened. And there were many who never found mates because of it."

Katla wanted to know if Merrill had someone in his life. She suspected she was about to find out.

"Dragon Kings are difficult to kill. On our world, only another Dragon King can kill a King, be they already crowned or ones the magic has tapped for the position. The Pinks are the smallest of the dragons, and the ones the humans singled out to hunt."

She tried to hide her wince as she thought about all the Pinks she had lured into the bramble forest.

"Their numbers diminished quickly. Their King rallied his clan and fought back, but it did little good. Then the real war erupted. We were divided at first, and it was during that initial skirmish that the King of Pinks was slain by another King. The other two Kings...perished when we chose different sides for a short time."

"Why didn't the Kings go with their families?"

Merrill's lips compressed into a thin line as he sighed. "It is a King's duty to safeguard Earth. We all wanted to go with our clans, but we couldna leave."

"You have now."

"No' all of us. Those who are mated remained behind to guard Earth."

Katla licked her lips as she glanced at him. "What of the rest of you? Will you stay on Zora?"

"I doona know."

She had been afraid that would be his answer. "The mates on Earth aren't dragons, are they?"

"They are no'. Those Kings found their spouses in humans, Druids, Fae, and others with magic."

"Humans?" she repeated.

Merrill looked at her. "That surprises you?"

"It does, considering you keep yourselves secret on your world."

"I suppose it is surprising. Every mate at Dreagan earned the right to stand beside us. They carry our secret, just as we do."

Katla turned her face into the collar of her coat when a gust of wind zipped past her. Her nose was frozen, and one side of it was clogged, making it difficult to breathe. It had been so long since she'd felt a change of weather. "Since there are no dragons on Earth, does that mean you'll remain Kings forever?"

"Possibly."

"That makes you nearly immortal. And if the mates are bound to the Kings, then they're immortal, too."

Merrill brushed a lock of hair from his face. "In theory. But you need to remember, the dragons here doona need Kings. Eurwen and Brandr, who are half dragon and half Fae, rule over them. If the current Kings are killed, there willna be anyone to replace us."

"The Kings aren't fighting each other, so that isn't an issue."

"No' quite. The Star People can take a King's life."

If Katla believed Merrill, she had Star magic. Which meant she might be able to kill him. She was horrified and took a step away from him.

He raised a brow in question. "What is it?"

"You knew I might be able to hurt you, and you still pushed me to lose control of my magic?"

Merrill dipped his head. "Guilty."

"Why would you do that?" she demanded angrily.

"I knew you wouldna harm me."

"I don't want to take that chance." Then it hit her. "Why would you dare go up against Villette and Miena if they can kill you?"

"Because they must be stopped. And I wasna alone. Dragons can kill hellhounds. And yet, Kora is Derek's mate. Lotti is a Star Person and mated to Alasdair."

Katla drew in a deep breath. "You're unbelievable."

"How so?"

"Those are *mated* couples."

Merrill halted. She went two steps past him before realizing he had stopped. She paused and whirled to face him, her hands clenched as anger sizzled through her.

His dark blue eyes were steady as they met hers. "Say what you're holding back."

With those words, the dam burst. "How *dare* you put your life in my hands, knowing I might be able to kill you? You know what I've done and what I'm desperately trying to make up for. You know the uncontrollable rage within me. Why would you do that to me?"

"As I said, I knew you wouldna harm me."

She was a riot of emotions. Her magic whipped through her, demanding to be released. She curled her hands into fists in her pockets, trying to keep it contained. "And if I had? Do you know what that would've done to me? Look at me now! I barely have control of my magic."

"You're aware of your magic and emotions. You're deciding when to unleash your power. You did it last night, and you're doing it now."

"Don't tempt me to prove you wrong," she bit out. Yet he spoke the truth. She had recognized her emotions a heartbeat before her magic welled. His instruction had given her the capacity to use that single beat to decide whether to release her power or not.

Merrill stepped toward her, his gaze piercing as he held hers.

"You see yourself as tainted, corrupted. Unworthy, even. That isna what I see when I look at you."

Her anger vanished like smoke, leaving her waiting with bated breath for him to finish. "What do you see?"

"An exquisitely beautiful Druid. A woman with untapped power, who has yet to comprehend her full potential."

He thought her exquisitely beautiful? No one had ever said such words to her. She couldn't catch her breath. Her stomach fluttered as she found herself leaning toward him. Her eyes dropped to his mouth. Just then, she saw something beyond his shoulder. She searched for it again, her eyes scanning the area behind him as she moved up beside him.

"What is it?" he whispered.

"I saw something. I'm sure of it."

He turned around to look with her. "I believe you. Can you describe it?"

"It was fleeting." Katla sighed and sniffed as she shook her head. "It was probably a bird."

"Probably."

But his voice held doubt. Merrill had been on edge all day but was even more uneasy now. So was she. Could she have seen the entity? She wished she could be sure, but she had been too engrossed in thoughts of kisses to know what flashed out of the corner of her eye.

They turned together in silence and continued walking. His head moved from side to side as he scanned the area around them. Even looking back every few steps. Katla was jumpy, too. No matter how hard they looked, neither saw anything again. That should have reassured them, but it seemed to have the opposite effect on Merrill.

In two hours, they reached the edge of the forest. Katla had thought that would ease some of Merrill's tension, but it didn't. Instead of continuing south, he suddenly turned them west toward the mountains.

"I doona want us out in the open at dusk," he explained when she looked at him. "We'll find shelter."

Katla had to admit she wouldn't mind getting out of the weather. It didn't seem to matter how far they walked, the cold clung to her. She could no longer feel her toes. She kept thinking about the hot bath she'd soaked in the previous night. It had eased her tight muscles. Right now, she'd love its warming properties.

Merrill's strides lengthened as he ate up the ground. She fought to stay with him. A couple of times, he realized he had gotten ahead and slowed. His impatience to reach the mountains also consumed her. Every movement she saw out of the corner of her eye made her jump. Most were falling leaves. A few were birds. Others, she wasn't sure about. Those might just be her imagination playing tricks on her. She couldn't be sure.

"There," he murmured when they reached the mountains.

Katla looked up but didn't see where he was pointing to in time. All she saw was a wall of rock rising above her. There wasn't time to get a good look at it as she concentrated on following Merrill up the incline. He moved with an agility that startled her. And there was no way for her to keep up.

He went ahead and then stopped and turned to survey their surroundings until she reached him. He stared into the distance behind her for a heartbeat, then scurried up the mountainside to repeat the process a second time. When she caught up with him next, he led her into the opening of a cave.

The wind stopped battering her the moment she stepped

inside. Only then did she grasp the complete absence of light. There was a flare of it as a fire erupted about ten feet from her. Merrill stood next to it, motioning her forward. She eagerly went to the waiting warmth, holding her hands to the flames.

"I'm glad to be out of the weather," she told him.

Merrill glanced at her before returning his gaze to the entrance. "I'm going to have a look around."

"So, if it is the entity, it can attack you without me to help? Is that smart?"

He blew out a breath.

"You said it can't go through walls. If there's an attack, it has to come straight at us."

Merrill twisted his lips. "If it does come, we'll have nowhere to go."

"Neither will it."

"A quick look," he said before striding out.

Katla watched him leave before sinking onto the cold stone ground. She smothered a yawn and propped her feet out toward the flames. She curled her toes inside her boots, trying to get some feeling back in them, but even that small movement hurt. She was settling back against the wall when Merrill returned.

"I didna see anything," he said.

He hadn't returned empty-handed, though. Merrill had a skinned ritbit in hand. He placed it over the fire to cook and added some seasoning before sitting beside her.

"What do you call that animal?" he asked.

"A ritbit."

"We call them rabbits."

She yawned again.

"Here," he said, scooting closer as he patted his shoulder.

Katla leaned her head against him and closed her eyes. It felt good to lean against him. His warmth enveloped her. Her thoughts were drifting, jumping from one thing to another, when she suddenly sensed the tension in him. She had been so eager to touch him again that she hadn't paid attention before.

She lifted her head and asked, "What aren't you telling me?"

"I can no' shake the sense we're being followed."

"By humans?"

He turned his face to the flames. "I didna find tracks."

"Entity or Villette?"

"Could be either."

Katla considered both options. "If this invisible foe attacks whenever it comes upon a dragon, my guess is its Villette."

Merrill's lips twisted as he lifted a shoulder in a shrug. "What would keep her from attacking? Nothing. And that's the problem. Neither option makes sense."

"Then maybe it's neither. It could be something else. If it hasn't hurt us. Maybe it doesn't mean any harm."

"Maybe," he replied unconvincingly.

TWENTY

Merrill closed his eyes and dared to live in that perfect moment. The weight of Katla's head upon his shoulder was satisfying. Calming, even. Weakness hadn't put her head there. The dawning of trust had.

And it profoundly affected him.

He was surprised but pleased at the new development. Merrill felt the weight of her shame and guilt. The fear she had for herself and her magic. It was why he had pushed her before. There was strength within Katla, but she had to find it again. The truth had set her free of Villette and the valley but trapped her in new, destructive ways. And if they were to go up against Villette, then Katla had to find that strength again.

As broken and damaged as he was, she thought him trustworthy. He had made some questionable judgments and shut himself off from his family. There was no guarantee anything he did would help him face the horrors of his past. His brethren might very well have to hunt him down and kill him if things went as badly as he feared. But until then, he would protect and watch over Katla. His lids lifted, and he stared past the fire to the cave's opening.

And destroy anyone or anything that dared to harm her.

Something was out there. What did it want? More importantly, which of them was it after? The Kings had plenty of enemies on Zora. Unless someone had seen him shift at Stonemore—and that was doubtful—no one should know what he was. Merrill turned his head incrementally and lowered his gaze. As for Katla, no mortal should know about her.

He listened to her even breathing as she slept. If someone was after her, they would have to go through him first. And nothing was getting past him. Not even the invisible enemy. Merrill looked at her hand resting upon her leg. He recalled how good it had felt to hold it earlier, how right. The urge to reach for her again was compelling. He could gently brush her fingers. It was a small touch. She would never know.

He cut off those thoughts before he did something foolish. The dark emotions he had let fester within him for too long tempted, cajoled. But he held firm. Barely. They roared through him like an uncontrolled blaze, demanding and directing.

Somehow, Merrill withstood it. Because if he gave in, if he dared even one solitary touch, he knew he wouldn't be able to stop. He would take all of her. And never let go.

He was drawn to her. Had been from the first time he'd spotted her. The sight had stopped him in his tracks. He had walked away then, never imagining he would see her again, but he had. There had been no stopping him from finding her after that. It would be worse if he let his desire take him now.

It wasn't wise to be around her as he fought not just the past but also the growing darkness within that had already taken him once. She stirred his lust and hunger, but she also kept his rage contained. He knew what would happen if his wrath were unleashed. He couldn't say for certain that anything would be different if he let loose his desires. Right now, it was enough that he was with her.

Merrill tilted his head and rested his cheek upon her head. When was the last time he had spent time with a woman like this? Just sitting. Being. Desire raged like a savage beast, but he wouldn't taint Katla. She was different. Exceptional. And she didn't even realize it. He had told her things he'd barely acknowledged to himself, but the words had flowed effortlessly past his lips. Something about being with her quieted his violence and quelled his ire.

The smell of the meat caught his attention. He raised his hand and turned his fingers, his magic lifting the rabbit—no, the ritbit—and flipping it to finish cooking. It would be done soon, but he wouldn't wake Katla. He would keep it warm until she roused.

Dusk had settled over the land while he was deep in his musings. Those who craved the night were about to stir to live, hunt, and thrive beneath the moon. He should be out there scouring the land for whatever tracked them, but he was loath to leave this small slice of bliss bestowed upon him.

Merrill tried to rest but kept thinking about what was out there. He wasn't keen on looking over his shoulder. He would rather face whatever it was head-on. Katla would demand to stand with him if he told her what he planned. But he had no idea what he might face, and he couldn't stand the thought of her being harmed. Besides, if it was something he couldn't handle, she could get word to the Kings.

He was about to move Katla when she sighed in her sleep and

slipped her arm through his. Merrill froze. He should remain and enjoy the moment—it might never come again. The last time he had lingered in such indecision, it had nearly resulted in Villette killing the Kings. His heart may long to remain, but his mind knew he had to leave.

"I'll be back," he whispered, gently laying Katla down.

Merrill climbed to his feet but hesitated as he stared at her. Then he walked out of the cave. Trees and the mountain were still distinguishable in the twilight. He looked skyward at the vibrant orange and red colors that melded. Stars were becoming visible. It was a special occurrence that bridged day and night. His mum had always called it the magic time.

He scanned the mountain's slope below before checking to either side and finally behind him. There was nothing there to see. He had sensed it before, but he felt it now. The presence was heavy, aggressive. Instead of assaulting him, it vanished. Which only confused Merrill. What was this thing? It had trailed them, which meant it was sentient enough to know what it was doing.

Merrill made his way down the incline until he reached the bottom. If he couldn't see this thing with his eyes, perhaps another of his senses could detect its location. He opened his hearing to pick up minute sounds, but there was no breathing or movement to distinguish. He breathed deeply and, for a second, caught a whiff of something. But it was gone too quickly for him to determine what it was.

He walked to the woods and strolled among the trees. It wasn't for peace or solace but to find a better position. He stopped and faced the mountain, looking between two large pines to see the cave's entrance. He remained there, watching. Waiting.

For something to come at him.

Or for Katla.

The minutes slowly ticked by, eventually turning into an hour. Then two. No matter how many times Merrill reached out with his senses, he detected nothing out of the ordinary. His instincts about something not being right had never been wrong before. And they weren't wrong now, despite everything pointing to the contrary. Merrill had lived too many lifetimes not to know the difference.

"I know you're out there," he said. "What are you waiting for?"

He didn't expect an answer, but there was a subtle shift in the forest's energy to hostility. It was so slight, he might not have noticed if he hadn't been searching for it. Once it registered, he knew his words had reached whatever was observing him.

Anger simmered in his veins. It wanted to unsettle him, irritate him. But it didn't realize that it had woken the darkness within him. The more Merrill contemplated being followed by this unknown adversary, the more incensed he became.

"Show yourself," Merrill taunted.

He turned in a circle, searching the night. Suddenly, the insects went silent. Then he caught an odor. He drew it in deeply, letting the aroma linger. He detected a hint of almonds. Then, the aroma of dried wood. The last time he had smelled the combination was when some wine had turned bitter. Now that he had the scent, he could find the being. Without a doubt, this was the invisible foe.

Merrill turned to the left, where the smell was the strongest, and stared. "Maybe you're too scared to face me."

The brutality and ferocity that blasted into him was all the warning he got before something collided with him. Merrill flew backward and crashed into a tree, his spine snapping as the impact bent him in half. Agony shot through him, even as he began to heal, before landing in a heap at the base of the trunk.

Merrill jumped to his feet and turned toward the stench. He gathered his magic but was pummeled again before he could release it. He staggered back with each strike, letting the entity get close enough to sense its location. Merrill absorbed the pain, allowing it to mix with the blinding rage rising inside him. Then he latched onto the entity.

He might not be able to see it, but the descriptions he had gotten gave him an idea of where to grab. And he had the fucker. If he thought it had been malevolent before, it was nothing compared to the belligerence that swarmed him now. It suffused his nose, his mouth, and his ears until he was choking with it, his head ringing. But he wouldn't let go. Merrill hung on, shoving his fingers into it and giving back as good as he got.

It would take more than he had to end the entity, though. He opened the mental link to call out to Varek when something pierced his spine. He shouted in pain, his nerve endings on fire. He waited for his body to heal, but the agony never stopped.

Merrill bellowed Varek's name but couldn't feel the mental link. He tried to shout Rhi's name aloud, but his vocal cords wouldn't work either. Though the entity didn't have a face, Merrill could've sworn it smiled. A trap had been set, and he had walked straight into it.

It was becoming harder to hang on to the entity. The pain was excruciating. It spread outward to his extremities, weakening him. He fought to hang on. He couldn't let the foe go. He might never get another chance like this.

Merrill tried the mental link once more. Something prevented him from reaching out to the Kings. But he didn't give up. Not when he was so close. All he had to do was reach out to his friends.

"Varek!"

No sooner had he managed to shout to his friend than he felt another sharp prick in his back. Then two more in quick succession. His knees gave out. Merrill dropped to the ground, his fingers beginning to lose their grip. The more blood that flowed out of him, the weaker he became. He was no longer regenerating.

Something pierced his left side.

One hand slipped off. He clenched his teeth and dug his fingers in deeper, calling to the anger—even greeting the darkness within—to stay in the fight. But it was too late.

He grunted as something impaled his right side, sliding between his ribs and into his lung. It filled immediately. He coughed up blood as he fought to breathe.

As his hand tumbled from the entity, Merrill heard Varek shouting his name in his mind. He tried to answer, but the entity barreled into him.

And the world went black.

TWENTY-ONE

Katla jerked upright. She looked around the cave, trying to figure out what had woken her. The instant she realized Merrill wasn't there, she jumped up and ran outside. She saw the torches through the trees and heard men's laughter, but the scent of blood propelled her down the mountain at breakneck speed. Her foot slipped, and she slid down a good portion of the incline before regaining her feet.

She burst into the forest to see ten men. Then she spotted Merrill lying on the ground, bloodied and still. Her focus narrowed on him and then the men. Fury surged, exploding from her. She recognized the violence and savagery she wrought. And she welcomed it. Greeted it. Just as she had when she faced Villette and at the tower with Miena.

Katla screamed Merrill's name and ran to him, sparks flying from her fingers to swirl rapidly around her before flashing outward—and straight through—three of the men, who immediately dropped dead.

The others circled, stepping over their fallen comrades. Out of the corner of her eye, she saw a ball of dark energy with long, wispy tendrils that looked like elongated limbs. This was the invisible foe Merrill had told her about. It had been tracking them, just as he'd suspected. And he had faced it without her.

Katla drew in her wild, violent wrath. The sparks flared and grew more intense. She turned her magic on the entity when it came at her. It slammed into the sparks, pushing against them. They moved to make a shield in front of her, and for a heartbeat, she thought she might hold the being back. But it kept shoving until it began curving the shield inward and broke through, aiming for her head. She ducked just as it barreled over her, the force whipping her hair into her eyes. The malice the entity exuded turned her blood to ice.

She turned and saw the being swing around. The men moved closer, their blades drawn and aimed at her. Katla stood over Merrill. A great swell of magic shot from her, along with a blinding light.

When Katla blinked, the men and the entity were gone. She dropped her arms to her sides and looked out into the moon-drenched, U-shaped valley with the dark, sharply chiseled mountains rising on either side. Her shoulders drooped as relief cut through her. She looked down at Merrill and dropped to her knees beside him. The silvery beams of moonlight showed blood—so much blood. Too much.

Her heart dropped to her feet. Katla put a hand on his chest and felt it rise, but his breathing was slow and labored. What had they done to him? He was essentially immortal on his world. Surely, it would be the same on Zora. It had to be.

"Merrill," she called softly. "Wake up. Please."

The roar cut through her like a blade. It sounded as if it were right behind her. She drew in a shaky, petrified breath and slowly raised her eyes, seeing dozens of dark dragon silhouettes flying around her. There was another roar, this one even closer. Katla was afraid to turn around. She glanced at Merrill, but he hadn't woken. And she worried he might never move again.

A puff of heated breath came from behind her, ruffling her hair as it enveloped her. Magic instinctively filled her palms, but she clenched her fists tightly. She wouldn't harm any more dragons. Not even to save herself. She hadn't meant to come onto their land. She wasn't even sure how she'd got from one place to another.

A low, ominous growl rumbled in her ears. Hot breath fanned around her. A dragon landed to her left, the impact shaking the ground. It shook its large head and snapped its wings against its body. Another came down in front of her. It left its wings out as it aggressively lowered its head to glare at her. Others remained in the sky, but they were all focused on her.

They had to know who Merrill was. All she could hope for was that they wouldn't attack him. Then again, he wasn't their focus. She was. The Kings may not have sought justice, but these dragons wanted it.

Katla glanced at Merrill and nervously licked her lips. She slowly got to her feet. "I understand," she told them. "I'm trespassing. It was unintentional. I promise."

All three growled angrily in response.

All right. So, they didn't believe her. "The invisible foe attacked. Merrill was hurt. I had to get us out."

She never saw the tail coming at her. It bashed into her side and sent her tumbling through the air. She landed awkwardly on her back, the air knocked out of her. She struggled to take a breath as she rolled onto her side. Katla spotted the fury in the dragons' eyes and knew this was about more than her crossing the border. They knew who she was, and they knew what she had done.

One of the dragons drew in a breath. She watched fire swirling behind its scales and knew she was about to die in a fiery blaze. Katla looked at her hands and the sparks there. She made fists and curled into a ball, covering her head with her arms.

Another roar came, this one long and deafening. It cut through the night, ringing out over the others. Her heart skipped a beat when the ground shook forcefully. The dragon moved closer. It was about to happen. She hoped the pain wasn't too bad. She waited, but nothing came.

Katla peeked out from beneath her arm to see a large claw and orange scales. She lifted her head to find an enormous dragon standing over her, its wings outspread, almost as if protecting her. She looked where Merrill had been on the ground, but he was gone.

Her gaze lifted to the dragon's long neck. She winced when he roared again. The dragons about to attack flew off, one by one until it was only her and Merrill. He didn't budge, so she remained just as she was. Katla saw dragons flying around them but wasn't sure if they were coming just to watch or to challenge Merrill.

Several tense moments passed before he eventually closed his wings and stepped back. She pushed up onto her hand and looked over her shoulder to get a better look at him. Unfortunately, Merrill had already returned to his human form. His bloodied clothes had been replaced by a beige shirt and dark trousers.

Their eyes met. There was a moment of hesitation before he walked toward her. "Are you hurt?"

Katla shook her head and accepted his hand to regain her feet. "You were the one bleeding and not moving."

"Why did you bring us here? It isna safe for you."

"It wasn't on purpose, I assure you."

He glanced up. "We can no' remain."

"They know who I am."

Merrill looked at her and nodded. "They're verra angry."

"They have every right."

"We can debate this later," he said. "We need to go."

"Which direction?"

"It would take days for us to walk to the border."

"Days?" she repeated in shock. How far had she taken them?

He looked at her oddly. "We'll have to fly out."

She had mentioned flying before, but Katla had never expected him to take her up on the suggestion. If she needed a reason to leave quickly, all she had to do was look up at the others waiting to exact their justice. "I never meant to come here. At least, I don't think I did. Will you tell them that?"

"It willna do any good."

"Maybe not, but I need them to know."

He gave her a flat look. "All right. I told them. Are you ready?"

"I believe so."

"Once I shift, climb up my arm and settle at the base of my neck. Unless you'd rather I carry you in my hand."

She wouldn't pass up the opportunity to see the realm as he did. "I'll ride on your back."

He hesitated. "None of the dragons will harm you. I give you my word."

After putting himself between her and the others, she had no doubt. He took several steps back. There was no warning. One moment, he stood there as a man. The next, a dragon towered over her.

Moonlight gleamed off his orange scales, making them look metallic in the light and black in the shadows. She stared into his large, umber-colored dragon eyes as they met hers. She hadn't known his eyes would change color, but the dark, yellowish-brown was beautiful next to the orange. Yet, there was no denying that his sheer size was intimidating. Even more so than the three that had surrounded her a few minutes ago.

There wasn't time for a long perusal, but she took as much in as she could as she walked forward. His skull was narrow, with several tendrils atop his head. A row of horns ran down the sides of his jaw. He had two thin slits for nostrils, with small tendrils on his chin. She nearly missed a step when she spotted the two massive teeth poking out from the sides of his mouth.

As she got closer, she saw that his underbelly was slightly lighter than the rest of him. He lay down. She did a double take at the size of his shiny, obsidian claws. They could easily cut her in two. It took her two tries to find a good place to set her foot so she could climb. His scales didn't just look metallic, they felt it, too. But they weren't cold. They were warm.

She climbed atop him to find the scales on the back of his body narrower. Small ones ran down his spine, which she grabbed to pull herself up. She followed the tendrils down his long tail and saw where it ended with a sharp tip.

Katla settled at the base of his neck as he'd told her and adjusted her coat. Then Merrill climbed to his feet. The action tilted her precariously to the side. She hastily reached for something, and her hand slid across his scales to latch onto a tendril once more. It was on the tip of her tongue to stop him as fear seized an icy hand around her heart. She recalled him standing over her, keeping the dragons away. Merrill wouldn't fly with her unless he thought it would be safe.

That confidence lasted until he jumped into the air. She watched him spread his huge, leathery wings and take them higher. Then, she looked down. The ground began to spiral dizzily. She shut her eyes and leaned forward.

The wind was cold on her face. It sucked away her breath and lifted her braid to fly behind her. The wide legs of her split skirt were molded to her. The act of flying was as exhilarating as it was terrifying. She tried to open her eyes, but she got dizzy again the moment she looked down.

Katla looked forward to stare at the dark strip of horizon. As long as she did that, she didn't get lightheaded. She lost sight of the horizon when he flew them through a cloud. She tried to grab some, but it vanished in her palm like mist. She looked up to the millions of stars above.

The rhythmic beat of Merrill's wings became hypnotic. She relaxed, and when she did, she felt the movement of his body as he breathed. The wind thundered in her ears so loudly it silenced her thoughts. She was riding a dragon among the clouds. It was surreal. And utterly amazing. All the while, the rest of the world was silent. Almost as if it didn't exist. She could pretend that her worries and problems had evaporated like the cloud in her palm. Because, up in the sky, there was freedom, unlike anything she had thought possible.

She felt wetness on her cheek, but the wind whipped it away before she could. Things were so clear and simple up here. If only they could be the same on the ground. But here, among the stars, she could let go of everything and just be. It was no wonder dragons and birds preferred the sky to the ground.

Merrill's trajectory shifted downward as he began their descent. She spread her palm over his scales, deeply moved by this gift he had given her. And deliriously happy that he was alive. As beautiful as the night was, reality was descending upon her. And with it, the memory of the entity and the men who'd attacked Merrill.

She clung to the peace of flying until Merrill landed. Katla unwound her hand from the tendril and climbed down. No sooner had her feet touched the ground than he stood as a man before her, dark blue eyes watching her.

"Your cheeks are red," he murmured.

"It was cold."

His brows snapped together. "Too cold?"

"Never. It was...perfect. If I could take to the skies as you do, I would never come down."

There was a hint of a smile on his lips. He glanced away. "I need to know what happened tonight. There was someone else there besides the entity."

"Men. Ten warriors."

He frowned again. "Men? Are you sure?"

"I came upon them standing around your unconscious body. They tried to attack, and I retaliated. I took out three and then saw the entity."

"Did it attack?"

She nodded, remembering the way its malice felt. "I fought back, but it went through my magic. The next thing I knew, we were in another place."

"That may have saved your life. Did you see what the warriors were wearing?"

"Sleeveless tunics and armbands."

He blew out a breath. "I knew we hadna seen the last of the Orgate warriors."

TWENTY-TWO

Katla started to ask about Orgate when she saw the vine forest over Merrill's shoulder. Her breath left her as she walked around him. The vines sat fifty feet from them, their thick branches weaving together to make a solid wall without a visible thorn.

"We needed somewhere we wouldna be bothered," he said from behind her. "I couldna think of anywhere else. Was I wrong to return here?"

Her feet took her toward the vines. As she walked, she looked left, where she had last seen her husband and daughter alive. Try as she might, she couldn't remember much about them. They were faceless images in her memories now. Katla didn't stop until she stood before the vines. She knew without looking that Merrill was behind her. If he had asked her earlier if they should come to the valley, she would've refused. They couldn't remain on dragon land, and the entity waited near Stonemore, which meant that wasn't safe either.

The valley had been a place of fear for all dragons for over a millennium. But now, it would give one shelter. If the vines allowed them to enter. Katla could force them, but she didn't want to do that. She had demanded much of the brambles over the years.

"I can take us to Iron Hall."

She shook her head and finally looked at him. "You made the right choice. I feared seeing this place again would drown me in misery, but it hasn't. I was the one holding on to all of that. I kept myself locked in a never-ending cycle." Katla surveyed the thick wall of vines and gently laid her hand upon one. "These were my confidants. They listened to my stories and heard my plans. They comforted me when I wept and heeded my pleas for revenge. And when it was time, they stood against me."

"No' against you, lass. *For* you."

Katla jerked her head to Merrill and his silhouette. His face was hidden in the shadows, but his eyes were on her. "For me?"

"They wanted your freedom. You wouldna get that by remaining in the valley. They heard Henry, and the vines pushed you to see the truth."

"*For* me," she agreed, nodding.

The vines parted, opening a path. She peered into the valley to find the vines weren't as thick as they used to be. They had spread out and up, becoming much taller than before. Only the perimeter along the edge was impenetrable, ensuring no unwanted entered.

Still, she hesitated to step inside. "Where is the border?"

"The moment you step into the vines, you'll be off dragon land."

"They moved." Katla swallowed past the lump in her throat. "I coaxed them over the boundary. They've returned."

Merrill stood patiently as she took it all in. A path continued to open for them, and he was right behind her once she entered the vines.

Katla spotted green on the ground and pointed it out to Merrill. "Henry did that. After I agreed to help Villette and the vines erupted, it became a desolate, barren place. I thought the vines did it, but I was to blame. Look at what has happened since I left. Winter is coming, and the ground flourishes with life." She sucked in a breath when she saw a small bud of green on a vine. She paused and bent to admire it. "Even these thrive."

"Why do you believe you made the valley barren?"

"It's obvious." She straightened and glanced back at him. "Henry's magic began life here again. I didn't remain to stamp it out."

Merrill grunted. "Have you considered that perhaps it had nothing to do with you?"

"I can't see how it doesn't."

"If you were to blame, would the vines so readily invite you inside now?"

Katla was brought up short by his words. "I hadn't considered that."

"Try it out," he whispered, his breath against her ear.

She shivered, but it had nothing to do with the nip in the air. She continued along the path, anticipating the sight of the valley in the daylight. When she resided there, everything had been dead and still. There was no rain, no sun, no moons, no sky. Just drab grayness. The songs of insects rang around her now, and she saw the night sky through the branches. The valley was alive again, and that delighted her.

Katla knew where the vines were leading her but didn't deviate from the trail. The past was gone. There was no changing it. Pain might forever remain, but it no longer brought her to her knees. One day, when she thought of her family, maybe she would smile instead of getting choked up. Perhaps she would even forgive herself for her actions and the pain she'd caused so many.

Merrill was quiet. Only the soft tread of his footfalls could be heard. Her mind was full of memories—both good and bad. It wasn't easy to face her transgressions and accept her part in it all. Denial would be easier. Simpler. But it would only make her sorrow linger. Owning up to her mistakes and cruel actions was a brutal, grueling journey and might very well be the end of her. But she had to do it. Not just for herself but also for her family and her people.

She knew the path they were on well. She had walked it thousands of times. So, she wasn't surprised when she saw her cottage as she rounded the bend. How had she not seen its age before? How had she not realized the passage of time and its toll on the structure? She saw it clearly now. Still, she thought it charming.

And it was all that was left of her village.

Merrill walked around her when she paused. He ran a hand along the stones that made up the outside of the cottage and surveyed the thatched roof. She was rooted to the spot as he walked around the dwelling until he stood next to her once more.

"It's in good shape," he said. "It needs a wee bit of work, but that's no' surprising after so long."

"I was so excited when it became ours. I forgot all the good memories in my grief. I didn't even think of it as a home anymore. It was just somewhere I came," she admitted.

He turned his head to her, a part of his face highlighted by the silvery threads of moonlight shining through the branches. "We doona have to go inside."

"I want to. I *need* to."

Merrill motioned for her to lead the way. Katla swallowed and headed for the door. It swung open with only a slight creak. The inside was dark and shadowy, but she knew where everything was. Katla walked to the kitchen table where a candle rested. There was much she could remember about the years with the vines, but there were other parts she couldn't.

"I don't remember lighting these," she confessed as she removed her coat and folded it over the back of the chair. "I must have. I never sat in the dark."

Merrill closed the door softly. There was a whoosh of light as he made flames erupt in the hearth, and every candle flare to life. "It was no doubt Villette's magic. She took it after the battle here."

"She made me think it was mine."

"Maybe it was."

Katla swung her head to him. "Then why can't I remember? That should be easy enough."

"We doona always remember details."

"Lighting candles isn't something I should forget," she argued.

He shrugged. "Why no' just assume it was Villette?"

"I don't know." She sighed in frustration. "I shouldn't get upset about something so trivial."

"You're looking for answers. It's understandable."

Was it, though? Katla scanned the cottage. It wasn't anything grand, just a bedroom off to the side and a spacious kitchen where she hung herbs and combined tinctures. The area in front of the hearth was cozy, and it even had a loft overhead where her daughter had slept.

"This is nice," Merrill told her. "I can see why you were happy here."

She rested her hand on the back of a chair. "I wish you could have seen the village. They were good people."

"I'm sure they were. Their memory remains with you." He tilted his head slightly. "Why no' get some rest? We have a few hours yet before dawn."

"I couldn't sleep if I tried. Not after everything. Tell me about Orgate," she said as she walked to sit in one of the chairs before the fire. She motioned to the remaining one.

Merrill lowered himself into it. The glow of the flames danced upon his face, highlighting the lines creasing his brow. "I told you Varek was brought to Zora against his will. The fact is, Jeyra began it. She wanted revenge on the Dragon Kings for the death of her family."

"I didn't think the dragons crossed the border," Katla said as she settled more comfortably.

"It isna a prison. Just as you were able to cross at will, so, too, can the dragons," he answered. "I doona know if any left of their own accord. They may have. I suspect the ones Jeyra and the Orgateans saw were those Villette freed."

Katla stiffened, the implications clear. "You mean the ones I trapped."

Merrill dipped his chin slightly as he looked her way. "Villette wanted fear, remember? What better way than to release dragons upon unsuspecting humans? Some in Orgate hunt such dragons and kill them."

She tried not to wince, but Katla couldn't hide her distress over the part she'd played in all of it. "Why did Jeyra blame the Kings? None of you were even here."

"My guess is that was Villette, too. Regardless, Jeyra isna one for patience. She decided to get justice on her own. However, she couldna do it by herself. She sought out an old crone, who pulled Varek here from Earth."

"I hope you found her so she couldn't do such again."

"Oh, we did," he muttered.

Katla quirked a brow. "What do you mean?"

"It was Eurielle."

"Villette's sister?" Katla asked in surprise.

Merrill nodded slowly. "Her siblings banished her to Zora as punishment for interfering with things. She changes her appearance and can appear old or young."

"Does she hate dragons that much?"

"Actually, Eurielle claims she believed if she brought Varek here, we would follow and stop her sister."

Katla wrinkled her nose. "Do you believe her?"

"She's done enough to help in other ways. So, we do."

"I'm not sure I could."

Merrill rubbed a hand over his mouth. "Jeyra is part of an elite group of Orgate warriors. She, with the help of her mentor, Rankin, brought Varek's unconscious body back to the city and imprisoned him there."

"He busted out, I'm sure."

"The metal that makes up the prison prevented him from accessing his magic. He remained in there for some time. Varek being Varek, he began digging for answers. Jeyra couldna answer some of his questions, and that got her wondering. She started looking deeper and uncovered generations of lies and cover-ups. Jeyra put Varek in that prison, and then she broke him out. Once he was free, his powers returned, and with them, his ability to hear the dragons' screams. One of Orgate's council members, Arn, was corrupt and had the warriors bring the captured dragons to him."

Katla folded her hands in her lap. "What would a mortal want with dragons?"

"He tortured them and was somehow able to take their magic and use it as his, all while killing or banishing anyone in the city with abilities. Varek and Jeyra fought to free the imprisoned dragons. A battle ensued that divided the city. Ultimately, the dragons were released, and Arn was killed. The remaining warriors have been determined to make the Kings—and anyone associated with us—pay ever since."

TWENTY-THREE

The fury that had burned through Merrill when he learned what Varek had gone through singed him still. It was a good thing he hadn't been there. He would've set the entire city ablaze for the actions of a few. A handful were *still* causing problems, it seemed.

"Surely, these warriors know they can't win against you—or any King. They don't have magic," Katla said.

He brought his right arm against his side, recalling the feeling of the blade sinking into his skin. "Their iron stopped Varek's magic. And I believe they've found another use for it."

"What?"

"If I'm wounded, my body begins to heal immediately. When I faced off against the entity, it kept me focused on it so I didna see the warriors. I ended up stabbed multiple times by something that prevented me from healing."

Her lips parted, and her brows drew together in a frown. "You think it was that metal?"

"I do."

"For what purpose?"

He sat up and pressed his lips together as he once more looked into the fire. "I've been mulling that over. Nothing makes sense. Had the entity struck me as it had the other Kings, it would've rendered me unconscious. It would be easy enough to attempt to take my life then. But it didna strike me. It...goaded me." Merrill slid his gaze to her. "I caught it. I had a hold of it. I was getting ready to call for Varek when I felt the first blade pierce my spine."

"You think they're working together?"

"I do."

She tucked her feet beneath the chair and crossed her ankles. "That is rather ominous."

"Even more so when I think about how it seemed the entity watched as they stabbed me. Each blow weakened me. I lost my hold on the entity and the ability to reach out mentally to the Kings. And it still didna attack."

"This is the same enemy that has killed other dragons?"

He nodded.

"Why did it trail us all day? Why is it working with others? And why not go after you itself? Why let the warriors hurt you?"

Merrill released a breath as he sat back. "Those are questions I've asked myself, and I doona have an answer."

"We can't go back. Have you told the other Kings?"

"I will."

She gaped at him. "Why have you waited?"

"I had to sort things out, and I needed to know exactly what you saw."

"Nothing more than I already described: ten men standing around you, laughing. I didn't see the entity until after I rushed to your side."

He shouldn't be elated that she had come for him, not after he had told her to run. "You were supposed to sleep through all of it."

"You would rather I had woken to believe you left me?" She gave him a flat look before turning her head to the fire.

Merrill sighed. She might not realize what her help meant, but he did. "You'll have a target on your back now."

"I likely already had one since I was traveling with you."

"Perhaps." He hoped to hell that wasn't true, but he planned to find out.

Katla's swung her gaze to him. "What now?"

"We can no' remain here for long. The entity can get to you. And while the vines might try to prevent the warriors, they'd find a way through. I'd rather leave the valley as it is." Merrill considered their options, which were few. "I spent the majority of my verra long life hiding. I willna do it anymore."

"You want to seek them out?"

"I want to stop the entity. I had it in my grasp. I might've been able to kill it."

Her gray eyes were troubled as she stared at him. "You told me Villette couldn't kill it."

"Neither could Lotti, and she tried multiple times."

"What makes you think you can?"

He lifted a shoulder. "A feeling. None of the other Kings have been able to make contact."

"For good reason, obviously."

"But if I can grab it again, I can hold it for you."

Her eyes widened in astonishment before she scrunched up her face. "Did you miss the part where I said it went through my magic?"

"It has to be stopped."

"It doesn't have to be by you."

Merrill put his elbow on the arm of the chair and leaned forward. "It targeted *me*. It followed us and waited until I was out of the cave. It was patient. Who knows how long it watched us?"

"My point exactly. You can't see it. You'd never know it was coming at you."

Unless she was with him. She had gotten closer to the entity than he liked. It worried him that the enemy had tracked them. Had it listened to their conversations? Had it come close enough to hurt them? He was afraid of what the answers might be.

"How many do you think there are?" Katla asked.

He ran his hands through his hair, tugging the strands away from his face before letting his hands fall to his legs. "No one has asked that question. We've all assumed it's just the one."

"And if it isn't? What if multiple attack you at once?"

"This one acted differently than the previous attacks. That leads me to believe there *is* more than one. Fuck," he muttered. The Kings couldn't catch a break.

Katla rose and walked to the hearth, where a kettle hung off to the side. She took it and brought it to the kitchen, pumping some water into it. Then she hung it over the fire and faced him. "You need to warn the Kings."

"They're already on alert for that thing, but you're right. They need to know the rest," he agreed.

She smoothed her hands over her split trousers and returned to the kitchen. He watched as she reached above to some hanging herbs and picked a few. She moved about the space easily, taking dried herbs before surveying others in jars. As she mixed and combined, he opened the mental link and called out to Varek.

"Where the fuck have you been?" his friend demanded. *"You screamed my name and then didna answer."*

"I couldna."

Varek hesitated before he bit out, *"Why could you no' answer?"*

"I was attacked."

Merrill spent the next few moments spelling everything out to Varek while studying Katla as she ground the herbs with a mortar and pestle. When he finished, Varek was silent.

Then he said, *"Bloody fucking hell."*

"I couldna have said it better."

"Con, Brandr, and Eurwen need to be brought up to speed."

"That's what you're going to do."

Varek made a sound. *"Is that right? And just what are you planning?"*

"I'm no' sure yet."

"You should come home."

Merrill's eyes followed Katla as she retrieved the heated kettle and poured some boiling water into two cups. *"If this thing is after me, I'm no' bringing it to everyone else. Especially to where the bairns are."*

"We'll handle that."

"I'm no' doing it."

Varek's voice was tight with worry when he said, *"Then I'm coming to you."*

His friend severed the link. Merrill tried to get Varek to talk again, but he had apparently said his piece. Varek wasn't one to rehash something over and over.

"Varek is coming here," Merrill told Katla.

"It's a soothing tea, nothing more." She handed him one of the cups. "You sound surprised about Varek."

"You are no'?"

"I'm not," she said with a soft chuckle, bringing her cup to her seat. "He's your friend, and you're in a difficult situation. Wouldn't you do the same for him?"

Merrill twisted his lips. "Without hesitation."

She flashed a quick grin before sipping her tea.

He inhaled the scent of the liquid, letting the delicate, sweet aroma fill his senses. "Jeyra willna let him come alone."

"If you think it wise, I can go elsewhere and let the three of you talk."

"Why?" he asked in confusion. "This is your home."

Katla dropped her gaze to the floor. "You know why."

"If they can no' be courteous to you in your own home, then I'll tell them to leave. And doona dare say you deserve it. You deserve nothing but respect and civility."

She focused on the cup and then the fire, not saying anything.

Merrill had gotten used to being with her. He liked being around her. He liked *her*. And if he had his way, that wouldn't end. He understood her reluctance to go against the entity with him and respected it. It would be harder to walk away from her than he thought. "I'm sorry you got dragged into this."

"It isn't your fault."

He wanted her to look at him. "I'll leave as soon as Varek gets here."

Katla's head swiveled to him. She stared at him for a moment, then pushed to her feet and walked to the sink. She set her cup inside and leaned her hands on the counter, staring out the window into the night. "You're leaving me here."

Merrill set his tea on the floor and stood. He took one step toward her and then stopped. "This isna your fight."

"You made that decision for me, did you?"

"I'll return as soon as we defeat the entity. You and I still need to find Villette, remember?"

She looked at him over her shoulder before facing him fully. Her eyes beseeched him, and her voice wobbled with emotion as she said, "I've experienced more in the last few days with you than I have in my entire life."

He took another step forward before stopping himself. This goodbye was harder than he'd thought it would be. He looked at her lips. God, how he wanted to kiss her. The pain cutting across her expression was like a dagger to his heart. "They've meant more to me than you'll ever know. You…"

"I, what?" she implored, taking a step closer.

As he stared at her beautiful face, he found himself leaning toward her. Once more, he stopped himself. "You…helped clear the noise in my head. You quieted my rage."

Her lips parted as she leaned forward, then pulled back. Desire had turned her gray eyes to liquid steel. He took the final step separating them, her face tilted up to his. He slid his fingers along the side of her face, then into her hair and around her neck. He was trying to find the will to leave when her body melted against his.

Merrill was lost then, adrift in a sea of yearning. Her lids slid shut as he lowered his head. Their lips met and lingered as his blood rushed loudly through his ears. He kissed her a second time, then a third. She moaned softly as he swept his tongue between her lips and tangled it with hers in a sensual, carnal dance.

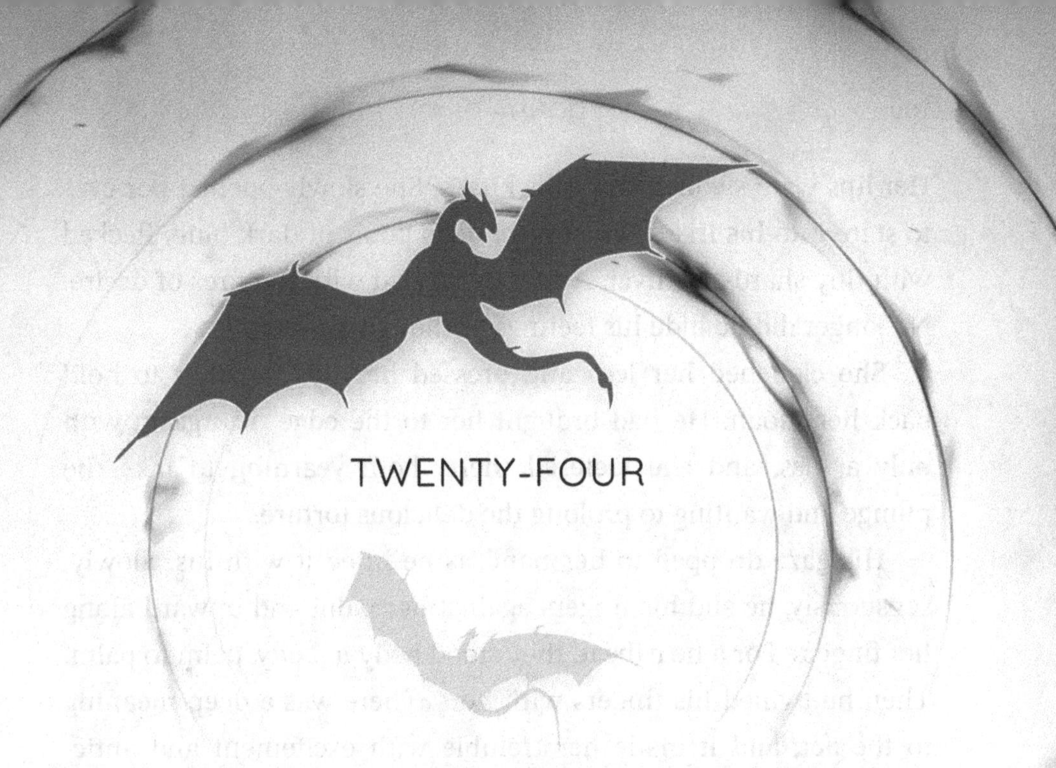

TWENTY-FOUR

No amount of fantasizing about the taste of Merrill's lips could have delivered such wanton passion or shameless abandon. Every nerve ending sizzled with a deep yearning. Katla's blood was molten as it ran through her veins. The desire heavy. Her need urgent. She was burning up, and only one man could douse the fire.

She slid her hands up his back when he brought her flush against him and deepened the kiss. His fingers tangled in the hair at her neck, holding her head as he ravaged her lips. Each kiss was deeper, hungrier than the last. Their breaths mingled, and their bodies pressed tightly together, seeking, needing to be closer.

She was drowning. She was flying. Passion slid sensuously through her in waves. The only one keeping her from disintegrating into a million pieces was Merrill. His large hand was splayed on her lower back, pulling her against his thick arousal. She moaned as wetness slicked her thighs.

The kiss ended, leaving her gripping Merrill to stay upright.

Her lips were swollen from his kisses. She slowly opened her eyes to stare into his irises. They were deep pools of dark blue, flecked with tiny shards of silver. And they sizzled with the fires of desire. No longer did he hide his feelings or thoughts.

She clenched her legs and pressed her lips together to hold back her moan. He had brought her to the edge of orgasm with only a kiss, and she teetered there, both yearning to take the plunge and wanting to prolong the delicious torture.

His gaze dropped to her hand as he lifted it with his. Slowly, sensuously, he slid his fingers against her palm and upward along her fingers. For a heartbeat, they stood body to body, palm to palm. Then he twined his fingers with hers. There was a deep meaning to the act, and it made her tremble with excitement and anticipation.

Longing.

His gaze swung back to her. "Katla," he whispered, his lips lowering to hers again.

Chills raced over her flesh at his husky voice saying her name. She rose onto her tiptoes, eager for another kiss—and more.

Just before their mouths touched, there was an explosion. The blast was deafening, the light blinding. She was ripped out of Merrill's arms and flung away. The world whirled and twisted as she flipped through the air. She dropped like a stone onto her stomach, and pain lanced through her. Katla couldn't hold back her anguished cry. She clenched her teeth as tears ran down her face. She attempted to move her hands beneath her, but her right arm wouldn't obey. The small movement brought another dizzying wave of agony.

Merrill. She had to find Merrill.

She lifted her head from the debris and saw the bone sticking out of the back of her arm above her elbow. Then she saw the fire. She stared in shock at the flames that burned what was left of the inside of the cottage. Her home was no more. Only one wall remained. The rest was scattered in all directions. Alarm rocketed through her when the fire jumped from the cottage to the vines and quickly spread.

"Nay!" she yelled, managing to sit up using her left arm. Katla hastily scanned the wreckage of the cottage. "Merrill!"

There was no answer, just the growing thunder of the flames. She struggled to get to her feet, but her body wouldn't respond. Katla had no choice but to drag herself with her left arm, shouting for Merrill. He was alive. He was made of fire. And he healed. He would be okay.

A cold shiver of apprehension ran down her spine. Katla stilled and looked up to find the entity watching her from the air. She felt its amusement. She rolled away the moment the being dove for her. Magic filled her palm just as the entity struck. The impact stole her breath and lobbed her into the burning vines. Her head slammed into the earth so hard when she landed it left her dazed.

Katla fought to keep her eyes open, but darkness edged her vision. The fingers of her left hand curled around a vine as she thought of Merrill.

Katla forced her eyes to open and looked through the smoke to the sky above. Every breath was agonizing. She couldn't move her arms or legs. She turned her head toward the roaring fire, and through the haze and unbearable pain, she saw men exiting the cottage, carrying Merrill.

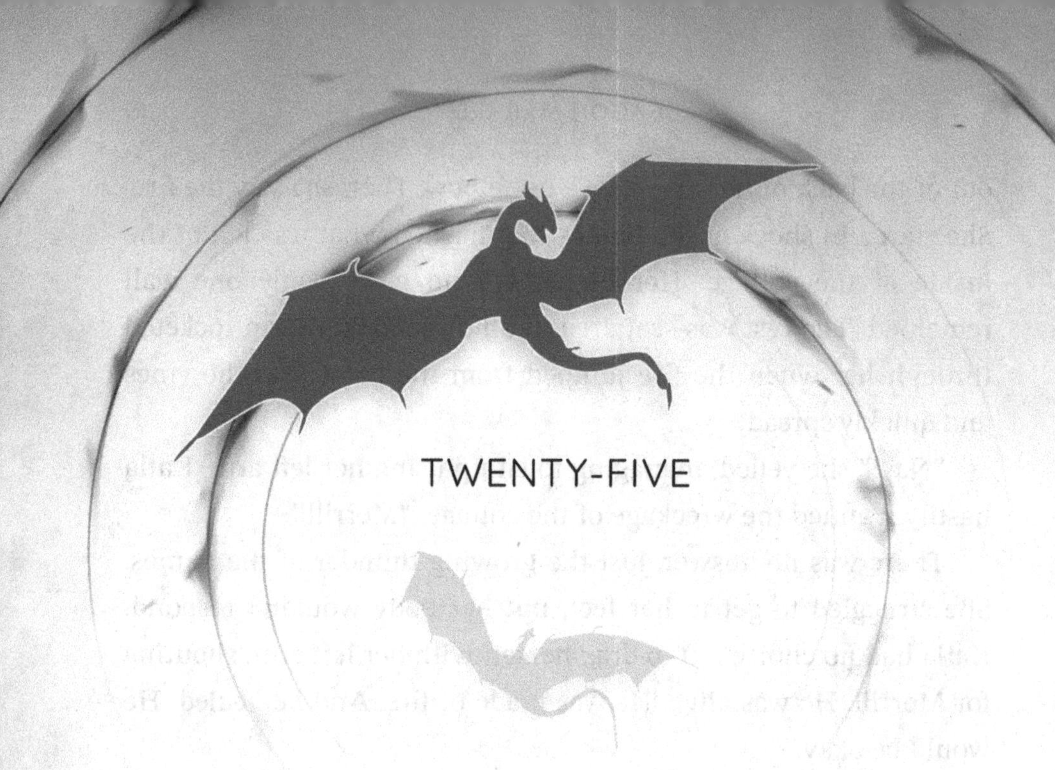

TWENTY-FIVE

Varek felt a sense of urgency to get to Merrill. Once he was in the air, he told Con about his conversation with Merrill, refusing to wait as the other Kings tried to catch up to him.

Jeyra rode on his back, draped over his neck as he flew low and fast. He ignored the other dragons hastily getting out of his path. Varek had been uneasy since Merrill returned to Stonemore. He hadn't been able to shake the feeling that something wasn't right. He'd assumed Villette would come for his friend, but they should've anticipated the invisible foe.

Varek was halfway to the northern border when he spotted smoke coming from that direction. He released a growl and pushed himself harder as he mentally shouted to every dragon through their mental link, asking them to join him. Then he tried reaching Merrill. No matter how often he bellowed his friend's name, he didn't respond. He wouldn't ignore Varek. Not now.

Varek was furious at himself for not getting Rhi or Lotti to tele-port him to Katla's. He was wasting precious time. He bared his teeth and flapped his wings faster, willing himself to get there quicker.

The closer he got, the thicker the smoke in the air became. Varek kept shouting for Merrill but got no answer. Then he saw the extent of the inferno as it ravaged the vine forest. Over half the valley was engulfed. It appeared as if it began at Katla's cottage and spread outward in a semi-circle. And it continued to expand at an unnatural rate.

Suddenly, a black dragon with silver-tipped scales moved up beside him. Varek glanced over at Derek. The King of the Dead nodded and dove toward the flames. That's when Varek spotted Kora on his back. They flew right over the tops of the vines as Kora used her hellhound abilities to put out the blaze.

Varek flew toward the cottage. He spotted a grouping of vines in a dome shape and remembered them making such a structure before. The first time had been to protect Henry and Melisse. Maybe Merrill and Katla were within. Though Varek had a hard time imagining Merrill hiding instead of fighting. Katla, too, for that matter.

He soared over the house. There was nothing left of the cottage but half a wall. Everything else was burnt or burning. The building itself looked like a bomb had gone off inside. The debris field made almost a complete circle, and there were no signs of any bodies.

Varek swooped to the ground. The moment he landed, Jeyra flipped off his back. He called clothes to himself as he shifted and surveyed the damage.

"What happened?" Jeyra whispered.

He shook his head. "Nothing good."

Derek and Kora flew over them, extinguishing the last of the fire. Varek looked at the sky and saw a wave of dragons approaching. His attention returned to the ground, searching for some sign of Merrill, Katla, or anyone else. The fact that no one was around had worry settling like a heavy stone in Varek's stomach.

Merrill, for all his years of good-naturedness, jokes, and uplifting comments, was a warrior of the finest caliber. He wasn't just a fighter. He was legendary among the dragons. Merrill saw a battlefield unlike others. He knew an enemy's weaknesses and just how to exploit them. Varek scanned the wreckage. If Merrill was here, he would've fought with everything he had.

Con shifted as he descended to the earth, landing on one knee. As he straightened, clothes covered his nakedness. His black gaze slid to Varek. Above them, more Kings crisscrossed the sky, each relaying what Varek already knew. Merrill wasn't here.

"Who did this?" Con demanded in a soft voice, belying his rage.

The question wasn't directed at anyone in particular, but Varek answered. "It could've been Villette. It could've been the entity."

"As well as the Orgate warriors." The wind ruffled Con's blond hair, drawing smoke around him.

"Possibly," Varek admitted.

He tried not to think about the time he'd spent in the city's prison, cut off from his magic and unable to shift. It had been stressful and terrifying. When Jeyra called his name, his attention swung to his mate. He found her walking among the remains of the cottage. She waved him over. Varek hurried to her, Con on his heels.

"Look," Jeyra said, squatting and moving a broken board.

He followed her finger to the orange scale peeking out from

beneath the rubble. A dragon didn't lose their scales easily. The fact that one lay there meant trouble.

"Con!"

Rhi's frantic shout cut through the night. Con spun and raced to his mate. Varek followed with Jeyra, seeing that the domed vines he had spotted earlier were now parted. He slid to a halt at the sight of Katla's body, bloodied and twisted.

"Is she dead?" Jeyra asked.

Con knelt beside Katla and laid a hand on her shoulder. Her face was turned toward them. Much of her hair had burned away, and half her face was blistered. Varek looked at her chest but couldn't see it moving. Everyone held their breath as they waited to see if Con could heal her. He could heal anything, but he couldn't bring someone back from the dead.

Varek saw Katla's burned hair return. After that, her wounds healed, one by one. She drew in a deep breath and opened her eyes. Her gaze lingered on Con for a heartbeat before she looked past him to the cottage.

"Merrill!" she screamed as she sat up.

She gained her feet and frantically shoved past Con and Rhi. Varek caught her when she tried to go around him.

"Easy," he told her.

Sparks shot from her fingers and swam in the air as she struggled. "I have to get to him."

Varek gripped her by the shoulders and gave her a gentle shake until she looked at him. "He isna there."

"I know."

He watched a single tear roll down her face. "What happened? Where is he?"

Katla stepped away, pulling from his grip. She scanned the

faces around her before looking at the dragons in the sky. "He brought us here, thinking we would be safe. We should have been. At least, for the night. There was no warning. Just an explosion. It threw me." She swallowed, her eyes never leaving what was left of her home. "I dragged myself to the cottage, but everything was on fire. That's when I saw the entity."

Varek exchanged a look with Con. It was the confirmation they needed that Katla had Star magic.

"It attacked me. It was fast. I had no time to do anything." She looked down at herself. Her clothes were still burned, but her body was healed. "I thought I was dead."

"You were close," Con said from behind her.

Katla twisted to look at him. "You healed me?"

"I did," he said with a bow of his head.

"Thank you."

Con walked to stand beside Varek. "Did you see Merrill after the explosion?"

Despair creased her face for a heartbeat. "They took him."

"Who?" Varek demanded, even though he knew what the answer would be.

Katla's gray eyes met his. "The Orgate warriors."

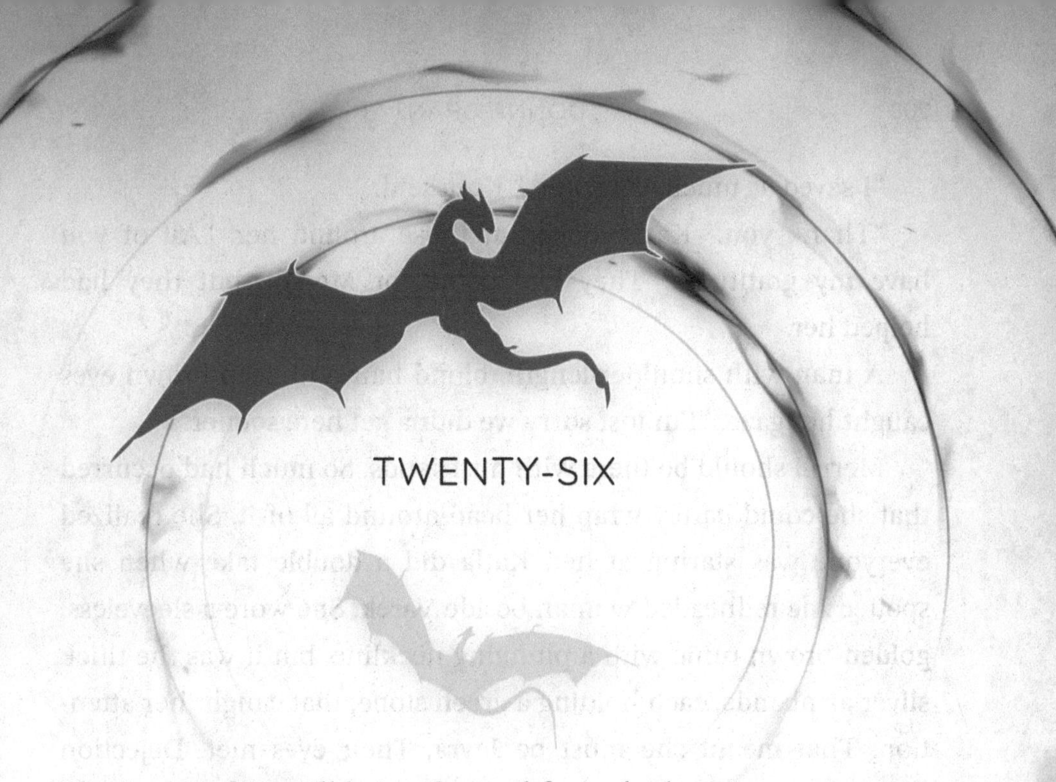

TWENTY-SIX

The image of Merrill being dragged from the burning cottage was seared upon Katla's brain. If only she had been able to stop the entity, she might have prevented the warriors from taking him. Her body tingled from healing magic. She shouldn't be alive, but she was. And she would find Merrill.

It hurt too much to look at the smoking remains of her home, knowing he was no longer there. She turned away, her eyes landing on the vines that had cocooned her. They'd packed themselves tightly together and were several feet thick, keeping the fire from reaching her. Many had sacrificed themselves to protect her. She placed her hands on the charred vines and felt another wave of tears for what had been lost.

"How badly is the valley burned?" she asked shakily.

"Badly."

Katla turned her head when she recognized the voice and saw Kora approaching. The hellhound's golden-brown eyes were filled with sorrow.

"I saved as much as I could," Kora said.

"Thank you." Katla looked at those around her. "All of you have my gratitude." They had come for Merrill, but they had helped her.

A man with shoulder-length, blond hair and deep brown eyes caught her gaze. "I'm just sorry we didna get here sooner."

Merrill should be there with his friends. So much had occurred that she could barely wrap her head around all of it. She realized everyone was staring at her. Katla did a double take when she spotted the redheaded woman beside Varek. She wore a sleeveless, golden-brown tunic with a plunging neckline, but it was the thick silver armbands, each holding a green stone, that caught her attention. That meant she must be Jeyra. Their eyes met. Dejection furrowed Jeyra's brow.

Kora touched her arm to get her attention. "Let me introduce you to everyone." She pointed to the blond King with black eyes who had healed her. "That is Con."

The King of Kings bowed his head to her. Katla returned it, knowing she owed him a considerable debt.

"This is Varek," Kora said as she motioned to the man who had spoken. "And beside him is—"

"Jeyra," Katla finished. "Merrill spoke of both of you. And of Orgate."

Jeyra's lips twisted. "I can't believe my people are doing this."

Varek put his arm around her and pulled her close. "I wouldna consider these warriors your people, or even Orgateans."

Smoke curled into the sky everywhere she looked. Heartache struck Katla at what she saw, no matter which direction she faced. The attack, Merrill's abduction, the burning of the vines. She couldn't stand by and do nothing. "Can someone point me in the direction of Orgate?"

"I can," Jeyra said with a defeated sigh.

"We'll both show you," Varek stated.

Katla met his gaze and politely replied, "That isn't necessary."

"You willna be going alone. No' after what happened here," he argued.

"I think I should." She held up a hand when Varek started to speak. "Merrill was right. The entity targeted him. He was attacked twice, but it didn't try to kill him either time. It wants something from him. Or it's a trap for more Kings." She licked her lips. "Or both."

"Fekking hell," Rhi muttered, crossing her arms over her chest.

Con said nothing. The only movement was the flare of his nostrils.

"Katla has a point," Kora said.

Varek shook his head and shrugged. "I doona care. I'm going. End of discussion."

Jeyra shot him a glare. "It's hardly the end of the discussion. You can't show your face in the city."

"And you can?" he retorted.

Con blew out a harsh breath. "Enough. Neither of you is going."

Fury contorted Varek's face. "They took Merrill."

"I'm aware," the King of Kings replied. "But the residents know your face, just as they know Jeyra's. Neither of you will learn anything of importance."

Rhi wrinkled her nose. "I hate to say it, but they likely know all of us. And with the entity following Merrill and Katla, who knows how often it has spied on us? We can't see it."

"Fuck!" Varek said, turning away to pace a few steps in anger before halting and returning.

Katla looked at the mountains on either side of her. She could either go over them or around. Because she wouldn't cross the border again. And she didn't know how to transport herself to another area when she wasn't angry. That was too bad. It would have come in handy.

Her valley had been destroyed once more. A fire had ripped apart her world again. Her rage was there, but the necessity to locate Merrill diminished it a bit. Was he in Orgate's prison? Or had he been taken elsewhere? She wouldn't learn anything by staying and debating the issue. If no one would tell her how to find Orgate, she would do it herself. Katla walked away from the group without saying a word.

"What are you doing?" Kora asked, falling into step with her.

A black dragon silently glided over them. The moonlight hit upon it just right, letting Katla see the silver along the edges of its scales, but Kora's smile told Katla who it was. Derek.

"What I must," Katla answered.

"All right."

Katla waited for her to peel off and return to the others, but Kora stayed with her. Katla shouldered her way through the burned vines, her heart heavy at their deaths. Derek stayed low, swinging around to fly over them again.

"This isn't your fight," Katla said as she glanced at the hellhound.

Kora's smile dropped. "You and Merrill were attacked. That makes it my fight."

"You don't understand this foe. The entity is..." Katla couldn't even find the words to accurately describe its malevolence.

Kora nodded as she looked forward. "It attacked Derek. He explained the assault to me. So, he understands. And he can see it."

"That didn't help me. I never saw it this time."

"You were inside."

"I should've been paying attention. Letting my guard down was a mistake."

Kora picked her way around a fallen vine. "I doubt it would've mattered. It didn't get Merrill the first time. It wasn't going to miss a second chance."

"I can't stop thinking about what they might do to him."

"I saw him go up against two of Villette's dragons. Trust me, he can hold his own."

At that moment, Derek flew over them again. Katla watched him as she thought about riding atop Merrill. "I'm happy to see you and Derek triumphed over Miena."

"It wasn't easy. I heard you went up against her, too. I have to admit, I was happy to see the tower destroyed," Kora said with a grin.

Katla tried to smile in return. "It wasn't on purpose. I was only keeping her away from the children."

"She wasn't planning to kill them. She wanted to take their magic."

"What?" Katla was so shocked that she stopped in her tracks.

Kora twisted her lips and stopped, as well. "Miena took people's magic. It was easier to take children's because they couldn't fight back. Apparently, she was even able to do it while locked up. So, Villette had the priests kill the kids before Miena could collect enough power to break free of her prison."

"And none of the other Star People stopped her?"

Kora shrugged as they began walking again. "From what we could gather, Villette was the only one who knew."

"I'm surprised she didn't try to do the same."

"Me, too, actually. I'm just thankful she didn't."

Katla glanced over her shoulder.

"What is it?" Kora asked.

"I guess I thought someone might try to stop me, but I've only just realized they can get to Orgate much quicker than I can."

Kora ducked under a burned branch. "Why would you think they would want to stop you?"

"I understand why Con healed me. They needed information about Merrill. I would've done the same. I'm also keenly aware of my part in Villette's grand plan."

"You were duped."

Katla shook her head. "Merrill said the same thing, but I saw for myself what the dragons think of me. If he hadn't been there, I'd be dead."

"But he was there."

"The dragons want justice, and they deserve it. It's only a matter of time before the Kings demand it."

Kora made a tsking sound and said, "You've got it wrong."

"How so?"

"If the Kings wanted you to pay, you would have already. It's that simple. Besides, Merrill wouldn't have traveled with you if he believed you were at fault."

Katla carefully walked around one of the fallen vines. She didn't want to debate her guilt or innocence anymore. Not when so much more was at stake. "Do you know how to get to Orgate?"

Kora shook her head. "Derek likely will, though."

"Will he share that information with me?"

"Of course. He wants to find Merrill just as badly as you do. If it weren't for Merrill, Derek might never know about the Kings."

Katla finally began to see some vines that only had minimal burns. She gently touched the ones she walked past. At least they weren't all damaged. "Kora," she began.

"I know what you want to say. If I were in your shoes, I'd probably say the same thing. But we're not going anywhere. Derek might be new to the Dragon Kings and trust and respect them, but he isn't obligated to Con or the twins as the others are." Kora grinned as she looked at Katla. "As for me, I stand by my friends."

"You hardly know me."

Kora held her gaze. "I know enough. Besides, you'll need our help. You can't get into the city alone."

"You may think differently when you go up against the entity. *If* it's only the one. There may be more."

"You've done things on your own for a long time. I was the same. I know better than most how difficult it is to ask for help. You don't have to ask. We're offering. Let us."

"You can speak to Derek mentally as the dragons can?"

Kora chuckled. "I'm afraid not. But I know my mate. He would say exactly as I am if he were standing here. Speaking of…"

Katla looked where Kora stared to find a tall man walking toward them. The darkness kept him in shadow until they stood before each other. Derek's straight, black hair was cut to just above his shoulders. He was tall and muscular, carrying himself with a confidence that warned others to keep their distance. But it was the marks covering every inch of exposed skin from his neck down that caught her attention.

He gave Kora a soft smile before turning pale olive eyes to her. "Katla," he said in greeting.

"Derek," she replied.

The three continued onward. The farther they went, the healthier the vines were. It gave Katla hope that they would cover the valley again one day. That knowledge eased her misery a little.

Alone with her thoughts, Katla tried to discern how the entity had gotten the warriors from Stonemore to the valley. Could it teleport like Rhi? Even if it could, it should've taken it longer to locate her and Merrill. Something more was at work here. Dread soured her stomach as she wondered if the entity, Orgate, and Villette were working together.

Katla wanted to free Merrill, but there was no telling how many opponents stood between them. To attempt something like that alone was foolish. Merrill needed to be freed. If she had to get on her knees and beg for help, she would do it. Kora had already offered, but Katla needed to hear it from Derek, too.

She swallowed past the nervousness and said, "I've been thinking. It doesn't seem feasible for the entity to find Merrill and me so quickly while also bringing the warriors."

"Aye. I'm thinking the same," Derek replied.

He didn't have the same accent as Merrill and the other Kings because he was from Zora, not Earth. But he had the same bearing. It must go hand-in-hand with being a Dragon King. "I think the entity has help," Katla said.

Kora's brow furrowed. "Who?"

"Villette," Derek answered.

Katla nodded. "It makes sense."

"Does she have her hand in everything?" Kora muttered angrily.

Derek grunted in response.

"I can't do this alone," Katla said.

Kora's brown gaze slid to her. "I've already offered."

"I know, but I need to ask. Will you help me find and free Merrill?"

This time, Kora didn't immediately reply. She swiveled her head to Derek.

"This won't be easy," Derek said.

Katla felt her stomach clench in dread. "I'll do whatever it takes."

The couple exchanged a look. She wanted to ask what that was about, but before she could, a roar sounded through the valley, bringing them to a halt. The three of them turned around and looked toward her cottage.

"What's happening?" Kora asked Derek.

Katla watched a gold dragon jump into the sky and fly upward before soaring over the valley, coming straight for them.

"It's Con," Kora told her.

Katla stared in awe at the size of Con as he got closer. He flew past them in a burst. She twisted to watch him dip a wing and swing around to zoom past them once more. Merrill was enormous, but Con was even bigger.

More dragons leapt into the air. The snap of their wings was so forceful she could hear it across the distance. Derek grunted and resumed walking. Kora and Katla observed Con and the others until they flew out of sight.

Kora turned to catch up with Derek. Katla remained a few moments longer, wondering if she might ever see the valley again. Merrill had allowed her to confront the past. And because of him, she had been able to release some of her guilt. She would never have been able to do that without returning. He had given her something else, too.

He had given her hope for a future she still wasn't sure she deserved. But she wanted it more than anything else. Even the revenge she'd once sought.

Her eyes burned with unshed tears as she thought about their kiss.

"You wouldn't leave me," Katla whispered into the night. "I'm not leaving you."

She turned and followed Derek and Kora.

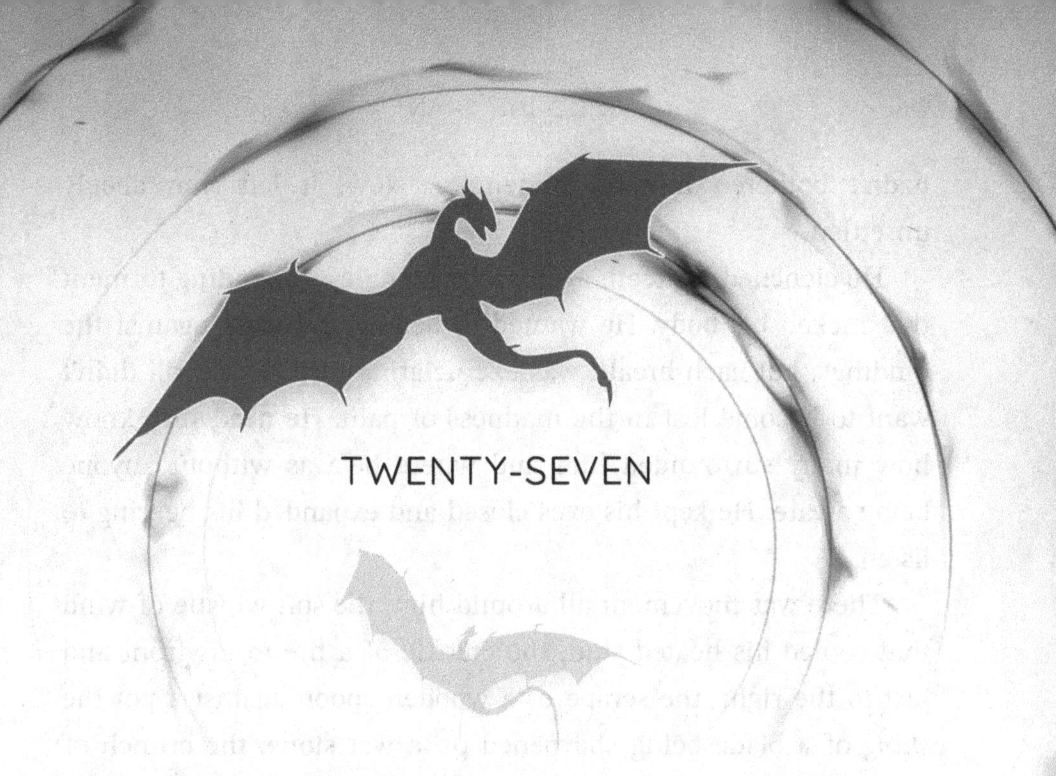

TWENTY-SEVEN

The climb from oblivion to consciousness was slow and a level of hell Merrill had never experienced. His head felt as if it was caught between the jaws of a dragon while also being ripped apart.

The rest of him fared no better.

He strove to shrink away from the unending, unbearable agony to no avail. He longed to sink into the darkness of nothingness, where the pain couldn't lash him with such fervor. Slumber was as distant as the days before the humans on Earth, forcing him to face the reality of his situation. He wasn't healing. And there was only one reason for that.

Dozens of cuts swathed his arms and upper body. Even his legs. But more than the blades had carved his skin. Cold, unforgiving metal bit into his wrists as he hung, his arms outstretched to the sides. His legs no longer worked, and his captors had made sure to suspend him so his knees wouldn't touch the ground.

Merrill clawed through the pain and attempted to reach Varek through their mental link—only to be met by silence. A quiet that hadn't bothered him at Stonemore. Now, it left him deeply unsettled.

He clenched his teeth against the merciless, unending torment that racked his body. He wanted to bellow and yank against the bindings, but each breath was excruciating torture. Merrill didn't want to become lost in the madness of pain. He needed to know how many surrounded him and where he was without anyone being aware. He kept his eyes closed and expanded his hearing to listen.

There was movement all around him: the soft whistle of wind that cooled his heated skin, the crackle of a fire to his front and just to the right, the scrape of a wooden spoon against a pot the *shing* of a blade being sharpened on a wet stone, the crunch of shoes on grass...

It hit him then that he wasn't in a dungeon as Varek had been but outside. And by the lack of noise, away from the city. In fact, his captors hadn't uttered a single syllable.

The air stirred to his left. There was rapid hand movement, and Merrill realized the Orgate warriors were communicating using some kind of hand signals. Then he caught a whiff of bitter wine. Anger churned as the scent circled him slowly, intently. The entity was focused on him, no doubt looking for signs that he was conscious. Merrill had a slight advantage for the moment, and he wanted to keep it.

He sought out any sound that would tell him if Katla had been taken with him. She had been in his arms after they'd shared a kiss like no other. He had smelled the entity a millisecond before it struck, giving him no time to warn her or retaliate. She had been yanked from his arms as everything exploded. He'd tried to shift, but everything went black.

Until now.

How had the entity found them so swiftly? More importantly, how had the warriors crossed several hundred miles through the Ferdon Woods, made their way across the rolling hills and into another larger forest, then over the mountains to the valley? They hadn't done it alone, that was for sure. Someone or something had brought the warriors here. Could it be the entity? Or was it Villette?

She had an alliance with a faction of Orgate warriors. They had attacked Shaw at the palace. All the Kings knew that. They should have anticipated that Villette would turn to that group. The Kings should have been prepared. Merrill, most of all.

He couldn't pick up any sounds that indicated Katla was there. She *could* be there and unconscious, but maybe they kept her else-where. He hoped she was still at the valley and unharmed. Because the alternative was something he couldn't consider. He should've brought them to Iron Hall the first time he sensed some-thing. At the very least, he should've called for Rhi. Instead, he had put Katla in the entity's crosshairs.

Footsteps drew near. Merrill kept his breathing even as someone stopped before him. He knew what was coming when he heard the *ssh* of a blade being drawn from its scabbard. He didn't jerk away when the weapon touched his neck, even though he wanted to. The warrior put pressure on the edge so it sank deep. Agony exploded like fragments from a bomb, hurtling through him in every direction, ripping tendons, burning muscle, and carving bone. Merrill bellowed inside his head, over and over, even as blood welled and rolled down his neck and chest.

The blade remained in his neck for several more seconds before the warrior withdrew it and walked away. But the pain didn't diminish. It rolled through him continually, like waves breaking on the shore. There was no respite, no second of relief. Just incessant, implacable torment.

How long had they been cutting him? Had it been hours? Days? Katla. He needed to know where she was.

Varek might have gotten to her. If she was injured, Con could heal her. And if she saw what happened, she could tell them.

If she was alive.

Another bellow roared inside his head, this one with a different kind of anguish.

He gagged at the bitter wine smell that infused his nostrils as the entity pressed against his cheek. The pain in his body and heart was too much. He couldn't pretend to be unconscious anymore. It was time he learned his fate. He had faced many enemies in his life, but he had been on top then. The one with the power and might, dominance and influence.

This time was different. He suspected it might be the end of him.

There were a great many things Merrill wished he had done. Even more things he wished he had said—not just to Varek and Con but also to Katla. He had gotten used to always knowing that another day would be around the corner. Knowing he had time. It had blinded him to the fact that he had let opportunities with Katla pass him by.

But if he had known her kiss would shake him to his very foundation, he never would have held back. Not once had he looked for a mate. He had known he would never find one. Then, he had.

Now, she was gone.

And his time had run out.

The pressure on his face intensified as the entity shoved his head to the side. Merrill had never cowered to anyone before. He wasn't about to start now. He yanked his head away and opened his eyes to the night. The pressure vanished as the smell moved to the side. Merrill looked around the camp. There were eighteen red-haired warriors, all wearing sleeveless tunics with gold and silver armbands around their biceps.

They were in a small forest clearing. Twelve men and six women stared at him. It took everything in Merrill to get one foot and then the other under him to stand against his enemies. Being upright took some strain out of his arms, allowing some relief. But the longer he stood, the harder it was to stay on his feet. The smiles on the warriors' faces said they knew exactly what was happening to him. Merrill lifted his chin defiantly.

He might not be able to say, "*fuck you*," but his expression said it for him.

There was movement behind him an instant before a blade sliced across his back. Dots edged his vision from the pain. He tried to remain standing, but his knees buckled, yanking him down. Blood poured down his back. The warriors walked toward him, drawing swords, daggers, and spears. He held his head high as they began stabbing him.

"We need to get there faster," Katla said as she hurried up the mountain. She had kept a hurried pace, sometimes even running, but it didn't feel as if they were covering ground quickly enough.

"I can't fly us there," Derek said. "They'll see us, and it will likely do more harm than good."

Katla ducked beneath a low-hanging tree branch and kept moving despite the surge of anger that made her want to lash out at something. Anything. Or any*one*. "We don't know what they're doing to him."

"He's a Dragon King. They can't kill him," Kora said.

Katla glanced at her. "Unless Villette is helping them."

"There's a way we can get there quicker," Derek said.

"What way?" When he didn't answer, Katla looked over her shoulder to find that the couple had stopped. She halted and swung to face them fully. "What way?" she demanded, her voice louder and her fury bubbling to the surface.

Derek took a few steps toward her. "You."

"Me?" she asked in confusion. Then it dawned on her. "You think I can jump us there?"

Kora glanced at Derek and shrugged. "You've done it a few times now."

"Without knowing what I was doing. And I was angry those times." Katla balled her hands into fists as sparks began to dance around her.

Derek quirked a black brow. "You're angry now."

She was, but she was also scared and worried. "I don't know what to do. If, by chance, I can do it, I might take us miles away and make things worse."

"Or you could take us right to him," Kora said in a soft voice.

Katla looked away as she wrapped her arms around herself. Merrill had held her just hours before, kissed her. Derek and Kora were right. She had to try. Walking would take too much time, and Derek in dragon form would only cause mass hysteria. And the entity would be on the lookout for dragons.

"I don't know where Orgate is," Katla said.

Derek pointed to the top of the mountain. "Don't worry about the city. Take us there."

That seemed easy enough. Katla faced the peak and concentrated on it as she held out her hand. Kora took it. Katla imagined herself standing at the top, but they didn't move. She closed her eyes and tried again, but they *still* didn't move.

"You're thinking too hard," Derek said.

Katla yanked her hand away from Kora and started walking again. "I don't know what I'm doing."

"And you never will if you don't try," he snapped.

"Derek," Kora admonished.

"She can't try it a few times and then just give up," he argued.

Katla knew they were right. Too much was at stake. But she was terrified of making a mistake. She had jumped locations three times now, each without knowing where she was going or how to do it. And all three had been in situations where she'd been facing off against her enemies. How did she recreate those scenarios without said adversaries?

"I'm not giving up," Katla replied.

"Prove it."

She halted at Derek's taunt. Katla wished she had held on to Merrill tighter. She wished she understood the power Villette had given her. She wished...for so many things.

"You said it was anger," Derek continued. "Use that."

Katla released a deep breath. "I can't fail."

"Then don't."

Kora walked around to face her. "You're scared. I know that feeling. It was my companion for entirely too many years. You aren't in this alone. We're here with you."

"Without any idea of what we're walking into," she said.

Derek came around to stand beside Kora. "Merrill walked into several of those situations to help Kora and me. We're willingly doing the same."

Katla swallowed. "All right."

"Good. Forget the fear," Kora said. "Concentrate on the anger."

Derek nodded. "Tell me about the last time you teleported."

That was easy enough. "Merrill was unconscious after being attacked. The entity came at me."

"What did you feel?" Kora pressed.

Katla stiffened as she recalled the alarm, but beneath it was a cold, uncontrollable rage.

"Let it suffuse you," Kora told her.

Katla closed her eyes as her magic surged through her arms and into her palms.

"What did you think about right before you teleported?" Derek asked.

She frowned and shook her head. She hadn't been thinking about anything. But...that wasn't true. She wanted to get Merrill somewhere safe. Dragon land offered that.

"Stay with it," Kora urged.

Derek's voice sounded as if it came through a tunnel as he said, "Keep that feeling close and think about where you want to go."

Katla let the rage boil over and focused on the top of the mountain.

"Open your eyes," Derek urged.

Katla did and found Kora grinning. Derek dipped his chin before looking to the side. Katla followed his gaze and found them standing atop the mountain. "I did it," she murmured in shock.

Once more, oblivion spat him out and forced him into waiting misery. Merrill opened his eyes to see daylight. How long had he been unconscious this time? He was weak and growing weaker each time they cut him. The blades were made from the same metal as the chains and caused unending pain. The manacles weren't making things any better, but there was no getting out of them. Not without help.

For the first time in his life, Merrill felt utterly defenseless. Vulnerable like never before. And he fucking hated it. Magic had always been a part of him, like his blood or organs. Yet he couldn't feel—or even sense—it now. He knew it was there, but it didn't stop the panic each time he reached for it, and it didn't respond.

It was more than his lack of magic, though. He could no longer hear the dragons' roars. Merrill hadn't realized it, but no matter where he went on Zora or how far from dragon land, his enhanced hearing always picked up the dragons. They were silent now, just as they had been on Earth. And it terrified him. He strained to pick up a distant roar or the flap of a wing.

But just as with his magic, nothing but spine-chilling, unnatural silence reigned.

What did the entity and the warriors want from him? Why hadn't they killed him? Maybe they had tried. The not knowing was almost worse. There was only pain and more pain, heaped upon uncertainty and panic.

And rage.

The longer he was here, the more riled he became. Merrill's heart raced as he spiraled out of control, pushing against the boundaries he had tested at Stonemore. That alarmed him more than anything. He couldn't tip past the point of no return. He wouldn't come back from it.

He seized upon the image of Katla's face. He recalled the feeling of her soft body against his and the sweet taste of her kisses as he plundered her mouth. Her sensual curves. The wanton moans that had fallen from her lips. The longer he concentrated on her, the calmer he became until the anger simmered. Yet it still festered.

The entity came up behind him, shattering his concentration. Its rancor was unlike anything Merrill had encountered, and it was directed at him. As if Merrill had personally done something to it. Whatever *it* was.

The warriors in the camp stared as if they knew what was coming. It was all the warning Merrill got before the torture began. The warriors descended like wolves upon a kill, cutting, hacking, and stabbing everywhere. He heard the crack of a whip before several barbs sank into his back, only to be yanked away, taking flesh.

Merrill held back his shouts for as long as he could, and swore he heard a laugh before his eyes rolled back in his head.

TWENTY-EIGHT

Somehow, they made it to Orgate. Katla stared at the gated entrance through the copse of trees. The gate was smaller than Stonemore's but no less intimidating. A tall wall surrounded the city, Orgate warriors stationed atop it every fifteen feet or so. The gates were open, but two warriors stood on either side, ready to prevent anyone who didn't belong from entering.

The longer Katla stared, the more she worried about the hastily formed plan they'd devised during their ten-minute walk. She had gotten Derek, Kora, and her down the mountain and through most of the forest with only a few hiccups. It would likely take several more attempts before she was comfortable using her teleporting ability.

"What do you think?" Derek asked.

Katla twisted her lips. "I don't have a good feeling about this."

"I always gave Orgate a wide berth," Kora answered.

Derek's eyes narrowed on the entrance. "Varek told me how to get to the dungeon."

"You're assuming that's where they took Merrill," Katla replied.

Kora shrugged. "It seems logical since it's where they held Varek."

Katla stepped away from the branches. "Maybe."

"Orgate warriors would bring prisoners to their city," Kora contended.

It was a valid argument. Why, then, didn't it feel right?

Derek turned his head to peer at Katla. "What are you thinking?"

"I don't know. It just feels too easy," she said with a shrug. "The warriors know I saw them. They had to know I would tell Merrill, and he would then pass the information on to the Kings."

Kora twisted her lips. "Maybe they don't care that we know who they are."

"Possibly," Derek mumbled and returned his gaze to the city. "Or they want us to believe they were from Orgate so the Kings would attack."

Katla frowned as she considered his words. "You think some are purposefully putting a target on their city because they don't like the decisions of their council?"

"I've seen mortals do much worse because of a lot less," Derek replied.

Kora drew in a deep breath and released it. "We're not going to find out staying here. I'll go in and have a look around."

"Not alone, you won't," Derek stated.

Kora smiled in response. "You should be more worried about those within the walls."

"I know you can handle yourself," Derek said. "I'm more

concerned about the invisible enemy and being able to warn you if it's there."

Katla watched the mates and found herself thinking about those few moments she'd shared with Merrill. What might have happened had they not been attacked? That couldn't be the last time she saw him. She refused to let it be.

"We'll be back as quickly as we can," Kora told her.

The two slipped away and took the path toward the gates. The warriors eyed them, but they weren't stopped. Katla watched until Derek and Kora vanished within the gates and were swallowed by the city's occupants.

She grew more anxious as each minute ticked by. What if Merrill was being held in the dungeon? How would they get him out? Worse, what if he wasn't there? Where would they even begin looking for him?

And would they find him in time?

Katla tried to remain calm, but the emotion remained elusive. Of all the Kings to target, why Merrill? More importantly, why now?

The thought that he was lost to her, to the Kings, was so upsetting that Katla had to turn her mind away from him. She wrapped her arms around herself against the chill and wished she still had the coat Merrill had given her. But it, like everything else in the cottage, had been destroyed. She wanted it more because it reminded her of him than to battle the temperature.

Merrill was strong. Nothing would break him. He would be able to weather whatever they threw at him. He had remained standing despite being dealt blow after blow on his world—and hers. There was no way he would crumble now. She had seen his resilience and strength. His power as a Dragon King.

Katla lowered herself to the ground and rested against a tree trunk. She scanned the area often, looking for any signs of other entities while fighting impatience for Kora and Derek to return with news. The not knowing was challenging. At least if they knew something, they could begin to plan better. Until then, there was nothing to do but wait.

The sun crept from its zenith toward the west. She had been waiting for over two hours. It was time she went looking for Kora and Derek. Katla got to her feet and turned, only to come face-to-face with the last person she expected to see: Villette. Surprise swiftly pivoted to fury as Katla lashed out with her magic. But Villette was quicker, vanishing before Katla's magic reached her.

Katla turned in a slow circle. "Hiding? Not something I expected from you."

"I think it prudent until you calm down enough to listen," came a disembodied voice.

Sparks danced erratically around Katla, mirroring her emotions. Where were Derek and Kora? They could kill Villette right now if they only returned. "Why should I listen to anything you have to say?"

"Because Merrill isn't in Orgate."

Villette had fooled her once. Katla had learned her lesson well.

"You know I'm right," Villette said. "You said it yourself."

"You've been spying on us?" Katla demanded as she spun around, hoping to spot the Star Person.

There was a loud sigh before Villette said, "Obviously. If I wanted to take your life—or Derek's or Kora's—I could have. A dozen times over."

That drew Katla up short. She hadn't sensed Villette. She could be lying again. Obviously, Villette wanted something. But what? "Why are you here?"

"You know why."

"Say it," Katla ordered through clenched teeth.

Villette materialized in front of her, wearing a long-sleeved, pale blue gown with icy blue adornments over the bodice. The dress skimmed her figure before falling to the ground. "I know where Merrill is."

"Because you took him?" Katla's magic surged into her palms. She fought the urge to lash out at Villette. Instead, she kept her arms at her sides and curled her hands into fists. She needed answers.

Villette's blond hair was long and lustrous, freely flowing over one shoulder while the rest fell down her back. She kept the golden locks covering the right side of her face to conceal the burns there. Even with them, Villette was exquisite. Her vibrant blue eyes scrutinized Katla. "It doesn't matter how I answer. You won't believe me."

"You're right. I won't."

Villette glanced toward Orgate. "You're wasting time—time Merrill doesn't have."

"Then let him go."

"It isn't that easy."

A wave of anger enveloped Katla as she glared. "You're a Star Person. You can do whatever you want."

Villette didn't reply. She simply stared.

"Fine," Katla said with a shrug. "If you aren't holding Merrill, then free him."

"As I said—"

"It isn't that easy," Katla spoke over her, repeating her earlier words. She shot her enemy a scathing look. "I don't believe you."

Villette briefly lowered her gaze to the ground and blew out an exasperated breath before locking her blue eyes on Katla once more. "Come with me. I'll take you to him."

It was a trap. And an obvious one at that. Yet Katla wondered why Villette hadn't taken her as she had Merrill. Could it be that she couldn't? Or—and this was a big leap—did she speak the truth? It also begged the question...if Villette knew Katla wouldn't believe her, why attempt any of this?

The mere idea that Villette might be honest about something was as far-fetched as Katla being able to touch the moons. Nonetheless, something within her said to hear Villette out. Cautiously, of course. But there might be a kernel of truth somewhere in her words.

She waited for Villette to say more, but she didn't. Villette had obviously said everything she would. That meant it was time for Katla to make a decision. She turned her head toward Orgate. Still no sign of Kora or Derek. They might still be searching, or they could be trapped somewhere like Merrill.

Like she might be shortly.

She had little recourse. She could remain and wait for Derek and Kora. If Merrill was there, they would return for her so the three of them could get him out.

But what if he wasn't in the city as Villette had said? She'd had concerns about Merrill being brought to Orgate, but it had been a destination. If the Orgateans didn't have him, then she had no other location to search. Not even an idea of where to go.

Then there was the second option. She could set aside her unease and go with Villette, a deceiver and destroyer, where a trap may indeed be waiting. In which case, Villette would end Katla's life quickly. But why not now? Why not engage in battle before? Or take her unawares? Villette had the power of a goddess. As she'd said, she could've killed Katla multiple times over today alone. But she hadn't. Could Villette really be telling the truth? Did she know where Merrill was? Or was it an elaborate ruse to muddle Katla's thoughts so much she couldn't tell up from down?

But there was hope. The tiniest, flimsiest shred. But Katla grasped it with everything she had.

There was a third possibility, though. She could strike out on her own. But there were so many disadvantages to that, she didn't really consider it a genuine prospect. She knew little about the realm and even less about the people. Besides, she had very little control of her magic to teleport.

The overwhelming odds of failure rose, threatening to bury Katla. She had been here once before and let fear take her. She couldn't—*wouldn't*—do that again. She had to be smart and think it through. There was no getting around the fact that emotions played a part, no matter what she told herself.

She slid her gaze to Villette. "There has to be a reason you've not helped Merrill yourself."

"I can't do it alone."

The admission surprised her. She was about to ask Villette why she had chosen her but realized it didn't matter. Katla wanted to be there for Merrill. "All right," Katla said, hoping she didn't come to regret the decision.

Villette held out her hand. "Take it so I can bring you to him."

Katla hesitated.

"Every second you delay is a second he suffers."

It was all the push Katla needed. She slipped her hand into her enemy's. There was no way to alert Kora or Derek. Katla was going on instinct—and excess emotion.

Katla blinked and found herself surrounded by different trees. Villette released her and put her finger to her lips before creeping forward, picking her way through the underbrush. As she followed, Katla looked around to get some idea of where she was. They wove through the trees as silently and quickly as wraiths.

The first time Katla heard the agonized bellow, it sent shivers through her and stopped her in her tracks. She instinctively knew it was Merrill. She was frozen, forced to listen to his tormented shouts. It went on for what felt like an eternity. She covered her ears with her hands, but there was no shutting out the guttural, searing screams. It was more than flesh and blood could bear.

How long had he been enduring it? She was here now. She could help. Katla dropped her arms and started forward to help Merrill, but Villette caught her by the arm. Katla swung around to face Villette and saw the Star Person's face was as pale as hers felt.

"Now, do you understand?" Villette whispered.

Katla swallowed the bile in her throat when Merrill finally went silent. It was then that she noticed the eeriness of the place. It was as if the forest itself feared to breathe. There were no animals. Apparently, they wanted no part of the area, and she couldn't blame them. She didn't want to be here either, but she would bear whatever she must to get to Merrill.

The crack of a stick echoed in the silence. Katla and Villette both looked to the right. Katla spotted the wide, gold armband through the foliage before she saw the warrior. She tried to shift behind a tree, but Villette's nails dug into her arm as she held her.

So, it *had* been a trap. Katla glared at Villette as she thought of a thousand different ways to end her enemy's life. To Katla's shock, the warrior walked past without noticing them. Villette released her when he was out of sight. Katla frowned, trying to figure out what was going on.

"I made us invisible to him," Villette whispered before moving forward at a slower pace.

Katla was unnerved at the rapid change of her emotions. There was no time to dwell on it, though, as she followed Villette. It wasn't as if she could turn back now. Especially not after hearing Merrill. She didn't want to see him being tortured, but there was no turning away. Katla would have to face it all.

Villette stopped next to a queen root tree, its spiraled trunk so wide three men wouldn't be able to link their hands around it. Katla flattened her palms against the rough bark and pressed her front against the trunk. Then she leaned to the side and peered around it. She squinted through the vegetation to the glade beyond to find a fire with men and women milling about. They were staring at something. No, some*one*. Katla waited for the warriors to move so she could get a better look. They finally parted, giving her the first sighting of Merrill from the side. The canopy above them was so dense only meager rays of sunlight filtered through it. But in the clearing, sunshine landed on Merrill like a spotlight as he hung from his arms by two vertical poles stuck in the ground.

She saw the bulky chains and the thick cuffs bolted around his wrists, but it was the dark splotches covering the ground that drew her gaze. Katla's heart hammered wildly when she saw how much of Merrill's blood had been spilled. If it were anyone else hanging there, they would already be dead.

Katla drew in a steadying breath, but nothing could prepare her for what she saw next. Tears stung her eyes, and her throat clogged with outrage and horror. Merrill's clothes hung on his body by mere threads, the rest cut and torn. Blood ran down his arms, face, neck, chest, and legs. There were so many lacerations and stab wounds on just the side of his body she saw she knew she wouldn't be able to count them all.

Finally, she lifted her gaze to his face. His head hung forward, his hair obscuring his features. Her eyes tracked down his neck to his shoulder and then up his arm to the shackles. His fingers were slack, and the entire weight of his body was on his arms as he hung, suspended with his knees just a few inches off the ground.

Katla straightened and pressed her forehead to the bark. She might have found him, but he was in rough shape. She needed to get the chains off so he could heal. But that wouldn't be easy with the entity.

She turned her head to meet Villette's gaze. Now, she understood why the Star Person had sought her out.

TWENTY-NINE

Images rolled through Merrill's mind like a movie. Most, he didn't recognize. He knew what his captors were doing. They were trying to make him go mad. Just as two of the Kings had done after being tortured during the Fae Wars.

And there was nothing he could do to stop it.

He tried. For a time, he held on to… He couldn't remember her name anymore. He could barely recall his. How much longer before that, too, was gone? It wasn't as if he would remember any of this.

Why had he even wandered around this cursed realm? What had taken him from the others? It must have been important, but he no longer recalled the reason. With every slice of skin and every drop of blood spilled, he was becoming something else. He had hidden it away, feared it. But even that was no more. He welcomed what he was becoming because the torture would be over.

As much as he sought the blessed oblivion, it no longer cradled him as it once had. Previously, it had taken him to that void where he felt nothing, and his mind was still. Now, it only brought him halfway, leaving him aware of the blood welling from his lacerations before skating down his skin to drip into the earth and the stinging of his flesh from being sliced and gored.

A quick, feminine inhale pierced through his musings. The sound was out of place in the camp. The women warriors would never make such a dainty, shocked sound. For just a moment, a face began to take shape in his mind. Thick, wavy, midnight locks that were cool to the touch. Stormy gray eyes.

He recognized her, but just as her visage came into focus, it faded like smoke, leaving him to drift half-conscious on the agony of his injuries. There wasn't much of him left. The next time they tortured him might be his last. He yearned for the end now, just as he had once longed for peace. Anything to stop the pain.

A cool blade pressed against the base of his neck above his spine. He waited for a taunt or two, but his captors never spoke. They let their weapons speak for them.

And they had a lot to say.

Merrill winced as the edge of the dagger pierced his skin, sinking all the way to the bone. There was a prick of pain, then wetness as warm blood oozed from the wound. Then came the flare of heat, followed by the stinging and burning. His flesh and muscles sizzled, and his body tensed, but there was no getting away from the agony. He tried to hold back the scream, but it burst from him, echoing around the forest as the blade carved a line down the middle of his spine.

THIRTY

Katla couldn't listen to Merrill's pain any longer. She had to do something. If Villette wouldn't, she would. Katla spun from around the tree but only got two steps before she found herself standing perilously close to the edge of a cliff. She stared down the drop and jerked back before she fell. Then she slowly turned her head to Villette.

"What are you doing?" Katla demanded as she backed away from the edge. "Take us back. Merrill needs us."

"Yes, he does. And quickly."

What little remained of Katla's patience was quickly dissolving. "Then what are we waiting for?"

"There are…things…you need to know."

"Then tell me," she bit out.

Villette stood composed, her features even, but there was a slight tremor in her voice when she began speaking. "I'm surprised Merrill has held out this long. They're trying to tip him into madness."

His screams reverberated in Katla's head, an echo that she feared would ring for an eternity. The utter anguish, the unending misery...

"It used to happen when we controlled the dragons."

Katla held up her hand. "We don't have time for a backstory."

"You've never seen the destruction a dragon can do when riled. You've never seen one filled with fury and the need to decimate everything around them until everything is on fire," Villette stated loudly.

A shiver of apprehension slid like an icy finger down Katla's back.

Villette drew in a breath. "Dragons live for thousands of years, but some of my kind had favorites and wished to prolong those dragons' lives. Various attempts were made, but each ended with the dragons going mad. Seven worlds were ravaged and turned to dust before the efforts were finally halted. I witnessed the destructive power of a dragon with a single mission: death. Merrill is nearly to that point. When he reaches it, they'll release him."

Nausea rolled through Katla's stomach. "Why would they do that? Merrill will kill them, as well."

"The entity is doing this."

"Why?"

"I don't know."

That wasn't what Katla wanted to hear. "How many of them are there?"

Villette's blond brows snapped together. "There's just the one."

Katla had been sure there were others.

"It's new to Zora," Villette continued. "I don't know where it came from or how it got here, but its hatred is all-encompassing. Don't let it touch you."

"Too late," Katla murmured as she rubbed her arm where it had struck her.

"There's more," Villette said, her eyes darting away for a heartbeat. "Miena found the ore. She's the one who had it tested on anything magical. However, I was the one who showed the Orgateans how to mine it, shape it, and use it."

Katla shouldn't be surprised to learn that both Miena and Villette had interfered in such a way. "That crime pales in comparison to others."

"You aren't listening," Villette said, her voice clipped with urgency. "It affects *everyone* with magic."

"And by everyone, you mean...?"

She drew in a breath and nodded. "Even me."

That meant Katla would also be affected. She put a hand to her stomach. The situation became more dire by the second. "We should be fine as long as we aren't chained."

"I wish that were the case."

"You mean we can't even touch it?"

Villette swallowed and subtlely shook her head. "The weapons the warriors use are also made of the metal. You hear what it's doing to Merrill. It'll do the same to us."

"Why not just kill the warriors? You can do that without even getting close to them. It might not free Merrill, but it would buy him and us some time."

"I already did. This is the second round of them. The entity brought them in within moments of my attack."

Katla shoved her hands into her hair to hold her head. Her mind was racing, every idea met by a thick wall. She dropped her hands and looked at Villette. "How is it doing that?"

"I wish I knew," Villette ground out.

"Someone has to get to Merrill before it's too late."

"You'll never make it. I brought us as close as possible. They buried strips of ore in the ground at the edges of the clearing to keep us out."

"Then we'll strike from a distance."

Villette shook her head. "And chance a confrontation with the entity?"

"Why did you bring me here, then?" Katla yelled. "Did you want to punish me further? Is that what this is? Showing me Merrill, but telling me we can't help him?"

"I brought you because I want to help."

"Then help!" Katla spun around and scanned the horizon. Which direction was Merrill in? She couldn't hear him anymore and didn't know whether to be glad about that or worried. "I can't sit here and do nothing. I don't care if I end up pitted against an army of Orgate warriors. I don't care if the entity comes for me. I'm not leaving Merrill to this fate."

"And if you can't save him?"

Katla closed her eyes. "I will end his misery." She opened her eyes and squared her shoulders before facing Villette. "I have an idea, but we'll need Derek and Kora."

"They won't work with me."

"This isn't about you. This is about Merrill."

Villette dipped her head. In the next moment, Katla stood in the trees outside Orgate. Derek and Kora startled at the sight of her. Villette had chosen not to reveal herself, which was probably a smart move.

"Where have you been?" Kora asked worriedly.

Derek's pale olive eyes scanned the trees as if he somehow knew Villette was out there.

"I found Merrill," Katla said. "There's a lot to take in, and time is of the essence, so I need you to listen."

She broke everything down as quickly as she could. The couple exchanged looks when Katla told them about Villette, but when they learned about Merrill and what the entity intended, they understood why Katla had gone with their enemy.

"What's the plan?" Derek asked.

Katla licked her lips. "The entity has magic, yet it isn't harmed by the metal in the ground."

"Because it flies," Kora said.

Katla nodded and looked at Derek. "Exactly. You can fly in and get Merrill."

"They'll see me long before I reach them," Derek said.

Katla knew Villette was there listening, but she wasn't sure how either party would react to this next part. "Not if you're invisible."

"You can do that?" Kora asked.

Derek shook his head. "She means Villette."

"We would all be passengers," Katla hurried to add. "Getting us in is just the first part. Kora, we'll use your fire to melt the chains, thereby freeing Merrill. Then we get out of there."

A tense few seconds passed before Derek bowed his head in agreement. Kora followed suit.

Only then did Villette appear in front of them. She looked at Derek and then Kora before her gaze came to rest on Katla. "It might work. The minute we drop from Derek's back, though, he'll become visible. I can keep us invisible, but they'll know we're there."

"It might be better if you stayed with Derek," Katla said. "That way, you can watch Kora and me and intercept anything."

Derek grunted. "I'd rather Villette stay with you two. You'll be able to move around easier if the warriors can't see you."

"That's assuming the entity won't be able to see us," Kora added.

Villette said, "It can't. At least I'm pretty sure it won't be able to. We have that small advantage."

"Will Kora's hellhound fire be visible? Will she even be able to use it?" Katla asked.

Villette lifted one shoulder in a shrug. "I don't know."

"We don't have a choice." Kora looked at each of them. "We have to do this for Merrill."

Katla blew out a breath. "We need to get moving before it's too late."

"Take to the skies and head north. I'll get Kora and Katla to you," Villette told Derek.

He ignored Villette. "It wouldn't be wise to shift so near Orgate."

"He's right," Kora said.

Katla looked at Villette. The Star Person rolled her eyes before teleporting them to the spot she had brought Katla to earlier.

Derek lightly touched Kora's face before diving off the cliff. Katla watched as he shifted in midair and spread his wings. He soared high into the afternoon sky after catching a current. Kora smiled as she watched him dip a wing and swing around toward them. For the second time in her life, Katla was about to get on the back of a dragon.

To have hated a species for so long, only to find them allies, wasn't as disconcerting as she'd figured it would be. All because of Merrill. He had shown her companionship but also friendship. He had bared his soul and given her the courage to do the same. It was only because of him that she was here at all. She would be on another path altogether if for Merrill.

The fact that the very person they had banded together against was now helping her free him was unsettling. She was discovering that alliances changed as quickly as the weather. The real question was whether Villette was being completely honest about everything. There had to be a reason she was risking so much for Merrill, especially when she had gone to such lengths to kill before.

Katla looked at Villette and found her staring at her. Derek soared over them. Villette grabbed her arm and then Kora's. In the next blink, the three of them stood on Derek's back, the wind whipping past them so fast it stole her breath. Katla gingerly lowered herself to sit. Kora sat at the base of Derek's neck while Villette remained standing between them.

To Katla's surprise, the Star Person had her eyes closed and a smile on her face, almost as if she were enjoying the ride. Katla grimaced at the thought and locked her gaze on the horizon. She didn't know how long the flight would take. Derek's enhanced vision and hearing would likely find Merrill before Katla knew they were upon him.

She remembered Merrill's gentle touch and soft words. That was the man she knew. He was already distraught over the actions that had led to him remaining at Stonemore. He wouldn't want to fall into madness now. Merrill had been looking for redemption. It wasn't right that he had ended up in the enemy's hands.

Then there were the Kings. The way they had come as a group to the valley to look for him was all the proof Katla needed that they loved him. If he went insane and their group couldn't stop him, the Kings would. His brethren would be forced to take out one of their own. It was its own kind of torture. Exactly like something Villette would think of.

Yet there was no denying she was equally unnerved about the entity and Merrill going mad. Everything Katla had learned about Villette was that she always had an ulterior motive for every action and decision. But no matter how hard Katla tried, she couldn't figure out what it was. And there was no time to speak to Derek or Kora about it.

That benefited Villette, but Katla didn't care. Everything now was about getting to Merrill before it was too late. They'd deal with whatever else happened after.

Katla wondered if Derek was informing the Kings of their plan. They had a right to know, but they might also come to help. While they could use the numbers, it could also make things difficult with the humans seeing dragons outside their borders again. The realm teetered on the brink of conflict already. It would only take the slightest push to ignite a war.

One Villette had spent centuries instigating.

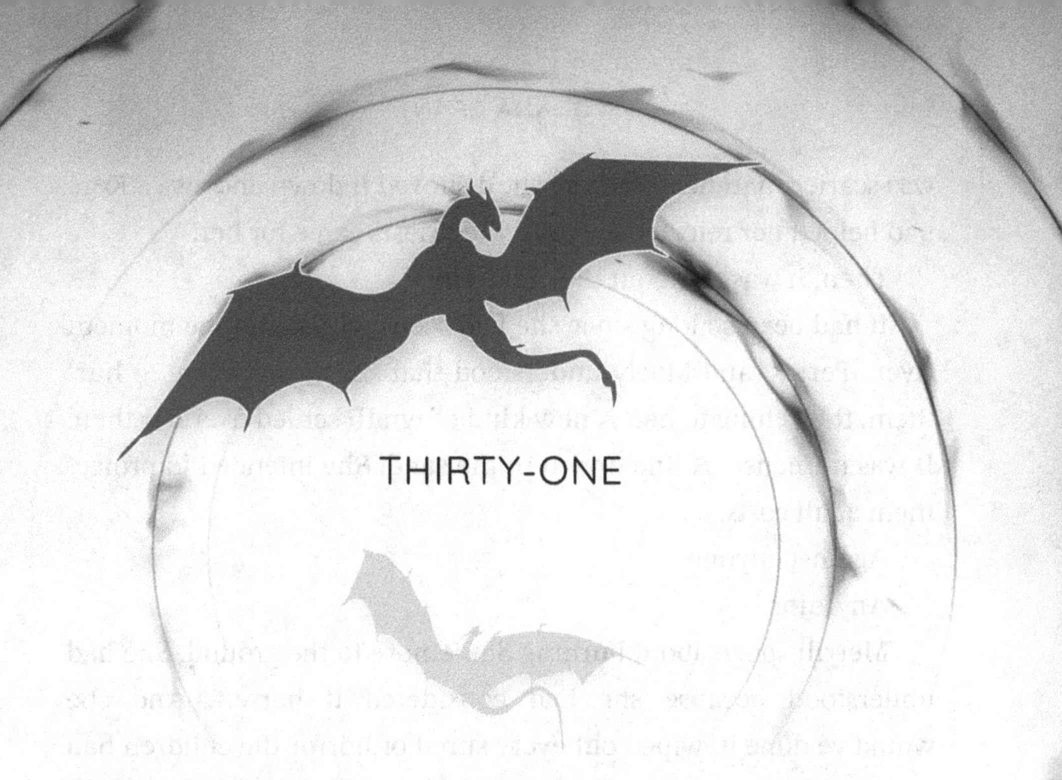

THIRTY-ONE

Katla had believed all her tears had dried up years ago, but it was an illusion. Much like most of her life these past fifteen hundred years. The truth had stripped away the deception and cleared her head, leaving her reeling.

Maybe she had gone to Stonemore on purpose after her clash with Villette. She might have subconsciously sent herself there to finish what she'd begun. All that did was turn her rage from the dragons to Villette. She hadn't learned anything in her many years of isolation. Anger was safe, easy. She was intimately familiar with it.

And she didn't have to delve deeper or peer inside her soul to see what she had become. What she had willingly and eagerly taken hold of and made hers.

Yet, for all her uncontrollable indignation, she had been frightened and panicked. The sight of Stonemore and all the people was a shock to her system that sent her reeling. The fear grew, and it was scarier than her anger, so she'd shoved it down and away. Kora had helped her refocus, but then the priests came for her.

Then, it was all about the children.

It had been so long since she had seen a child, and the moment Aven, Perick, and Maely understood that she wasn't there to hurt them, they clung to her. A new kind of wrath settled over her then. It was immense. A line drawn in the sand. She intended to protect them at all costs.

Against anyone.

Anything.

Merrill spoke about burning Stonemore to the ground. She had understood because she had considered it herself. And she would've done it, wiped out every shred of horror the children had endured and she had experienced within the city. Except her magic took her away again. But not far.

If she had gone farther, she wouldn't have returned to Stonemore and encountered Merrill. She wouldn't have watched him level the priests with that single blast of magic. He wouldn't have followed her, and she never would have known his friendship. Or his passion. So many things had to happen for them to meet. She'd once believed that everything happened by chance. Now, she wasn't sure. Could it all be by design? Had someone, somewhere in the cosmos, decreed that she and Merrill should meet? She liked to think so.

Yet if that was the case, it also meant his torture was part of the plan. And she couldn't abide by that.

The sound of his yell cut through her mind, and her eyes filled with tears. She squeezed them shut, but a tear leaked out. The wind caught it and dragged it across her temple and into her hair.

Another followed. Her throat tightened, and she held back her incensed, enraged scream, swallowing it.

There would be time later to give in to the wild emotions running amok within her. But not now. Merrill needed her. And she required her magic in every capacity she had—the parts she knew and those she hadn't explored before.

Katla opened her eyes. The wind dried the streaks from her cheeks. She glanced up to find Villette watching her. Katla quirked a brow. Villette looked away without a word, but she had seen the tears. Katla should be worried about her nemesis seeing such a weakness in her, but she didn't care.

A deep rumble vibrated through Derek, the sound holding a note of fury and indignation. Katla knew he had found Merrill. She placed her hands on the silver-tipped black scales and leaned to the side to peer around Villette and Kora. She saw nothing but trees. There were no screams of agony, at least none she could hear over the howling wind as it wailed past her.

Katla's heart battered her ribs, thumping hard and quick. Ice replaced blood in her veins as dread filled her. She wiped her clammy palms on her thighs. She looked down and spotted the clearing as they flew over it. Then she saw Merrill. His back was arched, head thrown back, and mouth open on a bellow she couldn't hear. But she felt it.

She trembled with fear. She needed her magic and wouldn't be able to use it. They were outnumbered and possibly outmatched, but it didn't matter. She would face a horde of entities for Merrill.

"Now," Villette urged Derek.

He quickly swung around. Katla had to lean to the opposite side to keep from sliding off. The moment he righted himself, she and Kora got to their feet. She eyed the warriors milling about.

"Ready?" Villette asked.

Katla locked her eyes on Merrill and the woman repeatedly stabbing him in the chest. Magic filled her palms, sparks rising around her. It exploded from her, shooting to the warrior. She grinned when the female crumpled. "Ready."

Then they were on the ground. Katla called to her magic, but the metal in the ground blocked it, just as they had feared. No shouts of warning filled the air, just the pounding of footsteps rushing up behind her. Katla ran to the woman she had just killed and grabbed her dagger as she spun to face her attackers.

She chanced a glance at Merrill. He was awake, the veins in his arms and neck bulging. She shouted his name, but there wasn't time for more as she faced two warriors. Without her magic, Katla could only bob and weave, ducking and rolling while keeping clear of their blades.

The pain became an ally, a companion. All the commotion in his head began to dim, bit by bit. He was falling into an abyss as black as pitch, and he welcomed it. Saluted it.

Embraced it.

Others moved around him. He didn't pay attention to their faces. None of them mattered. He no longer worried. Or cared. There was only him.

And the reckoning he would bring.

He got his feet under him, but his arms were still chained. He glared at the metal holding him. A woman caught his attention. Her black hair swung out around her like an inky curtain as she turned. Their eyes met. She called out something, but he couldn't hear her over the ringing in his head. One of the redheaded men who'd been torturing him knocked her to the ground.

Rage erupted, exploded. He furiously yanked the chains as the black-haired woman rolled out of the way of a sword aimed at her head. A large shadow fell over the clearing, followed by a thunderous roar. It was a familiar sound. One he recognized. He looked up to see the dragon. Chaos reigned in the clearing. He wanted—no, he *needed*—to join in.

Suddenly, his chains unlocked. His arms dropped to his sides. He rubbed his wrists, shook off the lethargy of his many wounds, and reached out to the first person who came near. His fingers wrapped around the man's neck. The warrior clawed at his hand. Merrill stared into brown eyes and squeezed until the bones broke, and the man went limp.

He was the first of many humans who would lose their life.

He tried to shift but he was still too weak. But not too weak to face the mortals.

Katla sank the blade into the warrior's side as they fell. He landed on top of her, knocking the breath from her lungs. She rolled him off. Another came at her, sword raised as she climbed to her feet. Large hands grabbed his head from behind and twisted, breaking his neck. She stared in shock as Merrill let the warrior drop. Their eyes met.

She dragged in a deep breath to fill her aching lungs and grabbed a fallen sword. She smiled, but Merrill didn't respond. He stepped toward her. They saw the woman at the same time. Merrill made quick work of her without breaking a sweat.

"Derek!" Kora shouted, his roar suddenly silenced.

Katla looked up in time to see Derek's dragon body tumbling from the sky. They had all known the entity would go after Derek first. Katla turned in time to see a woman swinging a sword at her. She leaned back, watching the blade as it passed so close it nearly touched her nose.

Katla straightened and rammed her shoulder into the warrior. The impact knocked the sword from the female's hand. Katla used the momentum to take them to the ground, but the female was stronger and quickly got the upper hand. Katla found herself on her back, using both hands to block the dagger now pointed at her throat.

She had lost the sword she had been using during the fall, but unlike her, the warrior had another weapon. Katla was using all her strength. Sweat broke out on her forehead. The female grinned as she leaned forward, knowing Katla's arms were about to give out. Suddenly, the warrior's head separated from her body. Blood sprayed Katla as the woman went limp. She tossed the body aside and surged to her feet.

Katla scanned the area for Merrill. She counted seven remaining Orgate warriors. It was easy to find Merrill because he was going after them. His shirt fell off, giving her a view of his back and the dragon drawn there.

"Merrill!"

No matter how many times Katla shouted his name, he didn't respond. She ran after him, catching up as he killed two more men. Villette dispatched hers as well as the one coming up behind Kora. Soon after, Kora ended the life of her opponent. They watched as Merrill effortlessly killed the final two warriors with a violence that shook her. Leaving the three of them with him.

"We're too late. There's no saving him now," Villette whispered.

Merrill's gaze locked on Kora, who was the closest to him. There was murder on his face when he stalked toward her. Katla moved to block his path. A shiver of terror went through her the moment his dark blue eyes focused on her. There was nothing of the Merrill she knew staring back at her. They had arrived too late. But she wasn't ready to give up.

"Merrill, you know me," she told him calmly.

He prowled closer, his head tilting to the side like a predator sizing up its victim. She retreated with every step he advanced. Everything in her told her to run, but she knew that was the worst thing she could do. If only she could get through to him. Maybe she could help him find his way back if he heard her.

"It's over," she told him. "Those holding you are dead. You can return to the other dragons."

He halted as a frown furrowed his brow. Dark blue eyes lifted to the sky.

"Derek is hurt. He needs us. We need to help him," Katla said.

Merrill's eyes lowered to her once more.

"Varek will be here soon." It was a lie. She had no idea where Varek was, but she hoped the name would trigger something in Merrill's memories.

He began advancing on her again—the opposite of what she wanted.

Katla had no idea where Villette or Kora were, but she didn't dare look away from Merrill. He was a predator now, one intending to take her life. She backed up another step. Her heel caught on something, and she went down. In an instant, Merrill was over her, his hands on either side of her head.

"Remember me," she whispered, reaching with shaking hands to touch his face.

The wildness she saw in his eyes made her heart catch. There was no warmth, no kindness. Just callous indifference.

"Merrill, I know you're still in there. Please, hear me."

It seemed her words got through. One moment, he was there with her, his eyes clear. Then, something slammed into him from the side, knocking him away. Katla rolled over and watched Derek tangle with Merrill. It was a savage, frenzied clash, unlike anything she had ever witnessed before. The violence, the brutality. The carnage.

She scrambled out of the way when their fighting brought them toward her. Katla caught a glimpse of Merrill's face. She didn't recognize him. It wasn't the blood or the bruises, it was as if Merrill's very essence was gone, replaced by something else.

"We need to go. Now. Before he sees us again," Villette said from behind her.

Katla knew she was right. Derek was giving them time to leave. He could hold his own against Merrill, unlike the rest of them. Yet she couldn't look away from the brawl. She still sought some sign that Merrill was still in there.

He grabbed Derek's arm and flipped him. She heard the loud pop of a bone breaking. Merrill shoved Derek away and fled without looking at her. A second later, they heard the crack of wood splintering before Merrill shifted and launched into the air.

Katla watched him fly, his orange scales bright against the afternoon sky. She lowered her eyes as Derek held his arm awkwardly and walked out of the clearing to heal with Kora by his side. Katla turned her head to Villette. The rest of them were dirty, their clothes torn, but Villette looked as pristine as ever.

"I lost the entity after it attacked Derek," Villette said.

Muscles Katla had never used before were tight and achy. She hid her wince when she tried to move. "It could still be around."

"If it is, it's hiding. Though we need to shift our concern to Merrill."

"Can you follow him?"

Villette glanced in the direction he had flown. "Doubtful."

"She won't." Derek's pale olive eyes were narrowed in anger and directed at Villette. "Tell us why."

Katla sensed that something had changed. She looked between the three, trying to figure out what was happening.

"Could it be you don't want to?" Kora shifted to the side, though she stayed out of the clearing.

Unease curdled Katla's stomach. There was no mistaking the undercurrent. What did Kora and Derek know that she didn't? Katla slowly stepped back to ease out of the clearing.

Villette ignored the allegations. Instead, she locked eyes with Derek. "How's the shoulder healing? Do you have any idea how hard it is to break that particular bone? Yet Merrill did it with ease. He's stronger and faster than before."

"Then help us stop him." Katla stepped into the tree line. She instantly felt her magic again. She eyed the edge of the clearing while wondering why Villette hadn't exited it like the rest of them.

"Was this your plan?" Derek demanded when Villette didn't answer. "Did you set all of this up?"

"You won't believe anything I say, so I'm not going to bother trying," Villette replied.

Kora shook her head. "I saw the fear on your face when the entity showed and went after Derek. I don't think you set this up. But you aren't telling us everything."

Villette couldn't teleport out of the clearing. Katla recalled the lengths Villette had gone to get her there. Now that Merrill was gone, Villette seemed reluctant to offer any more assistance.

Katla took a good look at Villette. Kora was right. She was scared. But perhaps Katla was wrong about *who* Villette was afraid of. She had pressed upon Katla the need to get to Merrill before he went insane. Villette had been eager to fight—right up until Merrill got loose.

Katla knew she hadn't freed Merrill. She never even got close because of the warriors. Kora and Villette hadn't been near him either. Derek had been in the air. So, who had released him? Her stomach roiled as the truth dawned on her.

"It's Merrill." Three pairs of eyes swung to Katla. She met Villette's blue eyes. "He's the one you're afraid of."

Villette tensed, the only indication that Katla's words had hit their mark.

"And there's only one reason for that. He can kill you," Katla stated.

Kora's brow furrowed with confusion. "Dragons can't kill Star People."

Katla recalled Villette speaking about how the maddened dragons had annihilated worlds. What else had they destroyed? "Not usually. Not unless they go mad." Magic pooled in Katla's hands as sparks danced in the air. Villette glared at her, blue eyes sparking with anger. "Isn't that right? You discovered that when you prolonged the dragons' lives. They went insane and slaughtered worlds. But you left out the part where they killed your kind, too."

Villette raised her brows and shrugged demurely. "Seems you

know everything. Which means you also know I won't go near Merrill."

"You'll leave it to the Kings, I suppose," Derek bit out.

Katla wasn't done with her questions. "What about the entity?"

"What about it?" Villette asked.

"Where is it?"

Villette briefly lifted her gaze to the sky. "If it was here, it would've come after us."

If it was here. Katla swung her head in the direction Merrill had flown. "The entity had tracked Merrill. It'd tortured him until he went mad. And it had released him, knowing he would kill." Katla swallowed the bile rising in her throat and met Villette's steady gaze.

Villette released a breath. "What does Merrill hate more than anything?"

"Humans," Katla whispered.

And they were everywhere on Zora.

"We lost," Villette stated. "We didn't get to him in time. The best thing for all of us to do now is leave while we still can."

Kora quirked a brow. "And leave everyone else to their fate?"

"Once Merrill finishes here, he'll go to Earth," Villette replied.

Katla wouldn't let it come to that. "You stopped the others who lost their minds. Do it again."

"Get your fucking siblings," Derek ordered furiously.

Villette shook her head. "Miena stopped them before."

Katla's knees went wobbly. She had to grab a nearby tree to keep herself on her feet. This couldn't be happening. There had to be something the Star People hadn't thought of. Merrill's wild eyes flashed in Katla's mind, and she fought the urge to give in to the tears.

Kora erupted in flames, her gaze leveled at Villette. "Then you've served your purpose. It's time to face justice."

They had Villette. All Katla had to do was call to Rhi. Perhaps Derek had already sent word to the Kings. They could end Villette right now. But at what cost to Merrill and any humans he encountered? Katla had gotten through to him. She was sure of it. And if she did it once, she could do it again.

Merrill or Villette. Katla couldn't be in two places at once. The longer she waited, the farther away Merrill got. Villette was a scourge upon worlds. She corrupted and killed, all for her own gain. She was the foulest of them all. The fact that Villette could move about the universe easily meant they should take the opportunity. It might not come again.

Then there was Merrill. He hadn't asked for any of this. He had to be stopped before he hurt innocents. She had set out on this journey seeking redemption. All this time, she thought she might get it by killing Villette. Maybe her path had been to pull Merrill back from madness all along—or, at the very least, stop him.

The memory of their kiss filled her mind. And it was all she needed to make her decision.

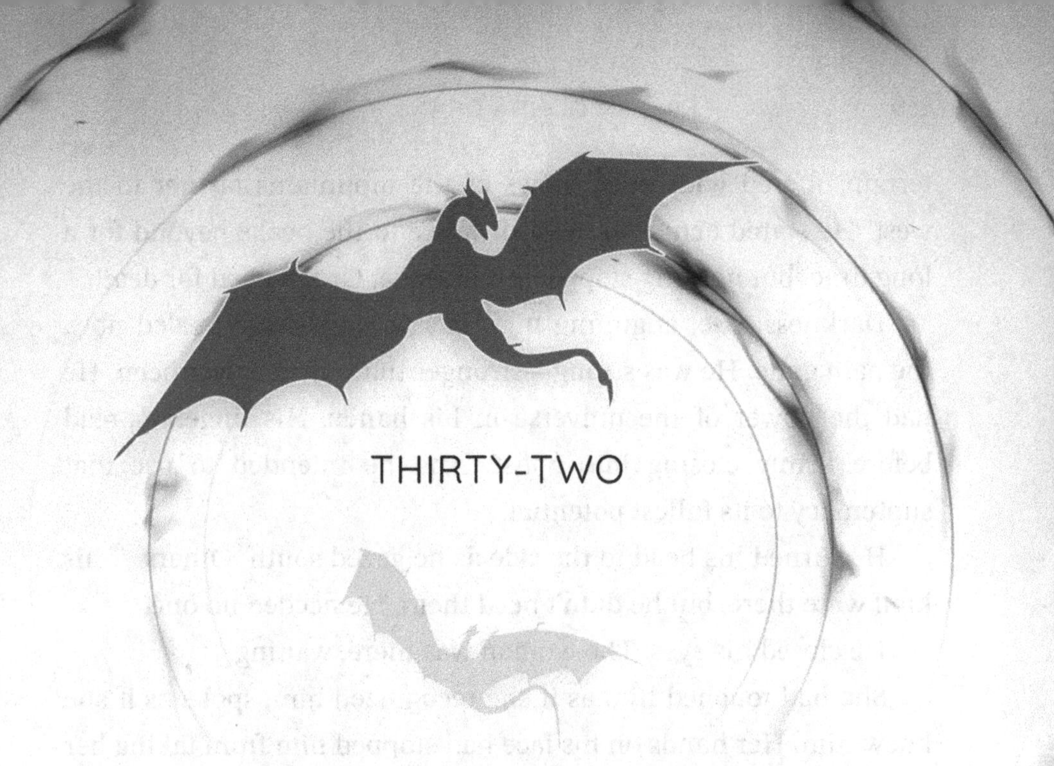

THIRTY-TWO

Violence still ravaged him, demanding to be released. It churned sadistically, mercilessly as it slid through his veins like slivers of glass. Relief lay in obliterating humans. They had to pay for their crimes.

And there were so many.

A woman's face filled his mind, her stormy gray eyes beseeching, her touch gentle. He faltered as he flew and dropped like a stone. He hurriedly flapped his wings to remain in the air but couldn't dislodge her image.

Druid.

He didn't know where the thought came from, but he knew the woman, whoever she was, was a Druid. How did he know what a Druid was, though? He was falling again. This time, he tucked his wings and dove. As the ground rose up, he shifted and dropped the last twenty feet to land, knees bent.

Light blinded him. He raised his hand to shield his eyes from the intense sunset. He blinked against the brightness. The hilly terrain offered wide-open views of the mountains farther to the west. He stared across the vast distance to the peaks beyond for a long time, but nothing stopped his outrage. Or the need for death.

Darkness rose, engulfing him. His wounds were healed now, the pain gone. He was strong—stronger than he had ever been. He had the power of the universe in his hands. His fingers spread before firmly closing into a fist. And he intended to use that supremacy to its fullest potential.

He turned his head to the side as he gazed south. Others of his kind were there, but he didn't need them. He needed no one.

He closed his eyes. The woman was there, waiting.

She had touched him as if she recognized him, spoke as if she knew him. Her hands on his face had stopped him from taking her life. The frenzy to kill had eased, much like now. But it wouldn't last. The need to mete out justice was too strong to ignore. Even now, he felt it building.

"Katla," he whispered, his voice rough and unused.

Her name came to him out of the blue, pulled from his chaotic mind. Memories bombarded him, but they vanished as quickly as they formed. The rage came like a great tidal wave, enveloping him. Engulfing him. He was lost to the storm once more.

The darkness within him growled with pleasure. He shifted and released a roar before taking to the skies.

THIRTY-THREE

Katla's first jump was easy, but it took her four attempts to teleport the second time. Each second wasted added to her anxiety, which made everything more difficult. It was a cycle she had to break quickly. She only managed to cross a short distance on her second attempt. She was about to try a third time when Kora burst through the trees, Derek right behind her.

"Wait," Kora said.

"What are you doing? You had Villette," Katla demanded when they stopped beside her.

Derek raked a hand through his black hair, shoving the thick locks away from his face. "Helping Merrill."

"What about Villette?"

Kora braced her hand on a tree trunk as she drew in long breaths. "We'll find her again. Merrill needs us. And it's like I told you. We owe him."

Katla sighed in relief. "I'm happy to see you both."

"Next time, tell us your plan," Kora said as she straightened.

Derek caught her eye. "I've alerted Con about Merrill."

It was the right thing to do, but that didn't mean Katla was happy about it. Merrill shouldn't have to face his brethren, and they shouldn't have to...remove him if it came down to it.

"There must be some way to reverse what they did to him," Kora said.

A roar danced upon the breeze, reverberating over the land. All of them knew it was Merrill. Katla grabbed the couple and tried to teleport again, but her ability failed her once more.

"If there was a way to reverse it, the Star People would've found it," Derek said.

Kora shook her head. "I don't believe that."

Katla shut out their words and concentrated. Merrill was in trouble. She needed to be there for him. Had to stop him from doing something that would do irreparable harm to his soul. When her magic let her down again, she threw back her head and yelled in frustration. The release of anxiety and fear helped, but only for a moment.

"You've teleported before. You can do it again," Kora said.

Katla shook her head. "I must get to him now. I can't wait."

"Then I'll get us there," Derek said.

Villette wasn't there to cloak them. They would be visible to anyone who looked up. It would incite more fear and hatred, but they had no choice. She couldn't take more time teleporting small distances.

Derek shifted. Within moments, she and Kora were situated on his back. Then he was in the air. She had really believed she could get to Merrill before he tipped into madness. She could blame

Villette for waiting too long to come to her or herself for not believing Villette sooner, but it didn't change the outcome. A new kind of apprehension gripped her. For the Dragon Kings. For the humans.

For Merrill.

It didn't matter whose plan this was. Katla didn't care who set things in motion. All she wanted was to stop Merrill—however possible.

The first scream that rent the air startled her. Kora mumbled something and looked down. Katla followed her gaze and saw the people. More screams joined the first. Had they made a mistake? Would this flight be what set the war into motion? Again, she couldn't find it in herself to care when so much more was at stake.

It wasn't just Merrill's soul. It was anyone he came in contact with. It was the innocents going about their days, not realizing that death was headed straight for them. It was for the dragons and all others with magic.

Maybe they had been in a war all along and never knew it. Merrill's capture and torture turning him into this might very well be the thing that ripped the curtain away and exposed the truth—a reality no one had wanted to see.

Kora looked over her shoulder, then nudged Katla to do the same. Katla turned and saw other dragons behind them. They flew higher but were headed in the same direction. She didn't know for sure what the Kings would do to Merrill, but she had an idea. Katla's eyes burned with tears when she spotted Varek's lichen scales. He was ahead of the others, flying fast to catch Derek.

"Hurry," Katla said, leaning over Derek.

A grunt rumbled through Derek as he sped up.

"What is it?" Kora yelled over the wind to be heard.

Katla leaned close to her so the wind wouldn't snatch her words. "It shouldn't be one of the Kings who has to stop him."

Kora stared at her for another minute before she nodded and turned to lay low over Derek's neck. It must have been some sort of instruction because Derek increased his speed even more. Katla had to grab hold of Kora to keep from slipping off. She searched the horizon, hoping to spotting Merrill. But the setting sun, with its vibrant colors, made it difficult to see.

"Katla!" Kora shouted and pointed up.

She spotted a dark shape just before it moved into the clouds, but there had been no mistaking the orange scales. It was Merrill. Derek altered his course to follow him. Katla's trepidation doubled when they flew into the thick, puffy clouds. It was a reminder of her ride with Merrill.

They burst from one cloud before disappearing into another. Then another. The clouds made it difficult to see, and the sun blinded her from the front. Katla had to turn her head to either side to make out anything.

She noticed one cloud that seemed to billow toward her. The next second, orange scales erupted out of it. Merrill's claws reached for Derek's wings. Derek jerked to the side to stay out of Merrill's way. Merrill swung around and headed toward them again. This time, his huge claws took aim at her and Kora.

Derek's wings snapped shut, and he angled his body as he dove. Merrill's claw was inches from Katla's face when she found herself suddenly plunging toward the ground. The force of the wind lifted her from Derek. Even Kora had a hard time holding on. Katla watched in horror as Merrill came at them again. Just before he reached them, Varek rammed him. The two locked together, talons and teeth slashing and biting.

Katla craned her neck one way and then the other to keep Merrill and Varek in sight. Derek spun around so the sun was behind them. It made it easier to watch the battle. The other dragons gave Varek and Merrill a wide birth. She wasn't surprised to see Con's gold scales. There was a dragon with sea green scales, another with sapphire scales, and a third with gold on top but beige on his stomach.

The battle was loud and wild, with a feral nature that took her aback. It was a fight with only one winner. She didn't know how they stayed in the air with teeth and claws cutting wings, but they somehow did.

It soon became apparent that Varek was dragging Merrill north, where they had been days earlier. The area was uninhabited, so if there was going to be a fight on this side of the border, it was likely the best place for it.

Katla winced when Varek slashed his talons across Merrill's chest, drawing blood. Merrill didn't even react, almost as if he didn't feel it. In retaliation, he clamped his jaws around Varek's neck, then threw him.

Right into them.

Derek tried to adjust but couldn't move quickly enough with her and Kora on his back. He wasn't able to get out of the way in time. All they could do was prepare as Varek collided with them.

The impact sent Katla tumbling backward, head over heels. The edge of Derek's wing knocked into her head. Dots edged her vision, and the wind howled ferociously around her. There was nothing to grab hold of. She tried to concentrate but was wavering in and out of consciousness. She was falling. At any moment, she would hit the ground and die, but there was nothing she could do about it. The answer was just out of reach. If only she could focus.

The wind suddenly quieted, and she was cradled in darkness. She thought she heard the flapping of wings but stopped caring as she lost consciousness.

THIRTY-FOUR

He had seen her too late. The dark-haired woman tumbled from the black and silver dragon before he could reach her. He dove the instant he saw her fall, but not even his speed could catch her in time.

The ground was rising up fast. He knew what would happen if he didn't get to her. He ignored the dragons and forgot about exacting justice on the humans. Nothing mattered but her.

He dove faster, willing himself to reach her. He extended his hand, scooping her into his palm moments before she would have slammed into the ground. His wings spread to help soften his landing as he brought his hand against his chest to protect her. He still stumbled. His shoulder rammed into the earth, sending dirt and grass flying as he slid, the ground forming a large hill.

He slowly regained his feet and then carefully lowered his arm, unfurling his fingers to find her. He felt her breathing against his palm. Her long, black tresses were spread against his scales in all directions. Her clothes were torn and bloodied. He saw a few bruises, but no wounds. He focused on her face, willing her eyes to open, but she was out cold.

The ground shook with the telltale sign of another dragon landing. He looked up to find the Lichen before him. Voices shouted in his head, calling him a name he didn't recognize. He shut them out, refusing to listen. No one would stop him from eradicating the humans as they should have been wiped out eons ago. Once he purged this realm, he would return to the other world and wipe it clean.

A Gold descended to the earth, followed by a Sapphire. The sea green one was next. Last was the gold and beige male. They surrounded him, but he didn't care. He could kill them all. He knew it. Just as he knew the woman had to be protected. Surely, they were aware they didn't stand a chance against him. He locked eyes with the gold dragon. Not even a Gold could stop him. He didn't want to kill them, but he would if they stood between him and his destiny.

There was no sign of the black and silver dragon. Yet. It would return. It seemed to always be there. His gaze dropped to his hand. Just as she was. Who was she? How did he know her?

He looked up in time to see the lichen-colored dragon glance at the woman. Maybe they weren't here for him. Maybe they wanted her. He issued a warning growl. That wasn't happening. He gently laid the female on the ground and stood protectively over her, looking at each of the dragons, another growl rumbling through him. If any of them dared to come closer, he would rip their throats out.

All but one of the voices quieted, but he still ignored the speaker. The words meant nothing. He had been stopped before. He had ignored and hidden his feelings about the humans for far too long. He would no longer conceal what he felt—or who he was. He would settle the score, once and for all.

The lichen dragon took a step forward.

Apparently, his warning wasn't enough. He spread his wings, his talons curving into the ground. His mouth opened, and he released a beam of searing light. The Lichen jumped into the air to dodge the blast. He readied for the next attack, but none came. The dragons held back, watching and waiting.

Something touched his arm. He looked down to find the woman's eyes open and locked on him. Gray eyes met his. The darkness called, but its voice was barely a whisper. Her arm was extended, her hand touching his scales. The rest of the world dissolved, leaving only her.

She sat up and winced as she touched her head. He didn't like that she was hurt. He wanted to take her pain but didn't have that ability. Another did. He tried to recall who but couldn't dredge up that information in the chaos of his mind.

The woman climbed to her feet. Her hand smoothed up his arm as high as it could go. She wasn't scared of him in this form. And her touch was sublime. It calmed the raging beast a fraction.

"Thank you for saving me," she said.

He tucked his wings, wanting more of her touch, more of her words. His mind cleared enough that memories peeked through. This woman was important to him. She meant everything. He would kill for her.

He would die for her.

"Can I touch your face?"

Her question surprised him. Still, he lowered his head so his chin brushed the ground. She placed her palm on his snout. The sensation of her magic glided over his scales like a caress. He held her gaze, drinking in her beauty and gentleness. She was an ember burning brightly through the fire. She was power and strength.

He needed to touch her. With a thought, he shifted to his human form. Her lips curved upward. He locked onto that sight because he had been waiting for her to smile for a long time. He didn't know how he knew that, but he did.

"Hi," she said softly.

Her hand had fallen away when he shifted, and his mind was becoming chaotic again. He reached for her, only to draw up short when a rumbling growl caught his attention. He turned his head to the side to retaliate, but she tenderly took his face in her hands and brought his focus back to her.

"Ignore them," she told him. "This is between us."

She dropped her hands to his shoulders before skimming her fingers down his arms to his palms. They linked hands.

"Do you remember me?" she asked.

He knew her face, her touch. Even her taste. He wanted to tell her he would never forget her but couldn't get the words out. He could only nod.

Her lips curved into a quick smile. "Do you remember my name?"

His heart lurched. How could he remember her but not what she was called? He didn't want to tell her that. He wanted her to smile, not frown.

"It's all right," she said quickly. "My name is Katla."

Katla. Aye, that's what she was called.

"Your name is Merrill." Her fingers tightened on his.

He stared into her gray eyes, noting the black that ringed her irises. There was dirt on her cheek and forehead, specks of blood here and there. Her hair was tangled, and her clothes were ripped. But he had never seen anyone so breathtaking.

"Do you recall the first time you saw me?" she asked.

An image of her on the streets of a city on the side of a mountain flashed in his mind. He dipped his head.

"Do you remember the first time we looked at each other?"

He started to shake his head when he caught a glimpse of a memory. It was Katla walking through rubble before turning, their eyes locking. He nodded again.

"What about when you followed me?"

He frowned at the question. Had he followed her? Aye, he had. That's when he saw the small ones. What were they called? Ba... bairns. She had been looking after three.

"You do," Katla said with a soft smile. "Then you know we're friends."

They were more than that. He was sure of it. His gaze dropped to her mouth. He brought a hand to her face. He had touched her like this before. He rubbed his thumb over her lips. He had kissed her.

Her eyes closed for a heartbeat as she kissed his thumb. His balls tightened with need as heat rushed through him. Her gaze smoldered with desire as she rose on tiptoe and pressed her lips to his. He was lost. Enraptured. Spellbound.

Desire flared. He wound his arms around her and held her against him as their tongues tangled. She tasted of passion and paradise. His hand moved down to the curve of her lower back, and he splayed his palm there, pressing her against his aching cock. She groaned into his mouth, inflaming his already out-of-control need to new heights.

The only thing standing between them was her clothes. But

those could be removed quickly enough. He tugged at the hem of her shirt that had come loose from her waistband and slipped his hand beneath the material. He laid his palm against her bare skin.

She gasped and tore her mouth from his. Her eyes were bright, her chest heaving, and her lips swollen as she looked up at him. She desired him. Just as he craved her.

"Merrill, I want this. More than you can possibly know." She swallowed and glanced to the side. "But now isn't the time."

He remembered then that they were surrounded. Being with her made him forget everything. Even his enemies.

Katla gently touched his face, her gaze serious. "You were taken from me. Ripped out of my arms."

A flash of fire and agony cut through him. He squeezed his eyes closed and jerked his head to the side.

Her hand rested on his chest over his heart. "I don't want to bring you any pain, but I need you to remember."

With her near, his frenzied mind was calm, allowing a few things to come through. Her words brought forth recollections he couldn't reconcile. He opened his eyes as the memories began to play.

They had been kissing—their first kiss. There had been an explosion, and then she was gone. He had shifted, only to be met by a terrible foe. "Entity." He didn't recognize his voice. It was deep and rough, like it hadn't been used in months.

She nodded slowly. "It and the Orgate warriors took you. They...they tortured you."

Those unearthed memories rose, drowning him in that awful torment once more.

"You're free of it," Katla hurriedly said. "You're free of it. You're here with me now."

He realized he was clutching her against him and loosened his hold. Someone had made him suffer, knowing it would drive him mad. They wanted him like this. No. Not they. The entity. It had wanted the dragon he'd once been wiped away.

Katla called him Merrill, but he wasn't him anymore. He looked up at the dragons. If he tried, he knew he would remember who they were. They hadn't moved. Enemies would've attacked, like he had with the black and silver dragon.

He wished to remain with Katla—for the calm she brought his mind, but also because she was...what was the word? He knew it. It was important to dragons. More important than anything.

"Mate," he murmured. She was his mate.

He wouldn't be able to live without her. But he couldn't be with her as he was now. There was enough of him left to realize that he needed to save her from himself. He took a step back.

"No, please," she said and held on to him. "Don't go."

He smoothed the wavy strands of her hair from her face. "Must."

"Then we go together," she stated.

He shook his head, but she wasn't listening.

"I can see the entity. We can find it together. We'll fight it," she insisted.

He would do anything for her but put her in a situation where she might die. She pressed her cheek into his palm and implored him with her eyes. She had his heart, his very soul. He would lay the universe at her feet. But he refused to put her in danger. Yet it was only because she was near that he could think clearly again, that the rage didn't consume him. The moment he left her, his mind would become a jumbled mess again. He was sure of it. He would be taken by a killing frenzy as he had been just moments before.

"You're stronger than before. You might even be able to kill the entity," Katla said.

The idea appealed to him. It needed to pay for what it had done to him.

"It followed us," Katla pressed. "It wants you to kill."

Why? The entity was capable of killing whatever it wanted.

"I don't know why, but it won't matter if we can stop it. You need me to get close to it."

He cupped her face in his hands. There were words he wanted to say, significant words. Things she needed to know. But they remained just out of reach. How did he tell her that he would rather die than see her harmed?

"I'm not without magic. I can take care of myself," she said.

He let himself imagine the two of them hunting—and ending—the entity. Then what? It wasn't safe for him to be out there alone. Worse, what if he turned on Katla? He looked up at the lichen-colored dragon before him. It had heard their conversation. All the dragons surrounding him had.

"If the entity isn't stopped, it'll keep hurting dragons," Katla said. "What if it takes Varek next time?"

He knew that name. It rolled around on his tongue, but no matter how hard he tried, he couldn't speak it aloud. He finally forced the name through his mind. *"Varek."*

The Lichen dipped his head in acknowledgment.

A voice pushed against his mind. He hesitated before opening the link.

"I know what you fear, brother. You have my word your death

will be swift if it comes to that. But it willna. You're strong enough to fight this," Varek said.

He'd called him *brother*. They weren't blood, but close enough. He had forgotten even that. The dragons around him were friends. He didn't want any of them to go through what he had. For them to lose themselves as he had. But he couldn't battle the destruction of his mind. It was already done. This brief reprieve was exactly that, and he needed to take advantage of it while it lasted. Before he forgot everything again. *"Promise...to...protect...her?"*

"I give you my vow that I will safeguard Katla."

With Varek's promise, he lowered his gaze to her. She watched him expectantly. A smile broke across her face when he nodded in agreement.

THIRTY-FIVE

Katla wanted to stay with Merrill in the field forever, and forget there were enemies out there who could cause someone so amazing to become something else. Sometimes, when Merrill looked at her, she saw the man who had befriended her. There were other instances where he seemed to withdraw.

When that happened, he held her tighter as if she was the only thing keeping him together. The last thing she wanted him to do was fight the entity, but someone had to stop it. Because if it wasn't stopped, it might do this again with another dragon. Since Villette feared Merrill because he could kill a Star Person, the odds were good he could end the entity.

At least, Katla hoped. She was banking everything on that theory.

Merrill's gaze moved over her shoulder. It wasn't long before she heard someone approaching. She didn't loosen her hold on Merrill. Not even death could make her leave him. She wished she had kissed him sooner, given in to the attraction. There was more to fret about now, however.

Varek came up beside her, his brown gaze coming to rest on her. "Merrill showed me a picture of the invisible foe. You can no' really think to go after it, can you?"

"You didn't see what they did to him," she replied.

Varek's lips compressed as he glanced at Merrill. "I have an idea."

"I don't know why the entity targeted Merrill, but what if he was a test? What if this is its plan?"

Varek turned his head to the side for a moment, a vein bulging in his neck. "We've no' been able to beat the entity."

"Villette is frightened of Merrill."

At the mention of the Star Person's name, Merrill bared his teeth, his nostrils flaring. Katla made a note not to mention her again. Merrill might not remember some things, but he instinctively knew others. Like Villette.

"In this state, he can kill a Star Person. I think he may be strong enough to end the entity," she continued.

"And if he isna?"

Katla licked her lips. "You know Merrill better than I do. Would he rather go out fighting or be taken down by his friends?"

"Fuck!" Varek said, shoving a hand through his blond hair. He blew out a breath and gave her a sad shake of his head. "He'd want to go out fighting."

She looked at Merrill and found him watching her. Katla smoothed some hair from his brow.

"Your presence keeps him calm. He's no' as lost to the madness when you touch him."

"It's a good thing I'm going with him then."

Varek scrubbed a hand over his mouth. "He's concerned about how long that will last."

Her chin lifted as she looked to Varek. "This will work."

It had to was left unspoken, but they all knew it.

"We could spend weeks hunting the entity," Varek said.

Katla shrugged one shoulder. "Then we bring it to us. It tracked Merrill for days. It planned this."

A frown marred Varek's forehead. "You think it has that ability?"

"I know what I saw each time it interacted with him. It won't be far from him."

"Which means it could be close even now."

She swallowed past the lump in her throat. "Exactly."

Varek released a loud sigh. "All right. We'll follow."

"It needs to know its plan worked. And for that to happen, Merrill has to be on his own."

"We're no' leaving Merrill to face it alone."

"Stay far enough back that the entity doesn't see you."

Varek's lips twisted. "We'll be close enough to help if its needed."

"Oh. Is Kora okay?" she asked as Varek started to walk away.

He paused and turned his head to look back. "She's fine. Derek caught her." Varek eyed Merrill and then dropped his gaze to her. "Good luck."

Merrill placed his finger beneath her chin and gently turned her face to him. It seemed to pain him to speak, but his face and eyes expressed enough for her to get the gist of what he wished to convey. The worry etched on his features mimicked her concerns.

"You don't have to do this," she told him. "You've done enough.

We can go back with the others and figure out how to reverse what happened."

His eyes closed as he shook his head. "Must," he murmured.

Katla felt tears prick the backs of her eyes. She forced a smile. "You're a good man."

He wiped away a tear that escaped before he lowered his head and kissed her languidly, tenderly, drawing out the kiss until she didn't know where she ended, and he began. She fought to keep their lips together even as he drew back.

"That won't be the last time we kiss," she stated for herself, but also for him.

Merrill jerked his chin to the sky. It was time to fly. Katla's heart thumped at the thought of falling again, but if he could fight back the madness, she could overcome her fears. She looked down at his bare chest and rippling muscles. All the wounds from the torture were gone. Physically, at least.

This wouldn't be the last time she touched him. They would have time for her to run her hands over his body at her leisure, bring him pleasure before their bodies joined. She believed this because, if she didn't, she wouldn't be able to follow through with her plan.

Katla released him and backed away. He shifted immediately, rising over her, powerful and deadly. His umber eyes locked on hers. She climbed up and settled on his back, only to notice that the other dragons were gone.

Katla placed her hands on him and leaned over his neck. "The entity's reign of terror ends tonight."

A rumble she assumed was agreement vibrated through him. His enormous wings unfurled. She glanced at the massive lengths that extended out on either side or her, then looked at the darkening sky. Merrill leapt, and then they were flying.

They remained in the air for over an hour without any sign of the entity. Katla had been sure it was out there. She shivered against the cold that numbed her fingers and toes. She didn't know how much longer she could endure the frigid temperature with nothing but her thin shirt. The air was much colder up high, though she had been out in it for so long that she wasn't sure she would ever warm up again.

Something brushed against her nose. She thought it was a bug until it happened again. Then again. She gazed out into the twilight to find snow falling. The fading light made it difficult enough to see. The snow would add another inconvenience.

It will work.

Katla had repeated that mantra since Merrill took to the skies. The entity had to be near. It had followed them, tracked them across mountains, and had been there when they tried to rescue Merrill. Where was it now?

What if it suspected their plan? What if it saw her with Merrill and knew he was no longer insane?

"This isn't going to work," Katla said to Merrill. "We'll have to come up with another plan."

He dipped a wing and swung around. Katla barely had time to raise her hands as the entity came at her face.

THIRTY-SIX

Sparks flew from her fingers as she fell backward on Merrill's back, barely holding on to him with her legs. He let out a roar and dove to the side. Her magic did little to stop the entity. Only Merrill's quick thinking saved her from a direct hit. Katla felt herself slipping again, but there was nothing she could do.

Merrill flew erratically, turning one way and then the other, moving up and then down. Each time she thought she could sit up again, she was forced to remain on her back, her hands gripping his scales in an attempt to remain atop him. She craned her head to the side and back and spotted their enemy. It was trying to reach Merrill's wing. Katla's heart jumped in her throat. One hit from the entity and she and Merrill would fall.

Finally, Katla could sit up. She instantly wished she hadn't when Merrill dove forward, his wings tucked to prevent the entity from reaching them. Their foe managed to keep up with them. She looked over to find it even with her. She knew it would be smirking with delight if it had a face.

Katla trusted Merrill, even when he dove toward the forest. She closed her eyes, hoping she stayed on when they crashed. But his wings whipped out at the last second, and he spun to the right, heading away from the entity. It was a great move that might have worked had she not overcompensated and tipped to the side.

She grabbed one of the tendrils along Merrill's spine, hoping to pull herself up. Merrill angled himself upward to help her. The entity used that moment to rush them. It was too much for Katla. Her hand slipped, and she bounced off Merrill's wing and onto his back. She hastily grasped for something to stop her fall, but her hands grabbed nothing but air each time. There came an instant where she hung in the air before bouncing down Merrill's spine and off his tail.

His roar reverberated around her, ringing through the night. Merrill spun around, and their gazes locked as he flew toward her. The entity smashed into him. Instantly, Merrill went limp and began tumbling to the ground. Katla screamed his name as he dropped like a stone, but the wind snatched the shout from her lips. She had seconds to attempt to teleport to safety. She didn't know if it was feasible, but she had to try. Over and over, she imagined herself on the ground. In the next heartbeat, she found herself standing on firm earth.

Her elation was short-lived, however, as she thought about Merrill. She raised her face to the sky and found him in a freefall, directly above her. Katla raced out of the way before he landed. He crashed so hard the ground trembled. The landing was followed by a blast wave that knocked her flat, her head smashing against the hard earth. She pushed to her hands and knees, dazed. Katla shakily climbed to her feet, holding her head. Then she turned around.

The sight of Merrill was like being doused with icy water. He lay in a crumpled heap, his wings bent at odd angles—one of them torn nearly in half as it lay twisted behind him. And he wasn't moving. Without thought, she ran to him. She only got two steps before the entity skated between them.

Its frenzied indignation rolled off it in waves as it hovered in the air. Face or not, she knew it was staring at her, its contempt clear. She had interfered with its plans, after all. A cold sweat covered her. There was no getting around the sinister threat before her. The entity wanted its pound of flesh.

But so did she.

The being moved quickly. She would have to be quicker—and ready for anything. She had the advantage of seeing it, but she knew its potency, had felt its power when they clashed before. But this wasn't about her. It was about keeping it occupied until Merrill woke.

Katla grinned as she lifted her chin. Magic warmed her blood as it skimmed along her body and pooled in her hands. "You can't have him. You can't have any of the dragons."

The entity had no face to speak off, no mouth with which to talk, but she still heard its enraged bellow, right before it shot forward. She turned her palms out, her arms slightly lifted outward at her sides. Sparks streaked around her dizzyingly in an X that formed a shield bigger and brighter than ever before.

The entity bounced off and immediately came at her again. Katla stood her ground, feeling her magic as it continued to grow. The second strike sent the being ricocheting away. This was the magic Merrill had tried to tell her about. The power she had ignorantly dreaded. She welcomed it now.

Katla brought her palms together before throwing her hands

out as magic exploded from her and through the shield. It plowed into the entity with such force that it spun the being around. She quickly fired off two more strikes. One struck a glancing blow, but the other missed entirely as the enemy shot straight upward. Katla turned, following it, but lost it in the darkness.

She blinked away the snowflakes that fell and tangled in her lashes as she looked at Merrill. He was naked, his human body lying in the deep depression his dragon form had made when he landed. Katla longed to go to him, but the entity was still out there. It wanted her to make a mistake and let her guard down so it could strike.

Katla held her ground. She pulled her gaze from Merrill and scanned the vicinity. What was the entity waiting for? The night was still, broken only by the gleaming snow in the moonlight. She used to love how the snowfall absorbed the sounds in the air. Now, it lent an unnatural, eerie atmosphere to the landscape.

The foe's wickedness pervaded the area, making the very heavens shrink away in protest. The malice that hung in the air waited to strike. Her trepidation grew with every moment she stood anticipating its next move. How much more of her magic was there? She dug deep again but got no response. If this was all she had, then she would make the most of it. All she had to do was stay alive long enough for Merrill to wake. Then they could fight the entity together.

It was a simple, uncomplicated plan. But nothing about this enemy was straightforward. Katla's nerves began to fray as she continued to scan the landscape and sky for the entity. She had taken Villette's word that there was only one. If Villette had deceived her again, then she could be out here alone with multiple beings. Would the Kings get to her quickly enough to help?

She turned her head to Merrill. It wasn't her she was concerned about. It was him. Every second she stood alone, she doubted her plan. She should've convinced him to go with the Kings instead of into a fight. Even if he could kill the entity, she might have unwittingly done more damage to him. She had been so sure they could do this. But it had been a mistake. Varek had known it. The others probably had, as well. She'd wanted to rid the realm of the entity so it couldn't hurt Merrill again.

Katla was never more aware of an uncertain outcome than she was in that moment. By the stars, what had she done, thinking to bring someone she cared so much about into such a battle? She swallowed past the lump in her throat, her thoughts forcing her to look deep into the feelings she hadn't dared acknowledge because she didn't feel worthy of them. Feelings she had kept closely guarded, tucked away in her heart where she could hold them against her.

She had to get Merrill out of here. Katla could call to Rhi so she could teleport Merrill out. But the entity would follow. Unless they took him back to their world. She might never see Merrill again, but she would lose him anyway if she didn't get him out.

"Rhi," she called.

The hair on the back of her neck prickled. Katla turned in a slow circle again. She caught movement out of the corner of her eye and jerked her head around, seeing the tail end of one of the entity's arm-like extensions as it whooshed out of sight. She had known it was still around. It was surveying the area and deciding on its next move.

Katla didn't like reacting. She'd much rather be the one delivering the assault. Her fingers ached from the cold, and she had lost feeling in her toes and nose. Her lips were chapped. The snow fell harder, silvery dots against the black backdrop of the sky. There was no sign of Rhi. She silently willed Merrill to wake.

The attack, when it came, happened swiftly. A blow to the left. To the right. The left again. And one to her back. The strikes were rapid and crushing. The shield took the brunt of three of the strikes, waning enough for the fourth to penetrate. The pain radiated outward from her spine, buckling her knees and sending her into a helpless sprawl forward.

Her mind screamed for her to flip over, but the command was slow to make it to her limbs. Her wound throbbed each time she shivered from the cold, doubling her pain. If she stayed down, she was dead. Katla gritted her teeth and rolled over. A scream ripped from her throat as she writhed at the contact of her injury with the earth.

Agony was dragging her to oblivion. She fought against it and focused her gaze to see the being coming at her. She raised her hands, calling to her magic to shield her face a second before it struck. The entity glanced off. She surged to her feet as thousands of sparks circled her but she couldn't stay upright. She dropped to her knees as her legs gave out. The pain was so intense it broke her focus. Katla shook her head to clear it, remembering then that she was in the middle of a battle. The sparks answered as they lit up the area as if it were daytime. They surrounded her, a wall between her and the enemy.

The entity languidly moved into view, suspended in midair. It was sizing her up. She didn't know how much more she had left in her, but she didn't plan to go down easily. She knew who she was now. She knew her potency, her might. So many times before, she had failed to protect those she loved in one way or another. This wouldn't be one of those times.

Katla gritted her teeth as she got one foot beneath her and awkwardly stood. She barely made it before the entity struck. It moved even faster, striking again and again until it finally pierced her magic. It wrapped one of its tendrils around her neck and lifted her off the ground as it squeezed.

She channeled her magic at the thing compressing her throat. When that did nothing, she focused it on the entity. All the while, it squeezed harder, suffocating her. She didn't want her last image to be of something so vile. Her gaze slid to the side to find Merrill.

Katla. She was the first thing he thought about when he came to. He had tried to catch her when she fell, but the entity had struck him down. He heard movement. Was it Katla? If she had fallen to her death, he would know. He would feel her passing as only mates could.

There was a soft grunt followed by the entity's distinctive odor. Katla must be nearby. Panicked urgency surged through him and battered his ribs. Katla needed him. He tried to move his limbs, but they wouldn't obey. He glared at the stars while silently screaming for his body to move.

A feminine gasp had him fighting his body to get to Katla. He struggled to curl a single finger until it ultimately obeyed, then focused on his hand until he could move it at will. Finally, he turned to his arm. Fear gave way to frustration, which melded into resentment that coalesced into a blinding rage. It raced through him like dragon fire, scorching every nerve and molecule.

He vaulted out of the sunken ground, ready for combat. Sparks hovered around a sphere-shaped presence as if lighting up for him. The entity. He lowered his gaze to find her on the ground. Seeing her like that was so devastating that it knocked him back a step. The lights moved, yanking his attention to them. The entity. It had hurt her. But she had made sure he could see their enemy.

And it wouldn't get away from him this time.

A bellow erupted from his lips as he launched himself at his foe. The dragon within called. He tried to shift, but his body remained in its current form. The entity didn't move, believing itself invisible.

Right until he latched onto it. He dug his fingers into the black-massed orb. The longer he held his enemy, the more incensed he became. It was fuel to an already out-of-control inferno, a storm that would devour anything in its path.

He knew rage. He knew hatred. He had carried them inside him for eons, suppressing them. Ignoring them. But this was different. This was a level of barbaric ferocity he hadn't believed possible. Once it had him, there was no turning back.

And it had him.

His rampage had just begun. There would be nothing but carnage left in his wake. His enemy was sadistic, but it was nothing compared to the darkness that had him in its grip.

He pulled at the entity, trying to tear it in half. It yanked against him, attempting to free itself. When that didn't work, its tendrils began slapping at him. He barely felt them. His enemy had once had the capability to knock him unconscious. Now, he had the power. And the day of reckoning was at hand.

The entity wasn't done fighting, though. It heaved itself upward, pulling him off his feet to dangle in the air. He didn't loosen his hold. One of his fingers punctured the orb. He heard his foe's bellow. The mixture of indignation and terror in the sound made him smirk. The pain was just beginning. There were layers of it, and he was ready to show it just how much awaited.

Suddenly, it dropped him. His knees bent on impact, but he fell onto his back. He didn't release the entity, not even when it pressed against his face. It had done that to him before, but it didn't have the same effect this time.

He released a battle yell and flipped over, pinning the enemy beneath his chest as he shoved it into the ground. He heard another scream, this one high-pitched. The foe shot into the air again, zooming left and then right, up and down, trying to dislodge him. Nothing would make him let go this time.

He tightened his grip. The entity flew into the night sky while lashing his eyes with one of its long appendages. The tendril penetrated his eyelid to sear his eyeball. He grabbed the offending limb and yanked it off. The entity then managed to wrench itself out of Merrill's grasp.

The wind roared in his ears as he fell. His body healed his eyesight a second later. This time when the dragon within called, he could shift. His wings unfurled with a snap as he glided through the sky, looking for the entity. The sparks still hovered around it, drawing his gaze. He spun around and sailed straight for his nemesis.

It zipped to the side, taking him on a wild chase as it rapidly flitted about. He sensed its urgency and terror. He smiled in anticipation. His neck stretched out as he opened his jaws, ready to snap his teeth around it. Suddenly, the entity dropped beneath him and slammed into his stomach. He roared and tucked his wings to roll onto his back, then arched, throwing his head back and flipping backward. As his body curved and righted itself, he flapped his wings to gain altitude. He was done playing.

The instant he caught sight of the sparks, he surged toward the entity. It darted to the side once more. He opened his jaws and let the searing light leave his mouth. The beam shot forward, laser-like as it struck the foe. The entity faltered but got away. His second strike took it down.

It didn't remain on the ground. The entity frantically lurched upward as Merrill landed beside it. He heard a voice then. It wasn't in his mind, and the entity had no lips from which to speak. Still, he heard it.

"No! How is this possible? I can't die. It should be you!" the voice bit out. "Your kind and the Star People shattered my world! You were my revenge!"

Merrill grabbed hold of the sphere once more. His fingers crushed the orb until his talons penetrated the mass. Its scream was wild and desperate. The sparks lingered over his skin before moving up to his face like a caress. His arms moved outward to stretch the entity to its breaking point.

Then he drew in a deep breath and felt fire rumble in his chest. He released it, letting it engulf the entity. He heard its screams as it feverishly fought to get free. Those screams diminished until, ultimately, they were silenced. The entity had been reduced to ash.

His arms dropped to his sides. His anger was satisfied, but there was no rejoicing. Something wasn't right. He was lethargic, as if his very soul were being bled. He took a step back and stumbled. His gaze swept the air and found her. She was still on the ground.

Nay!

He roared as he rushed to her, but his limbs wouldn't work right, and his wings barely held him. He crashed into the ground clumsily as he reached her. He had to crawl the last few feet to her.

Then he looked down at her pale form and the dark bruises around her throat. Denial rose, choking him with the truth.

His hand reached out for her. He drew back just as his talon was about to touch her. He tried to shift and failed. It riled him, sending him spiraling into emotions that pulled him down into a dark pit. He threw back his head and roared his anger. His need to touch her focused his thoughts. Still, it took him two attempts before he finally transformed.

His knees buckled. Carefully, gently, he gathered her against him. He held her head against his chest. There was no heartbeat, no breath coming from her lungs. But he knew that already. He should have been there to defend her. He was supposed to protect her.

He smoothed the midnight locks from her face. He couldn't remember her name, but he knew her. He would recognize her in whatever form they took, in however many lives they lived and loved. *Mate.* They were bound by the universe, by magic more formidable than any could comprehend. Their time here was done. She had departed first, but he would follow her soon.

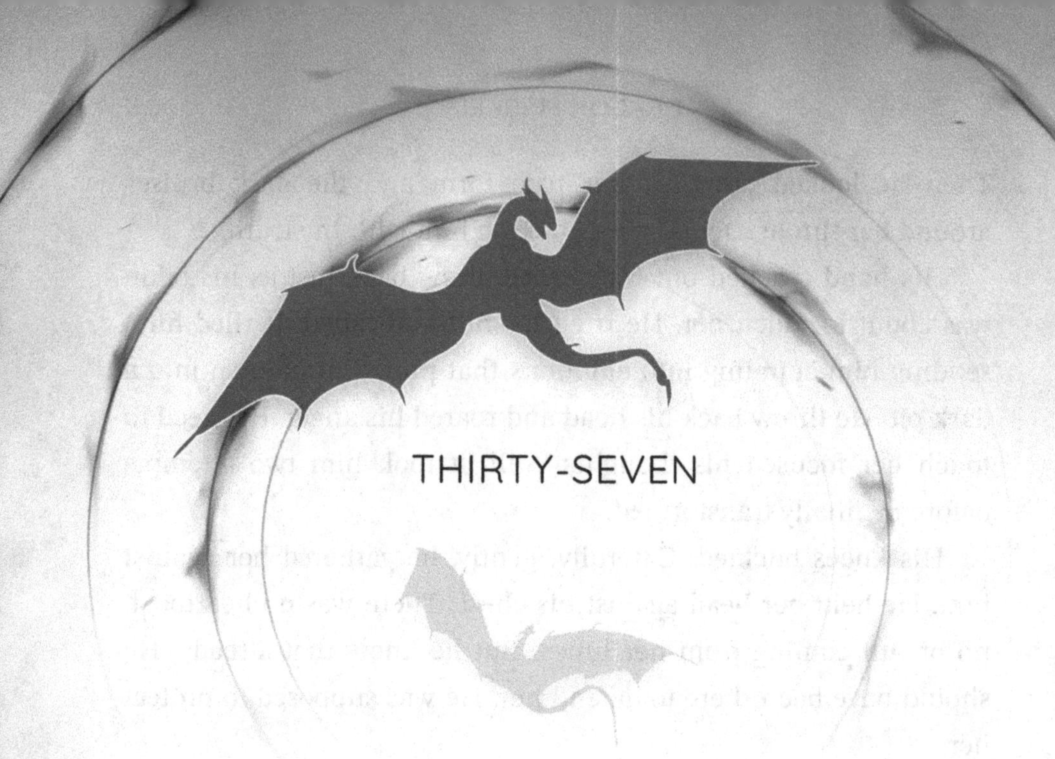

THIRTY-SEVEN

Varek watched the scene unfolding with horror. Merrill's sorrow-filled roar was like a gut punch. He knew what was coming, and there was no way he would allow his friend to suffer through it. He whirled around and strode to Con. The King of Kings slowly turned his head to him.

"Get Ulrik from Earth. Now," Varek demanded. When Con didn't immediately move, Varek got in his face so they were nose to nose. "You know what Merrill has done for us. For *all* of us. You can no' let him suffer."

Con didn't blink, didn't so much as breathe.

Varek shouldered past him. "Fine. I'll get him."

He didn't get two steps before Con's hand wrapped around his arm, halting him. "I sent Rhi for him the moment Katla fell."

All the anger left Varek. But with one problem solved, there was another. He looked at Merrill's hunched form. "We need to get to him now, then. Tell him. The madness will take him again if we doona."

"Nay, it willna," Con said softly as he released Varek. "There is no more anger in Merrill."

Varek didn't know what was worse: the raging Merrill, or the crushed one. Neither was the dragon he knew. He couldn't sit by and allow his friend to traverse things alone. Not after Merrill had sacrificed so much of himself for every King.

The entity had been defeated. There was no longer a reason for him to stay that way. Varek walked away from the others and burst into a run before shifting. He closed the distance between himself and Merrill in a matter of seconds. Yet as he flew over the couple, Varek was unsure what to say. Then he realized he wasn't alone. Con, Brandr, Hector, Alasdair, and Derek were in the air with him.

Varek landed, shifting into his human form as his feet touched the ground. He called clothes to him, but his footsteps halted as he stared at the couple. Merrill's head was bent over Katla. One arm held her against him, and he had intertwined the fingers of his free hand with hers. Sorrow permeated the air. Misery surrounded them like a wet cloak.

What could he say to a King who had lost his mate? A dragon who was slowly, painfully dying. Varek looked around for Ulrik. Where was he? Varek swallowed and ate up the last few feet between him and the man he considered a brother.

"Merrill," he called softly.

When Merrill didn't look up, Varek squatted, bending to the side in an effort to see his friend's face. All the air left Varek's lungs when Merrill's bleak gaze locked with his. Tears ran down Merrill's cheeks. The anguish staring back at Varek was visceral and gut-wrenching. He wanted to look away but didn't.

Then Ulrik was there. The King of Silvers glanced at Varek

before dropping down to one knee. "Merrill, hold on while I bring her back. I'm going to touch her now," Ulrik said as he tentatively rested his fingers on Katla's arm.

Ulrik's gold eyes closed as he drew on his magic to call Katla's soul back from death. It was a power Ulrik rarely used. Varek had known he would come to Merrill's aid without question. That's what family did.

His attention returned to Merrill as Ulrik worked. When he saw Merrill begin to tip to the side, Varek reached to steady him. Merrill went limp in his arms.

"Nay," Varek murmured as he laid his friend alongside Katla. "Hold on, you stubborn bastard."

Merrill's dark blue eyes met his before they drifted closed. And didn't open again.

"MERRILL!" Varek bellowed and shook his friend's shoulders.

But he was gone.

This wasn't how it was supposed to happen. Ulrik had come. He was giving Katla life again. That should have stopped Merrill's death.

"Wake up, dammit," Varek ordered, shaking Merrill again.

Someone touched his arm, but Varek couldn't look away from his brother. He couldn't be gone. He simply refused to believe it. Ulrik had come. Surely, he had brought Katla back in time.

Someone wailed, screaming Merrill's name. Varek's eyes swam with tears that dropped onto his face. His mind couldn't process the scene unfolding. He couldn't imagine a world without Merrill in it. The jokes, the laughter, his infectious smile. Merrill had defeated the entity. He had stood against Villette and Miena.

Varek drew in a shaky breath and blinked. It took him a

moment to realize that Katla was draped over Merrill. It was her wails he'd heard.

"She's alive, Merrill," Varek said, not wanting to give up. "Wake the fuck up! We're all here."

No matter how long Varek stared at his friend, Merrill's eyes didn't open, his chest didn't move with breath. He looked to Ulrik, who looked as shell-shocked as he felt. Above them, the Kings began their heartbroken roars. The sound spread as dragons across the border answered the grieving call. It had been so long since he had heard such cries that Varek could only sit and listen.

He wondered if Merrill had known how much he was loved—and how he would be missed.

Ulrik ran a shaky hand through his black hair. It was on the tip of Varek's tongue to ask Ulrik to bring him back, but it went against the rules for Ulrik to use his gift on a King—no matter the reason. They had spent so many eons without their dragons that they had all gotten complacent about their place. They had forgotten what it was to lose a King.

It didn't matter that Merrill had battled a terrible foe and won. They had failed him. Varek should've demanded that Ulrik be there from the very beginning. He shouldn't have let Merrill and Katla face the entity alone. It didn't matter the reasoning or how sound it appeared at the time. He had known it was a mistake. He should've listened to his gut. Merrill wouldn't be dead now if he had.

The last King of the Oranges. Varek closed his eyes and shook his head. Merrill would come back. He would sense Katla there and claw his way back. He was a fighter. He'd proven that as he kept a tenable hold on his sanity. He would've heard Ulrik. He wouldn't have given up. Not the Merrill Varek knew.

How many times had Merrill told him he wasn't that man anymore? Varek had dismissed his words then. He couldn't any longer.

Katla's keening howls pulled him out of his thoughts. Varek wiped his cheeks with the back of his hand before gently taking Katla by the shoulders. She didn't resist when he pulled her around to him. Her arms wound around his neck as she buried her face in his chest. He held her tightly as her shoulders shook with her sobs.

He had no words of comfort for her. This wasn't how things were supposed to turn out. The Kings had gone up against many enemies. They had taken a beating at times, but they always came out ahead in the end. Maybe a little worse for wear, but they made it. What had gone wrong this time? Varek needed to know where to place the blame. Someone or something had to be responsible for his best friend's life being extinguished.

Merrill should have waited for Katla to return.

Ulrik should have worked faster.

Rhi should have gotten Ulrik to Zora quicker.

Or maybe the blame lay with Con. He should've had Ulrik there days before.

If not him, then Villette, surely. She'd instigated all of this.

Nay, it was the entity and the Orgate warriors for driving Merrill to madness.

Maybe it was his fault. Varek should have seen the pain Merrill hid and helped centuries ago.

Varek looked over at Ulrik to find him staring white-faced at Merrill, tears rolling down his cheeks. He lifted his gaze to Varek. Neither had words for the anguish ripping through them. They should be celebrating Merrill's victory, not doing this.

Out of the corner of his eye, Varek saw gold scales descending from the sky. The King of Golds shifted as he landed. Con's normally unruffled composure was shaken. Grief cut across his face and shadowed his black eyes. He took a step forward, only for his leg to give out. He dropped to one knee, a hand on the ground to keep from tipping over. His breath billowed out of his mouth in a gray mist as he lifted his head. Varek watched Con's face crumple as he touched Merrill's arm.

"We need to take him to Iron Hall," Con said through their mental link.

Ulrik nodded numbly.

Varek dipped his chin when Con looked his way. Con was the first to his feet. He held out a hand to Ulrik and pulled him up. Varek helped Katla to her feet. She, too, had suffered. To have lost everything, only to find love and lose it again. It seemed unusually cruel for two people who had so recently found each other to be so viciously torn apart. It was worse for Merrill. He had never thought to find a mate, but in the end, he had. For an all too brief period of time, he and Katla had found happiness together.

Any questions Varek might have had about Merrill and Katla's relationship had ended the moment Con healed her wounds. Her first thought had been Merrill. Then again, after Merrill went mad, she had been the one to calm him. Only a mate could have reached Merrill in such a way.

Varek turned Katla so she didn't have to see Con and Ulrik lift Merrill's body. Ulrik touched the silver Fae cuff on his wrist, jumping them to Iron Hall. Merrill's body might have left the field, but the agony of his death lingered, hanging in the very air and scarring the ground.

Katla gripped Varek's shirt tightly. Her sobs had quieted, but not her tears. Nor, he imagined, would she stop for some time. He hadn't been able to help Merrill, but Varek intended to do whatever he could for Katla.

Rhi appeared beside them. Her face was pale, her silver eyes bright with tears. He gave her a nod when she lifted a hand. She jumped them to a chamber inside Iron Hall with a single touch. Katla didn't seem to notice. In some ways, Varek envied her. She was lost in a fog of despair and heartache. He couldn't delve into such emotions. Not yet. Some things needed to be taken care of first. It had been eons since a Dragon King had died, but they hadn't forgotten their traditions.

Varek longed to find Jeyra. He needed her arms around him, but his sorrow took a back seat until Katla was settled. Merrill would want her at Iron Hall. He would've fought for her to be welcomed, Varek was sure of that. Merrill had sought out the Druid and saw past her crimes to the woman beneath. He had freely given her his friendship. They would honor him by doing the same.

He walked Katla to the bed. There, he gently took her by the arms and leaned her back.

Katla's black lashes were spiked from crying, and her eyes were puffy. She looked lost as she gazed up at him. "He can't be gone."

Emotion swelled and lodged in Varek's throat. He couldn't stop the tears from rolling down his face any more than she could. "Merrill defeated the entity. He made sure it couldna hurt anyone again."

"How did it kill Merrill?"

Varek looked away, his chest tightening. She didn't know. And now he had to tell her. He couldn't find the words. It was too much.

Rhi approached. She gave Katla a gentle smile and peeled her hands from Varek's shirt before sitting with her on the mattress. "Did Merrill tell you about dragons and their mates?"

Katla nodded, her brow furrowed.

Rhi sniffed and took Katla's hands in hers. "A dragon can't live without its mate. If one mate dies before the ceremony to link them, the other will also die."

"Nay," Katla whispered as she shook her head. "Nay!" Her face crumpled, and a fresh wave of tears came.

Varek stood by helplessly as Rhi held Katla while she sobbed uncontrollably. Rhi motioned for him to leave, and Varek took the opportunity. He was too angry and upset at Merrill's passing to be good to anyone anyway.

He quietly shut the door behind him before striding down the corridor and into the great hall. Varek's feet halted at the top of the steps. He looked out over those below. Some cried, some spoke softly. His grief was too raw to share it with others.

Varek opened the mental link. *"Con?"*

"We're in the northeastern hall," Con answered immediately.

Varek turned on his heel and came face-to-face with Jeyra. She said nothing as she wound her arms around him. He crushed her against him and buried his face in her neck. Her hands were soothing, comforting as she stroked his hair.

She took his face in her hands. "Go to him. I'll be here when you return," she whispered.

He gave her a quick kiss and made his way through the maze of hallways. It would've been shorter to go through the great hall, but that would've meant talking with others. Con and Ulrik had brought Merrill to a private section of the underground city they'd recently found.

Walking was too slow. Varek started running, hoping to flee the hurt descending upon him. Which was absurd. He was running toward his best friend, who lay dead. There was no getting around the sadness and what the future would look like without Merrill. Varek couldn't even remember a time without Merrill in his life.

He slowed when he reached the corridor and walked along the hall until he found an open door. Varek spotted Ulrik first. He stood against the wall near the door like a silent sentry, his sadness creasing his features as his shoulders drooped. Con stood against the opposite wall. His devastation hanging like a dark cloud above him.

In the middle of the room, Merrill lay atop a table draped in an orange blanket from chest to feet.

Varek reluctantly made his way inside. His feet took him to the table. He gazed down at Merrill. Anger no longer contorted his features. But there was also no smile. Some would say Merrill was at peace, but only dragons knew the truth. Merrill's soul would search endlessly for that which he had so recently found. Katla.

The King who had helped each of them find acceptance in the loss of their clans, who never failed to know exactly what to say, and who had lifted others up had found little of it in his life. Family had meant everything to Merrill. He had proven that time and again when someone needed a shoulder and he offered his. Merrill made the world a better place, and everyone who knew him was better because of it.

But what would they do without him?

"How is Katla?" Ulrik asked.

Varek slid his gaze to the King of Silvers. "No' well. Merrill called her mate, but I doona think she understands."

"Bloody hell," Ulrik murmured.

Con walked to stand at Merrill's head. "In every battle, against every enemy, I always tried to prepare myself for such a loss. But nothing could've prepared me for this."

"It isna right," Varek said. "Merrill should be alive."

Ulrik shrugged. "I doona understand it. He just had to hold on a wee bit longer."

"Then we change it." Con and Ulrik looked at him. Varek shrugged. "He's no' supposed to be dead. Bring him back."

"There are rules…" Con began.

Varek sliced a hand through the air. "Fuck the rules!"

"It isna that easy," Ulrik said.

Varek crossed his arms over his chest. "It is for me." He shot Con a withering look. "It should be for you."

"There are things you doona know," Con replied.

Varek shrugged. "Then tell me."

"Enough," Ulrik said, pushing away from the wall and walking to stand at the foot of the table. "Varek, we all want this, but you know as well as I do that Kings can no' be returned."

Varek opened his mouth to argue.

Then Con said, "On Earth."

Ulrik's head swung to him. "What?"

"That's the rule on Earth," Con said. "We're no' on that realm."

Varek looked hopefully between the two. "Then do it."

"And the rest?" Ulrik asked Con without looking at Varek.

Con's brow creased in a frown.

"What?" Varek pressed. "What is the rest?"

Con ran a hand over his mouth and jaw. "The law on Earth is that Ulrik is forbidden to return a King once he dies. If he tries, the King will immediately die again. It's a cycle the magic set up."

"As we've already stated, we're on Zora," Varek said.

Ulrik's lips twisted. "True, but there may be other consequences. Merrill may never be able to return to Earth. Nor do we know if he will still be a King."

That wasn't something Varek had even considered. "Shite."

"Precisely," Con replied.

Knowing Con, there were other things, but he didn't plan on sharing. And right now, Varek had all he could handle. "Merrill always saw the best in everyone. Even when we couldna see it in ourselves. He had the innate ability to guide us toward whatever we sought. He did that with Katla. He saw something in her. Maybe he knew from the beginning that she was his mate. Maybe he didna. But he forgave her for her actions against the dragons."

"Because Villette deceived her," Ulrik said.

Con braced his hands on the table, his gaze on Merrill. "That doesna matter to the dragons. In truth, it didna matter to some of us. Katla had the ability to decide. But would we have made the same choices with the same information she had? Possibly. Merrill saw past all of that. He saw *her*. He befriended her and gave her what no one else did. Forgiveness."

"Because he sought it himself," Ulrik added.

Varek looked down at his closest friend. "Merrill was a protector. He stood between us and Katla when he thought we were going to hurt her. He would've stood between anyone and her. He found his mate. I say we bring him back."

"What about returning to Earth?" Ulrik asked.

Varek dropped his arms and looked at the King of Silvers. "Jeyra is here, and while we've made a few trips to Earth, I'm fine remaining."

"Aye, but you have the option. There's a difference," Con pointed out.

Varek grunted as he admitted the truth. Deciding when to return to Dreagan and never being able to return would change how he felt.

"And if he isna a King anymore?" Con asked, looking between Ulrik and Varek?

Ulrik shrugged. "I know what choice I'd make between remaining King or being with Eilish."

"I feel the same," Varek replied.

Con blew out a breath as he straightened. "Me, too."

THIRTY-EIGHT

Just when Katla thought she had cried all the tears there were, more came. She assumed she had forgotten how deep loss could cut, how shocking death could be. How unbearable it was to no longer be able to give love to the one who was gone.

The world kept going while she sat numbly staring at the walls while reliving the moment breath returned to her body, only to find the last had left Merrill's. It was unfair. Unjust. Merrill was needed. He could do great things. If one of them had to die, it should've been her. Not him. Never him.

She pulled her legs to her chest as she sat against the headboard. Rhi had offered her as much comfort as she could, but sometimes grief was better experienced alone. She didn't have a lifetime of memories with Merrill. She only had a few days. But she went through each one, cherishing every moment.

A knock on her door pulled her from her thoughts. She debated ignoring whoever it was, but they might return. It was better to find out what they wanted now and then let them know she wished to be left alone.

"Enter," she called.

The door opened to reveal Varek. He didn't look as devastated as before. In fact, he looked almost hopeful. He stepped inside with his hand on the door handle. "Did you put the sparks around the entity so Merrill could see it?"

Heartache surged in her chest, making it difficult to breathe. She pressed her lips together and nodded. "I knew I was dying, and if I wasn't there to show him, I wanted him to find the entity."

"You allowed him to find and defeat it. The entity tried its best to get away from Merrill, but he latched on and wouldna let go. I've fought beside Merrill. I know how powerful he is. What I saw today was something else entirely. I doona believe anyone but he could've destroyed the enemy. Then he saw you on the ground."

Her eyes burned as tears flooded them, distorting her view of Varek.

"I feared his madness would tip him into a killing rage," Varek continued as he walked to stand near the bed. "I was worried about my friend, and because of that, I forgot the despair and desolation that strikes our kind at such a loss. All he cared about was getting to you. Holding you."

Katla dropped her forehead to her knees and wept. She didn't want to hear any more. It was too painful. But she couldn't tell him to leave. It might be the last things she ever heard about Merrill, and as excruciating as they were, she needed every word.

"I doona know if he recognized me or Ulrik. But he knew you. His heart, his soul, they knew you. Maybe if he had recalled Ulrik, he would've known he was there to bring you back to life. Merrill may not have been able to understand me. If he had, he might have held on a little longer."

Katla's head jerked up. Her gaze met Varek's. "Why didn't Ulrik bring Merrill back as he did me?"

"It's a strict law we've never broken. At least no' on Earth."

His implication was clear. She dared to allow hope to blossom. "But not on Zora."

Varek licked his lips as he looked at the ground. "Ulrik is going to try to bring him back. We're no' sure if it'll work. It willna on our realm. It might be the same here. If it does work, there's a chance Merrill may no' ever be able to return to Earth."

"He loves Scotland."

"We all do. But if it's a choice between Dreagan and Jeyra, I'd choose Jeyra," Varek said.

"What about the Kings protecting Earth?"

Varek shrugged. "We'd figure something out as we are now. The worst part may be that he is no longer a King."

Katla didn't know what to say to that one. "So he would be a dragon, unable to shift?"

"Or a human, unable to be a dragon."

"That would destroy him."

Varek looked away. "We want to give him the option. And we'd like you to be there."

There was no way she would refuse such a request. Even if Merrill decided not to take the chances he may have to face for returning, she couldn't stay away. Katla slid off the bed and stood. Varek motioned for her to follow as he led her out of the chamber and down a labyrinth of hallways. There must have been identifying marks to lead him, but she got turned around immediately. She wondered if they were in Iron Hall, but the thought was quickly replaced by thoughts of Merrill. Except it wasn't tears that greeted her. It was hope. It was dangerous to hold onto that, yet she grasped it with both hands.

What seemed like an eternity later, they came to a room. Varek went inside, but Katla lingered at the entrance. Her gaze landed on Merrill's prone body and she had to grip the doorjamb to stay upright. Con stood near Merrill's head, his face tight and his dark eyes intense as they met hers. At Merrill's feet was the dark-haired man she had woken to see. He apparently had the ability to bring someone back to life.

Con nodded to the other man. "I doona believe you got a chance to meet the King of Silvers. This is Ulrik."

Katla met the Dragon King's gold eyes. "Thank you for what you did for me."

"My pleasure," Ulrik said, bowing his head. "I hear you're a verra powerful Druid."

"I didn't even know that word until recently. Merrill believed I already had magic and didn't know it."

Ulrik flashed a brief smile. "Merrill had an uncanny ability to see things like that in others. I've no doubt you did."

"Then Villette got involved," Varek said.

Katla grimaced at the reminder. "If I had known…" she began.

Con held up a hand, halting her words. "No one is demanding an explanation. None of us will. If there was any doubt about your true nature, your actions have disabused anyone of it. We know Villette deceived you, just as she did Merrill."

"As she has many," Varek added.

Ulrik's lips flattened. "I'm almost sad I've no' had the displeasure of meeting her."

"We had the chance to kill her," Katla said.

Con nodded solemnly. "No' anyone around will say you chose wrong. We can always find Villette later. The same couldna be said about saving Merrill."

Katla braced herself and lowered her gaze to Merrill again. The sight of him so still and silent was a sucker punch. She fought to catch her breath, even as her feet brought her to him. She reverently touched his hand, tears threatening again. She blinked them back and looked up at the men. "What now?"

"Now, I reach out to Merrill," Ulrik said.

She watched as he closed his eyes and placed a hand on Merrill's leg.

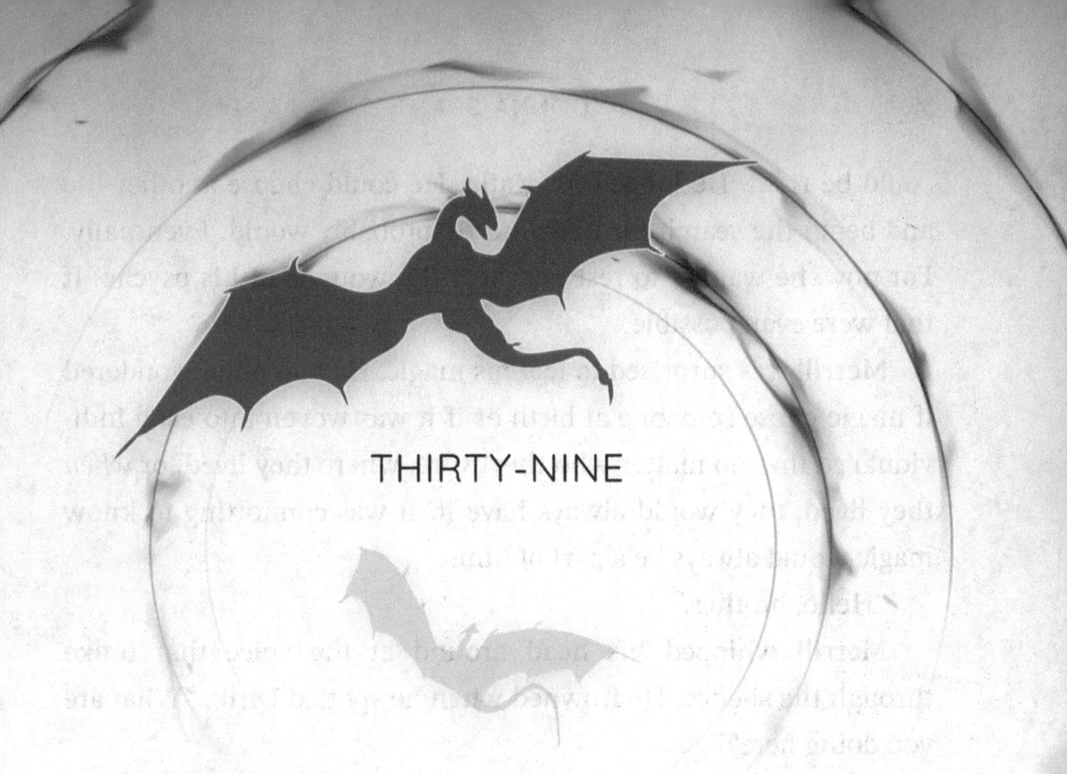

THIRTY-NINE

Death was a curious state. Merrill had never thought much about it. There hadn't been a need when the Kings were all but immortal on Earth. Going to Zora had changed everything. And revealed secrets and mysteries they had known nothing about.

He sat on the edge of a dock, the pink and purple colors below him moving languidly like a slow-moving river. The magenta sky was clear. There was no one else about. Just him. He drew in a breath and slowly released it. There was no more pain. No suffering. No madness. But there was an emptiness in his heart. He had hoped to find Katla on this side. Perhaps he needed to look harder.

His thoughts drifted to the Kings, specifically Varek. He wished he had been able to speak to Varek before he went insane. Instead, Merrill had shut everyone out. Regret was a bitter pill to swallow. The emotion was there but not as debilitating as he'd expected. Was he supposed to let such things go? It seemed the right thing to do in order to move on. But move on to where?

He had lived many lifetimes. Too many, some might say. They

could be right. He longed for Katla. He could choose another life and begin the search for her. And he probably would. Eventually. For now, he wanted to rest and heal the wounds of his psyche. If that were even possible.

Merrill was surprised to feel his magic. He had often wondered if magic chose someone at birth or if it was woven into each individual so that no matter who they were, where they lived, or *when* they lived, they would always have it. It was comforting to know magic would always be a part of him.

"Hello, brother."

Merrill whipped his head around at the voice that broke through the silence. He frowned when he spotted Ulrik. "What are you doing here?"

"Is it no' obvious?"

"You can no' bring me back."

Ulrik grinned. "On Earth. You didna die on Earth."

Merrill waited as Ulrik walked over and sat beside him. Then he said, "There's no way Con knows you're here."

"He's the one who pointed out the difference."

"If there's one you should save, it's Katla."

Ulrik met his gaze and smiled. "I already did. She returned seconds before you breathed your last. Varek tried to tell you. So did I."

"I didna hear either of you." He swallowed. "How is Katla?"

"Lost without you. We brought her to Iron Hall."

Merrill briefly closed his eyes and sighed with relief. "Good. She needs friends."

"She needs you."

"Returning a King from the dead is forbidden."

Ulrik twisted his lips and looked out over the magenta field.

"I'm willing to chance it." He cut him a look. "The question is, are you?"

"Of course, I want to return to Katla."

"Then you should be aware of some things that may change."

Merrill inwardly grimaced. Of course, there would be drawbacks to a King skirting the rules to return to life. "Like?"

"We're no' sure if you'll be able to return to Earth."

To not see Dreagan again? Not be able to walk the glens or swim in the lochs of his beloved Scotland? Simply because they found a loophole in the rules. But he would be alive and with his mate. "All right. What else?"

Ulrik hesitated. Merrill braced, knowing it would be a doozy if Ulrik paused.

"You may no longer be a King."

That one was obvious, but even Merrill hadn't considered it. He had been a Dragon King in life, so why not once he returned? Because of that pesky rule that no Kings should return from the dead.

He scratched his cheek. "Meaning I'll return as a dragon?"

"Maybe." Ulrik shook his head. "You could be human."

Unable to shift or take to the skies. How would he live without being a dragon?

"It's a lot to contemplate," Ulrik said. "How much are you potentially willing to give up for Katla?"

That was an easy answer. "Everything."

Ulrik grinned and turned his head to him. "I had a feeling that would be your answer."

"I'm willing to chance everything, but if I return as a dragon, this will all be for naught because I still wouldna have my mate."

Ulrik's smile faded. "True."

"We've no' discussed my madness. What point is returning if that takes me again?"

"You have control of that, brother."

"Trust me, I doona."

Ulrik walked a couple of steps closer. "You did it with Katla."

"Her presence calmed me and allowed me to think clearly."

"Is that what you think?" Ulrik chuckled softly. "She might be the catalyst that catches your attention, but you are the one who focuses your emotions."

Merrill snorted. "You were no' there. I clearly remember the slide into insanity. I couldna even remember my name."

"But you knew her."

"What if she isna always by my side?" Merrill demanded, his voice rising with his anger. "I willna chance harming others."

Ulrik grinned. "You have so little faith in your power."

"My magic can do many things, but it can no' reverse madness."

"How long have you lived with the resentment and wrath?"

The question made Merrill pause. He swallowed as he studied his friend. "Too long."

"Did you hurt anyone?"

"No' on purpose."

"Did you kill any humans?"

Merrill ran his hand through his hair as he realized what Ulrik was doing. "I didna."

"Then things are no' different."

"No' true. There was a primal urge, an elemental impulse to destroy every human. All of them. Innocent or no'. It was an instinct I couldna control."

Ulrik clapped his hands on Merrill's shoulders. "You forgot one thing. Who is behind all of this? Who manipulated even the mortals?"

"Villette." How could he have forgotten that?

"What if our places were reversed? Would you think I didna deserve my waiting mate?"

Merrill looked away. "You know I wouldna."

"Give yourself the same forgiveness and kindness you've given every King at least once through the eons, brother." Ulrik jerked his chin to the sparks. "Even now, your magic conjures her."

Merrill was brought up short. "I thought you brought them."

"That's all you."

He ached to see her face, to hold her again. She was alive. Waiting for him. "I want to be with Katla."

The corner of Ulrik's eyes crinkled. Something pulled at Merrill, tugging him away. He eagerly rose and followed Ulrik. Suddenly, a blinding light forced him to turn his head away. When he next blinked, he found himself staring up at a ceiling. Someone squeezed Merrill's hand.

He had a human hand. At least one of his fears had been alleviated. He didn't try to shift yet. He would face that one later. Merrill swallowed, waiting for the darkness to rise and the anger to swell and demand blood payment.

There was still anger, still some resentment, but it wasn't as it had been when he lost his mind. That meant he was still himself. Not the man from before Zora, but the one after. The one who still had many issues to address and repair. Another fear assuaged.

Hesitantly, he searched for his magic and felt its response. One more box checked. There was the final one yet, but he couldn't do it in the room and bust the walls. Nor did he want to do it with others around. Just in case. That was something to test at a later date.

He felt Katla's presence beside him, her hand in his. Merrill rolled his head to the side and saw her radiant smile. Tears welled up in her gray eyes and spilled down her cheeks as she whispered his name.

Merrill tugged her onto his chest. He wound his arms around her and held her against him. He had almost missed out on this. If not for his brothers, he would have. He looked over to find Ulrik, Varek, and Con. Ulrik winked before walking away. Con tipped his head, a grin on his lips as he followed Ulrik. Merrill stared at Varek, a wordless exchange passing between them. Relief shone in Varek's brown eyes as he nodded, smiling.

Then it was just him and Katla. Merrill tangled his hand in the cool length of her hair and closed his eyes. Her tears wet his neck. The madness he had feared hadn't returned, but that didn't mean it wouldn't. It meant he had to remain vigilant and have precautions in place. But that was for later. Now, he would hold his mate and revel in the fact that they were both alive.

Katla sat up, bracing her hand on the table as she stared down at him. "I thought I'd lost you."

"I would cross galaxies for you." He used his thumb to wipe away a tear, then cupped her face in his hands. "Surely you know how deeply I feel for you."

"I hoped. I dreamed. It was all I allowed myself."

"Then let me cast aside any doubt. You have my heart, my beautiful Katla. You alone pulled me back from the edge of madness. You calmed my rage and eased the storm within me. I love you. It's a deep love. The kind few believe in, and even fewer experience. Never doubt what I would do for you or the lengths I would go to for your safety."

She brushed her lips over his and whispered, "Never."

Merrill brought her face down to his and kissed her again. He was starved for her. He had waited an eternity to find her and would never let her go again. The rest of the universe could wait. This time was for them. He tugged her on top of him on the table. She rolled away. He hurriedly grabbed her so she wouldn't fall, only to feel a mattress beneath him.

His head lifted to find them in a bedroom. He looked at Katla. "You jumped us?"

She grinned, nodding. "Something new I've picked up."

"Impressive," he murmured as he looked around the room.

The ceiling and walls were a muted green, the floors wide, planked wood. The arched headboard was fashioned of thick vines. More of the vines made an arch from the wall, where the bed sat, over the middle of the bed to the opposite wall. An ivy-like plant wove through the vines to mingle with some small string lights. Two wall sconces sat on either side of the bed.

The wall facing him had a large pane of arched glass with a mural painted to appear as if it looked outside. There were lights that changed with the time of day to make it appear like sunlight. A vine as thick as his arm curved along the window with the ivy and lights hanging from it.

A dark green velvet comforter with matching sheets covered the bed. The same hunter green was used on a circular rug near the bed, and an oval rug alongside a copper clawfoot tub. A matching pedestal sink and toilet were nearby. A smile pulled at his lips when he saw the shower in the corner.

Merrill yanked aside the blanket and took Katla's hand as he rose from the bed. A frown flitted across her face as she parted her lips to speak. He dragged her to him, taking her mouth in a passionate kiss. She melted against him. With a thought, he removed her clothes so they were flesh to flesh, then bent his knees and slid his hands down her back and over her shapely arse to lift her. She spread her legs, wrapping them around his waist as he straightened. Then he walked them to the shower.

Glass surrounded it on three sides. The walls matched the rest of the room, and the trailing vine was also in there. The floor was tile that matched the planks on the floor. A two-foot square copper rain showerhead hung above them to match the copper faucet.

He released Katla's legs and let her slowly slide down his body. Only when her feet touched the tile did he reach over and turn on the faucet. Hot water fell down his back and trickled over his chest. She tore her lips from his and stared up in wonder at the shower. He watched as she put her hands under the water before walking beneath the spray.

Desire heated his already inflamed blood as she smoothed the water back from her face and over her midnight hair plastered to her head, the ends just skimming her hips. The water sluiced along her pale skin and mouthwatering curves. His hungry gaze locked on her voluptuous breasts where dusky pink nipples were hard peaks straining toward him. He followed the water as it slid into the indent of her waist and then over the swell of her hips to her shapely legs.

As his gaze traveled upward, he paused at the dark triangle of hair that hid her sex. His balls tightened with need. He moaned before pulling her against him and capturing her mouth.

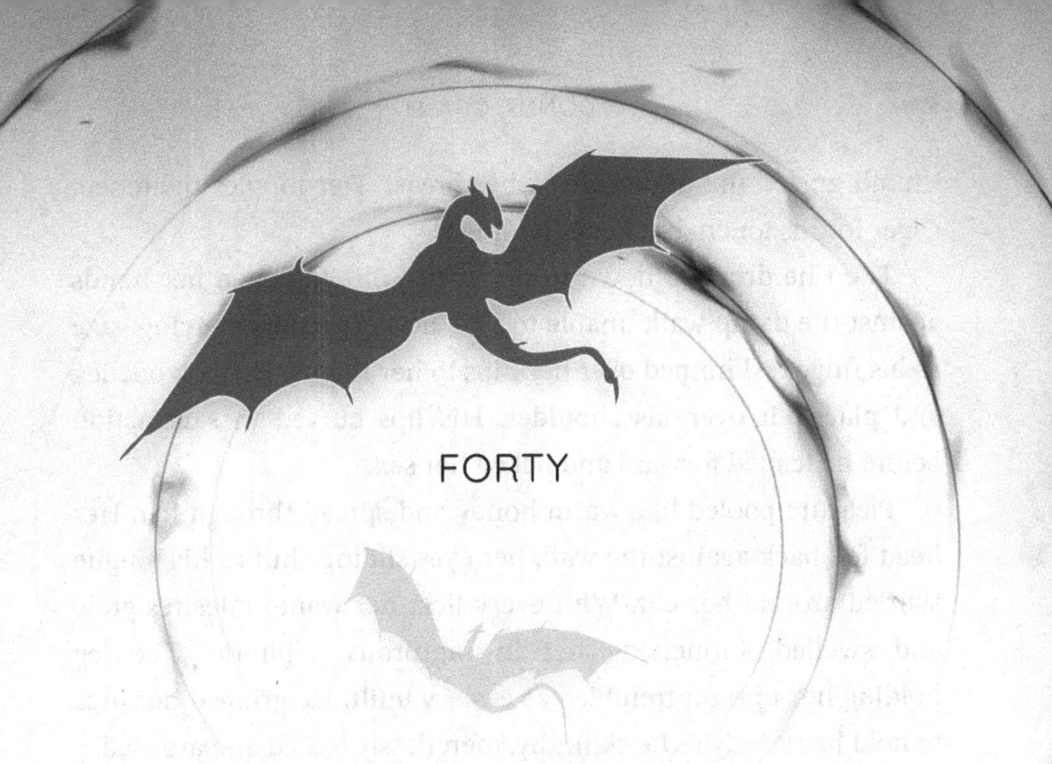

FORTY

Katla was flooded with desire. Everywhere Merrill touched left a trail of heat. He deepened the kiss, tangling their tongues in a wild, fervent kiss. Then she was against the wall, his hands holding her wrists by her head. He rocked his arousal against her, making her groan and her sex clench greedily.

Their hunger was too overwhelming, their need too great to take things slow. She arched her back to rub herself against him. He wrenched his mouth from hers with a moan. She was breathless and desperate to have him inside her.

Something possessive and ravenous flashed in the dark blue depths of his eyes. Her lips parted, her chest rising and falling rapidly. She trembled in excitement, the anticipation of the pleasure that awaited her reflected in his face. In his very touch.

He leaned forward, his lips finding her neck. She tilted her head to the side as his lips and tongue left a trail along the column of her throat. His fingers loosened on her wrists to slide along her arms and then down her sides. She sucked in a breath when his thumb grazed the underside of her breast. Her nipples tightened, eager for his touch, but he didn't linger.

Then he dropped down to his knees. She flattened her hands against the damp wall, unable to look away from his piercing gaze as his fingers skimmed over her hips to her thighs. He took one leg and placed it over his shoulder. His lips curved in satisfaction before he leaned forward and licked her sex.

Pleasure pooled like warm honey and spread through her. Her head fell back against the wall, her eyes sliding shut as his tongue swirled around her clit. With every lick, her wanton desires grew and swelled, immersing her in rapturous euphoria. The leg holding her upright trembled as ecstasy built. He gripped her hips to hold her steady as he skillfully, mercilessly teased and aroused.

The orgasm struck without warning. It shot through her, sweeping her along a river of unimaginable bliss. Wave after wave of rhapsody rolled through her, one on top of the other. She was powerless to do more than ride the surge until the very end.

She drew in a ragged breath and moaned as Merrill gently lowered her leg. He placed a soft kiss on each thigh and another in her curls before he straightened. She sensed him towering over her. She felt his longing, his desire. Her hands moved to his waist and then upward to his chest. Only then was she able to open her eyes.

His nostrils flared. His body taut, needy. The fever of desire roared to life again within her.

"Mine," he whispered before kissing her.

His arousal pressed against her stomach. She skated her hands around his back and pulled him close. His slipped between then and cupped a breast. A cry of pleasure ripped from her mouth when he thumbed her nipple. Desire shot straight to her swollen sex. She throbbed, ached. And she couldn't wait another moment to have him inside her.

Katla skimmed her palm over the ridges of his flat stomach to wrap her fingers around his erection. A bead of moisture formed on the head of his cock. He groaned into her mouth as she swirled her thumb around it. Katla moved her hand up and down his length as he continued to tease her nipples.

Need thrummed through her, demanding release. Just when she couldn't stand it anymore, Merrill gripped her hips and lifted her. She wrapped her legs around his waist and looked into his eyes as he pressed her against the wall. Then he slowly, sensuously slid his arousal against her clit. She cried out at the exquisite pleasure.

"Forever," he stated.

The head of his cock brushed against her entrance. He paused for a moment before sliding inside her. She sighed as her body stretched to accommodate him. Then he moved. Long, slow thrusts that pushed her closer to climax.

She clung to him, holding on as he gradually quickened his tempo. Their bodies slid against each other in a dance as old as time. The scrape of his chest against her nipples, his rod sliding in and out, their bodies meeting. It all heightened her passion.

He drove into her hard and deep, each thrust building her desire tighter and tighter. This time, she felt the orgasm forming. She reached for it eagerly, fervently opening herself to it. Even when she teetered at the precipice, it only enhanced the pleasure she knew was just out of reach.

The climax didn't slam into her like before. This time, it slowly rolled through her, gaining momentum and expanding as intense pleasure pulsed. The walls of her sex contracted around him. He didn't stop, didn't slow. He gave a final thrust, burying himself deep inside her, and she felt him touch her womb, felt his seed fill her as he orgasmed.

They remained locked together for long minutes, her body still tightening around his cock in the aftershocks of her climax. Finally, their breathing returned to normal. Merrill lifted his head. His crooked smile made her heart melt. He pulled out of her and lowered her to the floor, then positioned her beneath the spray of water.

He came up behind her, pressing against her. She leaned against him and smiled. She was deliriously happy. He took a bar of soap and began moving it over her, washing her. She never imagined she could enjoy someone bathing her, but she did. Merrill didn't just wash her. He touched, teased. Aroused.

Her head lolled when his mouth found a sensitive spot on her neck. He soaped his hands and massaged her breasts, paying particular attention to her nipples. He spent just as long on her back and her legs. He was gentle as he washed her sex then rinsed her with the same attention.

Katla took the soap from him and lathered her hands as they shared a look. It was her turn to inspect his body with as much consideration and care as he had hers. He grinned, his eyes sparking with desire. She wanted him again. She couldn't get enough of him, and she suspected it would always be that way.

She motioned him out from beneath the spray and put her hands on his chest, moving them in circles and spreading the soap across his pecs and muscular shoulders. His body was hard, each muscle honed to perfection. She moved lower over his chiseled abdomen to his narrow hips. She scrubbed back up his chest to wash each brawny arm from shoulder to fingers.

All the while, he watched her. She held his gaze as she dropped to her knees and skimmed her soapy hands down his front to clean one leg and then the other. His eyes heated when she slowly moved over his thigh and brushed his hard cock. He moaned the moment she wrapped her hands around him, then groaned her name when she used her thumb to twirl around the head, before stroking firmly down and then back up his length. She squeezed her legs together as she took great care in thoroughly washing his glorious arousal.

Katla rose and turned him around. Her eyes landed on the dragon. She had forgotten about it until that moment. Her hands lovingly caressed the design that took up his entire back.

The dragon was in mid-flight, its body curved as if turning. The wings were angled upward and extended to his neck and across both shoulders. The dragon's claws were positioned as if it were reaching for something. Its tail curled to end at the base of his spine. It was both beautiful and mesmerizing.

"It's called a tattoo," Merrill said as he turned his head to the side. "Each of the Kings received one the moment we shifted for the first time."

"How is this tattoo done?" she asked.

"It's inked into the skin."

She gazed at the color, unable to determine if it was black or red, finally settling on a mix of both. "Does every King have the same one?"

"We each have a different dragon placed on different areas of our body."

"Amazing."

Merrill couldn't take another moment of her hands on him. It had been the sweetest torture, but his body craved more. He turned to Katla and took the soap from her, rinsing her hands and then himself before shutting off the water. She shot him a knowing grin when he began to dry her off. He barely ran the towel over himself before he tossed it aside and lifted her in his arms.

She let out a squeak of surprise that turned into a laugh as he strode to the bed. He laid her on the mattress and followed to lay atop her. She rose almost immediately and turned him onto his back. Then she slid down his body to settle between his legs. He lifted his head, watching her hands skimming up his thighs. He held his breath, anxiously waiting for her to take hold of him. He couldn't get enough of her. Would never get enough of her. His beautiful, remarkable mate.

A moan escaped when her fingers wrapped around him. Her hand pumped up and down his length in slow, sure strokes. His head dropped onto the bed as desire licked his skin. Then her lips were on him, kissing his shaft.

He fisted the comforter as she moved up his length. He watched as she hovered over the head. Her lips parted, and she wrapped them around him to take him into her mouth. Pleasure rocketed through him. He groaned loudly, his body stiffening with need as she took him deep. Her head bobbed up and down, her mouth softly pulling while her hands worked him.

It was too much. He was at the edge already. Merrill flipped her onto her hands and knees and moved up behind her. He touched her sex and found her already wet.

"Please," she begged. "I need you."

He rubbed his cock along her labia before sliding into her from behind. She let out a soft cry of pleasure when he held her there, rocking gently. Then he gripped her hips and began to thrust hard and deep.

"Merrill," she called out in a shaky voice.

He reached around and rubbed her swollen clit. She cried out, rocking back against him. She was close. So very close.

He had dreamed of the many ways he would bring her pleasure. He flattened his hand on her stomach and caressed upward to cup her breast. He rolled a nipple between his fingers, wringing another low moan from her.

"Please," she pleaded.

He wanted the gratification as much as she did. Maybe even more. But it always felt better when it was earned. He fought against the rising desire and smoothed both hands down her back. She arched it, pressing her fine arse against him. His hands glided up her back, then he wound a hand into the long length of her wet hair. With the other, he skimmed his thumb down her spine and into the crease of her arse cheeks. Very gently, he pressed against the opening there.

She shattered instantly. The moment her body began to contract around him, he was lost to his orgasm. They were both out of breath when he finally pulled out of her. His body was sated as it had never been. They fell to the side together, and he flipped onto his back. Katla turned to face him, and he pulled her close. He loved the feel of her breath across his stomach and how she curled against him.

"I love you."

Merrill kissed her forehead. "I know."

"I never thought I'd love again. Never dreamed I could have something like this. I didn't know love could *be* like this." She rose to look down at him. "This may sound horrible, but I don't think I can be angry at Villette anymore."

He tucked a lock of hair behind her ear. "Oh?"

"If she hadn't interfered, I never would've met you. I wouldn't have known what it's like to be loved by or to love you. She did wrong. I'm not saying she didn't, I just—"

He put a finger over her mouth. "You doona need to explain. I feel the same. As odd as it is to consider, much less say aloud."

"Really?"

"Really."

She settled against his chest once more. "We're still going after her."

"Absolutely." Merrill stared at the ceiling. "Some precautions need to be put in place in case I can no' control my rage again, though."

"If it will make you feel better, of course."

"It will. I doona know what will happen in the future, and I want to be sure everyone is prepared."

She nodded. "What happens next? With us, I mean."

He sat up and rolled her onto her back to look into her gray eyes. "I wasna going to bring it up yet to give you some time to settle in."

"I'd rather discuss it now."

"All right," he murmured. "What would you like?"

She smoothed a lock of hair out of his eyes. "To stay with you."

"I want that, as well." He paused. "Eventually, I'd like more."

"Like?"

He wanted to find the right words. She had been locked away in the valley for so long and had just now found freedom. The last thing he wanted was for her to feel as if she were tied down again.

"Merrill," she nudged when he didn't immediately answer.

"I'd like us to do the mating ceremony."

A smile broke over her face. "I was hoping you'd say that."

He grinned, feeling joy the likes of which he had never experienced before. "Just let me know when."

"Is tomorrow too soon?"

He shook his head. "It can be arranged. I'll get things started right now."

"Wait," she said as she held him. "Does it have to be right this moment? Can it wait an hour or two?"

"Aye," he whispered before lowering his head.

She put a finger to his lips to stop him. "What about you?"

"What about me, lass?"

"There are things you should probably know for certain about...yourself...before we do anything."

Merrill put his forehead to hers. "Aye. You're probably right."

"It won't matter to me if you're still a King or not," she said. "I didn't fall in love with you because you're a dragon or could shift." She put her hand over his heart. "I fell in love with you because of the person you are."

"Thank you, lass. I needed to hear that." Not that it would help if he couldn't shift. He was in human form to be with Katla, and he had his magic. That should be enough. He told himself it was.

But it wasn't.

He was a dragon. No matter how long he was in human form, he never stopped being a dragon. Not in his heart. If he couldn't shift, if he couldn't take to the skies... He lay on his back, pulling Katla to him. She wound her arms around him.

"I want to ignore it, but that hasna done me much good." Merrill snorted. "Putting it off willna help me."

She rose and touched his face. "You can do this. I'll be right beside you if you want."

"I do. And I'd like to find out sooner rather than later. Somewhere no one else can see."

"I know the perfect place," she rose from the bed and held out her hand. "Shall we?"

He took her hand and stood. "Are you teleporting us?"

"We're going to find out," she replied.

Merrill called to his magic and covered them with clothes. Katla winked at him. In his next breath, he found himself standing in her valley. He gasped at the blacked and burned vines. There hadn't been time to ask what had happened to her after the attack.

"It's bad, but not all the vines were burned. Kora saw to that," Katla told him.

He looked down at her. "And you? Were you hurt?"

"Con healed me."

She wasn't telling him everything. Probably because she didn't want to talk about the details. He let it go for now, but he would ask Con later. "I'm sorry the destruction came here."

"The vines will recover. I plan to make sure of it," Katla replied.

Merrill stared out over the valley. The place had seen so much pain and death. It had been a prison for dragons in the past, but for him, it was a sanctuary. For whatever would happen.

Katla squeezed his hand. He flashed her a smile he didn't feel, then released her and walked away. He was scared. Terrified, actually. What if he remained human forever? Would he even remain at Iron Hall? It would be impossible to watch his brothers return to their true forms and not do the same. But he didn't want to be without them, either.

He was filled with gratitude for what had been given to him. If he couldn't shift, he would find a way to accept it. This time, he wouldn't ignore and deny it. This time, he would turn to those he loved and who loved him for the tools he needed to address it and heal. Even if he was still a King, he planned to focus on healing the pain of the past.

Merrill stopped amid a tangle of vines that leaned to the side. He looked back at Katla. She smiled and nodded encouragingly. Then he took a deep breath and felt inside for the dragon.

It roared loudly as his skin shed to reveal his orange scales. Merrill spread his wings, reared up on his hind legs, and let out a triumphant roar.

FORTY-ONE

Everything was ready. Except for her.

The last twenty-four hours had been a whirlwind. Katla hadn't known what to expect from the others at Iron Hall, but they had been exceedingly kind and welcoming. She would put her past to rights somehow. That was the least she could do for the dragons.

She walked across the bedroom floor and stood in front of the full-length mirror. Katla stared at her reflection, clothed in an off-the-shoulder orange, red, and yellow ombre gown. Its A-line cut was pleasing, and the deep V in the front showed off her breasts while the cinched waist flattered her. The bell sleeves added a dramatic flair, but it was the length that dragged behind her that she particularly loved. Rhi had called the material silk. All Katla knew was that it was soft and she felt amazing in it.

Katla touched her hair. She'd chosen to wear it loose down her back, though she had pinned the sides back. The woman staring back at her was nothing like the one who had left the vine forest, and she was miles away from the person she had been when she lost her family.

The future was uncertain, but she had Merrill to walk the path beside her. And a new family. She was ready for it all. The ups and the downs. The good and the bad.

Her door burst open, and Maely and Aven walked in with bright smiles. Katla's mouth dropped open when she saw them. Aven was in an ombre gown, the top red and the bottom orange while Maely's was orange on top and red on the bottom.

"Rhi said you'd enjoy the surprise," Aven said.

She went to the girls and wrapped her arms around them. "Both of you are beautiful."

"So are you," Maely said as she gazed at Katla's gown.

Katla looked behind them. "Where's Perick?"

"He's with Merrill. We cannot get him away," Maely answered with a roll of her eyes.

Aven chuckled. "And to think, not that long ago, we were wandering the forest homeless. Now look what we have."

"This place is pretty incredible," Katla agreed. "So are the people."

"Tamlyn said we're part of that now," Maely told her.

Katla smoothed her hand down the girl's black hair. "That we are."

Aven motioned to the door with her head. "It's time to go."

Katla eagerly walked out of the chamber with one girl on either side, holding their hands. Against all odds, she had found a family again. There was still much healing to do, but they had a good foundation now. They would continue to improve on it, and the future was brighter than it had ever been. But that's what happened with love.

Then there was Zora. The realm had some healing to do, as well. Katla planned to be right next to Merrill and the others to face Villette and any other enemies that rose up.

They turned a corner and found Con waiting. He wore a kilt with a black jacket over a white shirt. He nodded to the girls, who smiled at Katla and let go of her hands to keep walking.

"They were anxious to see you, so I sent them for you," Con explained.

She watched the girls vanish around a corner. "So much has been going on that I've not had a chance to speak with you alone. I know this must all be moving very fast for you—"

"I assure you it isna. However, I'm here now if you wish to talk."

Katla nervously clutched her hands together. "I don't think I'll ever be able to adequately repay all of you for what you've done for me and the children. Especially me."

"You love Merrill. That's all we need."

"Thank you." She blinked, her eyes burning with unshed tears. "I'll make amends for the actions of my past somehow."

Con dipped his chin as he smiled. "Now. It's tradition for me to walk the mate to meet her King. It's also tradition for every mate to receive a gift from me." He held out a small, black velvet box.

Katla stared at it. A gift. She wasn't used to those. Hesitantly, she took the box and opened it. Inside was a large, pear-shaped orange pendant hanging from a gold chain.

"On our world, the gem is called a spessartite garnet."

"It matches Merrill's scales." She excitedly took the necklace from the box.

Con held out his hands. "Shall I?"

She turned and moved her hair out of the way as he clasped it around her neck. Katla touched the pendant once it lay against her skin and faced Con once more. "Thank you. This is beautiful."

"You're very welcome. If we doona get there soon, Merrill will come looking for us. Ready?" he asked.

"Very."

They shared a smile before walking into the great hall. Katla would never get tired of looking up and seeing the enormous tree that hung above them, its roots shooting out in all directions to hold it up. And the pool below that collected the water that dripped from the roots. It was just one part of the amazing city that took her breath away.

Rhi was waiting for them by the pool, along with the girls. The Fae smiled in greeting. Katla had gotten to know Rhi over the last day since she had helped Katla find her gown. The other mates at Iron Hall had excitedly stepped in to help with everything. Love. A home. Family. Friends. It had seemed a distant dream until Merrill.

They halted in front of Rhi. The Fae was jumping them to Cairnkeep since Katla hadn't been there. She was hesitant to go to the capital since it was on dragon land, but Con and Merrill assured her that all would be well.

There was no time for Katla to say anything. Rhi touched her hand, and the next moment, she was outside. Sunlight streaked the ground between huge clouds while snow flurries danced in the air. Katla lowered her gaze and saw the guests lined up on each side of an aisle. At the front, near the cliff's edge, stood Merrill in his kilt.

"I'll see you up there," Con said.

Katla barely heard him. She saw Rhi leading the girls into the crowd. As Katla scanned the crowd, she caught sight of the other men wearing kilts. And then she spotted Perick, whose kilt matched Merrill's.

She looked at Merrill once more. He wore a bright smile. After that, he was the only one she saw. He gave her a small nod, and she started in his direction. Before she knew it, she stood before him. He took her hands as they faced each other.

"Wow," he whispered as he gave her an appreciative once-over.

Her heart was nearly bursting with happiness. "Wow, yourself."

"Welcome, all," Con said as he took his place to lead the ceremony. "There is nothing more joyous than a dragon who has found his mate. Sometimes, it comes easily. Other times, it doesna. But there is no denying the bond between two people who are destined to love. I know I'm no' alone is saying that Merrill and Katla have shown their love to one and all and earned their place among us."

A loud cheer rose up.

Katla glanced at the audience in surprise. A few had accepted her, but she never assumed others would.

"It's now time to welcome Katla as Merrill's mate," Con's voice boomed. "Merrill, do you bind yourself to Katla? Do you vow to love her, cherish her, and protect her above all others?"

Merrill's expression was serious and earnest as he stated, "Aye."

"Katla, do you bind yourself to Merrill, King of Oranges? Promise to love him, cherish him, and protect him above all others?"

Katla's heart filled with joy. "Aye."

A slow smile curved Merrill's lips. He had explained about the mark that would appear on her upper left arm. Pain seared her flesh, but it only lasted a moment. When she tugged her sleeve down, she saw the dragon-eye tattoo.

"The proof of your vows and your love. Everyone who sees this will know Katla has been marked as Merrill's mate for eternity!" Con shouted.

Her ears rang with the deafening cheers. But it was all quickly forgotten as Merrill kissed her.

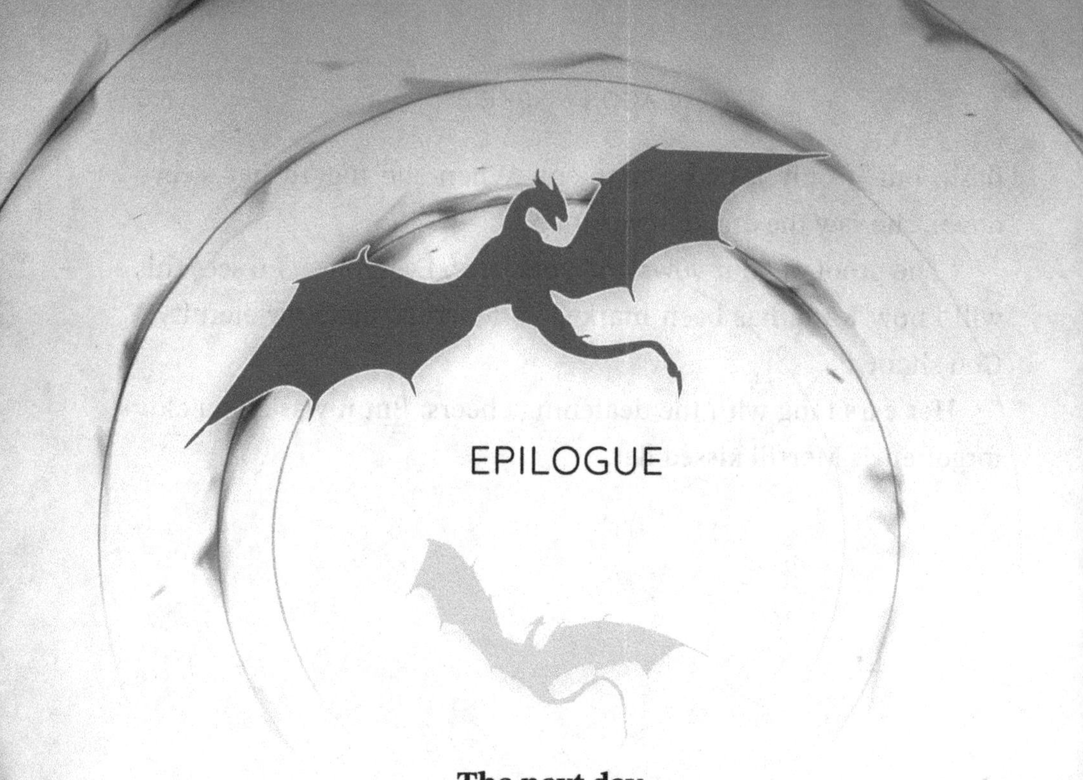

EPILOGUE

The next day...

Merrill stared at the field where he had killed the entity, the same one in which he had seen Katla dead. And the place he had died. The ground was white with snow. The blades of grass sticking up were iced.

Some might believe this was the place where everything changed. It was an important location, but the change had occurred earlier. The instant he decided to follow Katla. That was the catalyst. It'd sparked an entirely new journey that showed him his darkest fears and greatest joy.

His head turned to the side to look upon Katla, who stood next to him. She was swathed in a long, gray coat that matched her eyes. Thick fur lined the collar, lapels, and cuffs. He gazed in wonder at the incredible woman beside him. Her chin was lifted, her expression serene as she stared out at the grassland. She was searching for any sign that the entity might have survived.

Stormy gray eyes lifted to his. "I don't see it."

Con walked up on her other side. "Do you see anything that would lead you to believe it still lives?"

That's what this trip was all about. Merrill knew he had destroyed the being, but would it stay dead?

Katla said nothing as she walked forward. Her footsteps left tracks in the snow as she headed toward the location where he had ripped the entity in half. There, in a nearly perfect circle, the snow melted as soon as it landed. Brandr was there, squatting at the edge as he studied the ground.

Merrill hadn't seen anything drop from the being, but something must have. It was the only explanation for the area to be affected.

Katla stopped at the edge of the circle. "There are no remnants left behind. No bones or anything."

"Your sparks allowed me to see it being torn apart. I felt it, too," Merrill said.

Brandr lifted his gaze. "If it didna have a body, how can we know if it's dead?"

"We can no'. And that's the problem," Con replied.

Merrill frowned as he stared at the spot. "It spoke."

All three turned to look at him.

Merrill twisted his lips. "I'd forgotten until we returned here."

"What did it say?" Brandr asked as he straightened.

"At first it just screamed." Merrill touched his temple as the screech echoed in his head.

His eyes closed as he searched for the memory. His mind resisted. Did he really want to return to that night and the fury? Cold fingers of fear reached for him, clasped his heart. This was what he feared. To return and get a glimpse of perfect happiness only to have it snatched away.

Small hands took his free one. Merrill drew in a deep breath. Katla was his anchor. She showed him how to find his way when the darkness came. He had a long road ahead of him to be able to do this on his own, but he wouldn't be alone. He had his mate and his family. And with them, he could do anything.

He searched his recollections again. This time, when his mind resisted, he pressed onward, casting aside all doubts and fears. The memories had large holes of information missing, but he kept looking. It was important that he remember what the entity had said.

Merrill dug deeper, combing through every moment of their battle. And then he found it.

His eyes snapped open to collide with Katla's. He dropped his arm to his side. "I remember." Merrill looked at Brandr than Con. "The entity claimed we destroyed its planet. Us and the Star People."

"So, it was after revenge?" Brandr asked.

Merrill nodded.

Con's black eyes sizzled with fury, his nostrils flaring. "It wasna any of us."

"Exactly. Why go after Merrill?" Brandr asked.

Merrill recalled the hostility aimed at him. "I was an easy target because I no' only left the canyon, but my anger was out of control."

Con glared at the spot where the entity had died. "If there's any truth to this, we need to know."

"Bloody hell," Brandr murmured. "You want to ask Villette?"

Katla twisted her lips. "She did say some of the dragons they tried to extend their life went insane and destroyed worlds. The entity's might have been one of those?"

"I'd like to know if it was. And if there are more of them out there," Merrill said.

"I was really hoping there was only one of them," Brandr said.

Con glanced at the circle. "If there were, you'd think they would've banded together."

"True, but we should keep an eye out, just to be sure," Merrill said.

Brandr dipped his chin. "Agreed."

"One more enemy down." Con ran a hand over his mouth.

Katla put her back to the circle. "Does that mean we're done here?"

"Aye." Brandr looked at each of them. "I'll see you back at Iron Hall."

He was gone in a blink. Being half Fae, Brandr could teleport, just not vast distances like a full Fae or a Star Person could.

"Ready?" Katla asked.

Merrill saw her and Con exchange a look. He didn't have time to ask what it was about before Katla jumped them. Merrill tensed the moment he realized they were at Cairnkeep. His gaze shot to the sky, ready to protect Katla should any dragons come for her. When he didn't see any, he swung his head to Con.

"It was my idea," Con said. He slapped Merrill on the shoulder with a smile and walked away.

Merrill watched him for a moment before he looked at Katla. "What's going on?"

"The final question."

He looked up at the steep incline and the cliff above where they had been mated. Then he looked at the valley. He spotted the stacked stones that marked the Fae doorway that would take them to Earth.

"We don't have to try if you aren't ready," Katla told him.

Merrill shook his head. "I need to know."

That didn't stop the swell of fear, though. Scotland was in his blood. To never lay eyes on his beloved land, fly between the mountains on Dreagan, or walk the halls of Dreagan Manor would be unbearable. But he would endure it because he was alive.

He wasn't the only one going through—if he could. Merrill looked at Katla. "Are you ready? It's a vastly different world."

"I'll readily face anything with you by my side."

Merrill grinned. "You might go through alone. If that happens, just turn around and return. Or stay."

"I'm not going without you. Either we go together or not at all," she stated.

He licked his lips and looked at the space where the door was. He couldn't see it, but it was there. "All right."

"Go first."

"We go together."

Katla gave him a smile filled with love and slid her hand into his. "I'm a half step behind."

Just in case he couldn't go through. His heart was thudding against his ribs, his breaths coming quicker. The magic had chosen him as a Dragon King. It wouldn't reject him now.

Katla squeezed his hand. Merrill swallowed and stepped between the stacked stones. There was no resistance, nothing blocked him from passing through. One moment, he was on Zora.

The next, he stood in the Dragonwood. A heartbeat later, Katla was beside him.

"Oh, it's warm," she said.

Merrill stood within the forest and lifted his face to the sun as he drank in the magic of the realm. Excitement swept through him as he tugged Katla after him. "There is so much to show you, and so many people for you to meet."

Her laugh filled the Dragonwood as they started running toward the manor.

Sian set aside the glass tub and yanked off her gloves. She couldn't concentrate on anything since Katla and Merrill had told her about running into Jenefer. It had been so long since she had last seen her. Sian told herself to be patient, that Jenefer would return when she could, but she was tired of waiting, tired of worrying.

She left her lab and strode out of the double doors into the canyon. Usually, Sian was content to stride through the canyon, but not today. Something pressed her to get to the top. It wasn't an easy climb, even with the hidden rope ladder Cullen had fashioned.

Sian slapped away vines and large leaves as she made her way up. She was out of breath by the time she reached the summit. Her boot got caught in one of the vines and it made her stumble getting off the ladder. She fell to one knee. She was yanking her foot to get it out of the vines when she caught the flash of metal. Suddenly, she was free.

Sian lifted her head and stared into a face she feared she might never see again. "Jenefer."

Jenefer grinned and helped Sian to her feet. "You have no idea how much I've missed you."

"I have an idea," she said.

They fell into each other's arms then, their lips meeting in a passionate, hungry kiss. Someone cleared their throat. Jenefer ended the kiss, and they pressed their foreheads together.

"I missed that." Jenefer caressed her face. Then she straightened and turned to the side. "Sian, this is Narin."

Sian stared at the beautiful Amazon. Jealousy flared for an instant until she saw the love in Jenefer's gaze directed at her and not Narin. Sian gave Narin a welcoming smile. "Let's get both of you inside."

"We have a lot to tell everyone," Jenefer said.

"Merrill mentioned something about a girl you were looking for."

Narin shook her head. "We lost her."

"We'll look for her again, but I wanted to get home," Jenefer said.

Sian couldn't stop smiling. Jenefer was home. Everything was just as it should be.

Villette stood at the edge of the Ferdon Woods and looked out across the field. She watched the two Amazons with the other woman disappear into the canyon. A mighty civilization had once called it home.

Now she knew where the Dragon Kings were.

Thank you for reading **DRAGON MARKED**. I hope you enjoyed Merrill and Katla's book. I'm so happy Merrill finally got his HEA.

There's a bonus short story featuring Katla and Merrill. Grab it here: https://mailchi.mp/donnagrant/x45lpuxq1j

* * *

If you want more Dragon King stories, then you won't have long to wait. DRAGON FORGED will be out in July! Keep reading for a peek at DRAGON FORGED.

BUY DRAGON FORGED NOW
at www.DonnaGrant.com

* * *

If you love the Dragon King series, you'll love the next Dark Universe book set in the Elven Kingdoms series, STORM WOOD...

BUY STORM WOOD NOW
at www.DonnaGrant.com

* * *

To find out when new books release
SIGN UP FOR MY NEWSLETTER today at
https://www.tinyurl.com/DonnaGrantNews

* * *

Join my Facebook group, Donna Grant Groupies, for exclusive
giveaways and sneak peeks of future books.
https://bit.ly/DGGroupies

***

Keep reading for a peek of DRAGON FORGED and a glimpse at
STORM WOOD...

SNEAK PEEK AT DRAGON FORGED

DRAGON KINGS SERIES, BOOK 10

The next book in the Dragon Kings series by *New York Times* and *USA Today* bestselling author Donna Grant.

Keep reading for a sneak peek at DRAGON FORGED...

EXCERPT

Last days of Autumn
Iron Hall

Boredom had never been Hector's friend. He was a man of action. Not that he didn't enjoy rest. After all he and the other Dragon Kings had endured of late, a little respite was agreeable. But after a week of twiddling his thumbs, he was restless. He needed something to occupy him. He wasn't due for patrol rotation along the border for another six days, and he couldn't wait that long.

His bootheels thumped softly along the stone floors of the hallway. Iron Hall was enormous. Every time they thought they had explored all there was of the underground city, they discovered more. For the most part, the city had survived relatively well. However, there were sections that had some damage, and even areas that had caved in.

Hector had been exploring a portion that had the most devastation in an effort to curb his irritation and not get on anyone nerves but his own. Marcus rarely left the section Hector was exploring. Marcus was in his element putting the city back to its original glory piece by piece.

He found Marcus where he had left him three hours earlier. The atrium had a dome arched ceiling and sat in the center with five hall-ways branching off from it in a star shape. Three of the five had been extensive damage. Marcus' specialized ability was in architecture, and every aspect that went with it. He had designed and built Dreagan Manor as well as the distillery and every other building on their estate in Scotland on Earth. He was supposed to be constructing another manor at Cairnkeep, but his focus had deviated to Iron Hall. Hector grinned as he leaned a shoulder against a wall when he recalled how Marcus' eyes had lit up at the sight of the underground city.

"Tell me again why you doona just use magic?" Hector asked.

Marcus leaned over a table studying dozens of blueprints that were scattered about. Without looking up, he said, "That takes the fun out of it."

This was far from Hector's idea of enjoyable. He was a warrior, a fighter. Give him wide open skies and an enemy to vanquish over ruins to be put back together any day. He wasn't made to be stuck inside. Yet, here he was, doing just that.

He pushed away from the wall and walked to the last corridor to be cleared. This one was blocked, but Marcus saw things no one else did. It was why building and rebuilding were his fortes. It's also why, if they wanted a spectacular meal, they turned to Keltan. If someone needed healing, Con stepped up. All of the Kings had a unique ability. Even him. Though, he wouldn't call his all that special.

When the Kings first came to Zora, all that had mattered was discovering their dragons. Enemies had soon emerged, and they had been fighting one after another ever since. It kept them from exploring more than the fraction they had. Most of their time had been spent at Stonemore, a mountain-side city where several battles had been fought recently.

From what the Kings had seen of Zora so far, the realm was in a medieval-esque era. Stonemore had many beautiful buildings, especially the palace that sat at the very top of the mountain. They had glass for windows, plumbing, and even heated water. Yet, they still used horses and carriages.

Iron Hall was different in more than its architecture. The stones used for the floor glowed from within, and not with magic. Along the walls were sconces of flames that never went out. The aqueducts would've made Romans weep with envy. Everything about the city from the murals to the lighting made you forget it was deep under the earth. Yet, for all the wonders of Iron Hall, they hadn't discovered who built it, how long they might have lived there, or what happened to them. Hector was beginning to wonder if they ever would.

"The debris looks different in here," Hector called out as he walked to the entrance of the blocked corridor. "The tiles aren't cracked. They're smashed."

He walked the last few feet into the hall before the rubble began. Squatting, Hector picked up a small piece of broken rock. The edges were burnt like from a blast of some kind. Or fire. He tossed the rock into the air and caught it. He scanned from one side of the wide passage to the other, seeing deep into the darkness beyond as well as he would if it was lit. His enhanced dragon senses reached out, searching for what, he wasn't sure. But something wasn't right.

It occurred to him then that Marcus hadn't replied to his previous comment. He looked over his shoulder at his friend whose dark head was still bent over the designs.

"Did you hear me?" Hector asked.

"What?" Marcus briefly lifted his head and speared him with his green gaze. "Of course."

Hector grinned. "Did you now? What did I say?"

"Fine. I wasna listening. I have to…"

Hector didn't wait for Marcus to finish, because he wouldn't. Whatever was going on, happened inside Marcus' head and never made it past his lips. It was better to leave Marcus to his musings, and only interrupt if it was life or death.

Hector faced the debris field once more. The blackened stone bothered him. The few areas that had needed a bit of work to shore up a few cracks was nothing compared to this section. It was situated far from the main hub of the city and only connected by the corridors, which explained why the damage was so contained. They hadn't discovered what the location had been used for either. It would likely take the reconstruction of the last hall before they would be able to piece it all together.

Straightening, Hector picked his way around the rubble to get deeper into the corridor. And the more scorch marks he found on the rocks littering the floor. It confirmed that something or someone had blown up this hallway either by accident or on purpose. It would explain why three others on either side of it had sustained only minor damage.

It wasn't long before Hector had to duck because of the ceiling caving in. There was no telling how much dirt was settled above him. The Kings would survive a cave in with their magic, but others wouldn't be so lucky. He needed to bring this up to Marcus, just in case he hadn't inspected back here. At the very least, they needed to set up a barrier to make sure none of the bairns accidently found their way to this section. He was just about to turn back when he did a double take as he spotted an opening through a pile of rocks. He leaned to the side and tried to get a better look into the gap.

"Fuck," Hector mumbled when he struck his head on a rock when trying to get a better view.

He dropped to his hands and knees and crawled around and over large rocks with sharp edges. His skin stung from being cut, but his body healed instantly. If it wasn't for Marcus, he would've reached for his magic to clear his way, but he respected his friend enough not to make things more difficult for him.

It took some time before Hector reached the cavity. Once there he peered inside only to find more debris. There did seem to be space enough for someone to stand almost upright, but beyond that was a solid wall of rock and dirt.

Just as he was about to turn away, something made him pause. He scanned the space again, trying to decipher what it was that made him want to not just remail, but get inside. The pull was strong enough that he jerked away from the gap. As soon as he did, the overwhelming need to look against intensified.

Something was in there drawing him in, luring him. Hector looked down the hall to the center room and briefly thought about calling for Marcus. The moment that thought went through his mind, came a second that he would have to share whatever was found. Hector was at the opening in the next heartbeat. He eyed the width and breadth against his own body. It was going to be tight.

BUY DRAGON FORGED NOW
at www.DonnaGrant.com

GLIMPSE AT THE NEXT DARK UNIVERSE BOOK

STORM WOOD, ELVEN KINGDOMS SERIES, BOOK 3

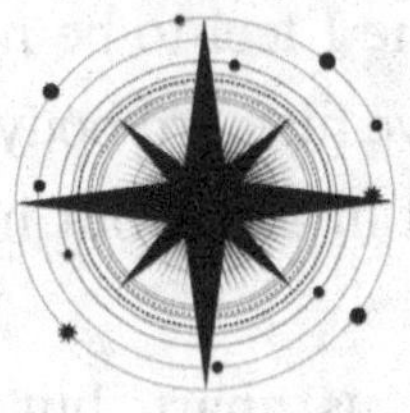

Deepest loyalty. Fiercest defiance.

I never wanted to fall in love. My sister's disappearance has damaged me for such things. All that matters is finding her—no matter where that leads me.

I could never have imagined it would bring me to him. A human with haunting celadon eyes and a determination that rivals my own.

Maybe that's why I wasn't prepared when he revealed he knew I was an undercover agent. And if word gets out, I'm as good as dead.

Too much rides on my identity remaining hidden. I have no choice but to help him navigate the perilous depths of the Below—

and all who reside there. For the time being, at least. Nothing will stop me from my mission. And he knows it.

But the lines that were once so vivid between us slowly begin to blur. We have only each other to survive and trust him with my life is one thing. With my heart...that's something I can't even consider.

Yet, I can't stop wondering what his lips would feel like against mine. I can't help the ache I feel to be near him. And I can lie to him, but not myself. I crave his hard body next to me.

I never wanted to fall in love...but he stole my heart before I had a chance to protect it.

Everything is pulling us apart, but I've never felt this way before. And I intend to fight for him. For us.

Even if it means my death.

New York Times and ***USA Today*** **bestselling author Donna Grant weaves a captivating story of daring choices, unlikely alliances, and the enduring strength of hope in the thrilling third installment of her acclaimed Elven Kingdoms series.**

BUY STORM WOOD NOW
at www.DonnaGrant.com

ABOUT THE AUTHOR

New York Times and *USA Today* bestselling author Donna Grant® has been praised for her "totally addictive" and "unique and sensual" stories.

She's written more than one hundred novels spanning multiple genres of romance including the bestselling Dragon Kings® series that features a thrilling combination of Druids, Fae, and immortal Highlanders who are dark, dangerous, and irresistible. She lives in Texas with her dog and a cat.

www.DonnaGrant.com

www.MotherofDragonsBooks.com

facebook.com/AuthorDonnaGrant

instagram.com/dgauthor

bookbub.com/authors/donna-grant

goodreads.com/donna_grant

pinterest.com/donnagrant1